Kevin – Ma

By David C Ayre

A story for children of all ages from ten to a hundred

Published by: -

SDS Publishing
7 Woodpark Avenue
Knaresborough
North Yorkshire HG5 9DJ

Email: davidcayre@ntlworld.com
Web: www.david-c-ayre.co.uk

First published February 2008 as separate books
New edition 2018

Other books by the same author

<u>For Young Adults</u>

Echoes Through the Mists of Time

<u>Books for small Children</u>

The Urgles (A picture book)

<u>Novels</u>

Follow the Dream
The Doomsday Machine

ISBN: 978-1-7286-6174-2

Kevin – Master of the Universe
Book 1

Chapter 1 - The beginning

Kevin Brown was a normal boy from a normal family. He lived a very normal life in a normal little town. He could not have been more normal. But although he did not know it, that was all about to change. He had woken that morning with a bad cold and his mother had thought he should stay in bed today rather than go to school. It had looked like rain when his mother had peeped out of his bedroom window.

"Looks like rain," she had said, "best to stay in bed today." Kevin did not argue. It was games today, football, and he was not too fond of football. He did not mind kicking a football around in the field at the back of his house. That was different. But football at school was organised; you had to take it seriously. Some of the other boys were good at it, or at least, they thought they were. They play 'striker' or 'mid field', but the likes of Kevin played full back. He was not hopeless enough to be put in goal. That honour was reserved for fat Freddie. He was really hopeless and usually managed to get Kevin into trouble with Miss Rodgers into the bargain.

Now Miss Rodgers had little time for Freddie and was always on the alert for an opportunity to chastise him and anyone who aided and abetted him in his misdemeanours.

One day, the game had been raging at the other end of the field for quite a time when Freddie had thought it would be interesting to climb up the goal post and swing from the crossbar. Kevin had not tried to dissuade him, as it was more interesting than the distant game of football.

However, it is strange how fortunes can change in an instant. The other side had gained possession of the ball and a giant swarm of small boys was stampeding in the direction of Kevin, Freddie and the goal. There was a thud as trainer made contact with plastic, a whoosh of air past Kevin's ear, a thud and a gasp as the ball hit Freddie, and finally, a splat as Freddie hit the mud.

"What do you think you are doing?" It was Miss Rodgers, face crimson from running, arms waving frantically.

"It was an ace save Miss," said Kevin. At this point Miss Rodgers' attention was drawn to Kevin.

"Oh, was it, indeed? Go and stand outside my room until I get back." Kevin left the field and made his way back to the school building. Well, it was better than football.

Half past three came. Children passed him in the corridor on their way home, but there was no sign of Miss Rodgers. At four o'clock he decided that perhaps, if he were to disappear, no one would be the wiser. So, he went home. It was just as well really, as Miss Rodgers had had to go to the hospital with fat Freddie. He had broken his arm.

So, staying in bed today seemed like a good idea. But by mid-morning Kevin was feeling better. He knew he was feeling better because he was bored. Maybe mum would not mind if he got up and went downstairs. He decided she would not, so he got up and put on his dressing gown. Then he crept downstairs to find his mother in the kitchen.

"What are you doing out of bed?" she asked, "If you're feeling better you had better get off to school."

"Oh, no," he replied, "I don't think I'm up to that yet. But I think I'm well enough to watch a bit of television."

"Well, all right then, but don't get under my feet, I've a lot to do today." She went back into the kitchen leaving Kevin to settle down with 'The Monster from Space'. It was quite frightening for a ten-year-old, but he held a cushion in front of him for protection and tried not to cry out at the very frightening bits.

The programme finished just in time for his mother to come bustling in with his lunch. He nearly jumped out of his skin, the nervous state he was in after watching his programme. But he soon forgot all about that when he started to tuck into his sausage and chips covered liberally with tomato sauce.

"There's not much wrong with your appetite," said his mother with a grin.

"Well, I'm feeling a lot better now, thank you," he answered seriously, "I think it might do me good to get a bit of fresh air this afternoon."

"There's plenty of fresh air on the football field," his mother replied with a grin.

"I don't think I'm quite ready for football yet," he answered gingerly.

At the back of Kevin's house was an old meadow leading across to the edge of the moor where the ground rose sharply in a short climb to some rocks at the top. Then after that it flattened out for a while. There were lots of little hidey-holes among the rocks where Kevin would play for hours on his own. So, when he had finished his meal, he strolled out into the garden. It was a lovely day; the sun was shining and the birds were singing as he made his way along the little stepping-stones that meandered through the shrubbery to the less kempt part of the garden, where brambles took over. It was more shaded here due to the enormous horse chestnut tree that stood in the corner of the garden. The blossoms had fallen but it looked as if there would be a good harvest of conkers, this year.

He made his way to the gap in the wall, where a few stones had been dislodged by cattle. The gap had been further widened by Kevin as he passed in and out of his garden to the fields beyond. He loved this place; it was like another world, his world, a world where he made the rules and decided what was to be or not to be. Here, he was the Ruler of the Universe. It is strange how dreams can become reality, for Kevin was to discover things stranger than he could ever imagine. But as yet, he was unaware of anything unusual as he made his way across the field to the hedge at the other side.

As he walked, he soon became aware that he was not alone. He turned and saw Billy plodding slowly towards him. Billy was an old pony that grazed in the field and was always on the lookout for Kevin in the hope that he might be given something nice to eat.

"I think you're out of luck, today," said Kevin as Billy nuzzled up to him. He rummaged in his pockets and found an old peppermint sweet which he gave to Billy who crunched it happily then sniffed around Kevin's pockets for more.

"Sorry, but that's all I've got," he said and turned to walk away. But Billy was not taking 'no' for an answer and kept nudging Kevin in the back as he walked away.

"Stop that will you," he shouted over his shoulder, but Billy kept pushing and nearly pushed Kevin off his feet. Kevin was getting a little alarmed now, as Billy was quite big, and although he was not aggressive as such, could be a little rough. Kevin turned and tried to shoo Billy away but Billy kept returning to resume his search for mints. Then Kevin began to panic and turned and fled towards the hedge which he cleared at a single bound before tumbling headlong into the long grass. He could hear the sound of skidding hooves as Billy decided that show jumping was not for him, followed by some impatient snorting followed by the sound of heavy hooves clomping slowly away.

Kevin scrambled to his feet and looked to see if all was clear behind him and saw Billy standing some way off watching him. Oh dear, he thought, I'll have to come back the long way round.

He turned and continued up the hill, winding his way through the gorse and heather. As he climbed, the air seemed to get cooler and he felt a gentle breeze brushing his face and hair. It took about half an hour to reach the rocky outcrop and by then he was feeling exhausted. He looked back down the hill expecting to see Billy still standing there waiting for him to return, but there was no sign of him. Perhaps he was hiding somewhere, waiting to leap out when Kevin returned, and catch him unawares. Anyway, that did not matter, as he was not going back that way.

He turned and squeezed between the rocks to find his own favourite place. Here he could be a king on his throne, or the pilot of an interstellar space ship fighting off the evil Garks. He could be anything he wanted. There was a rock just like a seat hollowed out by water in the dim and distant past, just for Kevin, or at least, that was how Kevin saw it. It fitted him so perfectly it must have been made to measure.

He sat down in the seat as he usually did, got himself into a comfortable position and picked up a small rock that had been placed by his right hand.

"Captain on the bridge," he said into it, "Warp speed five, full ahead." He put down the stone. Time for a short nap before we reach Arcturus, he thought and lay back and dozed. He did not know how long he had dozed or whether he had actually woken up again. There is that time between waking and sleeping when everything seems normal and you are sure you are awake but in fact you are not. So often his father had dozed off in the armchair in front of the television and had started to snore gently.

"You're snoring," his mother would say, and there would be no response. "I said, you are snoring."

"What?" his father would say in surprise.

"You were snoring, dear."

"No. I wasn't even asleep." And he was convinced that he had been wide-awake. What's more he could tell you what he had heard on television and he was usually right.

Well, that was how it was with Kevin. He had been dozing, no more than that, and he had been listening to voices talking softly nearby. It was part of his dream and he had been enjoying it.

The first voice had said "Are you sure he is the one?" and another had said, "Of course I am sure. Do you dispute the readings?"

"Of course not. You are the keeper of the Universal Crystal."

"Then why do you question my decision?"

"Well, it's so unusual. Firstly, it is the first time that we have been led to a primitive being. Secondly, he is so large, and thirdly, he doesn't seem very old."

"True on all counts. Just because the crystal hasn't brought us to a primitive world before does not mean that it shouldn't. Yes, he is larger than we are. Is this a problem? I hope not, because I am of the opinion that he still has much to grow. And finally, he is ten Earth years old which makes him about ten and a half universal years. Yes, that is young. The last Grand Master of the Council was five hundred and fifty-two when appointed, and fifteen hundred and twenty-seven when he retired. However, it would seem that these beings are very short lived; seventy to eighty years with luck."

"If he is not yet adult, we cannot expect him to leave his parents. Is this practical?"

"I agree there may be problems. We will not confront him now. Let us return to the ship and consult the crystal, and if it still tells us that this is to be the new Master, then we will return and appoint him. I think he may be waking. Let us depart immediately."

Kevin was aware of a scuffling noise nearby and became immediately alert. His first thought was that Billy had found a way out of his field and had followed him. He sprang to his feet and looked over the surrounding rocks into the moor land beyond but there was nothing to see. Strange, he thought, I could have sworn there was someone there, or was it just my dream. As dreams went, it was a strange dream with no pictures, just voices. It was as if a group of people had been standing nearby talking about him. But it made no sense. He looked around carefully to see if there were any signs of intruders, but there was little to be seen until he suddenly saw something sparkling in the heather. He went over and picked up what looked like an enormous diamond. *Wow*, he thought, *I'm rich*. But then again it was probably only a piece of glass.

Slipping it into his pocket, he looked at his watch and realised that he should be on his way back if he wanted any tea. He forgot all about Billy until he was half way across the field. He looked about in alarm, half expecting the demon horse to be charging at him from his hiding place. But all was quiet and peaceful. In fact, as he approached the wall of his garden, he saw Billy on the other side of the field, contentedly grazing. He felt a bit stupid for being so afraid of a horse that liked peppermints. Perhaps it was not such a good idea to watch scary television programmes.

Chapter 2 - The Deputation

"So, what have you been doing today?" asked Kevin's father while they had their tea.

"I kept him at home today," said his mother, "He didn't seem too well this morning."

"Oh, is that right?" Kevin's father looked at him suspiciously.

"I felt a bit better this afternoon, though and went out for some fresh air," put in Kevin quickly. He knew that grown-ups always thought that 'fresh air' did you good, especially if you would rather not have any. "I went up to the rocks." He put in as an afterthought.

"You'll be well enough for school tomorrow, then?"

"I think so," said Kevin.

"Good." His father carried on eating his tea while his mother chatted on about things that had to be done.

After tea Kevin went to play in his room before having an early night. He was really quite tired, but before going to sleep, he went over to the window and looked out over the moor. He could just make out the rocks in the moonlight, and as he looked, he felt sure that he could see movement up there. No, it must be his imagination. Suddenly he remembered the diamond, as he liked to think of it. He put his hand into his trouser pocket and pulled out the shiny object. What a find, just like in his dream, they spoke about the Keeper of the Crystal. Wow. He looked into it and could see all sorts of colours. They shimmered and sparkled. He wondered what it really was, probably nothing much at all. But his imagination would not let it be nothing. Something like this must be very important, at least in his make-believe world.

He walked back to the window still holding the crystal and looked up to the rocks. Surely there was movement up there. His imagination went into overdrive. Visions of aliens and monsters appeared before his eyes, but then there was a flicker of light. He looked more carefully and was sure that there was something up there giving off a glow of light. Must be the game keeper, he thought, doing his rounds. Then he looked back to the crystal in his hands and realised that it, too, was glowing. He gave a strangled squawk and dropped the crystal on the floor where it bounced and ended up under the bed.

"What's going on up there?" It was Kevin's father.

"Nothing, Dad. Just dropped something on the floor."

"Well, get back into bed and go to sleep." Kevin leapt into bed and pulled the covers up to his chin. Something was signalling to the crystal, something out there on the hillside. He wondered if it had been there this afternoon while he was asleep in the rocks. Supposing that it had found him and eaten him.

It is surprising how fatigue can take over when you think there is no chance of sleep. He had hardly finished wondering how he was going to get to sleep when he was woken by his mother shouting for him to come down to breakfast or he would be late for school.

School? How could he possibly think of going to school after all that had happened the previous day? He hurried downstairs, still trying to fasten his school tie.

"About time too," his mother scolded as he came into the kitchen, "Get this eaten." A bowl of cereal was thrust into his hands and he was propelled towards the table.

"You know, I really don't think…"

"Don't even think about it," said his mother, "Today, you are going to school." And shortly he found himself trotting down the road in order to catch the school bus. Supposing I should miss it, he thought. No, perhaps not.

At the bus stop he could not help looking this way and that as if he expected to see someone. He did not know why he did it, but he felt that he was being watched. Perhaps it was the owner of the crystal come to wreak vengeance on him for stealing it. The crystal. Oh no. He had forgotten all about it. It must still be lying under the bed. He hoped fervently that his mother did not decide to vacuum his room today. He was wondering whether he had time to run back home and retrieve his precious crystal when the school bus came labouring up the hill to pull up at the bus stop. Too late now. He would just have to hope for the best.

It was a long day at school, or at least it seemed so, and eventually he was on his way home again, sitting on the rickety old bus as it rattled down the dusty road towards Kevin's home. It was a lovely view out over the Yorkshire moorland, but Kevin hardly noticed. His mind was in another world. He hoped beyond hope that his crystal was still there. Why did this bus go so slowly? He could not wait to get home. It was Friday today, so he would have the whole weekend to play with his new acquisition. What adventures he was going to have. Little did he know.

Being an only child and living just outside the town, he did not have friends around to play with him, so he had to make do with his imagination. This was not a problem to Kevin. Imagination was not something he was short of. He was building up a great new story, in his mind, triggered off by his find and the dreams he had while dozing among the rocks. He was going to be the Master of the Crystal and there was no end to the possibilities this opened up for him.

The bus drew up at his stop and Kevin's feet were on the ground before the bus had stopped. He sped off up the old track that led to his house and arrived breathless.

"Good gracious!" exclaimed his mother as he burst through the door, "What's chasing you?"

Kevin looked puzzled. "Nothing," he said, "Just glad to be home."

His mother looked at him quizzically as he dashed out of the kitchen and made for his room. Once inside, he closed the door, listened to be sure that his mother was not following him, and then made a dive for the bed, almost disappearing under it. He looked around but could see nothing. The crystal had gone, and with it his hopes for an adventurous weekend.

His mother must have vacuumed it up. If that were the case he could retrieve it from the bag on the machine. He would have to be very careful not to be seen as he went down to the outbuilding where the vacuum cleaner was kept. Luckily, his mother was busy getting his dinner ready and did not see him creeping out of the back door.

In the outbuilding, which was a sort of lean-to, were kept all sorts of things, like the lawn mower, his bicycle, jars full of nails and screws that would 'come in useful' sometime, and the vacuum cleaner. It was an ancient monster and would be able to swallow his crystal in one gulp.

He felt the bag which seemed to be empty. It was empty. His mother had emptied the bag. He dashed round to the dustbin, threw off the lid and was confronted by an empty bin liner. The bin men had been. How unlucky could one boy get?

He turned and strolled inside again wondering how he could possibly find his lost treasure when his mother called to him from the kitchen.

"Oh Kevin," she called, "Is this yours? I found it under your bed." Kevin raced in to see his mother holding up his crystal. "Good thing I saw it before it got into the vacuum cleaner."

"Great," shouted Kevin, "I thought it was lost."

"What is it?" his mother asked.

"It's the great crystal of the Grand Council of the Universe," said Kevin proudly.

"Ask a silly question," said his mother, "Anyway, where did you get it?"

"I found it up in the rocks."

"Do you think someone might have lost it?" asked his mother.

"I don't think so. I think it is just a lump of glass or crystal or something like that." The last thing he wanted was for his mother to tell him he should take it to the police station and hand it into lost property. However, she seemed to have other things on her mind, like the pan on the stove which was about to go critical.

He picked up his crystal and walked out into the garden and made his way down to the bottom, out of view of the house. He walked to the wall and leant upon it as he gazed up at the rocks where he had found the crystal. He wondered if he had seen movement up there or whether it was just his imagination.

Billy was grazing in the middle of the field, but suddenly looked up and started towards Kevin. After some more peppermints, are you he thought?

There was a scuffling sound on the other side of the wall as Billy started to trot. Then he broke into a canter and it looked as if he meant to leap the wall. Kevin stood back as Billy skidded to a halt just short of the wall. A strange creature shot through the gap in the wall and rolled to a halt at Kevin's feet, followed closely by another, slightly smaller creature which was followed in quick succession by four more even smaller ones.

Kevin was so surprised that he hardly managed a squeak of alarm. The creatures slowly scrambled to their feet and stood before him in two neat rows. In the front stood the largest of the creatures who would have looked quite at home sitting cross legged on the lawn with a bobble hat and a fishing rod.

The second, who was slightly shorter but much plumper, stood to his left. The other four stood in a row behind the other two like hired retainers. These were only about half the size of Kevin but looked much older, in fact, they had quite wrinkled faces. All six of them were dressed as if they were in a pantomime.

"Please do not be alarmed," said the smaller of the two at the front. He was obviously subordinate to the taller one. "We mean you no harm."

"Who are you?" squeaked Kevin, and realising that he was sounding stupid, repeated in a much lower voice "Who are you?"

"May I present to you Borin Boranin, Keeper of the Universal Crystal and seeker for the True Master.

The taller one gave a stiff bow towards Kevin. "Pleased to meet you."

"How do you do?" said Kevin. This was all seeming very unreal to him. He felt sure he had dozed off again and had re-entered the dream he was having up in the rocks the previous day.

"I am Haranot Duplin, attendant to the Keeper of the Universal Crystal," he continued giving as much of a bow as he could manage due to his rather fat middle.

"How do you do?" said Kevin again, not too sure what you said to creatures out of a dream. Surprisingly, he was not feeling frightened of them, possibly because of their size, but mainly because of their comical appearance. "And who are your friends?" he asked indicating the four diminutive creatures standing behind them.

Haranot looked shocked. "They are not my 'friends'," he said with a shudder, "These are our attendants. They are Murin."

"Murin?" asked Kevin, "What's that?"

"The Murin are from the planet Muros in the Marrantine cluster. All our attendants and other servants are recruited from Muros."

"Oh, I see," said Kevin, "That's what my Father would call a gopher."

Haranot looked puzzled and turned towards Borin and spoke to him in a strange sounding language. Borin thought for a moment, then he turned towards Kevin and said "We do not see the connection between a small furry animal of your planet and the Murin. Please explain."

"It's a joke," said Kevin, "You know, 'go for' this and 'go for' that."

Borin and Haranot looked at each other. It was obvious that these creatures had no sense of humour. Borin cleared his throat, stood even more stiffly than he had before and started to make, what seemed to be, an official speech.

"Kevin, of the clan Brown, of the area known as Yorkshire, I announce that through the power vested in me by the Universal Crystal, I name you the designated Master of the Universe." At this point he stopped and said something in the strange sounding language that they had used earlier.

"We have a problem," said Haranot, "We have lost the crystal and it is essential in the naming of the new Master."

Kevin put his hand into his pocket and pulled out his crystal. "Will this do?" he asked. Haranot and Borin stared at the crystal in amazement. "Where did you get that?" asked Borin.

"Oh, I just found it lying around, up there in the rocks." He pointed across the field towards the rocks.

"Perhaps you would allow me," said Borin holding out his hand. Kevin looked at the hand with its long bony fingers and reluctantly placed the crystal into its palm. Borin closed his fingers around it and placed his other hand over it. "Now," he said, "We can proceed with the test."

Chapter 3 - The Test.

"What are you going to do?" asked Kevin. He was beginning to feel worried.

"We are going to carry out the test," said Borin, "Before becoming Master of the Universe, you must pass the test."

"So, if I fail, what happens then?"

"It is best not to ask," said Haranot.

Borin held the crystal higher and moved it close to Kevin's forehead.

"Just a moment," shouted Kevin in alarm, "What are you going to do?"

"I cannot tell you that. The test is the test and it is up to you to decide how you are being tested and what you have to do." Borin again held up the crystal which began to glow. Kevin could not take his eyes off it as it got brighter and brighter. It was getting painful to look at but still Kevin could not drag his eyes away from it. Then suddenly it went out and everything went black.

"Now you've dazzled me," said Kevin; "I can't see a thing." He rubbed his eyes and tried to focus them, but still could not see. He began to panic.

"What have you done to me?" he sobbed, "I can't see a thing. I think I've gone blind." But there was no response; not a sound. Then he began to make out shapes. He was not blind, but it had got dark. How could this be? Had he passed out, and if so, why had not someone come looking for him when his dinner was ready? But he could not have passed out because he was still on his feet. His eyes were coming back to life rather as they do when you go into a dark room from a brightly lit one. After a while your eyes become accustomed to the dim light and you begin to make out shapes. He ought to be able to see the wall as he was only a few paces from it, but it was not there, it most definitely was not there. He was standing in an open space, larger than his garden and a cool breeze had started to blow. It did not smell like his garden, either. The scent of the blossoms had gone and all he could smell now was damp rotting wood.

He moved his feet to see if he could get a better view of where he was, only to find that the ground was very wet and soggy. There appeared to be trees ahead of him and he made his way towards them. He was becoming very frightened, very frightened indeed. Something very strange had happened to him and he was beginning to realise that he was no longer in his garden. But where he was he had no idea.

He was now in reach of the trees which had very tall slender trunks and thin stubby branches at fairly regular intervals. Kevin was good at climbing trees and these were the easiest he had ever seen.

At that moment there was a blood curdling howl from just behind him, and before he knew what he was doing, he was twenty feet up the tree and climbing fast. Sheer panic had taken over and he was climbing for his life.

Eventually, the trunk had become too slim for him to go any further, but the branches had begun to spread, making a small platform as they wove themselves together in their struggle towards the light. Here Kevin stopped and made himself as comfortable as he could. He was hungry and it was getting cold, and he did not feel at all safe up here. However, there was nothing to be done until it got light, if it ever did.

He made himself as comfortable as he could and tried to doze, but he was scared stiff that if he went to sleep he would fall to his death below. He hooked his arm around a branch and closed his eyes. Occasionally he began to doze, but then awoke with a start in a cold sweat. After a while what had been a light breeze became a little more lively, and the tree, which was tall and slender, started to sway alarmingly. He was beginning to get cold and was feeling very frightened. Although he was a bit of a loner, he liked to know that his parents were at hand when he was worried about anything. But now he was beginning to wonder if he would ever see them again. He did not know where he was or what he was going to do next. He tried to look around him. It seemed to be getting lighter; a red glow had appeared on the distant horizon. As it got lighter, the breeze dropped and the tree swayed less and less. He shifted his position, carefully, making sure he had a good grip on a branch. There were more trees nearby and beyond, he thought he could make out a building of some sort. Perhaps he could get help there.

He looked down the tree and froze. He was much higher than he had thought, and the trunk of the tree was so slim it looked as if the slightest movement would snap it in half. But then, he told himself, it was all right when he had climbed up, so it must be stronger than it looked.

He started to climb down, but this was much more difficult than climbing up, as many a cat had found out to its cost, and there were no firemen here to help him down. Branch by difficult branch he struggled his way down. It seemed to take for ever and it was getting quite light by the time he reached the ground.

The sun could now be seen just above the horizon, glowing a brilliant red. It looked much larger than he was used to, but he thought it must be because it was so low in the sky.

He looked around him to find that he was standing in a large garden, but one like nothing he had seen before. There was a lawn of neatly mowed grass of a dark blue colour, and a gravel path leading around it towards where he estimated the building stood. It was hidden from his sight now by more of the slender trees like the one in which he had spent the night. Nothing was moving anywhere, so he started down the path very cautiously, looking to right and left as he went. He could not forget the creature that had howled when he first arrived here.

As he came to the end of the trees and tall shrubs that followed, he looked out across another wide lawn of the

19

dark blue grass to a house so strange he could but stand and stare at it with his mouth open. It appeared to be made completely out of glass, not just windows, but solid glass. In fact, it looked just like a row of bottles standing in a glass bowl.

"Awesome!" he exclaimed to himself.

"It is indeed," said a deep voice from just behind him. He spun round as if he had been pushed. There standing behind him was a creature just like Haranot, the smaller of the two creatures that had got him into this mess.

"Who are you?" said Kevin taking a step backwards.

"May I introduce myself?" he said politely, "I am Trinbar Nartop, Keeper of the Official Residence of the Master of the Universe." Kevin looked at Trinbar and then at the Building.

"Excuse me if this sounds rude, but there would seem to be rather a lot of work for one small person."

Trinbar smiled. "You jest Master. Of course, I have the usual staff of Murin and Dross."

"I have heard of Murin," said Kevin eagerly, "They are the attendants and servants, but I haven't heard of the Dross. What are they?"

"I hardly like to trouble you with such, but when we select our Murin, some do not meet with our requirements. These we call Dross. They do all the work that is beneath the status of even the Murin."

Kevin thought about this for a moment. "It doesn't sound as if they have a very nice time here."

"They are not here to have a nice time. They are here to do whatever needs to be done."

Kevin thought it best to say no more until he had found out a bit more about his own position. At the moment, they seemed to be treating him as if he were important, but he remembered what had been said just before he found himself here. He was to undergo some sort of test. He did not like the sound of that especially as he was beginning to find out how these people treated failures.

"Please follow me," said Trinbar, and started at a brisk pace towards the building. They followed the gravel path rather than cut across the lawn and walked past borders full of very colourful plants unlike anything he had seen before. It took quite a while to reach the front door of the building as it was larger, and therefore further away than Kevin expected. The doors were enormous, which seemed strange for such a compact people, with steps made out of glass or some sort of crystal leading up to a flat platform in front of the doorway. The steps were completely transparent and so shiny that Kevin expected them to be slippery. But they turned out to be just the opposite, almost sticky.

As they approached the door, it opened slowly and noiselessly to reveal a vast hallway with stairs ascending on either side. He expected to see armies of these servant creatures swarming around, but none was to be seen.

Trinbar stepped inside, raised his right hand, and snapped his fingers. Immediately a small figure darted out from wherever it had been hiding and stood before Trinbar.

"This is the new Master Elect," he said to the Murin, "Please take him to his room so that he can refresh himself before he eats." The creature bowed and made off towards one of the staircases.

"Please follow the Murin," said Trinbar, "You may wash and rest. He will bring you to the dining room when food has been prepared for you."

Kevin dashed after the fast disappearing Murin and followed him along winding corridors of shining crystal. The only decoration seemed to be in the form of carvings and statues in crystal.

Eventually they reached a room where the Murin opened the door and stood to one side so that Kevin might enter.

"Thank you," said Kevin as he walked into the room, "By the way, what is your name." But before he had finished speaking the door had closed with an ominous click. Kevin spun round and would have grabbed the door handle, had there been one, but the door was smooth. He could not get out.

He turned and looked around the room. It was not as large as he had expected. There seemed to be no furniture and everything was cold crystal. Not very comfortable, he thought. He walked over to the other side of the room where there was a small alcove. Inside there was what looked like a wash basin with no taps. Well that's not much use, he thought. How can I wash in that? He felt around the bowl to see if there were any hidden controls or levers, but all was smooth. He looked around thinking that the Murin would know what to do, but it had not come in with him. Then he thought about the way that Trinbar had summoned the Murin. Kevin raised his right hand and tried to snap his fingers. It was not something that he could do with ease, but after a few tries he made a resounding click which echoed around the room. Immediately a Murin was at his side. Kevin did not know where he had come from. It was almost as if he had materialised from nowhere.

"How do I get some water for washing?" he asked. The Murin turned and disappeared round the corner back into the main room. Seconds later, he reappeared with a jug of steaming water which he poured into the bowl. A small towel that was draped over his arm he placed beside the bowl and from out of a pocket or rather a pouch in his garment he produced what looked like a bar of soap.

"Thank you," said Kevin. The Murin looked puzzled but turned and left without saying a word.

He washed his hands and face and dried them on the towel. He felt very refreshed by this and was now beginning to feel very hungry. He had not eaten since well before he arrived in this place, wherever it was.

It would be nice to sit down, he thought, but there were no seats. He clicked his fingers again and immediately a Murin appeared. It was quite disconcerting how they appeared like that and then disappeared to leave the room completely empty.

"I would like to sit down," said Kevin. He was beginning to enjoy this. Instantly four more Murin appeared carrying an object that could roughly be called a seat. They put it down on the floor where it immediately unfolded itself into a chair.

Kevin sat down in it. This was comfortable, he thought and he lay back and closed his eyes. As he had had virtually no sleep the previous night, he fell fast asleep.

When he awoke, it was to find three Murin standing in front of him while another was shaking his arm vigorously. For a moment, Kevin did not know where he was nor what was happening. He leapt up in alarm before his memories came flooding back to him.

"Oh," he said, "Is it time to eat? I could eat a horse." At which the Murin looked horrified. As he turned towards the door he noticed that his chair had already gone. Two Murin opened the door and led the way out into the corridor. Kevin followed and two more Murin followed behind him. It must have been quite a sight as they walked down the corridor.

Eventually, they arrived at a large light room with windows looking out over the gardens. Trinbar was standing by a table laden with food. At least Kevin thought it must be food but it was like nothing he had ever seen.

"Please come and sit down," invited Trinbar amiably indicating a seat opposite the window. "The view from here is excellent, do you not think?"

Kevin had to agree. He was used to stunning scenery but this was something different. He sat down and looked out of the window across the sweep of blue grass to a break of flame coloured trees. Beyond, the ground fell away onto a wide plain of blue grass sprinkled with yellow and red bushes. There were herds of animals grazing there, strange animals, like none he had ever seen, and what is more, they were enormous as well as being brightly coloured.

"Aren't we in danger here from those animals?" Kevin asked,

"Oh, no," replied Trinbar, "They cannot cross the crystal barrier." This meant nothing to Kevin but it made him feel that things were under control.

"The Murin tell me that you have a liking for 'horse'. I am afraid that is not something we can provide, in fact, we do not eat animals of any sort."

Kevin looked puzzled for a moment before realising what Trinbar meant. "No, they did not understand what I meant. It was a sort of joke. We don't eat horses. What I meant was that I was so hungry I could eat that much food. A horse is very big, you see."

"Oh, good. I would not like to have to kill an innocent animal if I didn't have to. Anyway, I am sure you will find something here to your liking. Please taste various items and see if there is anything that suits you."

Kevin looked at the food and tried some of the things that looked palatable and found to his surprise that they tasted really good. He tried several things and found that he was soon satisfied.

"I was told there was to be some sort of test," said Kevin, "When is it to start?"

"It started the moment you looked into the crystal," answered Trinbar, "All aspects of your stay here go into the final result. In fact, you have now reached the final stage of the test. Had you not, you would have to remain here for ever and become one of the Murin. However, that is not the case. Please follow me." He stood up and made his way towards the door at the back of the dining room.

"This," he announced, "Is the Hall of Truth. The decision you take here will determine your future."

Kevin stepped through the door to find himself in a long narrow room. He had entered half way along one of the long walls. There was a door at each end of the hall.

"All you have to do now," said Trinbar, "Is to walk through one of these doors."

"But how do I know which one to go through?" asked Kevin desperately, "They both look the same."

"Just choose one and go," said Trinbar. Kevin looked first one way, then the other. What was he to do?

"What happens if I make the wrong choice?" asked Kevin.

"Who knows?" replied Trinbar, "Now make your choice. Time is running out."

Kevin began to panic. Which one should he choose? In the end he just walked in the direction he happened to be facing at the time and marched straight up to the door and pushed it open. There was a blinding light which made him screw his eyes up and when he, at last, managed to open them again, he was back in his garden at home.

Chapter 4 - Many Wonders

He blinked his eyes and found that Borin and Haranot were standing in front of him just as he last remembered them. Borin still held the crystal aloft, and behind them stood the four Murin. It was as if he had not been away.

"There, I told you so," said Borin to Haranot, "This is truly the new Master of the Universe."

"It would seem that you are right," replied Haranot, "My apologies for doubting you."

Kevin looked from one to the other. "What are you talking about?" he demanded.

"It would seem that the test has been satisfactory," said Borin stiffly, "We must now prepare for your investiture."

Kevin looked puzzled. "What's invest.. whatever it is?"

"You will have to come with us to the Crystal City to receive your crystal and be presented to the Universal Community. Then you will undergo your training to allow you to carry out your duties," said Borin.

"Training usually takes less than fifty years," said Haranot.

"Fifty years?" exclaimed Kevin, "That's no good. My parents would get worried if I was away that long."

"How long do you think you have been away this time?" asked Haranot.

"Well, all night and part of the morning I would think. In fact my parents will be frantic with worry by now." Kevin looked towards the house but nothing seemed to be amiss. He could see his mother in the kitchen, getting on with her work as if nothing had happened.

"Two minutes," said Haranot, "A bit longer than we expected. Why were you so long?"

"What?" cried Kevin, "I had to spend the night in a tree to avoid being eaten by wild animals. Then they took me to a big house to wash and rest, and then they gave me a meal. It wasn't until after that that they took me to the test room."

"Really made yourself at home, didn't you? said Haranot.

"It's not funny," protested Kevin, "I think it was a dirty trick sending me, wherever it was, and not telling me what to expect."

"That was the whole point of the test," said Borin, "Now it's about time we went to the Crystal City." He raised his crystal again.

"Wait," cried Kevin, "My parents will be waiting for me to go in for my dinner. I can't go off somewhere else now. If you want me to play your games you'll have to do it my way." He folded his arms and looked very determined.

"This is all very unusual," said Borin.

"But what choice do we have?" asked Haranot, "We can't force him if he doesn't want to co-operate."

Too true, thought Kevin, but he also felt very relieved that they were not thinking of whisking him off somewhere for the next fifty years.

"Perhaps, if I were to have my dinner, I could come out again afterwards for an hour or two."

"I suppose that will be all right," said Borin resignedly, "Go and eat and we'll wait here for you."

Kevin agreed readily to this and set off towards the house. He did not have much to say as he ate his meal. Somehow, he still had his appetite, even though he had only just eaten. But that was on another world, or at least, he supposed it was. Maybe that did not count.

After he had finished eating he got up and made for the door again.

"What are you going to do now?" asked his mother.

"Oh, I've got to be installed as Master of the Universe in the Crystal City," he said.

"That'll be nice," said his mother absently, "Don't be late back."

Kevin found the group of strange beings still standing at the bottom of his garden. The sight made him grin.

"Is something amusing you?" asked Haranot.

"Nothing really," answered Kevin, "It was just that something ran through my head when I saw you."

"Which was?" persisted Haranot.

"There are fairies at the bottom of my garden," said Kevin and burst into uncontrollable laughter again. Borin glared at him while Haranot smiled. "I don't really think that is very becoming of the new Master of the Universe."

"Can't the Master of the Universe joke if he wants to, then?" asked Kevin.

"Well of course he can," said Haranot, "If he is witty. But that was not witty. It was the humour of a ten year old boy."

"But I am a ten-year-old boy," objected Kevin.

"Quite so," said Borin, "I think it is time that we started for the Crystal City. Then the ceremony can take place immediately as they are expecting us and have been for some time now. Then we will return and I will introduce you to your facilities here on Earth. It is obvious that you are going to have to operate from here."

Facilities, thought Kevin. That sounds interesting. Borin held up the crystal which immediately started to glow. It got brighter and brighter and seemed to light up the whole garden, except that it was no longer his garden. He glanced around him and found they were standing on an enormous crystal platform which sparked and shone in the light that seemed to come from everywhere and nowhere. A large crystal globe drifted towards them and stopped in front of the group. Borin stepped forward.

"People of the Universe," he announced, "This is your new Master, Kevin." The orb drifted towards Kevin.

"Greet your people," whispered Borin and gave Kevin a nudge.

"Hi," said Kevin. Borin glared at him and indicated, by raising his eyebrows and inclining his head towards the globe, that he wanted Kevin to say more. "Greetings," he continued, "I am pleased to be your new Master and I will do my best to be a good one." At this point he ran out of words. "See you around," he said.

"Thank you Master," said Borin, "I am sure you have the thoughts and good wishes of the whole Universe." He held up his crystal and the Crystal City quickly faded and Kevin's garden reappeared.

"Oh dear," said Borin, "That was a disaster. Never in the last twenty-five thousand years has there been an acceptance speech like that."

"Oh, thank you," said Kevin looking quite pleased with himself.

"No, I mean it was really bad," he continued.

"I don't think it was that bad," said Haranot, "After all, they have never seen one of these creatures before."

"I wish you would stop calling me a creature," objected Kevin.

"I think it is time to move on to the Earth HQ," said Haranot.

"A good idea," said Borin raising his crystal again. This time it seemed to get darker and Kevin soon realised that he was in a cave. It seemed to be a natural cave cut into the native limestone by thousands of years of water seeping through. The air had a very damp smell about it. It started to get a bit lighter and Kevin could soon see that it was a very large cavern indeed. Borin strode off followed by Haranot and the four Murin. The illumination seemed to follow them so Kevin quickly followed before he was left completely in the dark, in more ways than one. At the other side of the cavern was a strange object. It looked rather like a small flying saucer, or at least, Kevin's idea of one. It was a lustrous silver colour and seemed to sparkle as if lit from within.

"This is your local transport," said Borin.

"Local?" asked Kevin.

"Yes," said Borin, "It will get you around the solar system quite quickly, but you will need your crystal for travel over greater distances. Also, you can use it to get you around the surface of this planet. It is very easy to use. I will show you. However, firstly, I must give you your crystal. This is the most important thing you will have, and it must never, I repeat never, leave you for an instant. It is on a chain so that you can wear it around your neck at all times."

He took a small sparkling thing out of his pocket and proceeded to place it around Kevin's neck.

"I feel silly wearing this," objected Kevin.

"Nevertheless," continued Borin, "You must never remove it under any circumstances. This is how you use it." He placed it on Kevin's forehead. "Hold it here," he said, "Now close your eyes and think of the other side of the cave."

Kevin did so. "What now?" he asked.

"Open your eyes," said Borin. His voice sounded a long way off. Kevin opened his eyes and looked around him. He was now on the far side of the cave from the others.

"Do the same again," said Borin, "But this time think of where we are."

Kevin did that and immediately something hit him and went rolling on the floor.

"Look where you're going," protested Haranot from the floor.

"Sorry," said Kevin, "I forgot where you were. Say, this is great. I could have all sorts of fun with this."

"That is not its purpose," said Borin, "I want you to take this very seriously. Now your transport. Please get in."

Kevin looked at the object that had been referred to as transport but could not see a door. He ran his hands over the surface, but it was perfectly smooth.

"Use the crystal," prompted Haranot. Kevin did so. He disappeared from outside the vehicle and a cry of pain came from inside.

"Mind the console," shouted Haranot."

"Thank you," came Kevin's voice from inside, "But you are a bit late."

Haranot used his own crystal and appeared in the seat beside Kevin.

"It's a bit small in here," said Kevin.

"Pull that lever back a little," said Haranot pointing to a knobbly thing in front of Kevin. Kevin did so and the shape of the craft seemed to change. He soon got the hang of it and had rearranged the dimensions to suit his proportions.

"Good," said Haranot, "Now for the driving lesson."

"But I'm only ten," protested Kevin, "I'll get into trouble if I drive. I can't do that 'til I'm sixteen."

"I don't think this will count," said Haranot, "Now let's get started."

"How can we go anywhere?" asked Kevin, ", we're in a cave."

"First you must use your crystal to get us out of the cave, and then use the controls to move the vehicle where you want it to go. I'll show you the controls before we start as you have to be able to take control as soon as we appear outside, otherwise we would just fall to the ground."

Kevin began to think that this was going to be too difficult for him, but after being taught how to hover and rotate the craft in either direction, he thought that, maybe, he could manage it after all. The 'Blob', as Kevin had christened the craft, was very easy to control and it almost flew itself.

"Now I think we can attempt a flight outside," said Haranot, "But first you must take the vehicle, along with the two of us outside. To do this you must concentrate. You must visualise the vehicle, with you and me inside, at a reasonable height outside."

"Can I try a short trip," asked Kevin, "Like across to the other side of the cave."

"If we must."

Kevin closed his eyes and visualised the Blob, complete with himself and Haranot, at the other side of the cave. When he opened them, he was amazed to find that they were now at the other side of the cave. This gave him much more confidence, enough confidence, in fact, to try for the big one. He closed his eyes again and thought, with all his might, of the Blob zooming across the sky with himself at the controls and Haranot beside him.

"I think it might be a good idea if you opened your eyes now," said Haranot with a trace of panic in his voice, "Open your eyes now!"

Kevin opened his eyes and found that they were tumbling through the clouds and approaching the ground very fast indeed.

"Take control, please," shouted Haranot, "Level out, quickly." Kevin set the controls to central position, as he had been shown, and the Blob immediately straightened out into level flight. This was great. Kevin's imagination ran riot. What fun he could have with this. Without really thinking what he was doing he put the Blob through a loop and then a couple of victory rolls.

"Stop it," shouted Haranot in terror, "You'll kill us both. Please be careful."

"Just putting it through its paces," said Kevin slowing the Blob and settling back into a nice level flight. "What next?"

"Back to the cave, I think," said Haranot, "But first we must slow to a stationary hover. Then we can transfer to the cave. We don't want to enter the cave at the speed of sound, do we?"

"I suppose not," said Kevin slowing until the Blob was hovering above the moors. Then Kevin closed his eyes and visualised the inside of the cave. This time he opened his eyes quickly to find that they had arrived back safely. He lowered the Blob to the ground and closed down the power. He then used his crystal again to transfer Haranot and himself outside to where Borin and the Murin were waiting for him.

"You have done well," said Borin, "I think that will do for now. Tomorrow we will carry on with your basic training, but now you must return home before you are missed."

Kevin was expecting Borin to transport him back but soon found that he was now expected to do this on his own, so he used the crystal again, and was immediately back in his garden. All was normal and no-one was looking for him, so he went in and watched television for a while until his mother told him that it was bedtime.

Chapter 5 - More to learn

When Kevin awoke the next morning, he was surprised to find his clothes laid out neatly at the foot of his bed. He was surprised because, although his mother always told him to keep his clothes neat and tidy, he never did. He distinctly remembered taking them off the previous evening and throwing them into the corner out of the way. A lad of his age would hate to get a reputation for being tidy. But there they were, neatly folded on his bed. Perhaps his mother had come in after he was asleep and tidied them up. But why? She never had before. Then, as he stood wondering, he caught a glimpse out of the corner of his eye, of something in the corner of his room that should not have been there. He turned and was amazed to see four small creatures standing to attention, or as near to attention as their fat little bodies would allow. They were the Murin, the little attendants he had seen with Haranot. He had also seen them at the strange crystal house he had been sent to. But what were they doing here?

"What do you want?" he asked sharply.

"We are instructed to attend the Master of the Universe," said one of the Murin without moving.

"Well, I don't need attending, thank you," said Kevin, "So you can go back to where you came from." The Murin looked perplexed. "I am sorry sir," said their spokesman, "but we have been instructed to attend you. The Master cannot be left unattended. We will not get in your way but are here whenever you need us."

"Oh, if you must," said Kevin, "but don't let anyone see you. That could be quite embarrassing."

"Of course not. You will not know we are there unless you need us."

The more he thought about it the more he thought that having a troupe of miniature helpers could be very useful. Anyway, today was Saturday and he was going to make the most of it. He got dressed and headed for the door. He could smell breakfast and it made him feel very hungry.

"While I'm gone," he said as he disappeared onto the landing, "you can tidy my room." As he left he caught a glimpse of frantic activity out of the corner of his eye. This could be good, he thought.

He went downstairs thinking what he was going to do today. He had the day to himself so he had plenty of time to see what the Blob could do. He had almost finished his breakfast before he realised that he was eating it. Better make the most of it, he thought, it could be a long day and he did not want to waste any of it having to come home for meals.

As he finished his third slice of toast, his mother came in looking very puzzled.

"Your room is very tidy," she said. "It's not like you to tidy up without being told."

"Well, I thought I would go on a long walk today, so I tidied my room first," he said.

"I suppose you'll want a packed lunch, then?" she said picking up the bread knife and starting to make him some sandwiches. Things were working out all right. His absence was not going to be noticed.

He got up from the table and headed for his room. When he opened the door to his room he stopped dead, his mouth open in amazement. The room had never looked so tidy. Suddenly there were four little figures standing in a row; the Murin.

"Look, you can't do this. Someone will get suspicious if you make my room look too tidy," he said crossly.

The larger of the Murin stepped forward. "We are sorry to displease you," he said. "We like to keep things tidy, it is what we are here for."

Kevin was in no mood to argue. There were much more interesting things to do today, so he set about packing his rucksack. He did not need much, really, but it had to look right. He could not go off walking without being fully equipped or someone would smell a rat.

When he had finished, he marched out onto the landing followed closely by four small figures.

"You mustn't be seen," he said pushing the Murin back into his room. "If you have to come you'll have to find your own way. Just don't let anyone see you."

He closed the door on them and set off down the stairs and into the kitchen where his mother was just closing the lid on his packed lunch. She took his rucksack from him and put the lunch pack inside and fastened it up securely.

"Have you got everything you might need?" she asked. It was just force of habit as she knew he would pack everything that he might need for a day out walking. He had gone off on his own since he was quite small and knew the moors very well and certainly knew what to do and what not to do. "Don't be too late back."

"I won't." he shouted back as he ran down the path to the hidden end of the garden. His mother watched him disappear into the foliage. "I wonder if he packed his waterproof?" she thought. "Perhaps I had better check." She ran down the garden to catch up with him but when she reached the wall, there was no sign of him. She looked across the field but he was nowhere in sight. "Strange," she thought as she turned and walked back up to the house. She did not see four small shapes scuttle out of the undergrowth and apparently burst like bubbles with a faint popping sound.

Meanwhile, Kevin had arrived at the hidden cave by using his crystal. He was getting quite good at it now but was quite surprised to find he had a welcoming committee consisting of Borin, Haranot and another creature he had not seen before. Before anyone could speak the four Murin arrived rather hastily, tumbling over each other in their badly timed landing. Borin ignored them while Haranot gave them a meaningful glare.

"Ah, Master," said Borin. "I hope you had a peaceful night and that these Murin looked after you satisfactorily?"

"Rather too satisfactorily, actually. My mother was very suspicious."

"Well, be that as it may," continued Borin. "I would like you to meet your new tutor." He indicated to creature at his side. It was a little smaller than Borin and had the features that reminded him of a pantomime cat. It did not have a tail, however, and if it had fur, it was very short and smooth. It wore a green and brown tunic and what looked like dark green tights. On his feet were a pair of boots that made him look even more like Puss-in-Boots. "This is Quartok Quanoga. He will teach you all you need to know about being Master of the Universe."

"Pleased to meet you Sir," said Kevin offering his hand.

"Greetings Master," he replied. "Please do not call me Sir, it is not fitting. You may call me Quartok if you wish."

"Thank you, Quartok. When do we start? I am longing to have another go with the Blob." They all looked puzzled. "The vehicle that you showed me yesterday. I call it the Blob."

"Oh, yes of course. Very apt." replied Quartok looking a bit dubious. "We could start with that right now, if you wish, and while we are travelling, I can give some more idea of your responsibilities now that you are Master of the Universe. It is a heavy burden you carry as many billions of creatures depend on you."

Kevin was not too sure he liked the sound of that. The word 'responsibility' had an ominous ring to it. They transferred to the Blob with no mishaps and then Kevin flipped, as they called it, the Blob and themselves out into the clear morning sky. It took him a second or two to gain control of it but it was not bad for only his second attempt.

"Where would you like to go?" asked Quartok.

"Where can we go?" replied Kevin.

"Wherever you like within the solar system," said Quartok. "We would need to flip to go any distance. How about a trip round the Moon?"

"Wow. Unreal."

"On the contrary. There's nothing unreal about this," said Quartok sternly. "I must remind you that this isn't a game. This is an important part of your training. Anyway, enough said about that for now. Firstly, we need to leave the earth's atmosphere. Take her straight up until I tell you to stop."

Kevin looked very surprised. Straight up? He was not too sure that he was going to like this but he pulled back the controls and sent the Blob hurtling towards space. It was quite amazing as there was no sense of acceleration, no being forced back into the seat and being unable to breathe. The sky grew darker and darker until it was completely black and the stars could be seen more clearly than he had ever seen them before. Then he saw the edge of the moon peeking out from behind the curve of the earth. As they sped out into space it came more and more into view.

"Now we will be able to flip," said Quartok in a matter-of-fact way. "Use your crystal and take us to a point to the side of the Moon, not too close and not straight at it. At this speed we would hit the moon with such a force they would see the dust cloud from earth. If you can judge it so that we are approaching the Moon on a path that will take us past it, that would be best."

Kevin held his crystal to his forehead and concentrated on the Moon, thinking of a path that would take him past it. Suddenly the Moon grew in size to almost fill his field of view making him gasp.

"You may well gasp," said Quartok. "That was much closer than I intended. However, now we're here you had better attend to your steering. Stay at this height and follow the curve of the Moon. You can reduce speed so that you have time to see what we are passing.

Kevin slowed down and flew the Blob in a curve around the Moon and when he was happy with his course, he looked out at the view. It was breath-taking. He could see all the craters in minute detail. It was absolutely amazing.

"Can we go closer?" he asked excitedly.

"If you wish. But slow down and go carefully. You seem to be able to control this machine quite well now, but don't get too sure of yourself."

"I won't." said Kevin setting the Blob in a downward direction. The Moon raced towards him but he slowed as the surface got closer until they were moving along quite slowly a few hundred feet up. He sat transfixed for a long time, watching the rocks and the craters slide silently past beneath his feet.

"I don't suppose we can get out, can we?" he asked already knowing that the answer would be no. He would need a space suit and there were none in the Blob that he knew of, and anyway, there would not be one to fit him.

"If you really want to," said Quartok. "You'll have to learn some time, so why not now? First bring the craft to a halt. You don't need to land."

Kevin did that. "But I haven't a space suit," he objected.

"And you don't need one. Hold your crystal in one hand and imagine a thin plastic bag completely surrounding you, full of air. Make it stronger with your mind until it is as strong as steel."

Kevin tried and found that he could do it quite easily. The crystal gave his mind powers that he would not have imagined.

"Now think yourself outside," continued Quartok. Kevin did that and immediately found himself standing on the surface of the Moon. It was amazing. He took a few careful steps and found that he virtually flew into the air if he pushed too hard. After a time, he had managed to judge it so that he could move along at a fantastic pace with very little effort. He could hardly believe he was actually on the Moon and felt sure he would wake up any minute.

Suddenly he felt that he was gasping for breath and his head began to spin. He did not know what was happening. He felt very dizzy and had to sit down as everything went black. Then he began to feel better and found that he was breathing again. He opened his eyes and found he was back inside the Blob. "What happened?" he gasped.

"You ran out of air so I brought you back in again. It was a harsh lesson, perhaps, but in future you will realise that you still have to be careful. When you created a bubble of air for yourself, you didn't make it very large so you ran out of air fairly quickly. Even so, you could have flipped yourself back in here when you needed to, but you panicked and didn't think. That would have been fatal if I hadn't been here."

"Thank you," said Kevin meekly. "But you could have told me before I went outside."

"In my experience, it is the things that you discover for yourself that are best learnt. Now, let's go back home, shall we. On the return journey I shall leave it completely to you. But bear in mind the fact that one wrong move could kill us both."

Kevin settled himself into his seat and set the Blob into a steep climb away from the moon and towards the Earth. He remembered what he had been told on the outward journey and soon they were on their decent through the clouds. He had managed to flip to an ideal spot above the North Atlantic and had been able to recognise the British Isles and head towards it. It was more difficult to navigate when they were closer to the ground but eventually he saw scenery that he recognised and brought the Blob to a standstill above the familiar moorland. Then using the crystal, he flipped them into the cave where the others were waiting for them.

Chapter 6 - The Council

For the next few weeks, Kevin spent every spare moment with Quartok learning all he could about his new powers and what was required of him as the Master of the Universe. He still could not really believe all that was happening to him and still seemed rather like a game, or perhaps, being in a play where some of the time he was a character in a different world, and the rest of the time he went back to his normal life.

At school, things were much the same as they had always been. He was the one that no-one took much notice of. So far, he had not risked using his crystal at school, but he had thought about it a few times. He wore the crystal on a chain around his neck so that no-one would see it. But then, the others took little notice of him so he felt fairly safe about it.

Quartok had told him that soon he would need to attend a council meeting at the Galactic Capital of Lume. The thought of being transported half way across the galaxy did not bother him half as much as the thought of having to speak to a bunch of strangers, and very strange strangers at that. Up to now he had met very few of these strange people and all had been friendly. However, it would seem that not all would be like this. He had been warned, particularly, about Duros, Governor of the Third Sector. He was of a quite different species, more related to lizards than humans, who had a history of violent and warlike activities. They had long since been pacified and brought into the galactic federation, but their personalities were still rather aggressive. Duros was against the appointment of a Master of the Universe chosen by a small group in the time-honoured way. He much preferred the Master to be elected by vote. That would give him a chance of achieving the coveted position of power.

The school holidays were approaching and it was during this time that Kevin would be expected to be able to get away for a day or two. He was sometimes allowed to go off with friends to camp for a few days, if the weather was good, and he was planning such a trip for this holiday. He had mixed feelings about going to Lume. He found all the other aspects of his new position very exciting, more than any boy could dream of. However, it was all beginning to have a serious side which was not so much fun. But, if he wanted to take advantage of the fun side of things, he would have to accept the responsibilities too.

Quartok had shown him video recordings of the Council in session and had shown him all the members until he felt he knew them all personally. Duros did not look as bad as Quartok made him sound and Kevin wondered whether the two of them did not get on too well. Now, as the time for his trip came closer, he began to feel more confident and was almost looking forward to it.

On the day of the trip, Kevin had his breakfast and tried to act as he would if he were really going camping with his friends. The Murin had packed his rucksack and put everything into it that he would need, both for a camping trip and a visit to Lume. He said goodbye to his mother and staggered off down the track to catch the bus, or at least, that was what his mother thought he was doing. His friends were going on their camping trip, but Kevin had told them, at the last minute, that he could not go, so they would be on their way by now.

At the bottom of the track, Quartok was waiting for him. They linked arms and Quartok used his crystal to transport them both to the galactic capital of Lume. There was no sense of having moved, but the surroundings suddenly shimmered and changed into a large open square with people bustling here and there, going about their business. Kevin and Quartok found themselves standing on a raised platform which had steps leading down to the square below. As Kevin looked around, other people were appearing and without taking any notice of him they hurried off about their own business.

"Follow me," said Quartok heading for the steps. Kevin leapt after him, not wishing to be left behind in a strange place, and nearly fell down the steps which were rather small for his feet. It was then he realised that everyone else in sight was smaller than he was and it made him feel rather conspicuous. However, no-one seemed to give him a second glance.

At the bottom of the steps they headed across the square towards a very tall and very impressive looking building that seemed to be made out of solid glass as it sparkled in the sunlight. And that was another thing, the sun seemed much larger than it should be and much redder. It was like you would expect at sunset, except that it was much higher in the sky.

On the far side of the square, Kevin could see Blobs, like his own, except they were of all different sizes. Some were just standing outside buildings while others were either leaving or just arriving from above. There were no roads, as such, as the Blobs did not require them.

When they reached the large building, Quartok carried straight on up the steps to the entrance.

"Where are we going?" asked Kevin.

"This is the government building where we will be staying and where the meetings are to be held," said Quartok.

Inside they walked to a large reception desk where people seemed to be checking in and out, rather like a large hotel. At the desk Quartok did not need to say who they were as the figure behind the desk suddenly started dashing around, summoning assistance from an army of Murin.

"Welcome Master," he said directly to Kevin. "I hope your stay will be a pleasant one."

"Thank you," replied Kevin automatically. The Murin picked up his baggage, which was larger than they were, and it took several of them to trundle it off at great speed. Several other creatures, not Murin, arranged themselves in front of Kevin and Quartok and led the way out of the large entrance hall and into the main body of the building. It reminded Kevin of the place he was sent to when he was being tested. That seemed a long time ago though it was actually only a few weeks. They passed along lofty corridors, through splendid halls before turning and going through a much smaller doorway leading into a much smaller passage way. At the end of the passage was a narrow staircase leading upwards. At the top of the stairs was a much smaller corridor than the ones in the public areas and much more to Kevin's liking. There was a carpet on the floor and the walls were covered in what looked like wallpaper, all in darker colours. It felt quite homely after the vast echoing halls.

At the end of the corridor, was a wider area with several doors in each wall and one in the end wall which the Head Murin opened and stood to one side to allow Quartok and Kevin to enter. Quartok stood to one side and indicated that Kevin should go first. After a short pause, he walked cautiously into the most delightful room he had ever seen. It was like something out of a fairy tale with quaint old fashioned furniture and a little table set with a jug and two cups on a tray and several plates of what looked like cakes. Although Kevin did not recognise them, they looked delicious.

The Murin then scuttled through with the baggage and disappeared into a back room.

"These are the rooms of the Master of the Universe," said Quartok. "They have been designed especially for you by the Craft Murin. I hope you like them."

"It's amazing," said Kelvin. "How did they know what I would like?"

"When you use the crystal, for any purpose, you tap into the energy of the cosmos and in so doing become part of it," said Quartok seriously. "And, as part of the cosmos your innermost thoughts can be read."

Kevin was not too sure that he liked people to have access to his innermost thoughts, especially the ones that involved getting up to mischief. Still it could not be helped, they would have to accept him as he was.

Quartok waved his arm towards a seat and sat himself comfortably into another. Kevin sat down also and looked at the cakes, or whatever they were.

"Please have one," said Quartok. "If there is anything else you require you just have to snap your fingers and a Murin will attend you." He picked up the ornate jug from the table and poured what looked suspiciously like tea into the cups and handed one to Kevin who sipped it cautiously only to find that it was, indeed, tea.

"Do not look so surprised," said Quartok. "It is what you usually drink, I believe."

"It is," said Kevin. "It's just that I didn't expect to find it here."

"Why not, indeed?" asked Quartok. "After all it is the most common drink in all the galaxy."

"Oh," said Kevin at a loss for words. Instead of discussing it further he just sipped his tea and nibbled one of the delicious cakes. Soon Quartok put down his cup, stood up and made for the door.

"A few things to attend to," he said. "Stay here and make yourself at home until I return." So saying he disappeared out of the door. All of a sudden Kevin became very alarmed. Here he was in a strange place, possibly on the other side of the galaxy, alone. It was rather like the time when he was small and his mother had taken him shopping and he had been looking at something in a shop while his mother paid for something she was buying. When he had turned round she had gone and he had panicked. He had run out into the street shouting for her and no-one had taken any notice of him. It was just like that and he felt like running outside shouting for Quartok to come back. But he did not do that. He just sat there, petrified.

After a while he calmed down a little and helped himself to more tea and cake. He told himself there was nothing to worry about as he could use his crystal to take him anywhere; home if the wished it. He stood up and walked around the room looking at things as you might do on your first visit to a strange house while your host was in the kitchen preparing tea. He hardly dared touch anything for fear of breaking it until he suddenly though, "I am the Master of the Universe. Why should I be worried about breaking something?" So he reached out his hand to pick up an ornament that had caught his eye and had almost taken hold of it when there was a knock at the door. He almost leapt out of his skin as if someone had caught him out doing something naughty.

He pulled himself together and walked over to the door and opened it, and there standing outside was a person he was sure he knew.

"Greetings Master," he said and bowed low making Kevin feel rather uncomfortable.

"Hello," said Kevin. "Don't I know you?"

"Alas, no, for we have never met," said the visitor. "However, I am Duros, Governor of the Third Sector, at your service."

Duros! So that is why he recognised him. He had seen his face on all those recordings that Quartok had shown him.

"Might I be permitted to enter?" asked Duros. "I have urgent business I would like to discuss with you."

"Of course," said Kevin. "Please come in." He stood aside and Duros walked in, took off his shiny blue silk gloves and sat himself down in the chair that Kevin had been sitting in.

"Please make yourself at home," said Kevin feeling a little annoyed at this intrusion.

"Thank you," said Duros. "Now to business."

Chapter 7 - Into Danger

Quartok had left Kevin to see to arrangements for the next day's Council Meeting and was now seated in a cosy little office with three of the Council officials discussing protocol. It was quite difficult as there had never been a Master before who was so young and had come from a planet outside the federation. To all intents, Kevin was a barbarian child with no knowledge of the civilised universe. Normally, the Master would have been aware of his duties and would know the intricacies of galactic politics, but Kevin did not even know much about the politics of his own planet. The discussion had gone on for quite a while when Quartok finally had to give his apologies and hurry back to Kevin's rooms. You can imagine his surprise and horror when he arrived there and found them empty. He rushed from room to room calling out for Kevin, but he had gone. He summoned the Murin and demanded to know where Kevin had gone, but as they had not been called by Kevin, they had no idea why he was not still there.

There was only one thing he could do and that was to use his crystal to contact Kevin, or at least to find out where he had gone. He fumbled feverishly in his pocket for his crystal and held it to his forehead and concentrated. Immediately he felt the link to Kevin's crystal burst into life but there was no response from Kevin.

"Where are you?" he shouted and almost in reply a pulsating glow came from the seat where Kevin had been sitting. Quartok darted for the seat and picked up Kevin's crystal.

"Oh no," he said and slumped into the seat, his head in his hands. "Oh no." Without the crystal Kevin was just a helpless earth boy, lost in a strange world. The crystal gave him powers that he had not yet realised, powers that would be his only when he had matured enough to use them. But now he had none, not even the crystal's power of speech translation. Without his crystal he would not be able to understand a thing anyone said to him.

Quartok went to the door and looked up and down the corridor, but there was no-one in sight. Where could he have gone? If he was on his own he could not have gone far, so Quartok decided that he must calm himself down and be logical. Where could Kevin have gone if he were on his own? The only route he knew was back to the entrance hall and there was nothing down there to interest a boy. Perhaps he had gone to explore the passages in the other direction. Quartok was sure that small earth boys would be just as inquisitive as small boys from any planet in the known universe, and this did worry him.

A careful search must be made and he would need help. He put his crystal to his forehead and mind spoke to the council members that he knew he could trust. It was imperative that Duros did not hear about it. The last thing he wanted was for Kevin to fall into the hands of Duros. As far as he knew, Duros was unaware of Kevin's presence here.

There was a clatter of feet running down the corridor and three small, but rather portly figures staggered round the corner, breathing heavily. The first, and youngest, was Snee followed closely by Larnock and Djie, all representatives of the Ganymede sector and close friends of Quartok. Immediately Quartok started giving orders to them so that an efficient search pattern could be employed without giving anyone cause to wonder what they were up to. They hurried to the end of the corridor and then each took a different path where the corridor split. Quartok went back to Kevin's room to wait, just in case he returned of his own accord. He kept his crystal to hand and received reports from the other three at regular intervals. Eventually Larnock returned to Kevin's room while the other two continued the search.

"It's no use," he said to Quartok as he entered. "He's not anywhere in this wing of the building, unless of course he's in someone's room."

"Why would he be in someone's room?" asked Quartok. "He doesn't know anybody."

"Maybe somebody knows him, though."

"What do you mean? Nobody knows him," snapped Quartok. "Not only that, nobody knows he is here."

"As far as we know," said Larnock. "There are people who make it their business to know what is going on, especially when it concerns the new Master of the Council."

"Not Duros, surely?" gasped Quartok. "If he's fallen into the hands of Duros we're in very deep trouble."

"Perhaps you had better call for an armed guard to accompany us to Duros' apartments," said Larnock.

"No! I don't want it to get out that we have lost the Master," snapped Quartok.

"We?" said Larnock. "I think that Kevin is your responsibility."

"Whatever. Still, I think it would be better to avoid a panic, and we certainly don't want to go throwing accusations about until we're sure. Especially where Duros is concerned. No, I think we'll have to go there ourselves on some sort of pretext and see if we can discover anything. Recall the others."

"They're already on their way," said Larnock.

When the others arrived at Kevin's room they sat down to decide what they were going to say to Duros. They would make it a friendly visit to let him know that Kevin was going to attend the next council meeting and see how he reacted. So they set off for the other side of the building where Duros had his sumptuous apartments. It was quite a long walk but none of them wanted to get there too quickly by using their crystals.

They eventually arrived and by this time they were feeling quite nervous. They looked at each other, hoping that someone else would knock at the door.

"I think you should knock, Quartok," said Larnock. "After all, you are the senior member here." The others agreed and pushed Quartok forward. He stood there for a moment, composing himself before reaching out and touching the bell plate by the door. A moment later the door slid silently back to reveal three Murin. The centre Murin stepped forward.

"You are welcome to the rooms of Master Duros," he said politely. "May I inquire who calls?"

"I am Quartok of the Council, and I am accompanied by three colleagues, Masters Larnock, Snee and Djie," said Quartok formally.

"Thank you," said the Murin. "Please come inside and make yourselves comfortable. I will inform the Master that you are here."

They followed the Murin into a sumptuous living room and sat down in the most wonderful seats they had ever seen. Duros made no attempt at hiding his vast wealth. There were valuable ornaments all around them from all parts of the known universe. The lighting in the room seemed to come from nowhere in particular but cast an even glow over everything in the room. The air was cool but fresh.

"What a room," said Snee in amazement. "Makes mine look like a peasant's cottage."

"You would think that he would have more taste than to flaunt his wealth like this," said Larnock with a sneer of distaste, if not a little envy.

"I'm glad you like my humble abode," a voice from behind them bellowed. "Cosy isn't it?" The four of them leapt to their feet as if the seats had suddenly become red hot. "Master Quartok, so pleased to meet you informally. I don't think we have allowed ourselves this pleasure before, have we?"

"No, I suppose not," said Quartok. "You know my friends, I presume?"

"Of course, although as I said, we haven't met informally before. To what do I owe the pleasure?"

"I, that is, we thought that it would be only polite of us to inform you of the presence of the new Master. He is hoping to preside over the next council meeting," said Quartok a little awkwardly.

"That is most kind of you Quartok. I shall look forward to seeing him in action, as it were. I am told that the new Master is rather younger than we are used to, and from a rather insignificant planet rather off the beaten track."

"Yes, that is true. In fact, we have been kept very busy preparing him for his responsibilities," said Quartok. "But he is shaping up well. I think he will eventually be a very good Master. In the meantime, I hope you will go easy on him as he isn't yet used to the cut and thrust of council debate."

"I will not go out of my way to upset him, of course," said Duros. "But I still have my responsibilities to my sector."

"Of course," agreed Quartok. "I wouldn't want you to neglect your duties."

"Good," said Duros. "So, if that is all, I'm afraid that I have pressing duties that need my attention, so I will wish you good day. The Murin will see you out." So saying, he turned and strode out, and before he had disappeared into the inner rooms the Murin were propelling each of them out of the apartment.

Chapter 8 - Panic

When Duros arrived, Kevin was thrown into panic. He had been warned about Duros and did not know what to do. On the face of it, he seemed quite a pleasant sort of chap. Perhaps Quartok had been exaggerating, so Kevin thought it best to act as if nothing were wrong. He invited Duros in and was a little annoyed at the way he made himself at home, strutting in and sitting in the chair that Kevin had just left.

"Now to business," said Duros.

"I think I should call Quartok if there are to be business discussions," said Kevin fumbling for his crystal.

"I don't think that will be necessary," said Duros sharply. What I have to say is for your ears only.

This Kevin found intriguing and it made him feel rather important. Why not hear what Duros had to say? Where would be the harm in that?

"OK," said Kevin. "Fire away." Duros looked startled but soon realised that it was just a figure of speech.

"I thought it was only fair that you should know some of the background information before attending the council meeting. So far, you will only have heard one side of the argument."

"I didn't know there was an argument," said Kevin feeling rather clever.

"Of course you didn't," said Duros. "You only know what they want you to know. The things that are in their interest for you to know. You see the civilised universe is not as civilised as you have been led to believe. It must all seem idyllic to you; little men at your beck and call to do whatever you wish. Crystal power to take you wherever you want to go. It must seem like some marvellous holiday that you are on."

"Well it is all rather different to what I have known at home," said Kevin. "So how is it different from what I've seen?"

"Perhaps I should show you," he said springing to his feet. "Come with me and I'll show you things that will make your hair curl."

Kevin was not too sure that he wanted his hair to curl. "Where to?" he asked lamely.

"Here and there, never mind where exactly. It wouldn't mean anything to you if I told you. Here, take my hand and we'll be on our way." He offered his hand in a way that was not to be rejected. Kevin took it and immediately the room faded and he was dazzled by a brilliant sun shining straight into his eyes. He slapped his hand over his eyes and looked down at the ground until his eyes had adjusted themselves to the brightness. Then he ventured a look around and was appalled by a scene of utter devastation. There was not a single plant or tree to be seen, just dust and dirt and dreary grey buildings as far as the eye could see. By this time the heat of the sun was becoming unbearable.

"Come with me," said Duros sharply and strode off towards the nearest building. Kevin dashed after him and had just about caught up with him when he opened a door and disappeared inside. Kevin followed and was greeted by the most awful sight he had ever seen. Hundreds of small ragged folk were working in terrible conditions while other larger, vicious looking creatures were hitting them or prodding them with long sticks. The noise was almost unbearable as hammers clashed on metal and metal crashed down on the hard, stone floor.

He suddenly realised that Duros was dragging him to one side and towards a doorway. Once through the door it was a little quieter and Kevin could hear what Duros was trying to say to him.

"This is what your friends are keeping from you," he said. "Did you think that all the nice things you saw in the civilised world were made by magic? Well, now you know differently." Duros grabbed his hand again and the factory, or whatever it was, disappeared to be replaced by a vast desert with only small tufts of vegetation growing in hollows where they could get some shelter from the biting cold wind. There was a solitary figure moving about among some rocks a little way off.

"What is he doing?" asked Kevin.

"He is one of the people who have managed to survive here after the planet was picked dry by the mighty production machine of the civilised world. This was once like the world that we have just seen, but it became worked out, just as the last one will be in a few years. That creature over there is looking for food amongst the rocks."

"Food?" cried Kevin. "What food could possibly be here?"

"There will be small amounts of moss and lichen, a few tough roots, and if he is lucky, maybe a small land crab or lizard." Kevin felt sick.

"And you say this is all down to the council?"

"Who else?" said Duros. The council is responsible for everything in the universe so it must be responsible for this. And of course, the Master is responsible for the council so must also be directly responsible for this. Don't you agree?"

"But that's me," said Kevin in alarm. "Are you saying this is my fault?"

Duros shrugged. "Who else?" he asked. Then as if he had been interrupted by someone, he put his hand on the crystal that hung around his neck and seemed to be listening. "You'll have to excuse me for a moment. Things to attend to." And before Kevin could reply he was gone leaving Kevin alone, goodness knows where. For a moment he stood transfixed glancing around him. Immediately, he groped for his own crystal. Perhaps this was his chance to get back home out of harm's way. He felt sure he had mastered the crystal well enough to do that. Where was the darned thing? He could not find it anywhere. He must have dropped it somewhere. Panic set in. He fell to his knees, scratching around in the sand for his lost crystal. Where was the thing? Perhaps this was Duros's plan all along to bring him to this God forsaken place and abandon him, and without his crystal they would never find him. He was at a complete loss what to think. Quartok and the others seemed decent people, but then again, so did Duros. Mind you, he had not seen so much of Duros so he might have been putting on an act for his sake, but why?

He was suddenly aware that he was not alone. He turned slowly to see a dark figure standing behind him, a mere shadow against the sky.

"What are you doing?" the figure asked. It sounded like a young person and did not seem threatening.

"I think I have lost my crystal," said Kevin.

"That was careless of you," answered the figure. Kevin climbed slowly to his feet to find he was looking at a young creature about three quarters his size. He had a course brown cloak wrapped around him and looked rather like a medieval peasant. He must have been of a similar race to Quartok but larger, or at least he would be larger when full grown. His skin was dark and rough, reflecting the harsh life he must lead.

"Yes, it was," said Kevin feeling a little foolish. "But I don't understand why I can understand you without it."

"On this planet everyone had a minute crystal implanted under the skin of their forehead at birth so that there was no problem understanding people from any part of the universe. And after several generations it was found that no crystal was needed. We can all understand anyone, wherever they come from though we haven't had the need for many years now."

Why is that?" asked Kevin.

"Well look at the place. Who would want to come here? It's all worked out now and was abandoned when I was quite young. I can just remember everyone leaving. My parents were frantic to be taken off but we were among the ones that were left. I don't know why. So why are you here?"

"I'm not sure," said Kevin. "I was with Duros from the Council. He was showing me what the Council had done to this planet. He should be back shortly."

"In that case, I think we should go quickly. I will explain later." Grabbing his hand, he raced off almost dragging Kevin after him. He was very agile and dodged in and out of the rocks very nimbly. Kevin was hard pressed to keep up with him, being that much larger, and did not fit so well between the rocks. He cracked his knees a number of times and was about to give up when the creature suddenly stopped.

"What's the matter?" asked Kevin.

"Shhh," came the answer along with a raised hand. Kevin stopped and looked in the direction the creature was looking. At first Kevin saw nothing, but then he thought he saw a movement. There was something moving between the rocks about a hundred yards away. It looked a bit like a lizard but seemed to be walking upright, if a little stooped. Suddenly it stopped and sniffed the air, looking about it. Kevin froze. It looked as if the thing had smelt him and was just trying to locate him ready for the kill. It had a very wicked looking face with large protruding teeth. Then suddenly it was away, moving in long one-legged bounds to pounce on some poor unfortunate creature that was snuffling among the rocks.

"Quickly," whispered his companion and darted off in the opposite direction. When they had put sufficient distance between themselves and the lizard thing, they slowed down to a brisk walk.

"What was that?" asked Kevin.

"Dzarr," came the reply. "There are not many of them about, luckily, but one is more than enough. Come, we are nearly there."

Kevin was not sure where they were going and could not see anything different in the scenery; a few larger rocks, maybe, nothing else.

"Where are we going?" asked Kevin.

"Here," came the answer as the creature rounded a large rock. When Kevin followed him, he was amazed to find that his companion had disappeared.

"Where are you?" shouted Kevin in alarm. He glanced feverishly about him but there was nothing. Then suddenly a rock moved back and the creature reappeared followed by several more similar but larger creatures. One, obviously the senior, stepped forward and looked fiercely at Kevin making him shrink back in alarm even though this creature was no bigger than he was.

"Who are you, and what do you want?" it said.

"I am sorry to intrude but I seem to have been abandoned here," said Kevin meekly. "My name is Kevin."

"Dahn said that you came with someone called Duros," the creature continued. "Is this so?"

Dahn must be the name of the boy who had brought him here. "Yes," replied Kevin. He was showing me what bad things the council had done to you."

"Huh," said the creature. "That's rich. We have been cut off from the civilised universe for many years and that is because we are in the Third Sector. Any planet unfortunate enough to be in the Third Sector will sooner or later meet the same fate as this one did. This was once a rich and beautiful planet. Then Duros came to power and everything changed. It took just 22 years for him to strip the planet of all its wealth before leaving it like this. We are probably lucky to have been left here, though we didn't think so at the time. I expect all those who were taken away became slaves in one of his industrial or mining planets. I don't suppose they lasted long. But then, if you know Duros you will already know this. So what do you want with us now?"

"No, I did not know about this," said Kevin. "In fact, I don't know much about anything. Duros was telling me that this was all down to the council. I think he was trying to get me to side with him."

"And why would he want to do that? What possible use could you be to him?"

"Well, I think it could be because I am the new Master of the Council," said Kevin. It still seemed impossible to him that he was saying that. However, incredible as it may have seemed to Kevin, it had a marked effect on the little gathering, for immediately they all went down onto one knee. Kevin felt quite embarrassed. It had not occurred to him that anyone would take all this seriously. He was fully aware that he was in an extraordinary situation, but he had not realised that people actually thought he was anything important. He had thought of himself more as a mascot or something like that.

"Look," said Kevin. "You don't have to do that. Please get up. Dahn, tell them to get up."

"Master," said the original spokesman. "Please forgive us for our ignorance. We didn't know who you were."

"That doesn't matter," said Kevin. "Now please stand up and tell me who you are."

They grudgingly got to their feet. "I am Petrog, Leader of this group. Dahn is my second son, and this is my first son, Brynn, and here is my daughter, Marlitta."

Brynn was very similar to Dahn in appearance. They both had their father's stocky build. Marlitta was smaller and more delicate looking. Perhaps she took after her mother. Kevin wondered why she had not been mentioned.

"Please will you do us the honour of coming inside where it is safe," said Petrog indicating the hole in the rocks from which they had recently emerged. Kevin stepped forward and cautiously climbed through the gap which was a little on the tight side for him and found himself inside a large cave. The floor was level and covered in fabric of some kind and there were piles of fabric which Kevin assumed were for sitting on. There was light in the cave, not bright, but it illuminated the cave adequately. Kevin could not make out where it came from.

The others had all followed him into the cave and the hole had been closed silently by swinging a rock, shaped exactly to fit the hole, in from one side. Kevin felt sure that no-one would be able to find the entrance from outside unless they already knew about it.

Petrog showed Kevin to a seat on a very comfortable pile of rags which he assumed was usually the seat of Petrog himself. As soon as he had settled himself, the others sat down around him. Petrog clapped his hands and three small creatures ran into the cave from a small opening on the far side.

"I hope you will join us in some food?" asked Petrog.

"Thank you," said Kevin. "That would be very nice." The three small creatures ran off, obviously to fetch food.

Chapter 9 - The Quest

As they sat and ate, Kevin listened to the conversation of the group. They seemed very nice people and Kevin was particularly struck by Marlitta who was remarkably pretty considering she belonged to a family of savages, or at least, that was how he saw them. She must have been older than he was though she was several inches shorter. At school he would not have owned up to having any feelings for girls, that was not 'cool'. But here it was different. He did not have to worry about what other people thought.

As they sat and ate, Kevin told them his story; about how he had been 'chosen', and about all that had happened to him since then. Petrog told Kevin all about life on Irma, which was what they called their planet, and how it had once been a beautiful place with lush green vegetation and a happy population. But that was before Duros had come to power. At first they saw no change, but they began to hear rumours about what was happening on other planets. Still they did not think it would happen to them until one day, it did.

Fleets of spaceships arrived and started unloading machinery. Immediately they started ripping up the beautiful countryside and flattening villages and towns only to build monstrous grey factories and mines in their place. People were rounded up and herded into the factories where they were sorted into groups depending upon their abilities and strength. The lucky ones went to the factories while those less lucky went to the mines. No-one knew what happened to the rest and no-one asked.

This went on for many years. Only the strong and the most determined survived until, finally, the planet was exhausted. The factories shut down and were dismantled and everything of value was loaded onto the spaceships and taken away. All those fit enough to be of use were taken away as well. Petrog begged them to take his wife and himself and not to abandon them on this lifeless planet. But it was not to be. They were too old to be of use, anyway, there would be plenty of younger people on the next planet they went to.

Not many were left, but those that were, grouped together with others they met up with and survived as best they could. It was hard, but they managed, and after a few years they had produced several children who had never known anything else and were ideally suited to this environment. So Brynn, Dahn and Marlitta had grown up on this planet and had never known civilisation, as such. They had heard stories of how it had been but found it very difficult to imagine what it must have been like. Their mother, it transpired, was away visiting friends across the valley and would not be back until the next day. Her name was Zerlinda, and Kevin wondered if she looked like Marlitta.

Petrog seemed very pleased that Kevin had arrived and could see great things coming of it.

"You must go back to the council," he said excitedly, "And tell them what has become of us." Realising he had spoken this way to the Master of the Universe, he stuttered an apology and looked most embarrassed. "I am sorry to presume so much," he said. "I did not mean to tell you what to do."

"Don't mention it," said Kevin. "That is exactly what I would like to do, only there is a bit of a problem,"

They all looked concerned but said nothing.

"You see," Kevin continued. "I have lost my crystal. I must have left it in my room when Duros came and fetched me. We came here using his crystal and now I can't get back unless Quartok, or one of the others from the council, comes and gets me, and they don't know where I am." He felt like bursting into tears, but it did not seem right for the Master of the Universe to burst into tears.

"Unless I can find another crystal," he continued, "I am stuck here. Unless I go back and wait for Duros to come back and find me. I could play along with him for a while, at least until he gets me back."

"I do not think that would be a good idea," said Petrog. "Duros will have realised by now that you have either met up with people like us, or that you have been eaten by a Dzarr or something similar. If it is the latter, he will forget all about you, but if he thinks you have met up with us he will do everything in his power to get rid of you. He was risking a lot trying to convince you that he was the good one. Maybe he was just trying to confuse you so that you wouldn't take a stand against him, at least, not for the moment."

The conversation continued well into the evening until Petrog eventually suggested that it was time to sleep. Kevin was given a comparatively clean pile of rugs and animal skins on which to sleep and, despite everything, he was soon sleeping soundly.

The next morning, he awoke and took a little while to remember where he was. The rock had been moved from the cave opening and a cool grey dawn filtered in. Smoke was rising from a small fire in the centre of the cave and Marlitta was prodding something in a pan over the flames. Everyone else seemed to have gone.

Kevin got slowly to his feet and stretched himself. Seeing that he was up and about, Marlitta emptied the contents of the pan into a rough earthenware bowl and took it to him.

"I hope this will be to your liking," she said with a hint of disdain in her voice. Kevin was sorry she felt like that about him and did not feel that he deserved to be judged by someone who did not even know him. Perhaps he had been right about girls all along. He sat down and tucked into his breakfast. He had no idea what it was, but it tasted good. When he had finished it he took his bowl back to Marlitta who looked at him with fire in her eyes.

"So, the Master of the Universe wants me to wash his dish, does he," she snapped snatching it from him.

"No," said Kevin looking startled. "I am quite able to wash my own dish, if I knew where the water was."

"Never mind," she said brusquely, "I'll do it anyway."

"Marlitta!" the voice came from the doorway and startled both of them. "That is not the way to treat a guest. I thought you had better manners." Petrog looked furious. "Go and get the water." Marlitta dashed out of the doorway and Kevin could hear her footsteps disappearing down the gravel path.

"I am sorry about that," said Petrog. "She will be severely punished as soon as she returns."

"No, please do not do that on my account," said Kevin.

"She must be punished for her behaviour whoever the guest. She has dishonoured the family by speaking so."

What will you do to her?" asked Kevin hoping it would not be too bad.

"She will be whipped when she returns. It is only right."

"No, I wouldn't want that," said Kevin in alarm. He still had a soft spot for her even though she had been rude to him. If she were punished on his account he could never be friends with her.

"Well she has to be punished in some way. I will leave it to you to decide. I must have your decision before we leave today."

"Leave?" asked Kevin. "Where are we going?"

"We have to find a crystal for you without delay, and also, I would like us to be as far away from here as possible as soon as possible. If Duros returns he will come with war machines and will kill anyone or anything he sees. I will have to find someone to guide you to the crystal caves as I need Brynn and Dahn to help me warn the others of the danger. Perhaps when we reach the next shelter someone could be spared."

"Why not let Marlitta guide me?" suggested Kevin. "Perhaps that could be her punishment?"

"I think she would prefer the traditional punishment," said Petrog with a grin. "But if that is your wish, so be it."

They went outside to find the others stuffing things into packs which they could carry on their backs. Marlitta returned with the water and went inside to wash the dishes and put everything away for their return when the danger had passed. When all was finished, Petrog slide the stone back over the entrance and kicked some rocks about to hide signs of habitation. He then gave instructions to the lads who made off quickly and were soon lost to sight among the rocks.

"Marlitta," said Petrog. "Your punishment is also an honour for you. You are to escort the Master to the Cave of Crystals and help him find a crystal capable of transporting him back to the council planet."

"What?" she gasped then thought better of it. "If I must," she said defiantly.

"You must," said Petrog. "Go now. I want us all to be well away from here before Duros returns."

Marlitta picked up the remaining pack and struggled to put it onto her back.

"Can I carry that," asked Kevin. It seemed the polite thing to do.

"Do you think I'm helpless?" she snapped. "Come on." She shot a glance of defiance at her father and stomped off.

"We'll meet up again soon," said Petrog, and turned and hurried off. Kevin had to run to catch up with Marlitta who was stomping along in a most determined fashion, muttering to herself about having to be a nursemaid to a stuck up little runt.

"I don't know why you are so angry," said Kevin as he fell into step beside her. "Surely this is better than being whipped?"

"No, it isn't," she shouted at him. "It is far worse. You're just laughing at me. You think I'm of no importance; just a useless girl. But I'll show you."

"No, I don't think you are useless," said Kevin. "Why should I? I don't even know you. When I first saw you I... well... I liked you."

"Well thank you very much for that. I'm glad you liked me. Should I be grateful?"

"Well I'm sorry you feel this way," said Kevin feeling he was getting rather out of his depth. "Let's just forget it, shall we? Where are we going?"

Marlitta explained about the Cave of Crystal, how there had once been a mine where the crystals of power had been quarried, but how the mine had become worked out many years ago. People had often searched for crystals, in recent years, in the hope of using one to escape from this planet, but no-one had succeeded. Kevin wondered how he was supposed to succeed when others had failed. Still, it gave him something to do, and he was in the company of Marlitta, even if she was not happy to be in his company.

They moved cautiously among the rocks, Marlitta always alert as if expecting something to jump out at them. They had crossed the floor of a small dry valley and had just reached the top of the far side, when Marlitta froze, listening intently.

"Look," she cried turning and gazing upward. "They're here already. Quick, follow me." She darted off over the top of the hill and threw herself to the ground behind a group of rocks. Kevin followed close behind. "Get in here," she whispered squeezing close to the rocks and pulling Kevin in after her. Kevin had not been in such close proximity to a girl before and felt himself going very red in the face.

"What is it?" he asked when he could trust himself to speak again.

"Duros is here. Look." She pointed upward between the rocks. Kevin could see the faint wisp of smoke from the braking motors of the landing craft. They must have been enormous to be so visible at this distance.

"We must get on quickly," she said as the ships got lower in the sky. "They won't be able to detect us if we keep the high ground between them and us." She crawled out from behind the rocks and started down the slope in a crouched position. Kevin felt quite disappointed when she moved away from him. He was just beginning to enjoy it. He hurried after her keeping his head down as she had and found her waiting for him as he rounded a large rocky outcrop.

"Come on," she said. "We can't afford to hang around here for much longer. They'll probably have sniffers."

"Sniffers?" asked Kevin.

"Large, quite vicious animals with large teeth and a keen sense of smell, trained to track, hunt and kill. You don't want to meet one."

Kevin agreed. He certainly did not want to meet anything of that description so he set off with a will. Marlitta reckoned that they should reach the cave before sunset and Kevin certainly thought that would be a good idea. He did not relish being out side after dark, especially with sniffers about.

Chapter Ten - The Crystal Cave

Late in the afternoon, after an uneventful day, they reached the foothills of what appeared to be a moderately sized mountain range. The ground became much rougher and the boulders were much larger making progress much slower. They were getting quite tired by this time and the constant scrambling over rocks made them quite breathless. They had said nothing to each other for the past hour and Kevin was beginning to wonder how much further it was to the cave. The sun was already disappearing behind the mountain peaks and Kevin could feel a distinct chill in the air.

"How much further?" he gasped at last. Marlitta said nothing but kept climbing. Kevin wondered if she actually knew where the cave was. He glanced over his shoulder in the direction they had come and caught a glimpse of the fading sunlight glinting on something shiny, then it was gone.

"I think we are being followed," he shouted at Marlitta who was beginning to leave him behind.

"Well come on then," she snapped back. "The sooner we get to the cave the sooner we'll be safe." It was obvious that she did not want to discuss it further, so Kevin kept quiet and clambered after her.

In the next half hour they must have climbed several hundred metres in height and covered about half a mile. At this point they were having to weave around between the rocks and squeeze through narrow gaps, which was becoming increasingly difficult as it was getting quite dark. Kevin was beginning to feel quite scared. He was cold, tired, and hungry and thought he was probably lost in the mountains of a strange planet with goodness knows what lurking in the shadows. Suddenly he realised that he could no longer see or hear Marlitta. He stopped and listened but could hear nothing. He hurried on again in an effort to catch up with her. It was now getting very dark;

the wind was rising and it was growing colder by the minute. If he did not find shelter soon he would freeze out here on the mountainside as he was not dressed for this sort of climate.

He stopped again and listened but could still hear no sound of Marlitta. He did not like to call out for fear of what else might hear him. Suddenly he heard a long eerie howl unlike anything he had heard before and certainly did not wish to hear again. He hurried on, steadily upwards, weaving between the rocks. Then he heard it again, closer now. He hoped it was not a sniffer following his scent. He broke into a run and almost immediately tripped and fell against the rocks. Pain shot up his arm and he thought it must be broken. Slowly, he pushed himself upright and rubbed his arm and wrist, waggling his fingers to see if they still worked. All seemed in order but it was still very painful. He felt something moving over his forehead and instinctively tried to brush it off with his hand. Whatever it was, it was wet. In the failing light he could see that it was blood on his fingers. He fumbled for his handkerchief and mopped at his brow. It was not as bad as he had thought, just a small graze.

He got to his feet again and stumbled onward. Then he heard that plaintive cry again. This time it seemed further away, as if it had passed by the foot of the mountain and was now ahead of him but much lower down. He felt relieved for a moment, then his thoughts returned to his real plight. He still had to find shelter, and soon.

He moved on, this time more carefully until he came to a level area, almost flat, with no large rocks. On the far side of this platform, as it would seem to be was a vast looming cliff, disappearing way above his head. There was certainly no way up there, at least none that he could see in this light. The best that he could hope for would be to find some shelter at the foot of the cliff and wait until morning, hoping that no hungry creature would find him before then.

He made his way carefully over the flat area, stumbling occasionally over small rocks, until he reached the cliff face. It was almost vertical and quite smooth. He walked along it looking for a crevice or small overhang that would give him some shelter, or maybe a raised ledge that he could climb onto. He thought he would be safer off the ground.

He rounded a curved section of the cliff and found the cliff face more broken. Perhaps he could climb up here. He tried several places, pulling himself up onto a higher level, but it was not until he had nearly exhausted himself that he found a place that looked as if it led somewhere. It was rather a scramble, but slowly, one rock at a time, he made his way upward into what seemed to be a narrow gully. It was now quite dark but it looked as if there were a moon behind the clouds trying to break through.

He stopped for a moment for a rest. He had not heard the cry again so he hoped that whatever it was had gone away. It was warmer here, partly because he had been working hard climbing, and partly because he was out of the wind. The moon was getting brighter as the clouds thinned and occasionally he got a clear view of the plain over which they had travelled, not in great detail, but enough to make him feel very lonely and vulnerable.

He decided it was time to move on again and started the long scrabble up the gully. The surface was getting quite difficult now as there were more and more loose rocks and gravel which seemed to be due to a rock fall further up. Every now and then he would lose his footing on the loose surface and fall cutting and bruising his hands and knees. In his fear of being caught out in the open, he hardly noticed when he hurt himself.

Suddenly, he found that he had reached the rock fall and could get no further. Tons of rock and rubble had crashed down from above, very recently and had almost filled the gully. It looked as if there might have been an opening, a cave or large fissure, which was now covered by the rocks. Perhaps he could remove some of the rocks from one side and squeeze in to safety.

He started lifting out rocks and moving them out of the way. Each one rattled down the slope sounding very loud in the dark. He tried to be as quiet as he could, but it was almost impossible. After what seemed like an age, he had opened up a gap large enough for him to squeeze into, and it was not until he had squeezed in that he realised how stupid he was being. He had no idea what was inside. There could be a vicious animal lurking in the darkness, or a vast pothole that would swallow him up, never to be seen again. Luckily, neither of these possibilities materialised. He was on firm ground and nothing had grabbed him as he slid inside the cave. At first, he could see nothing at all, but he could tell by the echoes when he scraped his feet on the ground that he was in a vast cavern. He wished he had a light of some sort as there was still the danger of falling down a hole. There might even be something lurking in the shadows waiting for him. But it was best not to think of such things; it would only frighten him more than he already was. He strained his eyes and his ears to see if he could sense anything in the darkness. All was quiet, there was not the faintest sound, but his eyes were becoming adjusted to the darkness and he could make out shapes, dim at first but getting brighter as he watched. It was amazing that so much light could filter through that tiny hole, even with a full moon. But it was not light from the entrance, it seemed to be coming from the rock itself; it seemed as if the rocks were lit from within. He could make out the far wall of the cave and see quite clearly the many stalactites and stalagmites that covered the roof and floor; some met in the middle to make strange pillars.

It was getting much lighter now and the walls were festooned with myriads of sparkling points of light. As he watched the lights grew brighter until it seemed as bright as day. On the far wall he noticed that one spark of light seemed much brighter than the rest. He watched it, bemused, as the colours changed. It was as if he were looking into a deep pool, through the ripples of reflected light and into a world beyond. He was transfixed by it. He gazed in wonder as a beautiful world unfolded before him. There were meadows and streams with delicate trees along the banks and sleek dappled animals, with long slender horns, grazing nearby. A large graceful bird glided down from the clear blue sky and settled by the stream to drink the cool clear water.

Kevin could see large silver fish swimming lazily in the water, but as he watched the picture faded into mist until he was back in the cave again. He rubbed his eyes, as if he did not trust what they saw, but everything stayed the same. He walked over to the bright object and found, as he approached it, that it was a crystal similar to the one that he had lost, but much larger. It must have been nearly three times the size. Kevin thought that if it were a diamond it would be worth millions of pounds, though money did not seem relevant here.

He reached out his hand to take the gem from its place in the rock and felt a warm tingle run through his fingers and into his arm. He pulled back his arm, momentarily, but then reached out and took the crystal and grasped it tightly in his hand. Warmth welled through his body and all his aches and bruises seem to be soothed. They did not go away, but were much more comfortable. This must be what he was looking for, only much, much better, much better even than his lost crystal. This was a crystal of power, he was certain. Now he could get back home again, or to the council and find Quartok.

He suddenly thought of Marlitta and her family and what was about to happen to them when Duros found them. But maybe they would be all right. After all, they knew the land and had places to hide. He could go back and forget about them. But that was the problem; he could not. He knew that Marlitta had been pretty rotten to him, but he still liked her and would like to show her that she was wrong about him. Anyway, she might be in danger out there on the mountain side. Until now he had not given her a second thought. He had been angry with her for losing him, but perhaps it was he that had lost her. No, he would have to see that she was safe first.

He slipped the crystal into his pocket, the one with a zip fastener, and climbed out of the cave again. The moon was shining brightly now and the sky was clear. Even with the extra light, it was not easy climbing down the gully. Every move he made dislodged rocks that went crashing down to the rock platform below. He thought he might manage better if he climbed out of the gully onto firmer ground and started up the steep side. It was more difficult than he expected and had to give up. Then it struck him. What an idiot he was. He reached into his pocket and took out the crystal. It glowed warmly in his hand. He focused his attention on the top of the gully wall and immediately he was there, looking down at the spot where he had just been standing and not a moment too soon. There was a rumbling sound and rocks came tumbling down the gully. There had been another rock fall. If he had stayed in the cave and not found the crystal he would have been trapped.

He looked down to the rock platform below and thought he could see something moving. Could it be Marlitta? But there was something else there; another shape in the gloom and it seemed to be threatening the smaller shape. Marlitta was in trouble. She had been cornered by a wild animal. He had to act quickly. Almost before he realised what he had done he was on the rock platform standing beside a terrified Marlitta and looking

into the eyes of the largest and most hideous dog he had
ever seen.

Chapter Eleven - Escape

Almost without thinking Kevin grabbed Marlitta's arm and visualised the rocky ledge above the gully and in the blink of an eye they were there, looking down as the creature leapt at the place where they had just been standing. It gave a startled yelp and started sniffing around, frantically searching for its prey. They froze, hardly daring to breathe, but in spite of that, a pebble started to roll down the rock towards the edge where it disappeared from sight. There was a moment's silence followed by a clatter of stones and rubble that had been set in motion by the one small pebble.

"Damn," said Kevin. "That's done it." The Creature looked up at them and then started to clamber up the rocks. Twice it fell back again, but on the third attempt it started to make headway.

Kevin slowly raised his hand, the hand that held the crystal, and extended his forefinger to point at the creature. Amazingly it stopped and stared back at Kevin. Marlitta stared in amazement as the two simply stood and stared at each other. Then Kevin slowly lowered his arm and the creature stood there and whimpered, lowering its head as if it had been told off by its owner.

"Good boy," said Kevin and reached out his other hand towards it. "Come on then."

The creature shuffled up the last bit of rock to lie at Kevin's feet, wagging its tail like a pet dog.

"How did you do that?" said Marlitta in amazement. "These animals are trained by Duros to obey his will and only his. They would rather die than go against his command."

"I don't know what I did," answered Kevin feeling slightly bewildered himself. "It's as if the crystal took charge and showed me what to do. It let me talk to the animal, not in words, more in feelings. I don't know but it seemed right at the time."

"So what do we do now?" continued Marlitta. "Will it stay like that for long?"

"I think it will obey me now, for ever, at least, I get the feeling that I am now its master; just like a pet dog."

"I'm not sure what you mean by 'dog'," said Marlitta. "I suppose it would be an animal from your world. Anyway, if this thing is here, then Duros can't be far behind. We must get out of here fast."

"I quite agree," said Kevin. "But where do we go? I can take us anywhere that I know, but I don't know where the others will have gone. Unless I can visualise where I want to go, I can't go there. If you see what I mean."

"I think so," said Marlitta looking a little puzzled.

"I could take us back to the place we were at this morning, he said.

"No, that wouldn't do," said Marlitta. They will have found that by now and we'll arrive in the middle of an army."

There was a small flash of light at the foot of the mountain and both of them saw it; ever the dog saw it and began to whine.

"Quite Sniffer," said Kevin sharply and the dog went quiet, resting its huge mouth on its paws. "What I can do is to take us to somewhere that I can see from here. It might not be a good landing if I can't see it clearly. Anyway, we have to try." He looked around. The plain below was too dark to risk, and anyway he did not know where Duros or his troops were. It would have to be upward. That way they could take smaller jumps. He took Marlitta's hand and put his hand on the dog's head. The dog looked quite pleased at this even if Marlitta did not. In a flash they were tumbling down a rough scree slope to eventually slide to a halt in a boggy pool at the bottom.

"What are you trying to do?" snapped Marlitta. "Kill us all?" The dog bared its teeth and growled at her. "And you can keep quiet too."

"Sorry," said Kevin clambering out of the water. "But how was I to know it wasn't flat behind the ridge?"

"Well put us somewhere you can see next time."

"OK, OK. There's a likely spot over there." He took her hand again and the dog nuzzled against his side as if it knew what to expect. This time the landing was almost perfect, so rather than stop and talk again, he took them to the next vantage point. This was a sheltered spot surrounded by tall rocks, one of which curved over to make a reasonable shelter.

"I think this will be a good place to stay 'til it gets lighter," said Kevin and shuffled himself into the shelter of the rock. Sniffer, as Kevin had called him, shuffled in beside him.

"What about me?" objected Marlitta. Sniffer growled.

"I think he is jealous," said Kevin. "Come on Sniffer, move over." The dog grudgingly moved over and Marlitta squeezed in beside Kevin.

"I don't see what he's got to be jealous about," she said. Kevin smiled but it was too dark for her to see.

When Kevin felt cold, the crystal seemed to create a warm glow, and when the wind managed to get into their shelter, the crystal seemed to deflect it. Kevin thought that there was much more to this crystal than there was to his old one. He would have to explore all its possibilities as soon as he had time.

"Why not do it now?" said a voice.

"What?" asked Kevin.

"I didn't say anything," said Marlitta.

Kevin was puzzled. Someone had said something and he felt sure it was not the dog.

"It was me," the voice came again, but Kevin had the distinct impression that it was coming from inside his own head. He must be more tired than he had thought and was hearing voices now.

I am Spectro," the voice said. "The voice of the crystal. I can tell you all you want to know."

"You can talk?" said Kevin, but this time he said it in his mind and not out loud.

"I can link into the mind of one who is receptive," said the voice in Kevin's mind. "And I can give advice when needed. Also, I have access to all the knowledge of the Universe but will only allow it to be used for the general good of all creatures. Duros is approaching, and he does nothing for the good of anyone but himself. He has been searching for me for many years so that he can use my power for his own ends, or so he thinks. And because of this, he has reduced countless planets to rubble in his quest. He must be stopped."

"I quite agree," said Kevin. "But it is going to take more than me to do it."

"True," said Spectro. "And I am here to give that assistance. When it is light I will show you some of my powers but it will need you to direct them. Now you must sleep or you will be exhausted. Duros will not find you tonight."

The words seemed to be echoing in Kevin's mind when he awoke and found that it was already dawn. He was rather stiff and could hardly move. Then he realised it was because Marlitta was snuggled up against him on one side while Sniffer had his head resting on Kevin's stomach. His attempted movements, however, woke the other two. Sniffer was immediately up and dashing around as if he were on guard. Marlitta stretched, and realising where she was, pulled herself away stiffly and crawled out of the rock shelter.

Kevin used the crystal to take him to the top of a nearby rock so that he could have a look round. It was the start of a bright day and the mist was just beginning to lift off the plains below. Kevin stared out across the flat lands beneath him but could see nothing.

"Allow me," said Spectro almost causing Kevin to fall off his perch. "Close your eyes and then look."

"How can I look if I close my eyes," he objected.

"You will see."

Kevin closed his eyes and to his amazement he could still see. Then it was as if he were swooping down from the rock, like an eagle, and skimming over the ground at a frightening speed. Then he saw them. Row upon row of wicked looking machines, rolling slowly towards him. In amongst them were hundreds of foot soldiers in black armour, carrying guns of some sort.

"That's what you are up against," said Spectro.

"Can't they see me?" asked Kevin.

"No, you are not actually here, you are still standing on the rock. It is just your sight that allows you to be here."

This made Kevin feel a little more secure as he zoomed past these wicked looking machines. Feeling a bit braver now he went in very close to the foot soldiers as they trudged along. Their black armour made them look very fierce and evil, but the way they moved made Kevin think that they were not as brave as they looked.

"Who are these people?" asked Kevin.

"The foot soldiers are people taken, by Duros, from his slave planets. You are right to think they do not look very brave, they are not. They are scared stiff and know that if anything goes wrong they will not survive."

"Let's go back," said Kevin.

"That's up to you," answered Spectro. "Take us wherever you wish."

Kevin realised that they appeared to go wherever he looked or thought. He knew that he was not actually moving. It was a bit like a computer game.

Back on the rock and seeing things as they actually were, he sat down.

"What do we do now?" he asked Spectro.

"That is your decision," came the answer. "I can give you information but cannot make decisions. However, there are several courses of action that could be taken. Firstly, you could wipe out the whole force by using the power of the crystal. Secondly, you could take control of their crystals and prevent them from leaving this planet, or you could leave and go back to the council, or even your own home planet, if you wished."

"I can't desert these people," said Kevin. "And I can't kill all those innocent people. After all, it isn't their fault that they're here. I can't leave them here because Duros would use them to hunt out all the other innocent people of this planet. I'll have to talk to Marlitta." He transported himself back to where Marlitta was waiting for him.

"Well?" she asked. "What have you seen?"

Kevin told her about the army and what possibilities he had. "I think we should get back to your people as quickly as possible," he said.

"But I thought you couldn't travel to places you can't visualise," she said.

"I think I probably can, now," he said. "This new crystal can do more than my old one and I can look at things that are miles away. Then I can go there. So, if you can explain where your people will have gone, I'll see if I can find them."

"Well they should be over in that direction," she said, pointing over to her left, much in the direction they were already heading.

Kevin closed his eyes and it was as if he had become a bird swooping over the edge of the cliff and skimming over the ground. "I can see a small river ahead," he said.

"They will have crossed that and followed it for some distance," she said.

Kevin swooped down to the river and sped along the far bank looking for signs of a footpath. After a while the path came very rocky and steep and it looked as if anyone walking that way would have to turn and leave the river bank.

Marlitta confirmed this. "They will now be heading into the direction that the sun will set," she said.

Kevin slowed his progress so that he would not miss anything. Soon he picked up a well defined path heading west as he judged the direction. Spectro confirmed this. The ground rose steadily and headed towards the mountains.

"They will not go into the mountains," said Marlitta. "They will turn and follow the flank of the hills until they reach the next settlement. You probably won't be able to see that. It is well hidden."

"Right," said Kevin settling at a spot that looked fairly flat. "Take my hand and grab hold of Sniffer."

When she had confirmed that she had a firm grip of Sniffer, the rocks faded and turned into a scene quite different from the one they had left. Kevin opened his eyes and saw the scene he had being looking at in his mind.

"Do you recognise this place?" he asked.

"I think so, " she replied thoughtfully. "I think we are quite close. Follow me." She set off along the path with Kevin walking just behind and Sniffer keeping close to Kevin. They walked for a while in silence when suddenly Sniffer leapt forward and bounded past Kevin and Marlitta and disappeared behind some rocks. There was a terrified scream and Kevin rushed forward closely followed by Marlitta. They rounded the rock to find Sniffer with his front paws on the chest of some poor unfortunate person who was terrified out of his wits. Sniffer was giving him a severe licking.

"Leave him alone," said Kevin and hurried forward to help the wretched fellow to his feet.

"Lartop!" exclaimed Marlitta and gave the startled fellow a big hug. "Where is everyone?"

Chapter Twelve - The rescue

Lartop was one of the 'locals' who Petrog and the others had set out to find and warn about Duros. But it seemed that none of them had arrived and Lartop was completely unaware that they were coming. He took them back to their dwelling, which was more like a rabbit warren than a village. About fifty people lived here and went out in small groups to forage and hunt. Several groups were out and would not be due back for several days.

Lartop took them to his house where he lived with his wife and son who made them welcome. Kevin was worried about Petrog and his group and hoped they had not been caught by Duros. He felt that he must do something urgently, but was not sure what to do or where to start. Lartop, who had now recovered from his fright and had made friends with Sniffer, suggested they should have a meeting of the elders as soon as it could be arranged. Kevin agreed and asked Lartop to arrange it as soon as possible.

"I don't know if I can get them to convene a meeting immediately, said Lartop. "I am not of very great importance in the village and they are not likely to drop everything on my say so."

"Perhaps you should tell them it is commanded by the Master of the Universe," said Marlitta.

"As if they would believe that," said Lartop. "I'd be in deep trouble if I tried that."

"I think you would be in even deeper trouble if you didn't." said Marlitta indicating Kevin. "This is the Master of the Universe and if we don't get some action immediately Duros will be here with his army."

Lartop looked dubious. It was a lot to expect him to believe such a thing, after all, the Master of the Universe was someone he had heard about in the dim and distant past living on some distant world at the centre of the Universe. It was not possible to imagine someone like that coming here, on his own without a great fanfare of trumpets and thousands of people in amazing shiny costumes.

Kevin thought a demonstration was called for so he gripped his crystal in his hand and closed his eyes hoping that Spectro could come up with something. A shimmer appeared around Kevin and, as he watched, Lartop saw Kevin transformed into an amazing shining image of what he expected the Master of the Universe to look like. He gasped, stepped back and fell to his knees.

"Forgive me," he sobbed. "I did not realise." Kevin snapped back into his normal form and pulled Lartop to his feet.

"You couldn't be expected to," said Kevin. "Now as quickly as you can." Lartop dashed from the room stopping to bow to Kevin and then turned and dashed out.

Kevin leaned back in his seat. "What are we going to do?" he asked Marlitta. "It sounds as if your father and the others might have been caught by Duros. If so, what would he do to them?"

"I don't know," she answered. "Normally he would just kill them without a second thought. After all, they mean nothing to him. But if he thinks they know where you are, he would keep them alive until they told him what he wanted to know. That doesn't mean that he wouldn't harm them if they didn't tell him."

"Well, we have to rescue them," he said thoughtfully. "So, I'll have to think while Lartop sorts out a meeting with the elders. Make sure I'm not disturbed." Surprisingly, Marlitta did not come back with a facetious reply, but she had more on her mind. In spite of her outward calm, she was very worried about her family.

Kevin closed his eyes and started a conversation in his mind with Spectro. He also allowed his mind vision to take him out and over the plains to where Duros had set up camp. He found that by taking a view from high up and then descending like a hawk towards what he thought might be Duros and his army, he was able to locate them very quickly. He still found it a bit daunting to get so close to these vicious looking soldiers. It looked as if they would see him, but of course, he was not actually there.

He drifted along, just above the ground, and wove around the various obstacles that appeared before him. Soon he saw some tents with guards standing outside. Could this be where they were keeping their prisoners? There was only one way to find out and that was to go inside. He then discovered that he could, in effect, pass straight through solid objects as if they were not there.

In the first tent were provisions and equipment. It was just a store tent. The next one looked as if it were the private quarters of someone important, perhaps even Duros himself, but there was no-one there so he could not tell. The other tents were meeting rooms and chart rooms with junior officers scurrying about, but there was no sign of the prisoners.

He thought he had better get a wider view of the camp so he rose up again, straight through the roof of the tent and hovered at a height that allowed him to see all round the camp. There were many rows of smaller tents, which were, probably, where the soldiers would sleep. But over to one side of the camp was another group of tents, all black, making them look rather grim. These must be the prison tents.

He swooped down to ground level and moved slowly into the first tent, not knowing what to expect. It was quite dark inside, and even with his special sight, it was difficult to see anything clearly. However, his sight slowly adjusted, just like his eyes would in similar circumstances, and he began to make out shapes of people tied to posts that had been driven into the ground. They looked in a bad way but they were all alive, as far as he could tell. He moved closer to see if he could recognise anyone, but the first two he saw were strangers to him, but the next one was Petrog.

What should he do now? He had to get them out before any more harm came to them. There was only one thing for it. He jumped. That was how he thought of the power of transportation that the crystal gave him. It was just like jumping, in his mind, without any sensation of having moved at all. And he was there, in the tent with Sniffer by his side. He must have had his hand on Sniffer's back as he lay there with his eyes shut.

"On guard," he whispered to Sniffer, though a command in his mind would have done. Sniffer darted to the door way and crouched down and waited while Kevin dashed from one recumbent form to another untying them as quickly as he could. They were only half conscious but he herded them into a group in the middle of the tent so that they were all leaning on each other.

Sniffer gave a low growl and Kevin called him back from the doorway and grabbed him by the collar while clutching one of the others with his other hand. Almost as the guard walked in he jumped and was immediately back at the village, just outside Lartop's house. Kevin was about to take them back to where he had just left, inside the house, but Spectro had intervened and diverted them. It was just as well that he had because this group would never have fitted into the house.

Marlitta, who had been sitting outside the house, deep in thought, sprung to her feet in surprise, then, seeing her father and brothers, she ran forward to support them, as they could hardly stand on their own.

Lartop returned to find his house surrounded by bodies lying on the ground. Kevin and Marlitta, with the help of Lartop's wife and son, had brought out bedding to make them comfortable. Then they had dashed around bringing out food and drink for them, though they could not eat much in their present state.

Lartop told Kevin that the Council of Elders had been called and would be ready to start in one hour. But the

Chief Elder, himself, would come and welcome Kevin shortly.

Lartop sent his son to get the village healer, as it was obvious that the newcomers would need medical care. Kevin was not sure what that would entail as he did not know the extent of the local medical skills.

In no time at all, the healer arrived and scurried around from one patient to the next, tut-tutting and talking to himself. He then took out a pot from the small bundle that he carried and gave instructions for the contents to be put into hot water and given to each of the patients to drink. Kevin found it difficult not to laugh as it reminded him of a fussy old man entertaining his guest with a pot of tea.

Spectro broke into Kevin's thoughts bringing him back to reality. "There is no need to laugh," he said sternly. "That is a very potent herb and will be very beneficial to these people. However, I think you could be of more help."

"How is that?" asked Kevin in his mind.

"The crystal can focus the life force of the universe if you will it. Think of the health-giving rays coming towards you from all around, and direct them, in your mind to each of these people. You will be able to feel the flow and be able to direct it where it is needed.

Kevin closed his eyes and let himself feel the flow of energy. It was strange that he had not noticed it before, but now it was there and he could control it. He directed it towards each of the patients in turn and felt the energy being almost pulled from him. It was actually quite hard work, and by the time that he felt all of them had had enough healing energy for the time being, he was exhausted. He lay, for a few minutes, flat on his back until a shadow passed over his face and he opened his eyes to find himself looking at a short, but very fat little man. This was obviously the Chief Elder.

Kevin got to his feet and tried to look serious. It was not easy to be serious when addressing what looked like an overgrown munchkin.

"Master," said the munchkin. "I am honoured to welcome you to Mountain Retreat." This was the first time Kevin had heard anyone mention the name of the village. "I am Rotunda, Chief Elder."

Kevin could hardly contain himself; Rotunda was an ideal name for this round little fellow. Perhaps it meant something different here.

"I am pleased to meet you, Rotunda," he said. "But I think we should start this meeting as soon as possible. I have just rescued these people from Duros and I think he will be rather upset. I don't know if he has any means of tracking them and finding us, but I am sure he will be starting his search very soon and I would like us to be as far away as possible by the time he gets here." Rotunda looked worried. He had not realised the extent of the problem and it was just beginning to sink in.

"Of course," he said. " Perhaps your Excellency would like to follow me." He gave a little bow and set off. Kevin signalled for Marlitta to come too and set off after Rotunda. Sniffer did not have to be invited. It seemed that he would go wherever Kevin went, whether Kevin liked it or not. It was a comical sight; a little round man striding out in front trying to look as important as he could, Kevin, half as tall again walking behind trying not to giggle, Marlitta walking behind Kevin trying to look as if she did not mind being bossed around by a mere boy, and Sniffer striding purposefully behind them all, sniffing the air as he went.

Chapter Thirteen - The Council of War

After a few hundred of Kevin's paces, they came to a cliff face with a small opening at the bottom, too small to call it a cave. Rotunda strode in. Kevin had to stoop to avoid hitting his head and Marlitta just managed to walk in without bending. Inside, there was a large hall with lamps burning around the walls. At the far end sat about twelve people in rows on the floor. Rotunda walked up to them and stood facing them.

"May I present Kevin, Master of the Universe," he said in his most pompous voice. The others stood up and bowed.

"Greetings," they mumbled. Then they all sat so Kevin sat down beside Rotunda with Marlitta beside him. Sniffer decided that he was not going to be left out so walked around in front of them and lay down. The assembled group looked very uneasy about this as Sniffer could have picked any one of them up and shaken him like a rat, if he had wanted.

"Gentlemen," said Rotunda addressing the Elders. "His Excellency has disturbing news for us. It would seem that Duros has returned and is searching for him. I do not need to tell you what this means to us. We are likely to be hunted down and tortured until we tell him what he wants to know and then we will all be destroyed." A loud muttering broke out among the Elders who seemed to be arguing among themselves. One of them stood up, his face red with anger.

"If Duros wants him," he shouted. "I think we should hand him over. Then we will all be left in peace."

"Hear, hear, " shouted several others who seemed to be friends of the spokesman. There was a great deal of noise and everyone seemed to be shouting at each other. Rotunda rose to his feet waving his hands in the air. "Quiet please," he shouted. "This is no way to behave." The noise lessened a bit but Rotunda could still not make himself heard, so Kevin spoke to Sniffer, using mind pictures and Sniffer jumped to his feet and growled at the riotous mob who immediately sank back into their seats and became very quiet.

"Gentlemen," said Rotunda looking at Sniffer very warily. "This is not the way to behave and it certainly is not the way to treat a guest. Duros can wipe us all out if he wants to, so it's better not to make ourselves known to him, at least for the moment. We have with us Kevin, Master of the Universe and he has great powers and I think it will be to our benefit, as well as that of all civilisation, if we were to help him. Duros must be stopped once and for all. He has desolated this planet as well as countless others and if we do not take this opportunity to stop him, he will devastate countless more."

"Fine words," said the troublemaker. "But how are we going to do that? Where is our army? Where are our weapons? I don't see any. No, I say that we must look after ourselves."

At that Marlitta leapt to her feet. "You snivelling coward," she shouted at him. "Kevin has already risked his own life for me and my family and he is willing to risk it again for you. Surely you can support him, or at least hear his plan."

Kevin was not so sure about this business of risking his life. He had not really thought of it like that. It was all still rather like a computer game to him, though he was rapidly beginning to see that it was not a game after all. And 'plan', what plan? He wished he had one.

"What should I do?" he asked Spectro in his mind.

"I'm afraid I cannot tell you what you should do," he replied. "But I can give you some possibilities, but it is you who must decide. It is possible for you to kill Duros and his army using the power of the crystal."

"But I don't know how to do that," said Kevin. "And certainly do not want to start killing people."

"Well, you could capture Duros and take him back to face the Council," Spectro continued. "But that is more difficult."

"Why's that?" asked Kevin.

"Because he also has a crystal," said Spectro. "Not one as powerful as yours though, but powerful enough to allow him to escape. To capture Duros, you first have to capture or, at least, take command of his crystal."

"But he will always have his crystal on him, won't he?" asked Kevin.

"He will, most of the time, but he will probably take it off to sleep or bath, or when he is changing his clothes," said Spectro. "But I think you would need help to distract him while you took charge of his crystal."

"Thanks a lot," said Kevin getting to his feet. There was a crowd of faces staring at him, waiting for him to tell them what was to be done. But Kevin had not spoken in public before and he felt very nervous about it, so taking a leaf out of Rotunda's book, he started in a very formal way.

"Gentlemen," he said in a rather timid voice. "I will need your help if we are to win and save everybody from Duros."

"What do you want us to do?" asked a rather smaller than average being at the front.

"I would like a group of you to come with me to Duros's camp and cause a distraction while I get his crystal from him." There was silence. Then a mumbling and then a grumbling and then the troublesome one stood up again.

"No," he shouted. "Do you want to get us all killed, or worse? If we just walk into Duros' camp we will all be captured and tortured before we know it. No! You cannot ask that of us."

"I'll go with you," said the little fellow.

"Thank you," said Kevin. "I'm glad you aren't all cowards here."

At that the troublesome one marched from the room followed uncertainly by a few of his followers. The others looked undecided, looking first at the departing group and then back at Kevin. One by one they agreed to help so Kevin sent them all back to their homes to dress up in warm clothing that would not easily be seen at night. Kevin returned to Lartop's house with Marlitta and Sniffer, and Rotunda went along too, as he did not want to be left out of the decision making. He was also very curious to know exactly what Kevin intended to do.

Back at Lartop's house there was food waiting so they all sat down and ate silently while Kevin gleaned as much information from Spectro as he could.

After they had finished eating, Kevin closed his eyes and had another look round Duros's camp. He fixed in his mind where the main tents were situated, and in particular, which one was Duros's own tent. He had a look inside and saw Duros deep in conversation with one of his generals. It would be some time before he went to bed so they would all have time to prepare and rest before their adventure.

Spectro reminded him, again, that it was not a game and could be very dangerous. Kevin knew this really, when he thought about it, but he sometimes forgot in the excitement of it all.

As there was nothing more he could do now he thought it would be a good idea for him to familiarise himself with the countryside between Mountain Retreat and Duros' camp. It was mostly flat with little vegetation, but quite rocky. Half way back he found that the ground rose into a low ridge which would be useful as a vantage point. Beyond the ridge it flattened into a flat plain right up to the foot of the mountains where the village nestled. About half way across this plain he thought he could see movement so he sped in that direction. Sure enough it was a small group of people from the village, heading towards Duros's camp. As Kevin approached he could see that it was a group of the village Elders led by the troublesome one who had wanted them to hand Kevin over to Duros to save their own skins.

Kevin was actually still in the village and it was only in his mind that he could see this little group trudging meaningfully over the rough ground. But Kevin could 'jump' using the power of the crystal and without further delay, that is what he did. The little group stopped in horror as Kevin materialised in front of them.

"Stop," he shouted. "Where do you think you are going?"

There was a moment's pause as they gathered their wits then one of them darted forward and grabbed Kevin. "Quick, all of you," he shouted to his friends. "Help me hold him." The rest of the group dashed forward and Kevin found himself pulled to the ground and being firmly sat upon.

"Right you," said the familiar voice of the ring leader. "You're coming with us."

Kevin did not think so. About five of them had hold of him leaving only the ring leader not in contact with him. That would have to do. He visualised the area outside Lartop's home and was immediately there. People who had been sitting around or getting on with little jobs to pass the time were startled to see this bundle of squirming limbs suddenly appear. Sniffer rushed out of the doorway, where he had been on guard and growled menacingly at the squirming mass that shuffled back in dismay.

Rotunda followed Sniffer out of the house and stood looking at the five snivelling creatures. "What does this mean?" he demanded.

Kevin scrambled to his feet. "It means," he said. "That these creatures were on their way to Duros's camp. Their leader is still out there. I don't know if he will carry on or come back."

"You are all a disgrace to the village," said Rotunda in his most authoritative voice. "Where is Gron?"

Kevin assumed that Gron must be the name of the one still out there. On seeing how angry Rotunda was, the five former Elders started grovelling as there were harsh penalties for traitors on a planet where life itself was harsh.

"I must go and find the other one," said Kevin. "This Gron, or whatever you call him. He mustn't get to Duros." Before any of them could say anything Kevin had closed his eyes and was sitting cross legged on the ground. In his mind he zoomed out over the plain to where he had left Gron but could see him nowhere. It was impossible for him to have walked far in the short time Kevin had been away, but he was nowhere to be seen. In desperation, he headed for Duros camp again and arrived just in time to see Gron being escorted into Duros's tent.

There was nothing he could do now but return to the village where his body waited for him. Seconds later, he was opening his eyes to see an expectant crowd waiting for him to speak.

"Too late," he said. "Duros has him. I don't know how he got there so fast. He couldn't have walked."

"Maybe a patrol found him," said Lartop.

Then one of the recently captured Elders came forward. "May I be permitted to speak?" he asked.

"Sit down worm," said Rotunda angrily pushing him back.

"No," said Kevin. "Let him speak." Rotunda pushed the unfortunate fellow forward again.

"I may be able to help," he said. "Gron had a crystal. Not a big one, but big enough to compel a few of us to obey him. Perhaps he could use it to transport himself from one place to another like the Master does."

"Nonsense, Dannu," snapped Rotunda. "Where would he get a crystal like that?"

"I believe it was one of the crystals used by the overseers when this was a slave planet," said Dannu.

"They were used to compel people to obey them but they didn't have the power of transportation."

"Yes," said Rotunda. "That is a possibility. He would have been able to use it to contact Duros. Overseers were able to report to higher authorities."

While this was going on, Kevin was listening to comments being made, in his head, by Spectro confirming what he was hearing.

"Why didn't I hear him, then?" asked Kevin in his mind.

"You weren't listening," answered Spectro. "And Gron would have beamed the message direct to Duros. If you had been aware that he could do that, you could have intercepted the message, and even blocked it. However, it is too late now. Duros will be heading this way as quickly as he can move his troops. He could come here himself using his crystal, but I don't think he would be that brave or foolhardy."

"You mean he is scared of me?" asked Kevin.

"Of you and your crystal."

Kevin held up his hands to quell the noise that had built up as everyone wanted to get a word in.

"Quiet," he shouted. "Duros is on his way here so we must either hide or get out as fast as we can. Is there anywhere near here that we can hide?"

"Well there is the ravine," said Lartop. "That would make a good place to corner them."

Kevin's mind immediately went into search mode. It was as if the crystal had taken over and was working automatically. Kevin searched the hillside beyond the village and could see what Lartop meant. A wide valley funnelled into a narrow, steep sided ravine which turned into a cave with no exit.

"I see it," cried Kevin. "If we could make them go in there we might be able to trap them. We must get going straight away. I'll work out what we are going to do as we go."

Chapter Fourteen - The Trap

Within minutes people were rushing about making ready to leave. There were too many of them for Kevin to transport using his crystal so he took Marlitta and Sniffer and 'jumped'. An instant later they were standing above the ravine looking down the steep slopes into the gully below. The valley narrowed sharply and large protruding buttresses of rock formed a narrow doorway into the ravine. Certainly the foot soldiers could get in but the mechanised troops would not be able to.

"Could I block that gap?" he asked Spectro. "Using the crystal."

"Easily," came the answer. "You just have to focus your mind on the lower part of the rocks and think heat."

"Think heat?" asked Kevin. "How do I do that?"

"Just imagine a blast of energy from your crystal beaming down onto that rock. Look, try it out on that small rock over there."

Kevin looked at the rock, concentrated, and visualised a beam of energy shooting out of the crystal into the rock. There was a shattering explosion and the rock was no more. Marlitta dropped to the ground hiding her head in her hands, Sniffer yowled.

"Sorry," said Kevin. "Just experimenting."

"Well you might have warned us," said Marlitta brushing the dust off her clothes.

Kevin explained what he was going to do and why he had needed to experiment with the rock.

"But how are we going to get them to go in there in the first place?" asked Marlitta.

"That's where your friends come in," said Kevin. "We need a fair group of villagers to lead the enemy into the gully."

"Won't that be dangerous?" asked Marlitta. "I don't want anyone getting hurt. And what happens when they're in there? They'll all be trapped."

"You see down there, at the end of the gully," said Kevin pointing. "Well that's the entrance to a cave, well I'll be waiting there. Our people will have to rush in and when they are out of sight, I'll bring them back up here."

"Will there be room in there?" asked Marlitta.

"Let's find out," answered Kevin grabbing her hand and touching Sniffer's head with his other hand. Instantly they were all in the mouth of the cave where it was very dark and damp. Kevin could hear water dripping somewhere inside and could tell that it was quite a large cavern by the way the sound echoed around. Kevin held up the crystal which began to glow quite brightly giving out a clear beam of white light. He was beginning to find that he could use the power of the crystal without really trying.

"That is because it was made for you," said Spectro in his head.

"How could it have been made for me?" asked Kevin. "I found it in a cave."

"Nevertheless, it is the crystal of the Master of the Universe. Each new Master must find his own crystal to replace the one he is given when he becomes Master. A special crystal, just for him."

While Kevin had been discussing the crystal with Spectro, Marlitta and Sniffer were exploring the cave.

"Doesn't seem to go very far back," said Marlitta, her voice echoing eerily around the cave. Sniffer was sniffing everything he could lay his nose on and really enjoying himself.

"Yes," said Kevin. "This will be fine. Now let's get back and get things organised."

Back at the camp Kevin got Rotunda to gather everyone together as quickly as possible. Marlitta joined her father and brothers who were fairly well recovered from their ordeal with Duros. Kevin walked over to join them.

"You have found a crystal then?" asked Petrog.

"Not only a crystal," said Kevin proudly. "But my crystal; the one that was meant for me."

"Well now you can go back to the council and tell them what Duros is doing," he said.

"Soon," said Kevin. "But first we have to deal with Duros ourselves." He told Petrog and his family what he had planned and they shook their heads but said nothing. "I am going to ask for volunteers."

"It's dangerous," said Petrog. "I wouldn't like any of my family to take the risk."

"Well that'll be up to us," said Marlitta.

"It certainly won't be up to you, my girl," said Petrog angrily. "You will be going nowhere."

"I think she's right," said Dahn. "We all have to do what we can or there will be no-one here to protect. Kevin may have a crystal, but I don't think he can defeat Duros on his own."

"Well I don't like the idea of my children being used as bait," said Petrog feeling a little shamed.

"Well we all have to get out of this village," said Kevin. "And everyone can do something to help. The fastest runners would be needed to lead the enemy into the trap, but we would need others to keep them there and stop them trying to climb out."

"All right," said Petrog. "Forgive me for sounding cowardly, but a father has to protect his children."

While they had been talking, a large crowd had gathered and Rotunda was trying to get them organised and settled in rows on the grass ready for Kevin to address them.

"They are ready for you now, Master," he said standing aside so that Kevin could climb onto the box that had been placed ready for him.

"Thank you," said Kevin, climbing onto the box which did not feel too safe. "Thank you all for coming, but we have to act quickly if we are to escape Duros and his army." He outlined his plan to them and, initially, received the same response as he had from Petrog.

"There isn't really a choice," said Kevin. "We must leave here immediately. If we just run away he will catch us, or at least he will catch you. I can always escape using my crystal. But I don't want to leave you to get killed. I want you to win, and I think we have a chance if you all do as planned. Firstly, we need a large group of runners to lead the enemy into our trap. This is probably the most dangerous job but if that fails no-one is safe anyway. Who will volunteer?"

At first there was no response, then Marlitta stood up. Everyone looked at her and then, one by one, all the younger ones got to their feet. Not to be outdone by the youngsters, several of the more elderly got to their feet.

"Can't leave it all to the kids," said one with long white hair and using a stick to help him stand.

"I think you are very brave," said Kevin. "But I think it would be better to leave the running to the younger ones. We need the brains at the top of the gully."

"Of course," said the old fellow sitting down again. "Of course."

The discussion continued and volunteers were found for every job, in fact many volunteered for several jobs and Kevin had to be firm with them, explaining that they could only be in one place at a time and, anyway, it was unfair of them to hog all the jobs.

Soon they were all eager to get started, so Kevin sent them all off to their allotted positions. It was quite a long walk to the gully but Kevin helped out by 'jumping' groups of them to their positions which gave them more time to get everything prepared.

The older ones gathered on the high ground on either side of the gully and started collecting rocks to use against the enemy, should they try to climb out. They also prepared places to conceal themselves so as not to be seen when the enemy approached. Two other groups hid outside the entrance to the gully, one on each side, in case any of the stragglers escaped or in case there was anything they could do to help if needed.

The main group, the runners, made their way directly from the village taking a path that could easily be followed. They spread out as they walked, leaving a wide band of flattened vegetation that looked as if a herd of buffalo had just passed that way. The vegetation was not thick, nowhere on this planet was the vegetation thick, but it was thick enough to leave a clear trail. The ground was also very dusty and the light breeze that blew across the plain lifted a dense cloud of it into the air that could be seen for miles.

When all was set, Kevin went on one of his mind journeys and swept across the plain to see if the army was on the move. He was surprised and quite alarmed to find that it was well on its way. It consisted entirely of foot soldiers as the mountainous region ahead would be unsuitable for the mechanised section. Anyway, Duros did not think it would take his full army to round up the escapees from the village, and as he was not aware of Kevin's crystal, he assumed he could just get them to hand him over when they were caught. He had little regard for the creatures that had been left to rot on a worked-out planet and did not realise what it took to survive here.

There was one mechanised vehicle which, presumably, held Duros who would rather ride than walk. It would not be long before they could see the cloud of dust, if they had not already seen it. The runners were going at a steady pace, not wanting to get too far ahead of Duros and yet not wanting to be caught before they reached the ravine.

The day wore on and the sky darkened as clouds began to form. This was not something that happened often, as rain was rather sparse on this planet, but it was welcome now. The wind was getting up too and that would reduce the visibility as it whipped up the dust from the arid ground. Kevin hoped that it did not rain just yet as the dust would quickly turn to mud and it would become very difficult for the runners to keep going at any speed.

Kevin, using his mind sight, could see the rows of black armoured soldiers moving at a steady pace across the plain. They were spread out in a wide fan shape with Duros's vehicle following steadily behind. They were catching up with the runners and looked as if they might reach them before they could get to safety. But the runners had spotted them now and were picking up their pace. But it was still a long way to go. Another hour passed and the runners had reached the flat plain leading to where the high ground divided, leading to the ravine. The pursuing army was now on higher ground and had a good view of its quarry. Kevin could see flashes of light from the army followed by puffs of smoke from the ground near the fleeing runners.

"They're shooting at them," shouted someone in alarm. Kevin used his mind sight and could see quite clearly the leading troops firing hand guns of some sort, laser weapons perhaps. He wondered desperately what he could do to help.

"You could set up a shield," suggested Spectro.

"What?" asked Kevin. "How do I do that?"

Spectro flashed a series of images through Kevin's mind showing him how to create a layer of air behind the runners that was denser than the normal air. This would deflect the laser beams upward and scatter the energy, but it would need to be constantly renewed as the wind scattered it.

Kevin concentrated and could see, in his mind, the layer building up. He could also see the laser beams being deflected so that there were no more clouds of dust thrown up when the beam struck the ground near the runners. But as he watched, he could see his shield being torn apart by the wind so he had to keep replacing it, which was very tiring.

The runners had reached the opening to the ravine and most of them had passed through into the relative safety between the rock walls when Kevin noticed that one of the runners had collapsed and was lying on the ground unable to get up. Then, to his horror, he saw Marlitta turn and run back to help the unfortunate runner to his feet. But no sooner had he stood up he staggered and fell again. The pursuing troops were now getting very close and almost without thinking, Kevin had 'jumped' and was standing beside Marlitta and the unfortunate fellow who had again collapsed.

"Grab his hand," shouted Kevin as he himself grabbed Marlitta's hand. Then he visualised his previous position at the top of the cliff and they were there.

"Can't stop," he shouted and before they could respond, he was down in the cavern waiting for the runners to appear. As they staggered, exhausted into the cavern, they quickly formed a chain, hand in hand, which Kevin dashed over to join. As soon as they were all there he 'jumped', or at least he tried to but he was not expecting it to be so difficult. He had not tried to move so many people before.

"Break the chain in the middle," he shouted, and as soon as the burden was reduced he was gone leaving half the runners still in the cave.

When the first group were safely settled on the cliff top he returned for the rest. It was a close-run thing, though as he could hear the pounding feet of the pursuers echoing in the gully as he transported the second group to safety.

Still he had no time to waste. The hordes were pouring into the gully and surging into the cave and did not stop until the cave could hold no more. Yet still they tried to push their way in.

Kevin watched as they rushed past the pillar rocks at the entrance. He needed them all to be inside before he collapsed the entrance, but he could see that the leaders were now emerging from the cave and telling the others to go back. Some were looking up the sides of the gully for another route out.

At last the tail end of the pursuing horde had passed through the entrance but there was no sign of Duros and his vehicle entering. In fact, Duros had no intention of going in, himself. So, it was now or never and Kevin thought it had better be now. So he put all his energy into directing a destructive beam straight into the rocks below.

There was a shattering explosion then a rumble and the whole side of the ravine collapsed and slid down to block the entrance. The trapped troops began to panic and tried to scale the rock walls, but it was too difficult and several slipped and fell. It looked as if the first part of the plan had worked.

Chapter Fifteen - Cat and Mouse

When the entrance to the ravine had collapsed, Duros had decided that things were not going his way, so he had 'jumped' back to his base camp. There was only a small force left, but these were all mechanised troops which were of no use to him in the mountains and he could not transport them using his crystal as it did not have the power that Kevin's had. What to do next? That was the question. The game had changed somewhat and he was now up against a powerful force. He did not know how powerful and he did not know how Kevin had come by this power, but he would have to be careful.

So he sent the remains of his force back to his ships to return to their home planets while he stayed to make his further plans. He certainly did not want Kevin to return to the council as he did not know if he could beat him in open debate and he did not want them to investigate anything Kevin might tell them.

This was going to take cunning, and that was something Duros had in plenty, but for any plan to work he had to be able to communicate with Kevin and that was the difficult part as he did not know how powerful Kevin's crystal was. He knew it was no ordinary crystal by the way Kevin had exploded the rocks in the gully, but all crystals were different and had different powers and capabilities. Yes, he would have to think very carefully before he made his move, and in the meantime, he would lie low and observe.

Kevin, on the other hand, had his work cut out organising the villagers and dealing with the captives. Kevin had made a narrow path out of the gully and the villagers were bringing the prisoners out one at a time. At first they were very careful in case the soldiers tried to attack them, but without the control of Duros's crystal, they had become frightened peasants and were no threat to anyone.

Several had hurt themselves trying to climb the sides of the ravine, but none seriously. Kevin looked at the sorry bunch.

"I think we had better get them all back to the village," he told Rotunda who had pushed himself to the fore now the danger had passed. Rotunda resumed his official stance and strutted around giving orders to everyone who set off with groups of captives in the direction of the village.

"I don't think these will be able to walk back," he said to Marlitta who had come over to join him after helping round up the captives.

"Can you transport them?" she asked him. Her whole attitude towards him had changed and she now treated him more like an adult rather than a stupid child.

"Yes," he answered. "That shouldn't be too difficult. Get them all to stand in a line holding hands, then you and Lartop can join the chain too. I'll need some help with them back at the village."

Marlitta ran off and collected Lartop and several other villagers that were still busy with the prisoners and rounded up the wounded ones. When they were all in a chain Kevin joined the end and with his other hand on Sniffer, who would not leave his side, they 'jumped'. Immediately they were standing in the deserted village square, at least some were standing. The others were so surprised by the sudden change of scene that they fell in a heap pulling the others with them.

When they had calmed themselves, scrambled to their feet and dusted themselves off, Marlitta and Lartop led them back to his house and sat them all down outside. It was not too cold and they were all dressed in warm clothes so they would be quite comfortable. Kevin sat down with them while Marlitta and the others tended the wounds, which mostly comprised cuts, abrasions, bruises and twisted ankles.

The one nearest to Kevin looked distinctly miserable.

"What's the matter with you?" asked Kevin. There was no reply so Kevin shuffled nearer. "I asked you what the matter was?"

"What d'ya think?"

"I don't know," said Kevin. "Tell me."

"It's obvious, I would've thought," he said. "We've failed Duros so he's abandoned us. Good riddance to him, I say, but what happens to us now? We'll be your slaves now I s'pose."

"No," said Kevin indignantly. "We don't have slaves, you'll be free to do whatever you wish."

"Here?" he did not seem any better pleased with this thought. "There's nothing here. We'll all starve."

"I don't think so," said Kevin. "But one thing at a time. We'll worry about what happens to you when the others get back. But for now, here comes some food." One of Marlitta's helpers was heading towards them with steaming bowls which put a weak smile on the fellow's face.

"Don't get too excited about it," said Kevin getting up and taking one of the bowls for himself. Everyone else seemed to be eating and he had only just realised how hungry he was.

He walked over to Marlitta and Lartop and the three took their bowls of food into Lartop's house where they sat down. It was warm but dark inside but Kevin found it pleasantly soothing.

"What do we do now?" he asked. "Will your village be able to take them all in?"

"Not permanently," said Lartop. "But I'm sure we could house them all for a while. Then we would have to send some of them to other villages. But what about Duros? Isn't he still a threat?"

"Yes, I suppose he is," said Kevin. "But he's sent all the rest of his army away now, so I expect he is going to try to get hold of me himself. I expect he is afraid of the crystal but he can't risk me going back to the council and telling what I know."

"How can he stop you?" asked Marlitta. "Surely you can just go any time you like now you have your crystal."

"I don't know," said Kevin thoughtfully. "I'm sure Duros has thought of that and I don't know what he would do if I did just go. Maybe he could get back at the same time and stop me, or he might stay here and harm you to get his own back. I just don't know. First of all, I'm going to see if I can find out where he is. Could you leave me alone for a while so that I can concentrate."

The others left and Kevin lay back, made himself comfortable and closed his eyes. In his mind he sped across the ground towards where Duros camp had been, but as he had expected it had gone. There were tracks on the ground where the heavy mechanised troops had left but no other signs that meant anything. All he could do was to follow the tracks back to where the space craft had been waiting to take them off. He found that he could move quite quickly and still concentrate on the tracks which were very plain. A wide column of vehicles had ploughed across the fragile terrain flattening everything in its path. Suddenly the tracks widened into a large circular area and stopped. There was no sign of anything.

He 'jumped' and found himself standing amid the furrows made as the vehicles had manoeuvred to enter the waiting craft. A cool breeze blew across the plain and he could see for miles and there was nothing to see. They had gone, but surely not Duros? He would not just leave; he must still be here somewhere, but where?

Spectro answered startling Kevin who was deep in thought.

"You can trace his path using the power of the crystal," he said.

"How do I do that?" Kevin snapped. He felt quite irritated by Spectro at times. He seemed to know everything but never volunteered information unless asked.

"You need to go back to the last place that we know Duros was," he answered. "Then you can pick up the trace."

Kevin thought for a moment. Where had Duros been that Kevin knew? Then he remembered. Duros had been waiting outside the ravine in his vehicle, and then he had 'jumped', vehicle and all. Kevin visualised the place and 'jumped'. Yes, this is it, he thought. At first, he could not see the tracks of the vehicle but after scanning the ground for a while he saw the tracks where Duros has crept across the ground keeping well out of harm's way. After following the tracks towards the ravine, Kevin soon found the point where they stopped.

"Now what?" he asked Spectro.

"Look at the marks on the ground and try and imagine the vehicle standing there."

Kevin tried but could not quite see the vehicle. He had not really taken too much notice of the actual appearance of it, just where it was and what it was doing.

"I can't see it," he said. "So, what now?"

"Keep trying," said Spectro. "Try to empty your mind and see if it starts to appear."

Kevin thought he would be wasting his time, but what else was he to do. So he stared at the ground where the tracks ended and tried to think of nothing. At first he could see his father's car standing there, then the school bus, then the milk float that trundled up the drive to his house. It was strange that, until now, he had hardly thought about his home. It almost seemed like a fantasy world from his dreams, and as he was thinking this he suddenly realised that in front of him, he could now see the black vehicle that Duros had been in.

"Good," said Spectro. "Now let it drift away in your mind and as it goes, follow it with your mind sight."

Kevin watched it closely, but it did not move. It just sat there, stubbornly looking back at him, or so it seemed. An age seemed to pass and it was not until his concentration began to lapse again that the vehicle started to fade. First it blurred around the edges and became like smoke which seemed to drift in the breeze. Then it began to move faster and it was all Kevin could do to keep it in sight. Away it shot, straight as a die, away over the ridge and off over the plain. Faster and faster it sped and the scenery became a blur. It was all Kevin could do to keep his mind focused on the misty vehicle as it sped onward.

Then, at last it began to slow down and eventually came to a standstill on a rocky ledge.

"Now what?" asked Kevin.

"Same again," said Spectro. "Each time he 'jumped', he would leave a new trail, so we have to follow each one until we find him. Now you must 'jump' to this place so that we can follow the next 'jump'."

Kevin had almost forgotten that he was only seeing this new place in his mind. Almost immediately he was actually there. He could still see the ghostly outline of the vehicle standing there, and then they were off again. This time they arrived at an area different from any that Kevin had seen on this strange planet, for here there were trees, of a sort next to a small stream.

Duros must have expected to be followed as he had 'jumped' many times to places Kevin had never seen, and it was all he could do to follow the track. Finally, at the end of a particularly long 'jump', Kevin suddenly found himself face to face with the evil black vehicle. It was standing in a low gully surrounded by rocks. Kevin 'jumped' to a spot out of sight of the vehicle, behind some boulders. From here he could see it quite clearly without being seen, himself. There was no sign of life, but it was impossible to know what was happening inside so he settled himself amongst the rocks to wait.

It was getting a bit chilly and he hoped it would not take too long for something to happen when suddenly, he noticed that the door in the side of the vehicle was slowly opening.

Kevin froze and waited. First a leg appeared, then another one followed by a small body as it climbed slowly down the ladder to the ground. It was not Duros, that was for sure. He would have used his crystal rather than climb laboriously down that ladder.

When he reached the bottom of the ladder he turned and walked out into the flat space between the vehicle and the rocks where Kevin was hiding. He had not seen Kevin but he seemed to be waiting for someone. As the little fellow stood there, Kevin realised that he had seen him before. In fact it was the trouble maker from the village elders. He could not recall his name for the moment, but that did not matter. Now was his chance to do something, so he 'jumped' and landed right behind him.

"Right you!" said Kevin. The fellow nearly jumped out of his skin as he spun round to see who had crept up behind him.

"Oh, it's you is it?" he said. "I've got a message for you."

"I know you, don't I?" said Kevin. Where's Duros?"

"Of course you know me," he continued. "Gron's the name. And Duros is waiting for you back at the village. That's the message I've got to give you. But," he said suddenly as he saw that Kevin was about to leave, "I've also got to tell you that he has everyone in the village held prisoner, so be careful and no tricks."

"He had better not hurt anyone," said Kevin, "or he'll regret it."

"Oh, big words," said Gron. "You don't think you can get the better of Duros, do you?"

Kevin did not bother to reply and was back in the village before Gron had stopped talking. He arrived outside Lartop's house. The place was deserted so he crept up to the doorway and slipped inside.

"Kevin!" It was Marlitta. Kevin could not see much as it was quite dim inside the house.

"Stay where you are." This time the voice belonged to Duros. "Do not move a muscle or your little friend here will suffer."

"Leave her alone," he said trying to sound brave.

"Or what?" asked Duros. "I know you have a crystal, of sorts, but it won't be able to master mine. So stay where you are and listen." Kevin stayed where he was and listened. "You are going to return, with me, to the Council," he continued, "And you are going to tell them nothing of all this."

"Why should I?" said Kevin defiantly.

"Because I am going to hold this planet hostage," he said. "And should you put a foot wrong everyone here will suffer."

"You must give me time to think about it," said Kevin.

"No," shouted Marlitta. "Don't do what he wants."

"Quiet you," said Duros throwing Marlitta to the ground. "I'll give you one hour and then you must decide." So saying he strode to the door. "Stay in here and no-one will get hurt." Then he was gone.

"You can't give in to him," said Marlitta indignantly.

"I don't intend to," said Kevin.

Chapter Sixteen - Return

"It's like this," said Kevin. "We have to get word back to the Council and they will send help."

"But if you leave," said Marlitta. "Duros will kill everyone here out of spite."

"I know," said Kevin. "That's why I can't go. Someone else will have to go."

"But who?" said Marlitta. "No-one else has a crystal."

"Well I thought you could go," said Kevin. "And you won't need a crystal."

"But how can I go without a crystal?"

"I'll take you," he said. "Anyway, you couldn't go on your own as you wouldn't know where to go or who to speak to. We've got an hour before he comes back, so I'll take you there, find Quartok and leave you to explain. Then I'll come back here and keep him occupied until help gets here."

"Will that work?" she asked. "Will he listen to me? What if he doesn't?"

"Well he's got to and you'll just have to make him. When he knows the situation, he'll know what to do."

"Well if you're sure," said Marlitta, "We'd better be off."

Kevin took her hand and closed his eyes. Only a few days ago he would never have dreamed of holding her hand, now he hardly gave it a second thought. Sniffer's howl disappeared in an instant and they were both back in Kevin's room at the Council headquarters. Nothing had changed but the room was empty. Kevin snapped his fingers and immediately they were surrounded by Murin. Marlitta stepped back in alarm. "What are these?" she shouted.

"Don't worry," said Kevin. "They are Murin." Then turning to the Murin he asked where Quartok was.

"He is with the Council," came the answer.

"Well bring him here quickly," he snapped. "This is urgent." The Murin disappeared leaving Kevin and Marlitta alone.

"We may as well sit down and wait," said Kevin. "I don't know this place well enough to go looking for him."

They sat down and Kevin tried to answer all Marlitta's questions, though it was difficult to keep up with her. He had forgotten that she had never been away from her home planet and all this was very strange to her. He also told her more about his crystal and the powers it had and before he had had time to answer all her questions the door opened and in came Quartok looking very flustered and out of breath.

"Kevin, Master," he gasped. "Where have you been?"

Kevin explained, as quickly as he could, what had happened and what had to be done. "Now," he said, "I must get back or there's no knowing what Duros will do. Marlitta will fill in the gaps." And with that he was gone.

Back in Lartop's house he had hardly arrived when Sniffer leapt upon him and gave him a good licking. He had taken it very hard being left like this.

"Good lad." said Kevin stroking his head and making a fuss of him. "Now sit down and be quiet while I have a think."

By that, Kevin meant that it was time that he had another discussion with Spectro. He needed to know what he could do to overpower Duros and hold him prisoner.

"You could neutralise his crystal," suggested Spectro.

"Now he tells me," said Kevin. "How do I do that?"

Spectro explained in mind pictures what Kevin had to do.

"As easy as that, is it?" asked Kevin.

"Yes," said Spectro. "I would have told you sooner, but you didn't ask."

Kevin was getting a bit fed up with this, but decided there was nothing for it but to ask more questions in future. "Is there any chance this won't work?" he asked, thinking it would be better to know all aspects now rather than when it was too late.

"It is possible," said Spectro. "It depends on whether your will power is greater than his."

"Oh great," said Kevin, his spirits dropping into his boots.

"But you do have a more powerful crystal," Spectro continued, "even if I do say so myself."

Kevin did not seem to have much choice; he would have to give it a go and hope that Marlitta was successful in persuading Quartok to do something quickly. He did not know how long he had been sitting thinking but he was shaken out of his reverie by a low growl from Sniffer.

"Quite boy," he whispered. There was someone outside moving towards the door. Surely it was too soon for Duros to return for his decision. He waited as the door opened and Duros entered.

"I got fed up with waiting," he said. "I will have your decision now."

Sniffer sprang to his feet as if to attack, then sank to floor with a whine. Duros had stopped him with a single mental command. That seemed to be the power of Duros' crystal; the power to subjugate people and animals. Kevin hoped it was not powerful enough to stop him doing what he had planned.

"Do I have any choice?" said Kevin playing for time.

"Not really," said Duros with a sneer. "I know you have found a crystal, I can't imagine how because there are no more crystals left here, except perhaps very small ones. Give it to me." He held his hand out to Kevin as if he expected him to do as he was told.

"No," said Kevin defiantly, "You'll have to take it from me if you want it." Kevin felt an overpowering feeling that he wanted to give the crystal to Duros, and before he had realised it he was reaching into his pocket to find the crystal. He tried to fight it but found that he could not.

"What can I do?" he implored Spectro.

"You must destroy his crystal," came the answer in his head, "like you did the rocks."

Kevin knew what he meant but found it very difficult to concentrate on two things at the same time. He could see Duros's crystal in his mind and he tried to send a beam of energy at it, but Duros, sensing this put more pressure on Kevin's mind to make him stop. At least this removed the desire to give his crystal to Duros, but it left them in stalemate. Neither could make an advance on the other. Beads of perspiration appeared on Kevin's forehead and Duros was gritting his teeth as if he were in a tug of war and was slowly being dragged forward.

Kevin did not know how long he could keep this up and hoped that Marlitta came back quickly with reinforcements. However, in the struggle, Duros had let slip his hold on Sniffer who was now looking very puzzled. He was not sure what was happening. If Duros had been physically attacking Kevin there would have been no problem. He would have known immediately what to do. But here they were just sitting looking at each other. But Kevin looked as if he was being hurt and this bothered Sniffer. His doggy intelligence told him that his master was being threatened but he could not see how.

Suddenly Kevin started to shake with the exertion and this was enough for Sniffer who leapt at Duros who immediately diverted some of his power to stop the dog, and this was all Kevin needed.

There was a blinding flash as Duros' crystal exploded into a million pieces. Sniffer stopped in his tracks, yelped, and ran back to Kevin in terror. Duros fell to the floor clutching his burnt chest, and Kevin collapsed into a heap on the floor. When he finally had recovered enough energy to sit up and look around him, he found Duros cowering in a corner groaning while Sniffer stood guard over him.

"Good lad," said Kevin weakly, "Guard him."

At that moment the door burst open and Lartop, followed by several others poured into the room.

"What happened?" shouted Lartop. "We heard a loud bang."

Kevin explained what had happened and Rotunda seeing it was now safe, pushed himself to the fore. Until Duros's crystal had been destroyed, all the citizens of the village had been under its power and had been unable to leave their houses. However, as soon as it had exploded, they were released from its hold and the first thing they heard was an almighty bang.

"Take him and lock him up," he commanded pointing at Duros. Two men stepped forward to carry out his order and immediately stepped back again when Sniffer growled at them.

"It's OK Sniffer," said Kevin. "You can leave him now." Sniffer gave Duros one last growl and went back to sit beside Kevin. "You can take him away now and lock him up. He won't be any more trouble. And I think he will need a little first aid as well."

The men grabbed Duros and dragged him from the room.

"Don't be too rough with him," said Kevin, "He's harmless now. But while I think about it, his friend is still lurking out there. I'd better go and get him."

"What friend is that?" asked Rotunda.

"I think you know him," said Kevin. "His name is Gron."

"Oh him," said Rotunda. "He deserves all he gets, the traitor."

"Come Sniffer," said Kevin. Sniffer, eager to go with his master pushed himself against Kevin's leg and in an instant, they were gone.

The vehicle was still there but there was no sign of Gron.

"Come out of there, Gron," shouted Kevin. At first nothing happened, then slowly the hatch opened and Gron's face appeared.

"What do you want?" asked Gron looking puzzled. "I would have thought that Duros would have dealt with you by now, or were you too scared to go and find him?"

"Duros is in prison at the village," said Kevin, "and that's where you're going so come here."

Gron looked at Sniffer. "Not with that beast sitting there," he said. "Do you think I'm a fool?"

"Yes," said Kevin, "and you'll be even more of a fool if you stay here. You'll either starve or one of the wild animals will get you, or worst of all, you might be caught by your old friends. I don't think they're too pleased with you."

Gron slowly started to make his way down the ladder from the hatch, keeping a wary eye on Sniffer who sat watching him intently.

"Keep a firm hold of that beast," said Gron as he reached the ground. But Kevin had plans of his own and he meant to teach this little toad a lesson.

Gron was half way between the vehicle and the place where Kevin was waiting for him when Sniffer leapt at him. With a startled cry, Gron was off at a gallop. Kevin never would have thought that little fat legs could run as fast. If it had been Sniffer's intention to catch Gron he would have had him before he had gone two paces. However, Kevin had put a little thought into Sniffer's mind and it did not include actually harming Gron, but it did include frightening the life out of him.

Gron had disappeared over one of the rocky dunes and Sniffer had let him go. After a short delay Gron appeared again running up the side of the next dune, scrabbling for all he was worth. Occasionally he fell and slid down to the bottom of the dune again only to scramble back onto his feet and start again, continuously looking over his shoulder for the ferocious dog.

Sniffer, however, was sitting at the bottom of the first dune waiting for Kevin's command.

"OK," said Kevin. "Go fetch him."

Sniffer bounded off in a wide circle heading for a point well ahead of Gron. As soon as he reached a point directly ahead of the terrified creature, he sat down and waited. Shortly, Gron's red face appeared over the dune and a look of horror spread over it as he saw Sniffer sitting there waiting for him.

He turned and fled back the way he had come with Sniffer trotting along behind him.

When he finally got back to where Kevin was waiting Gron was on the point of collapse and he crawled the last few yards to drop at Kevin's feet.

"Mercy," he cried. "Save me from that brute, please."

"He only wants to play with you," said Kevin. "Don't you like playing with him?"

"No. Please keep him off."

"Well, perhaps that will teach you what it feels like to be the victim of someone like Duros, " said Kevin. "Here Sniffer."

Sniffer bounded to Kevin's side and Gron gave a strangled scream. But Sniffer was not going to hurt him. Kevin just wanted to make contact with both of them so that he could take them back to the village.

As soon as they arrived at the village, an angry crowd gathered shouting for vengeance on the traitor.

"No," shouted Kevin. "Leave him alone. He will be dealt with by the Council as soon as they arrive. Take him and lock him up with Duros, but make sure he isn't hurt."

"He looks as if he has already had rather a rough time of it," said Lartop walking over to Kevin. "What have you done to him?"

"Never touched him," said Kevin innocently. "He just decided to take Sniffer for a run."

Lartop grinned but said no more about it. He did not have the opportunity as a commotion broke out at the other side of the gathering. At first Kevin could not see what was causing it, but then the crowd parted and Marlitta dashed through to him.

"I've brought them back with me," she said. "Thank goodness it isn't too late."

Close behind her came Quartok with two other important looking people who Kevin half recognised, followed by ten armed guards.

"Kevin," said Quartok. "We had given you up for lost. What's happening here?"

"It is all under control now," said Kevin. "We have Duros locked up in the village. I have destroyed his crystal so he can't escape."

"Is there somewhere we can go?" asked Quartok. "We have a lot to discuss."

Lartop offered his house, which was close by, much to the annoyance of Rotunda who was trying to wheedle his way to the centre of things without much success.

"Thank you everyone," shouted Kevin. "We will have a full meeting of the whole village as soon as we have had a private discussion. I will leave Rotunda to organise it."

Kevin then led them to Lartop's house and took them inside. He also invited Lartop, Marlitta and her father and brothers to come in as well. The ten guards took up their positions outside the house.

Chapter Seventeen - Making Amends

After Lartop had provided everyone with food and drink, the discussion started. Kevin told them all that had happened from the time Duros had taken him from his room. He also told them all about the plight of the third sector which had been controlled, until now, by Duros. Quartok and his two friends, Snee and Larnock, were amazed by this. They had had no idea that this had been going on. They had known that Duros was a trouble maker but had thought that this went no further than the debating chamber.

"I can't imagine how he managed to keep it secret," exclaimed Quartok. "Although his crystal gave him powers, it also should have acted as a restraint and reported any misbehaviour to the council. I don't understand it."

"It is my belief that Duros had a special crystal that had been modified for his own use," said Kevin. "My own new crystal seems to know about everything, but it is sometimes difficult to get it to give me the information. It seems that each crystal is different and made to suit one particular person. This crystal of mine was meant for me and I was led to it so I could find it when I needed it. I don't know how Duros got his, but at least he hasn't got it now."

"That must be a very powerful crystal you have there," said Snee. "I have never heard of one that could destroy another crystal before."

"No," said Quartok sternly, "you must use it with care. Anyway, we have much to decide and the sooner started, the sooner mended. I think we must first of all see to the evacuation of this planet. There aren't many people left here so it shouldn't be too much of a problem."

"Excuse me," said Petrog apologetically, "but may I say something?"

"Of course," said Kevin. Then turning to Quartok he said, "This is Marlitta's father. He took me in when I was first abandoned here. What is it Petrog?"

"Well," he said hesitantly, "we don't actually want to leave here, well not all of us that is. But it would be nice if something could be done to restore the planet to its former self."

"A good point," said Quartok. "It would be possible, though it could take some time and a great deal of effort."

Kevin consulted Spectro silently while the others waited for his reply. "Spectro says that it can be done but it would need someone to have the right crystal for the job."

"That could be a problem," said Quartok. "I don't know where we would get one to suit."

"According to Spectro," continued Kevin, "a crystal can be found right here on this planet, but first we must appoint a leader and then he will find the crystal himself."

"I suppose we will have to stick with the fellow who's in charge now," said Quartok. "What was his name?"

"Rotunda," said Kevin, " but I don't think he would be suitable. He's too pompous. I could ask Spectro?"

"A good idea," said Quartok relieved that he did not have to make the choice himself. After all, that's how we chose you isn't it?"

"Yes," said Kevin. "I suppose it is."

So when the general discussion was concluded they all went out to meet the assembled population of the village. Kevin explained to them what was to happen and gave them all the choice of staying or leaving. They all chose to stay.

Kevin then walked past each of them in turn and spoke to each one and Spectro told Kevin of the person's suitability. When he had spoken to everyone, which took quite a while as they were a talkative lot, Spectro came to a decision.

"There has been a decision," announced Kevin and he noticed Rotunda pull himself up to his full height and prepare to come forward to receive the honour. "The new leader is to be Petrog."

There were general cries of agreement which made Rotunda look most put out, but before he could say anything Kevin looked straight at him and said "However, we still need someone to head the village and see to all the civic duties, and I think Rotunda will do that very well."

There was another cheer, though not quite as enthusiastic this time.

"You will both need a great deal of help," continued Kevin, "so I'll let you each choose your own helpers. Of course, there will be a great deal of help from the Council if we are to make this planet more comfortable to live on, but we'll have to see to all that as soon as we get back there."

The meeting broke up then and groups gathered together to discuss things. Rotunda went round trying to get all the best people to help him, but Petrog stayed with Kevin and the Council members to discuss things less publicly.

"Are you sure I'm the right person for this job?" he asked Kevin. "I'm not one for making speeches and such like. Perhaps you should find someone else."

"I think you're just the right person," said Kevin. "We don't want people to make speeches. I think it's better to have someone who'll just get on with the job, not like politicians who talk a lot but never seem to do anything."

"Quite right," said Quartok. "You seem to be getting the idea of this job more quickly than when I was trying to teach you."

Kevin looked surprised as he had not really thought about it until now. "Well," he said, "I've been getting a lot of help from Spectro."

"Yes," said Quartok. "You've mentioned him before but have never told us exactly who he is."

"Well he's the voice of my crystal," said Kevin. "I don't think he's an actual person though, but he says he has the knowledge of all the crystals in the universe. I don't really understand it myself, but he is quite useful when I remember to ask for his help."

"What are we to do about Duros?" asked Snee suddenly.

"I suppose we'll have to take him back to the Council," said Quartok. "What does Spectro say?"

Kevin went quiet for a moment as if deep in thought. "He says it would be better to keep him here away from possible help. He has no crystal now so he shouldn't be much trouble. It would do him good to help put right what he has spoilt."

"But I suppose we still have to find his replacement," said Quartok. "That could be difficult. The third sector is quite a responsibility and we don't know yet just how much damage he has done."

"How was he chosen?" asked Kevin.

"He was voted in by a Council majority," said Quartok.

"Most important posts are filled in that way," put in Snee.

"Why didn't you use a crystal to find the right person," asked Kevin, "like you did when you found me."

"I don't know," said Quartok. "It's never been done that way before. Perhaps you should consult Spectro again."

"What do you think?" Kevin asked Spectro. "Can you choose the right person?"

"I can give you the logical options from my store of data," he said, "but I my thought processes are different from yours."

"Well give me the options then," said Kevin.

"The most effective way to find out what someone is suitable for is by first finding their crystal; the one that matches their mind and personality," continued Spectro.

"You found me because we were attracted to each other by the life force of the universe. It is the same for others. You would need to take the possible candidate to the cave where you found me and see if they can find their own crystal."

"But how do we decide who to start with?" said Kevin getting a little impatient.

"Well, the personality that fits the requirement best, as far as I can detect," said Spectro, "is that of Marlitta."

"Marlitta?" repeated Kevin in amazement. The others all stared at him and he realised that he had spoken out loud.

"Is that the choice?" asked Quartok.

"You must be wrong," said Marlitta. "What do I know about being in charge of a galactic sector? I don't even know what it is."

"You might say the same about me," said Kevin.

"I did," said Marlitta with a grin. "But I was wrong. Anyway, you have a crystal to help you."

"But that is what Spectro said," continued Kevin. "We must take you to the cave where I found Spectro and see if you can find your crystal. You see everyone has their own personal crystal somewhere in the universe. You just have to find it."

The discussion continued all that day and long into the night, interrupted only by food brought in by Lartop and his family and friends. Finally they were all found beds for the night and they all were soon enveloped in a much needed sleep.

The following morning the assembly gathered again with the exception of Kevin and Marlitta who were to go to the cave again. They took Sniffer with them as they were not too sure exactly where it was. Kevin could visualise the flat ledge were they first met Sniffer, and he transported them there with little effort.

"It's somewhere up here," said Kevin looking up a steep little gully full of loose rocks.

"It looks a bit dangerous, though," said Marlitta looking doubtful.

"I think I can 'jump' us up to that level bit up there," he said pointing upwards. When they landed it was not as level as it had looked and it was all they could do to hang on and not slide over the edge to plummet to the rocks below.

"I think you should judge where you're taking us a bit better next time," said Marlitta, "if you don't want to get us all killed."

"Sorry," said Kevin. "It can't be far from here."

Sniffer started snuffling around and Kevin sent little doggy type messages to him to encourage him to find the cave. He scrabbled over the rocks sniffing all the time and Kevin and Marlitta did their best to follow him, though it was not easy.

Eventually Sniffer became very excited and started clawing at the ground with his front paws sending rocks tumbling down behind him.

"Careful," shouted Kevin as he dodged one of the flying rocks. "What have you found?"

"He's probably found the scent of a brubru or something," said Marlitta. Kevin did not know what a brubru was but assumed it was a small burrowing animal. Almost as she spoke something darted out of a hole in the ground and ran up the vertical rock face above them at an amazing speed.

"There! What did I tell you?" she said with satisfaction.

"I don't think he was after that," said Kevin. "Look, he's still digging."

"Probably a whole family of them," said Marlitta.

"I don't think so," said Kevin. "Come on, let's help him." So they both started pulling rocks out with their bare hands. It was hard work, but they soon could see that it was the opening to a cave.

"I think this is the place," said Kevin. "We must make the opening big enough to be able to squeeze in."

"Can't you use some of the power of that crystal?" asked Marlitta. "It would save a lot of time."

"I never thought of that," he said. "I'll have a word with Spectro."

"If you open up the cave," said Spectro, "it will be available for all and sundry to wander in and find crystals. Wouldn't it be better to 'jump' in and leave the cave sealed?"

"But I can't remember what it looks like in there well enough to do that," said Kevin.

"Well why not take a look, then," continued Spectro. "Use your mind sight."

Kevin had not thought of that. He still kept on forgetting the many powers of the crystal but having been reminded he closed his eyes and looked inside the cave. Then taking hold of Marlitta he jumped and they were immediately inside the cave. Kevin's crystal produced a clear white light that made the walls of the cave sparkle with reflected light. Marlitta gave a startled cry. "You might have warned me you were going to do that," she chided.

"Sorry," said Kevin. "Now, it's up to you. All those sparkles of light are crystals, some big, some small. Choose one for yourself."

But how will I know which is the right one?" she asked, bewildered by the array of glittering crystals. "They all look the same."

"Your crystal will find you and draw you to it," said Kevin.

Marlitta looked about her. The walls were awash with glittering crystals, some bright white ones, some dull red. The suddenly she noticed one pale blue stone that seemed to be winking at her. She moved closer to it and it seemed to be giving off a warm glow. She reached out for it and it almost fell into her hand. She stood gazing into its soft blue light. "This is the one," she said, almost to herself. "Will it speak to me like yours does?" she asked.

Kevin consulted Spectro. "It will speak to you in its own way," he said. "Not necessarily in words. Spectro says that it will most likely communicate through feelings and emotions as this will match your own personality."

"Can I use it to 'jump', as you do?" she asked.

"Yes," said Kevin. "You just have to think of the place you want to be and then just imagine yourself there. I can also see places in my mind; like my own built in television."

"What's television?" she asked.

"Oh, never mind that," he said. "Let's get back to the village. See if you can do it on your own. I've got to collect Sniffer first."

Almost before he had finished speaking, Marlitta was gone. Kevin jumped outside again and was immediately leapt upon by Sniffer who was becoming frantic at the loss of his master.

"Steady on, Sniffer," said Kevin pushing the dog off him. "Let's get back to the village." He took hold of Sniffer and they were back in the village square where Marlitta was surrounded by an eager crowd wanting to know what had happened. Kevin went to Marlitta's rescue and took her into Lartop's house where Quartok was waiting to hear the good news.

Chapter Eighteen - Back home

The next few days were spent organising things for the restoration of the planet which was to be called 'Eden' at Kevin's suggestion. Then it was time to return to the Council and the party gathered in the village square to make their farewells. Petrog said his goodbyes to Marlitta. He was sorry to lose her but pleased that she would be doing something important with her life.

"Don't worry," she said. "You'll be seeing quite a lot of me while Eden is being rebuilt."

"I hope so," said Petrog. "I'll need all the help I can get."

"Goodbye Petrog," said Kevin. "Thank you for everything, and you Lartop. I expect I'll be back from time to time. Make sure Duros does something useful for a change."

"I will," said Petrog.

The group then all joined hands and was gone. Back at the crystal city, they arrived in the Council chamber in the midst of a heated debate. There were two contenders for the position previously held by Duros and each was arguing his case in a very heated way. The sudden arrival of the group startled everyone into silence. Quartok went straight to his position at the table and addressed the council. He explained what had happened and that they now had a new candidate to take over from Duros. There was immediate uproar, but Quartok called them all to order.

"May I remind you," he said, "that we now have a new Master of the Council and while he was away he has found his own crystal. A crystal, I may say, which is more powerful than any known before. I therefore hand this meeting over to the Master."

Kevin went to the place Quartok indicated at the head of the table. Everyone went quiet waiting for him to speak. He told them of Spectro and what he had said concerning the appointment of a new leader for the Third Sector. He explained about the selection of a crystal for this person and how they have found their crystal.

"So now," he continued, "may I present the new Leader of the Third Sector." He indicated that Marlitta should come forward. There were gasps of amazement. "But she is just a child," someone shouted.

"Maybe," said Kevin. "But so am I, I suppose. But it is the crystal that makes the difference. Marlitta has found her crystal and it will make her the best person for the job. But she will need your help because she can't do it all on her own."

Marlitta was given a place at the table and they continued to discuss what had to be done to undo all the damage done by Duros. Quartok took on the job of training her in the use of the crystal and the way in which the Council worked. He said that Kevin did not need him anymore as he now had Spectro to advise him.

Kevin was in a unique position as he came from a planet outside what was known as the civilised universe, and what is more, he was still no more than a child even if he was bigger than most of the people he had met so far. It was, therefore, important for him to continue with his schooling on Earth before he could leave home for good. It was also very important that no-one on Earth found out about his new powers. He was going to have to be very careful what he did and make sure that no-one got suspicious.

He spent a few more days at the capital seeing Marlitta start on her training. But he eventually had to make ready to return home. Strangely, he was not feeling home sick. At home he spent a lot of time on his own and did not rely on others as much as he might have done had he lived in a town. And here, he had made more friends in a few days than he ever had at home in his whole lifetime. He could not believe that he felt attached to a girl. It was not the done thing, back home, to be soft on a girl, not when you are almost eleven years old. But he did not want to leave Marlitta.

"I'll be back soon," he said "to see how you're getting on."

"Good," she said. "I'll miss you."

Kevin went bright red, or at least he felt he must have. He said all his other goodbyes before closing his eyes and thinking of home ready to make the 'jump' back again. At first, he found it difficult to get the picture in his head, but finally decided on the field at the bottom of his garden. He knew that well. But as he was about to 'jump' he felt something touching his arm but he ignored it and 'jumped' anyway.

He opened his eyes and was back home, standing in the middle of the field at the bottom of his garden, and there, half way between him and the garden wall was that wretched horse, Billy.

"Oh dear," thought Kevin. "Now what?" It was only then that he noticed he was not alone, for sitting patiently by his side was Sniffer. "What are we going to do with you?" he said. Sniffer was not the sort of animal people were used to seeing. Kevin had grown used to him now and had thought of him as a household pet, but other people were not going to think of him as a pet. He made a rottweiler look like a toy poodle.

"Oh, come on then," he said and started walking towards Billy who looked at Sniffer in a very suspicious way and backed away as they approached. Kevin felt quite relieved by this but then wondered if his new crystal would allow him to communicate with Billy but could get no response when he tried.

"No-one at home," he thought and looked at Billy who seemed to look a little indignant.

They carried on into the garden and made their way up to the house. Kevin could see his mother moving around in the kitchen but there was no sign of his father. When he entered his mother seemed surprised to see him.

"You're back early," she said. "The bus isn't due for another hour yet."

Kevin had forgotten that he should be returning on the bus and, anyway, he was not sure what time it was. It was then that his mother noticed Sniffer in the doorway and she let out a startled scream.

"Oh don't worry about him," he said. "This is Sniffer."

Sniffer walked forward and with some mental prodding from Kevin sat and offered his paw for her to shake.

"What is it?" she asked in amazement still not sure she was safe.

"He's my new friend," said Kevin. "Is it OK if I keep him?"

"Well I don't know," she said. "I'll ask your father what he thinks. Anyway, where would he live? He can't stay in here."

"I'm sure he'll be OK in the shed," said Kevin. Sniffer looked doubtful.

"Where did you get him?" asked his mother looking for a way out of keeping him. "Doesn't he belong to someone?"

Kevin made up a long tale about how he had been given him as his owner could no longer look after him. "He was great company when we were camping."

"You still haven't told me why you have arrived early," said his mother remembering what she had been saying before she saw Sniffer.

"We hitched a lift," said Kevin.

"Now I've told you before about not accepting lifts from strangers," she said sternly. "Anything could happen to you these days."

"Not with Sniffer to look after me," he said.

"Right. You'd better go upstairs and have a bath," she continued. "I expect you'll be needing one after ten days camping. Did you have fun?"

"Oh yes," said Kevin. "We got stranded on an almost deserted planet with a villain who was trying to catch us. But we got the better of him in the end."

"Yes dear," said his mother. "I'm sure you did."

Kevin went upstairs to wash and change followed by Sniffer.

"I don't know," he said. "Here am I, Master of the Universe, and I get told off for not having a bath."

Kevin was not quite sure, but it looked as if Sniffer was laughing at him.

* * *

Part 2

The Revenge of Duros

Chapter 1 – A surprise visit

It was several months since Kevin's escapade on the planet of Eden and it all seemed like a dream. He had now turned eleven years old and was in his final term at the junior school. He had had a bit of fun with his crystal but was always careful that he would not be found out. It had been particularly useful when they went for a cross country run. Kevin would wait until all the others were out of sight, and then 'jump' to somewhere near the end of the run and wait until the others caught up with him. Then he would join on at the back as if he had been there all the time.

'Jumping', as he called it, was something the crystal let him do. All he had to do was to imagine the place he wanted to 'jump' to and think he was there, and immediately he would be there. Distance was no object but you had to be careful.

People had been somewhat surprised when they saw Sniffer for the first time but they soon got used to him and accepted him as a dog, if a rather unusual one. Sniffer would stay at home while Kevin was at school and would run down the drive to meet him from the school bus in the afternoon when he returned. At first, he would not stay at home and followed Kevin to school causing quite a stir when he walked merrily into assembly. Kevin used his crystal to tell Sniffer that he must not do this and to go home immediately. He did not use words to talk to Sniffer but rather communicated in pictures. Anyway, it did the trick and Sniffer shot off in the direction of home and never tried to follow Kevin to school again.

One day when Kevin returned home from school, Sniffer seemed to be extra pleased to see him.

"What's the matter, boy?" asked Kevin as they walked up to the house. But Sniffer could not communicate well enough to make Kevin understand so he gave up.

The house was an attractive country cottage about a quarter of a mile from the road that wound its way up the hill out of the town. There were several large trees at the front of the house so that you could only see part of it from the road. At the back there were more trees and a garden leading down to a dry-stone wall beyond which was a small meadow leading to the moors where Kevin had first heard the voices talking about him while he dozed among the rocks.

As he reached the house his mother came out to meet him.

"That dog of yours has been acting very strangely today," she said looking at Sniffer. "He's been under my feet all day."

"Perhaps he wanted a walk," suggested Kevin.

"I don't have time to take him for walks," said his mother following him into the house. "You'll have to take him after you've had your dinner."

Kevin did not mind that, in fact he rather liked the idea. He enjoyed being out on his own with Sniffer. It was fun. So, after he had finished eating he put on his old clothes and set off down the garden with Sniffer at his heels. It was a pleasant evening and the birds were singing in the trees as he climbed through the gap in the wall and out into the field. Once in the field, Sniffer raced off into the distance. Kevin thought it was because he had been shut up at home all day and he was just pleased to be able to stretch his legs. He was not worried about calling him back as he could do that at any time using his crystal. He could also listen in to Sniffer's doggy thoughts, if he wanted to, to find out what Sniffer was trying to tell him, which he did from time to time. Kevin was not actually listening in, but he got the feeling that Sniffer was eager to show him something.

"Probably after rabbits," he thought and sauntered after him.

Sniffer seemed to be heading for Kevin's favourite rocks at the top of the slope. That, in itself, was not surprising as they often went up there. Since his last adventure the novelty of the crystal and its power had worn off a little and Kevin did not find it quite so much fun to 'jump' from place to place using its power. He had not even been back up to the cave where he kept the blob, as he called the strange vehicle he had been given. He really could not be bothered. It was quite pleasant just strolling along, alone with his thoughts without a worry in the world. It was just as well that he was making the most of it as that was soon going to change.

As he reached the rocks, he became aware of someone else nearby. He could sense the presence of Sniffer, but there was someone else, and that in itself was strange. No one he knew would go anywhere near Sniffer and certainly would not stay near him unless Sniffer had him by the throat.

"Oh no," he thought. "I hope he hasn't hurt someone."

He rushed forward into the space between the rocks and was amazed to see Sniffer being stroked by a girl. As he approached her she turned to face him and he stopped in amazement. It was Marlitta.

"Hello Kevin," she said smiling broadly. "Bet you didn't expect to find me here, did you?"

"Marlitta," stammered Kevin unable to think of anything else to say.

"I thought you would like to know have things were going on Paradise," she said. "I thought you might have come and had a look for yourself, actually." She had a slight edge to her voice even though she was still smiling.

"Well it isn't long since I was there," he said, "so I didn't think much would have happened yet."

"It might not have been long here," she said, "but it has been over a year on Paradise."

Paradise was the planet where Kevin had met Marlitta. It had not been called that then as it was far from being paradise when Kevin had first arrived. In fact, it had been a very bleak and desolate place. When he left they were about to transform the planet back into the beautiful place it had originally been before Duros has arrived and ruined it by mining and plundering all its wealth. Now Duros was being held prisoner on Paradise and was being made to help repair some of the damage he had done.

"Why don't we go now?" she said with a look that would not accept 'no' as an answer.

"Why not?" said Kevin holding out his hand to her. No sooner had his hand grasped hers than the scene had changed. There was a slight chill in the breeze after the warm sun that had just been beating down on him, but the sight that met his gaze was far different from what he had expected. There was a covering of pale green over everything now. Small trees were springing up and there was the sound of water trickling over rocks.

"What do you think?" asked Marlitta excitedly.

"Amazing," was all that Kevin could say.

"Of course, it is only a start, but once the new vegetation takes hold there will be no stopping it. The climate will improve which will help the plants, and so on." She was really proud of what she had achieved and hoped that Kevin would be as pleased as she was.

"Where are we, exactly?" asked Kevin looking around.

"Not far from where we first met," she said. "I thought you would remember what it was like here."

"Well, it's certainly changed since then," said Kevin. "What about the village?"

"All in good time," said Marlitta. "That is still being rebuilt, but it's coming on fine. But first, I thought you would like to see what Duros has been doing."

"I hope you're keeping an eye on him," said Kevin.

"Not so much now," said Marlitta. "We did at first, but he is a really changed man now and has done some marvellous work over in the mountains. He's done so well that we have given him more freedom and I think it has paid off."

Kevin did not look so sure. "Perhaps we should have a look," he said.

The mountain country had truly been transformed. There were trees on some of the slopes and pleasant sheltered valleys lush with new grass where animals were grazing. The climate was less severe than it had been last time he was here and small animals and birds were in evidence here and there. Kevin looked around him. The place seemed familiar; he felt sure he had been here before. Then it hit him. This was the place where he had found his crystal.

"Where's Duros?" asked Kevin suddenly.

"Back at the village, I would imagine," answered Marlitta surprised. "Why?"

"Take me to him," said Kevin. "Quickly." His abruptness surprised her but she did what he asked.

The village had not changed as much as he had expected. Many of the old houses were still as they were though a new complex of buildings was part finished on new ground outside the old village. Marlitta immediately led him to a building that had the look of the site hut on a building site. There were building materials stacked all around and people were coming and going with a sense of urgency.

"This is where Duros operates from," said Marlitta walking into the small doorway.

It was dimly lit inside. In the corner was a makeshift desk piled with papers and plans. There were more boxes full of papers staked around the room. At first it seemed as if the room were empty, but as his eyes grew accustomed to the dim light, Kevin realised that there was someone sitting behind the desk studying some papers. He looked up as they approached and smiled at Marlitta.

"Welcome, welcome," he said getting awkwardly to his feet. "We have progressed well since your last visit. Would you like to inspect the building work?"

"Not at the moment, thank you," she said. "I would like to speak to Duros. Where is he?"

"I believe he is in the mountains inspecting the work there," said the little person. Kevin did not like him. He looked shifty, as if he had something to hide.

"Call him back, then," said Kevin losing patience. "I want to speak to him now." The creature looked at him as if he had just noticed him standing there.

"And you are?" he said.

"Not very impressed," said Kevin.

"May I introduce you both," said Marlitta sensing that things were getting a little awkward.

"Please do," said the creature.

"Gnarlop," she said. "This is Kevin, Master of the Universe. Kevin, this is Gnarlop, site foreman in charge of the building works here in the village. Gnarlop blanched visibly and tried to smile at Kevin.

"I'm honoured, sir," he said and bowed his head.

"Right then. Now how about getting Duros for me?" said Kevin. Gnarlop fumbled in his pocket and brought out a grubby piece of cloth, which he carefully unfolded onto his desk revealing a small crystal, which he picked up and held to his forehead. He concentrated for a moment then began to frown.

"I'm sorry sir," he said. "But I don't seem to be able to contact him."

"Don't be stupid," said Marlitta stepping forward and taking the crystal from Gnarlop. "This crystal is individually tuned so that Duros can be tracked at any time wherever he might be on the planet."

"And if he isn't on the planet, what then?" asked Kevin.

"It's not a powerful crystal but good enough to track someone anywhere on the planet," said Marlitta. Even if he were in the caves it could find him."

"Caves?" said Kevin. "Which caves?"

"Well any caves," said Marlitta looking puzzled. "They come with the mountains. What's the matter?"

"Well if you remember, it was in one of those caves that I found Spectro, my crystal," said Kevin. "So, if Duros has been allowed in the caves, it is quite likely that he has managed to find a crystal powerful enough to get him off the planet. If so, we're in big trouble."

"But he can't have," said Marlitta.

"If he can't be found on the planet," said Kevin, "he can't be here any longer. I think you had better go straight to the council and start a search. I'll get straight back home. There's not much I can do here. Let me know what is happening."

Chapter Two – The Stalker

Kevin hoped that he would not have to get involved with Duros again and soon fell back into his daily routine. It was as if he were two people; the twelve-year-old school boy and the grown up with responsibilities. When he was at home or at school, the other side of him seemed like a dream, but when he was on another planet, the schoolboy seemed to disappear and he became someone different. Maybe it was because he was treated differently in the two different places.

It was about a week later when he began to have the feeling that someone was watching him, but he never could see anyone who it might be. It was silly really. There was no reason why he should have this sort of feeling. Then shortly after it had started, he noticed someone standing on the pavement watching him as his bus sped off towards his home. It was no one he knew or had even seen before so he could not think why the person should have been looking at him. Perhaps he was looking at someone else on the bus. Yes, that must be it.

At home that evening, when he should have been doing his homework, he sat in his room wondering if Duros was trying to track him down. He took out his crystal and was about to use its distant vision when Spectro spoke to him. He had not spoken to Spectro, the voice of the crystal, for quite a while and it startled him.

"It would be best not to use the power of the crystal," it said.

"Oh," said Kevin, "and why not?"

"If Duros has tracked you to this planet," continued Spectro, "he will be looking out for signs of your power. It would be very easy for him here on Earth where no one else has a crystal. Besides, that is not the only reason."

"And what is the other reason?" asked Kevin impatiently.

"All the power that is used by the crystal comes from the centre of the galaxy where most of the civilised worlds are situated. Earth is right at the edge of the galaxy, a very long way away from the source of power. So, you do not have the same power here as you had on the other planets you have visited."

"But I still have quite a bit of power though?" asked Kevin feeling a bit alarmed at this.

"Only if you conserve it," said Spectro. "Also, the Earth is moving into a position where your sun comes between it and the source of power. During that time your powers will become very weak, so I must conserve every bit of energy I can in case you have need of it during that time."

"How long will this last?" asked Kevin.

"Three to four weeks. So, during this time you will have to remain as inconspicuous as possible and hope that Duros has not followed you here," said Spectro. "If he is here, he will not show himself because he is so different from the Earth people. But he might find someone he can control and get him to find you."

"I think someone was watching me when I got on the bus this evening," said Kevin. "But I don't know for certain."

"Well keep your eyes open and try not to do things to a pattern," said Spectro. "What people look for is a pattern. That allows them to predict what you are going to do and where you are going to go."

The following days he kept his eyes open and noticed everyone who might be watching him but did not see anyone who he really suspected. He never saw the man at the bus stop again so he decided it must have been his imagination. School was much the same as usual, a bit boring, especially after his recent adventures. At times he was tempted to use the crystal to cause mischief, but decided against it, usually at the prompting of Spectro. He always did well at his schoolwork, even better than he had in the past, now that he had Spectro to help him. He could easily get full marks at all his tests, but Spectro suggested that it would not be such a good idea. It would only draw attention to him.

One day, at break, Kevin was strolling around the playground, minding his own business when a girl from year nine came up to him.

"Got any sweets?" she asked.

"No," said Kevin and walked on.

"What about money, then?" she asked. She did not sound unfriendly, but Kevin did not like the way the conversation was going.

"Just my bus fair," he said.

"That'll do," she said. "Hand it over."

Now it was at this point that Kevin should have handed over the money but it really annoyed him that he could be threatened by a girl, even one two years old than he was. So, before Spectro could stop him he had blatted her with the power of his crystal. He was not sure what he had meant to do, but what he did do was to cause all her hair to fall out and disappear in a puff of smoke. The girl at first looked frightened and surprised, but then her features hardened and she glared at Kevin but did not move. He was not sure if she was scared of him or was just deciding which form of torture she should apply first.

"So, it is you, is it?" she said in a measured way. "You're going to be very sorry about what you've done. Very sorry indeed."

It was at this point that the small crowd that had gathered started to laugh and jeer at her. Glaring at them, she strode off towards the school.

"How did you do that?" asked a girl from the crowd.

"Me?" said Kevin feigning surprise. "I didn't do anything."

"I don't think she sees it that way," said one of the boys. "I wouldn't like to be in your shoes when Tracey gets her friends together. They'll eat you alive."

Tracy. Yes, that was her name. Tracy Bagshott. Not a nice girl at all. She had been in trouble before, mostly for bullying, but always seemed to get away with it.

"Just what we wanted," said Spectro. "All this attention, a blast from your crystal which could be picked up half way across the solar system and a nasty girl who seems to know more than she has let on."

"Oh no," said Kevin. "Surely you don't think she could be working for Duros, do you?"

"Why not," Spectro continued. "She's just the sort he would pick on; so easy to control."

Next day was Saturday so Kevin decided to head off onto the moors. It would be quiet up there and there would be no-one about, at least, not where he went. So, after breakfast he got his coat on and was about to go out when his father came into the kitchen.

"Where are you off to?" he asked.

"Thought I would go up onto the moors," said Kevin noncommittally.

"I thought you might like to come shopping with us this morning," continued his father.

"Shopping, me?" said Kevin indignantly. "I would much rather go onto the moors."

"What's so special about the moors?" asked his father. "You can go up there any time."

"Well, I've got this project to do for homework," he said thinking desperately. "About conservation and all that sort of thing."

"Oh well if you must. But you'll have to take some sandwiches with you as we'll be out 'til mid-afternoon," said his father. "And don't stay out too late."

Kevin made himself some sandwiches and put in a bit of cake too and a small can of Fanta and set off up onto the moors. It was a nice day and he was pleased not to have to go to school because he had started to worry that

Tracey Bagshott would cause him trouble. At least up here he would not have to worry about her.

He was soon out of sight of his home and his step lightened as he walked through the heather. There was a lark singing overhead and every now and then he heard the grumbling sound of the grouse and occasionally the call of a curlew. A slight breeze ruffled his hair which took the edge off the heat of the sun which was rising quite high in the sky by now.

He crossed the little brook that chattered over the rocks in the gully and climbed the steep bank on the other side. Luckily it hadn't rained recently and the ground was quite firm. When wet it could be quite slippery.

He clambered to the top onto the flat ground beyond and made his way over to an outcrop of rocks but as he stepped onto the flat ground he felt sure he caught a glimpse of something moving behind him. He turned and looked into the gully but it was in shadow and difficult to see clearly. Nothing could be seen and there was no further sign of movement so he continued his walk towards the rocks. It was further than it looked and when he reached them, he was ready for a sit down. He found a nice cosy little nitch and settled himself down to eat his lunch. The sandwiches weren't as good as the ones his mother made but not too bad for all that. Anyway, he had worked up quite an appetite so he probably would have eaten anything.

When he had finished his lunch he just sat and stared out over the moors. It was very peaceful. There were some sheep munching the grass down near the gully and a few birds flitting around as usual, but nothing out of the ordinary so he sat back and closed his eyes for a doze in the sun. He didn't know how long he had been dozing, or if he had actually been asleep, but he opened his eyes suddenly just in time to see the little group of sheep bounding off across the heather.

"I wonder what startled them?" he thought to himself, but there was nothing to see so he closed his eyes again and continued to doze. He had almost dropped off when something grabbed him by the throat. He opened his eyes in alarm to see Tracy Bagshott grinning at him.

"Now what are you going to do?" she asked menacingly. Kevin tried to answer but couldn't speak as she was nearly strangling him. "What's that?" she said mockingly, "I can't hear what you're saying."

Kevin thought of using the crystal but Spectro beat him to it.

"Don't even think about it," said Spectro. "There isn't enough power, and anyway it's just what Duros wants you to do."

"Why didn't I bring Sniffer with me?" he thought. "He would have seen Tracy Bagshott off and no mistake."

"Can't help you there," said Spectro, "and he is too far away to summon. It would take too much power."

At that moment she loosened her grip on Kevin's throat and he gasped for breath. "What do you want?" he gasped.

"Revenge," she said with relish. "Do you think you can make a fool out of me and get away with it?"

"What are you talking about?" he said. "I haven't done anything."

"What about my hair?"

"How could I do that?" he asked.

"I know about the crystal," she said. "Give it to me, now."

"I don't know what you're talking about," he said desperately. "Who said anything about a crystal?"

"What can I do?" he asked Spectro in his mind. "She can't take the crystal."

"True," said Spectro. You will have to use it to persuade her; make her think she is wrong. That's what Duros does. He uses the power of his crystal to persuade people to do what he wants them to do."

Kevin thought about how he used the crystal to tame Sniffer that first time they met and started to concentrate on Tracy. He stared into her eyes and glared. Then he started to think things at her.

"What's the matter with you?" she said looking a bit alarmed.

"There is no crystal," he said in his mind. "You are wrong. There is no crystal. You are making a fool of yourself. You had better get out of here as fast as you can."

She stood up and stared at him and her face went white with fear.

"No," she said. "No. Get away from me. No. No." She was backing away from him as she spoke, then turned and ran as fast as she could, straight across the moors.

"Well that worked better than I thought it would," said Kevin.

"What do you mean?" said Spectro. "You didn't do anything."

"I must have," he said watching Tracy disappear into the distance. He could hear her faint screams as she ran. "Why would she run off like that if I didn't do anything?"

Chapter Three – Another Surprise Visitor

"I think you should look behind you," said Spectro. A shadow had fallen across Kevin from behind and he suddenly felt cold. He slowly turned his head and there standing just behind him was a sight that turned his blood to ice. He staggered back and tripped on a small rock falling backwards onto the ground. He tried to get up but his arms and legs wouldn't work.

"What's the matter?" asked Spectro.

"What do you think?" answered Kevin. "Do something can't you?"

Kevin lay there staring at the thing. It was almost as big as a small pony; a thing from nightmares. He wasn't too frightened of spiders as a rule, but this was quite different. It was like a giant tarantula, standing there looking at him with its segmented eyes. The little feelers around its mouth busily moving as if getting ready for its next meal.

"I'll have to use the crystal," said Kevin. "There's no other way."

"Of course there is," said Spectro. "Why not just talk to him?"

"Talk to a spider?" shouted Kevin in his mind. "I don't think it'll take much notice of that."

"Oh, I see the problem," said Spectro. "That's not a spider, as such."

"Well it looks like a spider to me," said Kevin.

"This is an emissary from planet three of the Poseidon Cluster in the third sector. I think he wishes to speak to you."

"You mean it is from another planet?" said Kevin.

"Yes. The Collandan people inhabit most of that cluster," said Spectro. "This is Mondarwi Maloo, an emissary who wishes to speak to you. He will not speak until you address him yourself. It is not etiquette for him to do so."

"What should I say?"

"Tell him who you are and greet him to Earth and ask how you can help him," said Spectro.

Kevin cautiously got to his feet and looked at the beast that was standing there staring at him.

"Greetings," he said haltingly. He cleared his throat and continued. "Welcome to the planet Earth. I am Kevin, Master of the Universe. How can I help you?"

"Greetings Kevin," it answered in a rather breathy voice. "I am Mondarwi Maloo, emissary from the Poseidon Cluster. We are in need of your urgent assistance."

"What is the problem?" asked Kevin who could hardly believe he was having a conversation with a spider.

"We have been attacked. Two planets in the system have been taken and my home planet is now under attack," said Mondarwi.

"Who is attacking you?" asked Kevin, though he had a good idea who it was.

"It is Duros. He has escaped from the planet where he was held captive and has enlisted the help of creatures outside the Galactic Federation. He must be stopped before he gets too powerful. He could threaten the whole federation." Mondarwi was getting quite agitated which made Kevin feel rather uneasy.

"Something must be done urgently," said Spectro.

"Yes, but what?" asked Kevin. "You said we can't use the crystal, so what can I do?"

"Well it would seem that Duros has his mind on other things at the moment," said Spectro, "so that leaves us free to use the crystal without fear of being traced."

"Does it have enough power to get me out of here?" asked Kevin.

"Not enough to get us to the Poseidon Cluster," said Spectro, "at least not directly from here."

"So how can we do it?" asked Kevin growing a little impatient.

"Well we could 'jump' to somewhere outside the energy shadow," continued Spectro, "and then jump again from there, but the problem there is that you don't know anywhere suitable so you can't 'jump' there."

"I don't know of anywhere near here that we could jump to," said Mondarwi.

"Why don't we jump to the cave where the 'Blob' is kept and use that to go to somewhere like Mars?" suggested Kevin. The 'Blob' was the space craft he had been given for local use.

"Not far enough I'm afraid," said Spectro, "but there is another option."

"Well what is it then?" said Kevin. He found it quite irritating the way Spectro didn't volunteer information and had to be asked directly, except when the information was to stop him doing something he wanted to do.

"We could contact Marlitta," said Spectro. "That doesn't take as much energy. Then we get her to come here with her crystal fully charged with enough energy to take us all to Poseidon."

"Right I'll do it straight away," said Kevin. "But should I have some excuse for being away for a while?"

"If you aren't away for too long," said Spectro, "you should be able to get back in less than two hours, Earth time. There will be a lot of time compression on this trip."

"Right," said Kevin, "I'll get on with it." He sat down and concentrated on Marlitta to make contact through the crystal. It seemed harder work than last time he did it and he realised that this was due to the fact that his crystal was almost out of power. It would be good to see Marlitta again. He had missed being with her and now he was set for a new adventure with her.

He soon made contact with her and explained to her that she must charge her crystal with as much power as it could hold and then home in on his position and then 'jump'. They had to wait for a while as it took time for her crystal to absorb energy, so while they waited Mondarwi told them more about the problem on his home planet.

"My planet is an agricultural planet basically, but we do a lot of trade in ropes and bindings of exceptional strength. We use the material we use for spinning our webs you see. We have lived like this in peace for thousands of years and we don't have much in the way of armaments. We have never needed them. So you can see that we are very vulnerable. When the first planet in our system fell to Duros, we bought as many weapons as we could from a neighbouring system. They were very expensive and we couldn't afford enough.

"At the moment we are just able to prevent any of the enemy space craft landing on our planet. But we can't stop individual troops 'jumping' in if they have crystals. We don't know if they do have crystals but we can't rule it out. The other problem is that we cannot cover the whole sky all the time and it's possible for the odd ship to sneak through our defences unseen."

There was a sudden flash and Marlitta appeared. She looked at Mondarwi with alarm then realised that Kevin was not looking threatened and realised that the fearsome looking creature must be friendly. Kevin introduced them and then they prepared to 'jump'. To do that they had to touch each other and Kevin didn't like the idea of touching Mondarwi even though he knew him to be friendly, so he took Marlitta's hand and left her to take hold of Mondarwi, which she did without a moment's hesitation.

Suddenly the sky went dark and the air became colder.

"We are here," said Mondarwi. It is night at the moment but dawn will not be long in coming. "We must make our way to the web."

"Web?" said Kevin in alarm.

"Of course," said Mondarwi. "That is where we live. It is better than staying out here until dawn. Follow me."

He scuttled off at alarming speed and it was all that Kevin and Marlitta could do to keep up with him.

"Hey, not so fast," shouted Kevin. Mondarwi stopped.

"Sorry," he said. "I wasn't hurrying. I hadn't realised that you moved so slowly."

It wasn't far to the Web and it took Kevin completely by surprise. He didn't know what he had expected, but it wasn't what he saw. Ahead of him lay a vast city made of a shimmering silver-grey material. There were twinkling lights everywhere. They entered through a huge archway into a wide street where other spiders, or Collanda people, as they were called, scuttling about at alarming speeds. Some went in and out of wide doorways, while others seemed to run straight up the sides of buildings and enter at another level.

Although Kevin knew that they were intelligent people and were friendly towards him, he still felt uneasy about them. Marlitta walked quietly by his side and he couldn't be sure if she was worried about them or not, and it was difficult to talk with Mondarwi walking along beside them.

It was quite a long walk to the large open square which they crossed. Now the Collanda started to take more interest in them and started to gather round and look at them chattering together in their strange clicking language which the crystal didn't seem to translate. Mondarwi spoke to one or two of the newcomers who moved away and spoke to others in small groups.

Soon, they reached a tall building on the far side of the square and, when they reached it, Mondarwi started to walk straight up the side of the building.

"Wait," said Kevin. "We can't do that." Mondarwi stopped and started down again.

"I am sorry," he said. "How do you get to the higher levels in your buildings?"

"We have stairs," said Kevin. Mondarwi wasn't sure what they were but it didn't seem to bother him.

"Well we have to get to the eleventh floor," said Mondarwi. There is a conference room there and some guest apartments.

"Perhaps," said Marlitta, "if you were to go up there first we could use our crystals to locate you and then 'jump' to where you are."

"Good idea," said Kevin wishing that he had thought of that. So Mondarwi set off up the side of the building while Kevin and Marlitta closed their eyes and followed him using the sight that the crystal gave them. When he reached the eleventh floor and went inside Kevin and Marlitta 'jumped' and when they opened their eyes found they were in a large reception hall. Mondarwi was waiting for them.

"I will show you to your room first so that you can rest until the meeting has assembled," he said moving off down a side corridor. "Follow me, please." They followed. There were quite a few other Collandans moving about in the corridor. Kevin still found it difficult not to think of them as spiders.

It was a strange sensation walking along the springy yet slightly sticky surface that made the floors and walls of this strange building. He also found it difficult to come to terms with the doors that led out of the building, even at this height. But the Collandans just scurried in and out and went straight up or down the outside walls without a moment's hesitation.

They were both so busy taking in all their surrounding that they hardly noticed that Mondarwi had stopped at an opening. There was no door, as such, but there was a sort of curtain made out of a similar material to the building; a sort of spider's web, but thickly woven.

They went into the room, which too was sparsely furnished. Kevin supposed that spiders did not need to sit down as we did, but there were some humps in the floor which could be sat on.

"If you would be kind enough to wait here I will return shortly to take you to the meeting," said Mondarwi. "Would you like to eat while you wait?"

Kevin wondered what they ate on this strange planet. All he could think of was enormous flies buzzing as they were held fast in a tangle of web.

"I am not sure you would have the sort of food that we eat," said Kevin not wishing to be rude.

"Perhaps a little fruit would be to your taste?" asked Mondarwi.

"That would be nice. Thank you very much," said Kevin.

"Yes, thank you," said Marlitta. Almost immediately a swarm of small spiders rushed into the room carrying all sorts of dishes containing the most unusual looking things.

"I will return shortly," said Mondarwi moving towards the door. "Please make yourselves at home."

After he had left and all the little creatures had scurried out, Kevin and Marlitta examined the things on the dishes.

"I wonder if these are OK to eat," said Kevin.

"Well I recognise some of them," said Marlitta. "These are rather nice." She picked up a bunch of small round yellow things that looked rather like grapes. "You can get these all over the galaxy."

She handed a few to Kevin who looked at them rather suspiciously. Marlitta was tucking into hers so he thought he would give it a try. They were very similar to grapes but were sweeter and had more of a taste of melon. He ate them quickly and took some more.

"These are quite good too," said Marlitta handing him something covered in spikes.

He watched her peal the prickly shell of the fruit to reveal something like orange segments, except that these were green. He pealed his and found it very tasty.

After they had tried quite a few of the fruits, they settled down on one of the hummocks to rest.

"I will have to get back home as soon as I can," said Kevin. "Then I'll arrange to be away for a bit longer. You will have to go straight to the council and get them to send a fighting force out here to stop the fighting. I'm sure Duros is here somewhere, not on this planet, but I think he will be somewhere with the attacking forces."

"I don't think he will be putting himself in any danger though," said Marlitta. "I expect he will be hiding on the home planet of the invaders. We'll have to wait for the meeting to find out more."

There was a sudden explosion and the whole building shook. Then another, nearer, and another. Suddenly there was the sound of gunfire nearby and a loud screaming noise as something big went by overhead.

"We're under attack," said Kevin in alarm.

"So it would seem," said Marlitta. "Perhaps we should help."

"How do we do that?" asked Kevin thinking that there wasn't much they could do.

"We have our crystals. We must make a shield."

"But I don't know how to do that," said Kevin in desperation.

"Well ask Spectro."

Kevin did just that and Spectro talked him through the procedure. Soon there was a shimmering force screen covering the whole of the city and the sound of fighting disappeared.

"You can also fight back if you wish to," said Spectro. "You will need to use your mind travel to see where the enemy ships are."

Kevin knew how to do that so he closed his eyes and his mind leapt up out of the building and into the sky like a bird. His body didn't move but it seemed to Kevin as if he were flying. Then he saw them, the enormous black flying machines. They looked like big black wasps and they moved at an alarming speed. Kevin concentrated his energy on one of them. There was a blinding flash and the machine started to tumble from the sky. He then focussed on another until that one went the same way as the first one. As they fell they seemed to gather themselves up and change shape before zooming out into space. All the others followed them until he was alone.

Chapter Four – Council of War

As soon as Kevin opened his eyes he was back with Marlitta in the strange little room. They sat and ate some more of the fruit until Mondarwi returned to take them to the meeting.

The conference hall was smaller than he had expected. Sitting in a circle, if sitting was the right word, were some of the oldest and ugliest looking spiders he could have imagined. Mondarwi ushered them to a raised lump in the floor where they sat as best they could.

"They look an ugly lot," said Marlitta. Kevin realised she hadn't actually spoken but was using her crystal to communicate. "I thought it best to talk through the crystals. I don't trust this lot."

"What do you mean?" asked Kevin also through the crystal. "They are under attack and need our help."

"I don't know exactly, but be careful what you tell them."

Kevin noticed one of the smaller spiders moving to the front. He came right up to them and spoke to Kevin.

"Master, welcome to Collandar. The council of Elders would like to thank you for your help," he said.

"I am pleased to help you," answered Kevin feeling that he should be polite.

"We would also like to thank you for your help in the recent attack," he continued. "We are hard pressed to defend ourselves."

"That's all right," said Kevin. "But why did you not go straight to the Galactic Council and ask for help?"

"We have had some disagreements with the Council in the past and we didn't think they would be very receptive to our request," he said. "So we thought it would be better to contact the Master of the Universe, himself. We knew that you would not be involved in the politics of the Council and would, therefore, be more likely to view our problem sympathetically."

"But I can't do much, myself," said Kevin. "I will have to go to the Council to organise help for you."

"That would be much appreciated," said the spider. "However, we noticed how powerful your crystal was and we thought that maybe you could lend it to us for a while."

"Be careful," said Marlitta in his head. "Don't agree to anything."

"Besides," said Spectro, "the crystal is matched to your personality and cannot effectively be used by anyone else."

"That would not be very practical," said Kevin to the spider. "Only I can use the crystal to any effect, and besides, I will need it myself."

"Perhaps you would like to think about it for a while?" said the spider. "Mondarwi will see you back to your room while we debate."

Mondarwi came forward and they followed him back to their room.

"I really think it would be better if we involved the Council," said Kevin as they entered the room.

"Perhaps," said Mondarwi. "But I think we should wait to see what the Elders say first. There could be other options. Please make yourselves comfortable until they have finished."

He turned and left quickly spinning a fine web across the doorway as he went out. Kevin went over to it and found that it had effectively made them prisoners in the room.

"They've sealed us in," said Kevin.

"Probably just the way they close doors in this place," said Marlitta. "Maybe it is to keep people out. It certainly won't keep us in."

"No, I suppose not," said Kevin.

"Perhaps we should speak through the crystals," said Marlitta in his head.

"Why?" asked Kevin also using the crystal to speak. "I wouldn't think they can hear us, could they?"

"Probably yes," said Spectro. "The arachnid species can communicate through their webs. In your own world, when an insect flies into a spider's web, the spider hears it through the vibrations in the web. It has very sensitive feet and sits there with one foot holding the web and it can hear anything that gets caught."

"You mean it has ears in its feet?" asked Kevin in surprise.

"You could say that," replied Spectro. "And these spiders are much more developed than those of your planet. If you look outside you will see there are fine single strands of web stretching between the buildings. Those are their telephone lines. They communicate with them. So I'm sure they will be able to hear anything they want to in any room in any building."

"Right," said Kevin. "We'll talk through the crystals then. Now, why don't they want us to bring in the Council. They can't expect me to sit here fighting off invaders with my crystal, can they?"

"I don't know," said Marlitta. "But it doesn't make much sense does it? They must have known they couldn't use your crystal, and they must have realised it would be impractical for you to stay here to defend them. After all, it could take years."

"If I might make an observation," said Spectro. "It might be that their purpose is to separate you from your crystal."

"And why would they want to do that?" asked Kevin.

"Well it could be," interrupted Marlitta, "that Duros is behind this. Once you don't have your crystal you are at his mercy."

"I suppose so, yes," said Kevin thoughtfully. "But you still have yours."

"Yes, said Marlitta. "But I don't think they were expecting me to be here. They sent Mondarwi to Earth to fetch you and didn't realise that there was a problem with the crystals there and that you would call for help from me. And now I'm here, I think they are wondering what to do. I expect they will be contacting Duros at this moment to get further instruction."

"We must get out of here," said Kevin suddenly. "Spectro, have you fully charged up your energy supply?"

"As much as I can, yes," answered Spectro.

"Then I must return to Earth," said Kevin. "I am expected back and will have to make arrangements to stay away longer. Marlitta, you must go to the Council and speak to Quartok and tell him I will be there as soon as possible. Explain the situation to him."

"But what are we going to do?" asked Marlitta. "If we bring a task force here Duros will just disappear and then we will have to start again."

"I don't know," said Kevin. "I'll have to think about it. You can get all the information you can glean about this sector that might help us."

"Don't mind me," said Spectro.

"OK, I know you know everything," said Kevin. "But it's like getting blood out of a stone getting information out of you."

"I should feel insulted," said Spectro. "But I am not capable of feeling that emotion."

At that moment, there was a noise outside the door. After a few moments the web was removed and Mondarwi came in.

"Will you come with me quickly please," he said. "The council needs to speak to you again."

Marlitta made a move towards the door but Mondarwi put out a leg to stop her.

"No, they just want to see the Master," he said.

"No," she said. "We go everywhere together."

"I am sorry but that is not possible," said Mondarwi.

"It's all right Marlitta," said Kevin, "I'll go with him to see what they want."

"All right," she said in his head." But keep in contact using the crystal."

Kevin went out with Mondarwi and followed him down the corridor to the conference room. It was still as he had left it and it didn't seem that anyone had moved at all. But this time it was rather different. Everyone seemed to be talking at once, some talking to each other, while others seem to be shouting at him.

"What's all this about?" he said to Mondarwi.

Mondarwi didn't answer that the noise in the room seem to get less as he took his place on the mound in the middle of the floor.

"What do you want of me now?" he shouted at the assembled mass of spiders. "I have told you that there is nothing I can do myself. I must go back to the Galactic Council and see what help can be arranged for you."

One of the larger, older spiders came forward slowly towards him and stared at him for a few moments.

"We know what you said, but that is not what we want," he said slowly." We want you to help us directly."

"But I have already told you that I cannot do that," said Kevin. "I have to go back to the galactic council and see what they say."

"But we insisted that you stay," said the wizened old spider. "You see, we are holding your friend hostage."

"Marlitta? What have you done to her?" said Kevin. He then tried to contact her using his crystal, but there was no reply.

"Our little runners are very fast," said the spider. "One small jab of venom and she is helpless."

There was a sudden movement in the far corner of the room and Kevin noticed a small white spider scuttling across the room towards him. He didn't have time to think, so he 'jumped' to the last place he could remember, the clearing outside the town where they had first arrived. He was only just in time as the little white spider had almost reached him. If it had touched him he would have been too late. But what should he do now?

"And we are no energy to get back to earth?" he asked Spectro.

"Yes, I am fully charged now," he answered.

"But first I must find out what has happened to Marlitta," he said. First, he looked around him to make sure there were no spiders lurking in the undergrowth, then he closed his eyes let his mind wander back to the city. Soon he found the building had been in and went straight to the room where he had left Marlitta. She was no longer there, so he started to search the rooms round about, but she was nowhere to be found. Then he tried the floor below, but she wasn't there either. He tried the next, and then the next until at last he found a small room where there were lots of small bundles of spider's web, each one a wriggling and squirming. This must be their larder. He looked at each of the squirming bundles until eventually he found one that was Marlitta.

He looked around and there were no spiders in the room, so he 'jumped' again and was instantly standing next to Marlitta.

"Marlitta," he said thankfully. "Are you all right?" Marlitta groaned and wriggled a bit.

"Can you hear me, Marlitta?" he asked desperately and grabbed the web to try and tear it off her, but it was far too tough to be broken like that, and what's more, he found that his hands were stuck fast to the web and the harder he struggled, the tighter it held him. He began to panic, and then he remembered the crystal. He focused his mind on the web and tried to burn it. It worked a bit but as soon as he stopped, it stuck together again. He wasn't going to have time to free both himself and Marlitta before one of the spiders found him. In fact, he could hear scurrying noises just outside at that very moment. He had to 'jump' and right away, but he didn't know what effect it would have while he was attached to Marlitta and the web which was attached to the ceiling.

There was no time to worry about that, so he 'jumped' back to the place outside the town where they had first arrived. The shock of it nearly pulled off his arms, but when he managed to scramble upright again, he found that he was still attached to the web, but Marlitta wasn't in it. He couldn't use the crystal to contact her because he assumed the spiders would have taken her crystal after they had captured her. What was he to do? Firstly, he must get this web off his hands, so he started work with the crystal, melting it off bit by bit. He burnt his hands once or twice but he hardly noticed in his desperation to free himself.

After he was free he 'jumped back to the room where he had found Marlitta, but she wasn't there so he 'jumped' out again. He didn't know what to do but he had to wait for a while, anyway, for Spectro to charge himself up with energy again. Then he 'jumped' back to Earth, to the place he had met Mondarwi.

Chapter Five – Manhunt

He had been away for quite a while, but on Earth, the time had been less. Even so, an hour or more must had passed since he had left. Now he had to make arrangements to be away for a while, the weekend would probably be enough. It would give him several weeks on one of the distant worlds he needed to visit. He was just about to 'jump' back to his home when he remembered that he must conserve energy to be able to 'jump' out again. So he started walking. As he reached the crest of the hill and looked down into the valley below, he was surprised to see a line of men with guns, fanned out across the hillside coming towards him. He had a moment of panic. Had Duros landed here with his army?

"It would appear that you have been missed," said Spectro unexpectedly.

"You mean they're looking for me?" said Kevin. "But why are they carrying weapons?"

"I do not have knowledge of who or what they are," continued Spectro. "But they would appear human and therefore are natives of this planet, and Duros hasn't had time to take control of humans yet, so they must be members of your law enforcement people, maybe the police?"

"But the police don't carry rifles."

"It is possible that the girl who confronted you last time we were here has raised the alarm," said Spectro.

"But I still don't see why they would need rifles to look for me," said Kevin getting a bit annoyed.

"The rifles are because the girl would have told them about the Collandan, or spider as she would call them. She probably thinks that you have been eaten by it and the authorities are taking no chances."

"I am surprised that anyone would take any notice of her," said Kevin. "I know I wouldn't if I didn't know these things were possible. Anyway, what am I going to do? Can I use the crystal to 'jump' back to my home?"

"No," said Spectro. "We must conserve energy to 'jump' out again. You'll have to walk."

"Thanks a lot," said Kevin. It's going to be difficult to convince my parents to let me go off for the weekend with a scare like this going on."

"You'll just have to convince them that it was a joke or something like that."

Kevin set off down the hill towards the line of men. He hoped Spectro was right about them, because if they weren't ordinary policemen, they might start shooting at any moment and then he would have to 'jump' out and then he might be trapped here and not be able to help Marlitta.

The men stopped and one of them seemed to be looking at him through binoculars. He seemed to give an order and the main group continued up the hill while two of the group broke away and headed towards him. As they got closer, he could see that they were armed policemen and didn't seem to be too threatening. When they were close enough, one of them asked "Are you Kevin Brown?"

"Yes," he replied. They came up to him and stopped.

"We have had a report that you had been threatened by something up here," he continued. "But the girl wasn't very coherent."

"Oh, you mean Tracy Bagshott, I suppose," said Kevin. "I think she's nuts."

"You mean this is all a hoax?" asked the other policeman.

"Well yes, I suppose it must be," said Kevin. "She's been bothering me for a while now. I suppose she thought it would be funny to get you out here to give me a fright."

"Well I'm afraid we don't see the joke," said the first policeman. "We'll come back to your home with you to put your parents' minds at rest." He lifted the microphone attached to his mobile radio to his mouth and said "Panic over. Return to base." He gave a few more detailed instructions as they moved off. On the way back down to his home, Kevin tried to sound relaxed and told the policemen how she had been bothering him recently and that he often came up here on his own and had never been in any danger at all.

When they reached his house, his mother and father both came out into the drive to wait for them. His father looked concerned and a little angry while his mother just looked worried.

"Right, my lad," said his father as the group walked up to him. "What's been going on?"

"Don't be cross with him," said his mother. "Let him tell us what's been happening."

"Well, it'd better be good," said his father. "I've had to come home from work specially, and I was in a very important meeting."

"Well don't blame me," said Kevin. "It was that stupid Tracy Bagshott that caused all the fuss. I know nothing about it. I've been up there quietly enjoying myself."

"So, what's she been making all the fuss about?" asked his father, calming down a little.

"Don't ask me," said Kevin. "It's the sort of thing she does to try and get people into trouble."

After a bit of further discussion with the policemen, Kevin and his parents went inside and the policemen left in their van. Kevin's father decided that he had better get back to his meeting and Kevin sat down to have his tea with his mother.

"It really was a lot of fuss about nothing," said Kevin.

"I know, dear," said his mother. "But it was rather alarming to have armed police arriving on our doorstep saying that you were in trouble."

"I suppose so, yes," said Kevin. "But I wasn't in trouble. It was all a stupid story put about by that stupid girl."

"Well, that's as may be," said his mother. "But I think it would be best if you didn't go off on your own for a while. Just to be on the safe side."

"But Mum," he protested. "I was going to go camping this weekend."

"I don't think your father will agree to that," she said. "Better wait 'til he's cooled down a bit before you mention it to him."

Kevin kept quiet. He thought it best to say no more for the time being. After tea he decided to go down into the village and face Tracy Bagshott. She was beginning to be quite a nuisance to him, and he still didn't know if Duros had had an influence upon her.

When he reached her road, he could see her sitting on a bench in the park opposite her house. She looked deep in thought and didn't see him coming until he was a few paces from her. She looked up, startled and her mouth opened and closed, but no sound came out.

"Hello Tracy," said Kevin. "Surprised to see me?"

"You.." she gasped. "How.. how did you escape from that thing?"

"What thing?" asked Kevin pretending not to know what she was talking about.

"That thing up there," she said pointing to the hill. "It was a spider. Enormous. It was horrible. How did you get away from it?"

"I think you must have been seeing things," said Kevin. "The police were very cross with you. I expect they will be round to see your parents later."

"Well I only told what I saw," she said. "He told me about you so you can't fool me."

"Who told you about me?" asked Kevin. "What are you talking about?"

"Nothing," she said realising that she shouldn't have said that. "I don't know."

"Who told you about me?" he continued. "It is very important because if it is who I think it is, you are in great danger."

At this Tracy turned quite white.

"I can't tell you," she said. "Please don't make me."

"I think you have told me what I want to know already," said Kevin.

"Who is he?" asked Tracy looking even more frightened.

"He is a very nasty person," said Kevin. "Very nasty indeed, and you don't want to have any more to do with him if you know what's good for you. When will you see him again?"

"I don't know," she said. "I don't really remember seeing him the first time. It all seems like a dream."

"What did he want you to do?" asked Kevin.

"He said I had to hassle you. I don't know why."

"I think I do," said Kevin. "You see, he is after me and he thought if you hassled me I would use the crystal and then he'd know where I was."

"Bad move," said Spectro unexpectedly. "You've told her about the crystal."

"What crystal?" asked Tracy looking puzzled.

"Never mind," said Kevin. "You wouldn't understand."

"You'll have to take her with you when you go back," said Spectro. "Just to keep an eye on her and you need some help if you are to track Marlitta down."

"I'm going on a camping trip tomorrow," said Kevin. "Perhaps you should come too. Just to be safe."

"I don't think so," said Tracy getting back some of her old spirit. "What makes you think I'd go camping with you?

"OK. Stay here then and see what 'he' does when he finds you made a mess of things. I don't think he'll very pleased with you."

"What do you mean?" she looked worried again.

"If you come with me he won't be able to get at you. So you'll be safe. OK?"

"I suppose so," she said. "But no funny business. Right?"

"Right."

Kevin arranged to meet Tracy first thing the next morning up on the hill behind his house. She wasn't too keen on this as she still had an intense fear of the creature she had seen earlier that day, but Kevin eventually managed to convince her it wouldn't be there anymore.

Back at his home, he went up to his room early, before his father returned, and started to pack some things into a small haversack ready for the morning. Then he went to bed and slept surprisingly well considering what had happened that day.

In the morning he went down to breakfast and found his father had already finished his and was about to go out. He seemed in quite good spirits considering how he had been the previous afternoon.

"See you later," he shouted through to his wife who was busy in the kitchen getting Kevin's breakfast ready. "And don't you be getting up to mischief either," he said to Kevin as he went out of the door.

That was one problem solved. He didn't have to convince his father to let him go camping.

After he had finished his breakfast he asked his mother if she would make him some sandwiches to take with him.

"What did your father say about going camping?" she asked.

"He didn't seem to be against it," said Kevin evasively.

This seemed to satisfy his mother who set to making him some sandwiches which he packed into is haversack along with some cans of fizz and an apple or two. Then he went outside and collected Sniffer from the barn and set off across the field towards the hill. He still hadn't decided exactly what he was going to do so asked Spectro for the options.

"Well, there are many options," said Spectro. "But I would suggest that the best one is to go to the Council and speak to Quartok. He is the best one to advise you."

"And you still think I should take Tracy with me?"

"I don't think you can risk leaving her here," replied Spectro. If Duros can contact her there's no knowing what he might get her to do."

"But if he can contact her using his crystal," said Kevin. "He might be able to use her to get me into trouble wherever we are. And he could probably use her to keep track of me."

"Maybe," said Spectro. "But at least you will be able to do something to prevent it. Your crystal, even if I say so myself, is more powerful than anything he might have and can block its effects."

"OK then," said Kevin. "She comes with us."

At that moment she came into view just over the crest of the rise. She was waiting near some rocks and was looking around her in a very nervous manner. When she saw Kevin, she started towards him until she saw Sniffer when she froze and started to back away. Then she turned and ran for all she was worth.

"Oh no," said Kevin. "Go get her Sniffer but be gentle."

Sniffer dashed off and Kevin hurried up the remaining slope after them. Soon he could see Sniffer sitting looking pleased with himself, but there was no sign of Tracy. But as he got nearer he could see arms and legs sticking out from under Sniffer.

"OK Sniffer," he said as he approached them. "Let her get up."

Sniffer stood up to reveal a very frightened Tracy.

"Don't let him touch me," she sobbed.

"It's all right," said Kevin. "He won't hurt you."

"He already has."

"I don't think so," said Kevin. "Come on, let me help you up." He pulled her to her feet and she sidled round behind him to get as far away from Sniffer as possible.

"Look," said Kevin. "He won't hurt you. Let me introduce you. Sniffer, this is Tracy. Tracy, this is Sniffer. Why don't you shake hands?"

Sniffer raised a paw and Tracy backed away.

"Shake hands with him," said Kevin. "Then you'll be friends."

She reluctantly put out her hand and took his paw and shook it. Sniffer looked pleased and raised his head and licked her face.

"Ugh," said Tracy. "That's gross."

"Right it's time to get going," said Kevin. "There's a lot you're going to have to learn but you won't believe me if I just tell you. Right, take my hand."

"What?" she said. "You're weird."

"Do as you're told." He took her hand and touched Sniffer's head. Suddenly everything got brighter and the hills and rocks had gone, to be replaced by shining glass buildings and metallic roads.

Chapter Six – The Crystal City

Tracy stood with her mouth open, staring about her.

"Don't be scared," said Kevin. "It's OK here. This is the Crystal City where the Grand Council of the Universe sits. We have to see one of them to get some advice. Come on."

He moved off still holding her hand and she followed meekly. After a while she began to feel more at ease, and realising she was holding Kevin's hand, she shook him off and tried to look confident.

"Right," she said. "Where are we going?"

"See that building over there," he said. "That's the Council building. That's where we're going."

They walked across the square towards the building and it was only then that Tracy realised that there were other people scurrying about. Not only that, they were small. Even smaller than she and Kevin.

"Who are these people?" she asked.

"I don't know them personally," said Kevin. "I expect they live and work here in the Capital."

"But they're so small," she said.

"Most people in the universe seem to be," said Kevin. "I think we are unusual in being bigger. Mind you, the Collandans were quite big."

"Who?", she said.

"The Collandans," he repeated. "You saw one up on the moors. They look like spiders to us."

"So, I wasn't imagining it," she said. "You mean we could meet something like that?"

"Yes," he said. "But not here. They live in a system at the edge of the Galactic Union."

"Oh good," she said with relief. "I wouldn't like to see one of those again."

"I didn't say we wouldn't see any," said Kevin. "I just said we wouldn't see any here. We'll see plenty of them when we go to their planet."

"We?" she said in alarm. "I'm not going anywhere. If you want to see giant spiders, you can go on your own."

"Sorry," he said. "Not possible. Where I go, you go."

By then they had reached the steps up to the Council Building and had started to ascend. They went into the foyer and Kevin went to the reception desk, but before he could say anything, the girl behind the desk jumped to her feet and bowed to him.

"Your Excellency," she said. "Welcome back. Who shall I summon to greet you?" Tracy stood with her mouth open.

"Could you let Quartok know that I'm here, please," said Kevin.

"Immediately," she said, and within seconds Quartok appeared before them. Tracy stepped back in alarm, and then seeing that the newcomer was only quite small she relaxed a little.

"Greetings Master," he said. "I am surprised to see you here. I thought you were trying to avoid being detected by Duros. Coming here might broadcast your whereabouts to him, don't you think?"

"A lot has happened recently," said Kevin. "Can we go to your rooms. I have a lot to ask you. Oh, by the way, this is Tracy Bagshott from Earth. I had to bring her with me."

"Had to?" asked Quartok.

"I'll explain in your rooms."

They linked hands and were suddenly in a very plush living room. Tracy looked around in amazement and Sniffer just sniffed.

"I see you have taken over Duros's old rooms," said Kevin.

"Why not?" said Quartok. "It was a pity to waste them. Now tell me what's been going on."

Kevin told Quartok all that had happened. Quartok sat and listened quietly, nodding his head occasionally, and Tracy sat with her mouth open. She was beginning to think she was dreaming and would soon wake up.

"You mention Collandar," said Quartok when Kevin had finished his story. "You realise that we haven't heard from there for a while now. The Collandans are a quiet peace-loving community of farmers. The creatures you describe can't be from that planet."

"But Spectro said they were Collandans," protested Kevin.

"That's what they told me," said Spectro.

"If they are from Collandar," said Quartok. "They must be a species that was not in the union. It's a possibility. Duros must have contacted them and stirred them up to take over the planet."

"The species is indigenous to that system," continued Spectro. "Their main strength is on a neighbouring planet."

"The main problem is that they have Marlitta," said Kevin. "I have to get back there to rescue her. I'll need a lot of help."

"Here we have a problem," said Quartok. "If we send the fleet, they will have to go under their own power. Even your crystal couldn't transport them all. That means it will take quite a time to get them there. The best we could do is to take a small scout ship with a small squad to see if we can get in and rescue her. That's assuming she's still there."

"Why? What do you mean?"

"I mean they could have taken her to somewhere more secure," said Quartok. "And don't forget, they will have her crystal now. I think we should summon a meeting of the Inner Council immediately. If you and your friend would like to make yourselves comfortable here, I will go and organise things."

Almost as he finished speaking he vanished.

"I wish people wouldn't do that," said Tracy. "So what happens now?"

"Quartok has gone to summon a meeting of the Grand Council," said Kevin. "We need to get something organised quickly."

"Well I don't see why that should involve us," said Tracy. "I'd like to go home now, please."

"Sorry Tracy," said Kevin. "I'm afraid not. I have to do this myself, and you have to come with me."

"But why?" she moaned. "Why can't I just go home. I don't like it here, and I certainly don't want to go chasing giant spiders."

"Well it's like this," said Kevin. "There's this rather unpleasant fellow called Duros. He used to be a member of the Grand Council but he used his power in a most evil way. He destroyed thousands of planets but we eventually stopped him. But now he's escaped and wants revenge. He is trying to get at me, but it's difficult for him while I have my crystal so he got in touch with you. He has a crystal that can influence people to do what he wants and he tried to get you to get at me, but it didn't work so he sent one of the Collandans. You remember the spider? That was a creature from the planet Collandar. But that didn't work either but he did manage to capture a friend of mine called Marlitta. So, he will be expecting me to try and rescue her and will probably set some sort of trap. He could try to cause a diversion as well, and if you were still on earth, he could use you to cause harm."

"How?" she protested. "What could I do?"

"I don't know," said Kevin. "But I don't want to take the risk so you will have to come with me so that I can keep an eye on you."

"So, what are we going to do?" she asked.

"I'm not sure yet," said Kevin. "That's why we are calling a meeting of the Council. I expect it will involve going to Collandar. Quartok said we could take a small scout ship and a small task force. If we are quick that might be enough."

"I don't like this," said Tracy. "I don't like it at all. Anyway, how did you get into all this?"

"It's a long story," said Kevin. "But when they need a new Master of the Universe they take a special crystal around the galaxy and it leads them to the chosen. And this time it led them to me. It's the first time it's taken them to someone outside the Galactic Union, and as I'm rather young and live in a world that has no idea that there's other life in the universe, I have to spent part of my time going to school and leading my normal life and part doing what a Master of the Universe has to do."

"Weird," she said. "Really weird."

Suddenly Quartok was back in the room with them. Tracy made a strangled squeak and then tried to look unconcerned.

"I'm sorry if I startled you," said Quartok.

"No, it's all right," said Tracy. "I'm beginning to get used to it."

"Good," he said, then turned to Kevin. "The Council will assemble as soon as possible. There should be time for you to have something to eat before then, so if you would like to come with me?" He turned towards a door at the far side of the room and ushered them through into another lightly lit room with sparkling and glittering ornaments everywhere."

"I think you're enjoying all this glitter," said Kevin. "Not too much I hope?"

"As I said," Quartok answered. "It was a pity to waste it, but as it happens, I am not here often. I have been quite busy recently."

They went into the room and were shown to seats around a large circular table and, as they sat down, there were suddenly hordes of Murin scurrying around placing food on the table.

"What are those?" asked Tracy in astonishment.

"Murin," said Kevin. "They live to serve. I used to think it was exploitation, but it seems it is all they want to do and they seem quite happy to be of service." Tracy watched them until the last one had disappeared, though she wasn't sure just where they had gone. Then she looked at the table and her mouth dropped open.

"Please help yourselves," said Quartok.

"But what is it?" asked Tracy. "I've never seen anything quite like it."

"Food," said Kevin.

"But what sort of food?" she insisted.

"Don't ask," said Kevin. "It's OK. I think you'll like it."

She tentatively tried something from the nearest dish and her face lit up.

"Yep. It's OK," she said tucking into more of it. She really had quite an appetite and Kevin sat in amazement as she stuffed food into her mouth.

"So I See," he said.

After they had finished and were sitting back in the living room, Quartok asked more about what had happened on Collandar. Kevin told him that two of the other planets in the Poseidon Cluster had been taken by Duros with the help of an alien culture and that Collandar was under attack, at least that is what he was told by Mondarwi.

"That is strange," said Quartok. "I wasn't aware that any other planet in that system was colonised. It is possible that some of the Collandans were mining the other planets but you couldn't say they were inhabited. Did you speak to any of the Plubarwi?"

"Sorry," said Kevin looking puzzled. "Who are they?"

"The Plubarwi," said Quartok. "Are the other race that lives on Collandar. They are a friendly peaceable people. They were the original inhabitants before the creatures you met moved in."

"I didn't see any of them," said Kevin. "And no-one mentioned them to me."

"Perhaps we should contact them first," said Quartok. "They might be able to put us in the picture." He paused as if listening. "We are required in the council chamber," he turned to Tracy. "Would you mind waiting here for us?" he said not expecting an answer.

"Yes, I would mind," she said indignantly. "If I'm to be involved in all this I want to have a say."

"It is not possible," continued Quartok. "This is business for the Master and the Council. I insist you wait here."

"No. Kevin, you can't leave me here," she pleaded. "I want to come with you."

"I think that would be all right," said Kevin. "As long as you promise to keep quiet. If you interrupt you will have to leave."

"Well if you a sure?" said Quartok looking a little bit annoyed to be overridden.

"I'm sure it will be all right," said Kevin. "After all, if she is to be involved with this it is only fair that she should hear what is decided."

Sniffer, who had been lying in the corner of the room looked up expectantly as they all got up.

"No not you Sniffer," said Kevin. "You wait here for us. We won't be long." Sniffer looked disappointed but lay his head down again in a resigned way. Quartok touched each of them on the shoulder and the scene changed abruptly and they were standing just outside the Council Chamber where little people were scurrying around.

As they appeared, a portly fellow in bright yellow robes stepped forward to greet them.

"Welcome Master," he said. "It is nice to see you again." He looked at Tracy in a Questioning sort of way.

"Hello, Snee," said Kevin. "This is a friend from Earth. Her name is Tracy Bagshott."

"Greetings Tracy Bagshott," said Snee offering a hand for her to shake. Tracy stood transfixed for a moment then took his hand and shook it.

"Hello," she said. At that moment they were joined by another similar creature, much thinner than Snee, dressed in plainer clothes of a dull grey and brown material.

"Hello Larnock," said Kevin. "This is Tracy Bagshott." He gestured towards Tracy. "Tracy, this is Larnock."

"Pleased to meet you," said Larnock. "If you are ready," he said to Kevin. "Perhaps we should go in."

"Fine," said Kevin, and as everyone else seemed to be holding back, he walked into the chamber. It was just as he remembered it. The room was long and narrow with a long table at the centre and chairs arranged all around it occupied by little people of varying sizes and colours. Kevin walked up to the large chair at the top of the table and sat down. Larnock pointed Tracy to a chair at the side of the room away from the table which she reluctantly sat in. Snee and Larnock took their seats on either side of Kevin. Kevin would have liked someone to have started the proceedings, but everyone was looking at him waiting for him to speak. At last, he cleared his throat and stood up.

"Hello everybody," he said. "I am pleased to see you all again.

Chapter Seven – Decisions

Having opened the proceedings, Kevin sat down and Snee got to his feet.

"I would like to officially greet the Master," he said. "He brings news of the whereabouts of Duros. However, as you will notice from the empty seat, he also brings news of Marlitta. I will pass you over to Quartok who will give you all the details."

He sat down and Quartok stood up and told the assembly all that had happened to Kevin and how Marlitta was now in the hands of the Collandans. There were murmurs amongst the delegates as Quartok's story unfolded and as he finished, a small rather hairy creature stood up. He looked very old and had brown wrinkly skin and looked rather bad tempered.

"May I ask why the Master took it upon himself to go to Collandar and then to risk one of the Council in this way?" he asked. He would have said more but Quartok stood up again to answer.

"I think that is a matter for the Master," he said. "And I think you will find that he was misled by the Collandans into believing that they were being attacked. Also, I think you will agree that the purpose of the Master is to deal with problems without involving fleets of warships which could only result in mass destruction. After all, that is why he is the keeper of the Master Crystal. No, I think he acted perfectly correctly, and now we need to decide what action is to be taken next."

Another person leapt to him feet and waited for Quartok to acknowledge him.

"Blarnog. What would you like to say?" asked Quartok looking a bit worried. Blarnog was larger than most of the others round the table, being both taller and fatter. He had a pale green complexion and rather pointed ears. His hair was short and black and he was dressed in shiny blue material with a flowing coat rather like a dressing gown. He reminded Kevin of a Leprechaun.

"I think we should send a task force immediately," he said. "These people need teaching a lesson."

"I think not," said Quartok. "A task force would take too long to get there. We need to act immediately if we are to rescue Marlitta. Besides, Duros would be aware of a large force well before it arrived and would be able to take Marlitta somewhere hard to trace. Also, we do not know just how involved the Collandans are. Duros may be forcing them to co-operate with him. We don't know."

"So, what do you suggest, then?" asked Blarnog.

"I think we should send a small scout ship," said Quartok. "With the use of the Master Crystal we could be there instantaneously and probably without the knowledge of Duros. That will give us the chance to gather more information."

"And who would be fool enough to go on such a mission?" asked Blarnog. "I'm sure I wouldn't want to risk it."

"I'm sure you wouldn't," said Quartok pointedly. "No, I will go and so will the Master, obviously, and he will take his friend from Earth." He indicated Tracy. "I will then ask for volunteers. We will need another three people at most."

Another person stood up. He looked a bit like Blarnog but was a little smaller.

"Who is this Earth person?" he demanded.

"She is called Tracy Bagshott," said Quartok. "The Master has brought her with him as Duros has been in contact with her and he wanted to prevent her causing mischief at his prompting."

"What?" shouted the standing figure in a high-pitched voice. "Why have you brought her in here? Don't you realise that Duros is probably using her to listen in to our meeting?"

"Please calm down," said Quartok. "She is no danger to us while she is here. She has no crystal so cannot contact Duros. If he wants to contact her, he will have to get very close to her to do that. His crystal isn't that powerful.

"Now, are there any volunteers to come with us?"

They all looked at each other, but no hand went up. Kevin looked around the line of hostile faces, then slowly got to his feet.

"Well if you are all too scared to come with us," he said. "We'll just have to go on own. But remember that if any of you were in trouble, we wouldn't hesitate in coming to you aid." He sat down.

Then one small person sitting at the far end of the table slowly raised his hand.

"Thank you, Crispin," said Quartok. "I'm glad someone is willing to help."

"I was not afraid of the mission," he said in a small voice. "I just thought I would not be of any use to you. I am not a warrior type, you know."

"I think you will be just fine," said Quartok. "We will be pleased to take you with us."

"I will join you also," said Larnock.

"Excellent," said Quartok. "I don't think there is anything more to discuss. We will retire to make preparations for our quest. You need do no more than keep a look out for any sign of Duros in any of your sectors and report back to the Council. If we need further action to be taken, we will contact the Council and tell you what we require. Thank you all for attending. The meeting is now closed."

The meeting dispersed amid a lot of muttering and Quartok took the small group of volunteers back to his rooms to make their plans.

"I think we should use one of the small scout ships for this venture," said Quartok. "We have a small fleet of them here. They are usually stowed on board the larger cruisers for local use in planetary systems, but I think if we can harness the power of the Master Crystal, it should serve us admirably."

"Does that mean that I will have to 'jump' the ship and all of us to Collandar?" asked Kevin. "The reason I ask is that to 'jump' I have to have a clear picture in my mind of the place we're going, and I could only take us to the landing site that we arrived at when I went there with Mondarwi."

"What would be wrong with that?" asked Larnock.

"I'm sure it would be watched continually," said Kevin. "We really need to arrive without them knowing."

"Very true," said Quartok. "That is more difficult."

"Excuse my butting in," said Crispin meekly. "But why doesn't the Master use the mind sight to find a suitable place to 'jump'?"

"I don't think I know how to do that," said Kevin.

"But it's a good idea, Crispin," said Quartok. "It shouldn't take long for him to learn how to do it. Now, I'll just send a message to Snee to get the Scout ship prepared and provisioned. It won't be ready until tomorrow, so I think you can all go and prepare for the journey. I'll see if I can teach the Master how to find a 'jump' site using the mind sight."

Crispin and Larnock left saying they would be ready for the morning departure. Tracy went into the other room and tucked into some of the food that was laid out there and Kevin and Quartok got down to working with the mind sight.

"You see, Kevin," he said. "It's like getting ready to 'jump' except you don't. You just get the picture into your mind. Now I know you can do that starting from here, for instance, and move out into unknown areas as if you were actually there."

"I think I see what you mean," said Kevin.

"Good," said Quartok. "Then we'll start with something not too difficult. Can you visualise the Council Chamber?"

"Yes. No problem."

"Right," Quartok continued. "Think of it now and close your eyes and see if you can move your point of vision. Move about the room."

Kevin closed his eyes and disappeared. A few seconds later he reappeared.

"Oops," he said. "I think I 'jumped'. Shall I try again?"

"Yes," said Quartok. "But try to think like you do when you are just looking. We don't want you to 'jump' when you start looking at Collandar, do we?"

Kevin closed his eyes again. This time he didn't disappear.

"I can see the Council Room," said Kevin.

"Good," said Quartok. "Now move to the other end of the room and go through the door at the end. Then tell me what you see."

Kevin floated across the Council Chamber, or at least he did in his mind. His body stayed exactly where it was.

"I'm through," he said. "It's a small room with shelves. There are boxes on the shelves and there's a desk in the corner."

"Good," said Quartok. "Now open your eyes and return." Kevin opened his eyes. "You were in the archive room. Now let's try something else a bit further away. Do you remember the place you went to for the test you were put through when you became Master?"

"I think so," said Kevin.

"Right," said Quartok. "Let's try that then. Visualise the front of the building and then move into it and tell me what you see."

Kevin closed his eyes and thought of the strange building he had visited when he was being tested. At first it was just his imagination, then slowly it swam into focus and became crystal clear. He drifted forward towards the building, floated up the steps and into the building which he then began to explore, telling Quartok what he was seeing.

Next, he tried more difficult places until Quartok felt sure he could do it without 'jumping'. Then they went for the real thing. Kevin closed his eyes and thought of the place where he had arrived on Collandar. He felt quite nervous as he didn't want to open his eyes and find himself surrounded by spiders. Slowly the picture crystallised. It was early morning there and the sun glinted off the trees round about. The clearing seemed to be empty, but as he looked around he became aware off pairs of eyes in the shadows, looking out to where he was looking from. He felt sure they must have seen him, but they took no notice. It was all right. He hadn't 'jumped' and they couldn't see him, or even be aware he was watching them.

Time to look around, so he drifted upwards until he could see the small spider town. From this distance the spider web buildings seemed to be dull grey boxes with black dots where the windows, or rather doors, were. Each building cast a shadow that fell onto the next one and he could make out the scattering of small trees around and between the buildings. He could also make out dark shapes scurrying across the ground towards the edge of the town.

It was then he noticed the ships. Five sleek shining saucer shapes were gliding down towards the open ground just outside the town. As each one landed a group of spiders raced forward and started unloading objects from the ship and hurrying off with them towards the town.

Kevin floated down to take a closer view. It was difficult to see what it was he they were carrying. It wasn't boxes, the objects were not rectangular and looked more like bundles of rags. As he drifted closer he realised what he was looking at. The bundles were wriggling. They were creatures bound up in spider web being carried off to the pantry.

As the unloading of each saucer was completed, it rose silently into the air and sped off into the sky. When the last one was unloaded, it didn't take off as Kevin had expected but remained where it was. Then he saw why. A wriggling bundle was being carried out of the town towards the ship. He sped in to get a closer look and got up close to it just as it was carried into the craft. He felt sure he had heard a muffled cry that sounded just like Marlitta.

He didn't know what to do. Should he 'jump' now and rescue her or should he wait until he had back up? But now it was too late. The saucer was lifting off and he wasn't yet skilled enough at the 'mind sight' to manoeuvre himself into the space craft, especially at the speed it was now going.

He turned his attention to the stream of spiders disappearing into the buildings with their bundles. He wondered who these beings could be and what would be their fate. He certainly couldn't do anything about them single-handedly, so he turned his attention to the hills behind the town. If they were to 'jump' with the scout ship to a low position behind the hills, they could move in quite close and conceal the ship in the little rocky gorge out of sight and make their way on foot to the town. Then with a combination of 'mind sight' and 'jumping' they could get to where they wanted to be.

He looked around the area carefully so that he could find his way back again, then opened his eyes again and the scene faded and Quartok's room reappeared.

Chapter Eight – Task Force

Kevin wasted no time before telling Quartok all he had seen. Quartok looked concerned.

"It seems we have more to do," he said, "than simply rescuing Marlitta. And that is going to be more difficult now she has been taken somewhere else. We must give it much thought."

"Perhaps we should start at the spiders' town," said Kevin. "If we can get control of that we can find out where they have taken Marlitta."

"Yes," agreed Quartok. "I think that is our only option. But now, I think we should all get some sleep so that we can be ready to get off first thing tomorrow."

Tracy was shown to a room and left to settle in and after discussing things a little more, Quartok showed Kevin to his room where he settled down for the night. He felt rather restless and couldn't get off to sleep so he thought he'd have another look at what was happening on Collandar. He was finding it easier, now, to shift his point of view to the distant planet without fear of finding himself actually there in person, but he thought he would take no chances and focused on the proposed landing sight behind the hills. He closed his eyes and visualised the scene. At first it was just like a picture in his mind. Perhaps he hadn't remembered it correctly. Then it started to become clearer, rather like a photo developing. Soon it was crystal clear. The sun was higher in the sky now and the shadows were shortening. The land behind the hills was very flat with only sparse vegetation as far as the eye could see. The hills were rocky and steep with moss and stunted vegetation clinging to the steep surfaces.

He drifted slowly upwards until he could see over the top. It was then that he realised that there were little lookout posts nestling among the crags near the tops of the hills. They were using the natural features to give shelter with the aid of coverings of their sticky web. It was lucky he had found out about this, as they would have been spotted as they walked through the passes between the peaks on their way to the town.

He made a note of where they all were, then drifted down towards the town. The buildings were all the same so it was difficult to remember which ones he had seen the bundles being taken to. There was one that stood out because of its position, slightly away from the other buildings, so he headed towards that one.

It was easy to drift in and out of the rooms, even through the walls, as he wasn't actually there. It was a bit like using a remote TV camera. He headed towards the area he knew from experience was the pantry where they kept the bundled prey and when he found it he was amazed by what he saw. It was packed with wriggling bundles, each hanging from the ceiling. He moved in as close as he could and could just about make out small figures rather like Quartok in size and shape, enclosed in a binding of spiders' web. Some were quite still and Kevin wondered if they were still alive, but some were moving as if trying, in vain, to free themselves. He wondered where they had come from and why they were here. Well, he knew why they were here. They were to be food for the spiders, but he didn't know who had brought them and why.

Eventually he was feeling very tired and left the grisly scene and returned to his bed, where he quickly fell asleep.

In the morning he woke to find Murin bustling about. When they realised that he was awake they hurried out of the room to allow him to get up and get dressed. When he had washed and dressed he went through into the room where they had eaten the previous evening. Quartok was standing talking to Larnock and Crispin while Tracy sat nearby looking bored. When she saw Kevin, she jumped to her feet and hurried over to him but before she had chance to speak Quartok stepped forward to greet him.

"Good morning, Master," he said with a smile. "I hope you slept well?"

"Fine thanks," said Kevin. "Well I did eventually."

"How do you mean?" asked Quartok.

Kevin told him about his other attempts using the mind sight and what he had seen.

"That sounds serious," said Quartok.

"Do you really think it was Marlitta that you saw being taken away?" asked Larnock.

"I don't know," said Kevin. "It is difficult to say. But it seemed to move like her."

"I wonder where they have taken her?" said Crispin.

"What were the ships like?" asked Larnock. Kevin described the saucer like ships and Larnock and Quartok nodded to each other.

"Sounds like the Chetmock," said Quartok.

"Who are they?" asked Kevin.

"A particularly nasty species from a neighbouring star cluster outside the Galactic Federation," said Quartok. "It's a pity you didn't follow them using your mind sight. Now we will have great difficulty finding out where they have gone."

"I'm sorry," said Kevin, "I never thought."

"Can't be helped," said Larnock. "We'll have to find out from the Collandans when we get there."

"How are we going to do that?" asked Kevin.

"We'll have to storm their main building," said Larnock. "It'll be the one they took you to, where the conference room was. Anyway, have some food. We must get started as soon as possible."

Kevin sat down next to Tracy who had decided that it would be a good idea to get some food before they decided to rush off somewhere.

"So what next?" she asked Kevin.

"We have our breakfast," said Kevin, "and then we go to the space port."

"We're going in a spaceship?" she said, her face lighting up.

"Yes. We'll need a ship at the other end," said Kevin.

"Coo," she said. "Wait 'til I tell them all back home."

"Oh no," said Kevin. "That's one thing you can't do. When we get back home – if we get back, that is – you can't tell anyone what has happened."

"How can you stop me?" she said looking smug.

"There are many ways," said Kevin as he tucked into his breakfast. "If I thought you couldn't be trusted to keep quiet we might have to leave you somewhere and not take you home at all."

"You wouldn't do that?"

"Try me," said Kevin.

They finished their breakfast in silence and then, standing in a line holding hands, Quartok 'jumped' them to the spaceport. Suddenly they were surrounded by ships of all shapes and sizes. They were nothing like any spaceship Kevin could have imagined. Sniffer padded off to sniff everything.

They had arrived on the flat observation roof of a large building. There was a railing around the edge and there were a few groups of people standing watching ships arrive and leave. Most of the people were smaller than Kevin, but he was used to this by now. Sniffer sniffed them and most of them hurried off to somewhere safer.

"Which is our ship?" asked Kevin.

"We can't see it from here," answered Quartok. "If we walk over to the railing at the other side of the building we should be able to see it."

They set off across the roof towards the other railing, and as they got near the edge Kevin began to realise just how big this spaceport actually was. There were ships as far as the eye could see. Some were enormous fat things looking more like barrels than ships. There were sleek ships with sweptback wings that looked as if they were for use as aircraft rather than spaceships.

"Quite right," said Spectro unexpectedly, "though they can be used in space as well, mostly for local work."

"Which one is ours?" asked Kevin out loud. Quartok pointed.

"That's ours over there," he said. Kevin wasn't sure which one he was pointing at. "Perhaps we should go down to the departure hall and see if everything is ready for us."

They followed Quartok across the roof to a doorway in a raised section of the roof. Inside was what looked like a lift shaft but there was no lift.

"That looks a bit dangerous," said Kevin. Quartok looked puzzled and kept walking. Kevin grabbed him just before he stepped over the edge and fell to his death.

"What are you doing?" exclaimed Quartok pulling Kevin's hands off his shoulders.

"Trying to stop you falling down that lift shaft," said Kevin.

"Oh, I see," said Quartok smiling, which was something he didn't often do. "Of course, you won't have seen one of these before. It's a vertical transporter; used to take people to different levels in a building. Follow me, it is perfectly safe."

He stepped forward and walked on air, apparently, to the centre of the shaft.

"Come on," he said, "there's nothing to be scared of.

Larnock and Crispin stepped forward and stood next to Quartok while Kevin tentatively put his foot out and tapped the air trying to feel an invisible floor.

"You won't get me on that," said Tracy backing away.

"It is perfectly safe," said Quartok getting a bit impatient. "Please get on."

"But I can't feel the floor," said Kevin still tapping nothingness with his foot. "There's nothing there."

"Of course there's nothing there," said Larnock walking back to where Kevin was standing. "It is a force field and you have to apply a force before it acts. Here, take my hand."

Kevin took Larnock's hand and was pulled onto the invisible floor. It felt very strange, just like an ordinary floor but a bit spongy. Tracy was still standing looking perplexed, so Kevin gave a quick mental instruction to Sniffer who bounded forward and pushed Tracy bodily into the lift. She let out a scream and grabbed Kevin and clung on to him for all she was worth. Kevin felt embarrassed, then quite pleased at being grabbed. After all, when you got to know her she was really quite a nice girl.

At that moment the invisible floor started to melt, or at least that was how it felt, and they started to descend. Tracy let out another scream and Sniffer let out a howl. Their downward slide got gradually faster and the sides of the shaft moved past them at an ever-increasing rate. Kevin tried to look unconcerned but he wasn't sure which bothered him the most, the speed of descent or Tracy squeezing the breath out of him.

Suddenly, the invisible floor seemed to thicken and turn to treacle as their descent slowed down until they drifted the last few metres to a standstill at the bottom of the shaft. At least there was a solid floor beneath their feet now. Quartok, Larnock and Crispin strode out of the lift. Sniffer leapt out in one bound while Kevin half-supported Tracy as she tried to walk out with as much dignity as she could muster.

"I wasn't really frightened," she said.

"Of course not," said Kevin with a grin.

"I wasn't," she said glaring at him. Sniffer growled and Tracy decided to back off and strided off after the other three.

They went past what looked like the public area with its check-in desks, which looked rather like an earth airport. When Kevin mentioned this, Quartok said that they were much the same over all the known universe.

They walked past this area and into an area where there were no people who looked like tourists. There were a few Murin scurrying about and a few of the typical diminutive people walking purposefully about with clipboards or folders under their arms. It seemed that bureaucracy was universal as well.

They turn off into a narrow passage with a small door at the far end, which they entered into a small room.

"Another lift I'm afraid," said Larnock.

"No problem," said Kevin.

"Of course not," said Tracy trying to look brave as she stepped through into the recess with no floor. Kevin had to give Sniffer a mental push before he would enter.

This time did no more than clutch Kevin's arm as they started to descend but this still gave him a warm glow inside.

At the bottom of the shaft there was a horizontal transporter which took a bit of getting used to, but which wasn't as alarming as the vertical ones. At the end of the tunnel there was another lift, this time going up, which wasn't as bad as the ones that went down. At the top they went through another door, out into the bright sunlight right next to a very sleek silver fish shaped object.

"This is out ship," said Quartok and set off up the steps into shining machine. The others followed in silence.

Chapter Nine – Collandar

The ship was quite large. There was a main cabin with seats and tables where they could relax. Hatches at the sides led into the individual cabins, which were more like cupboards, which were actually quite comfortable. Two had been adapted to take Kevin and Tracy who were larger than the usual occupants, and there was a special one for Sniffer.

At the front was the cockpit, or control section as Quartok preferred to call it. There were five padded seats facing forward, but apparently there was no window so it was difficult to know how it would be flown.

"We'll go into that later," said Quartok. "Firstly, you should settle into your cabins and, perhaps, have something to eat and drink. It will be a little while before we are ready to go."

They each went off to their cabins and made themselves comfortable, though Kevin didn't really see the need. After all, they would get there in seconds and wouldn't be spending much time in their cabins at all. Anyway, they hadn't brought much with them; just what they had in the small packs they had left with.

He adjusted his bunk so that it felt comfortable and investigated the other fittings in the cabin. It was possible to wash, though with difficulty, and there were little cubbyholes where he could stow his possessions. He pushed his pack into one of these and then went out into the main cabin where he found Crispin sitting. There was some food on the table and some flasks of liquid.

"Come and have something to eat," said Crispin.

Kevin wasn't really hungry, as it hadn't been long since he had had his breakfast, but he sat down and poured himself a drink from the flask and picked up a biscuit shaped thing and started to nibble it.

Tracy appeared and joined him at the table. She seemed to be quite hungry, but then she normally did.

"Tell me, Crispin," said Kevin, "why there are lifts and transporters when it is much easier to 'jump' from one place to another?"

"Not everyone can 'jump'," he answered. "Everyone has some kind of crystal simply to be able to communicate with others. There are millions of languages in the universe and it would be impossible to speak to everyone that comes here if we didn't have the crystals. These are mostly very small and wouldn't allow you to 'jump'."

"So, who has the powerful crystals then?" asked Kevin.

"Well, you do, for one," said Crispin. "In fact, yours is the most powerful crystal in the known universe. But that is because you are the Master of the Universe. The council members each have a crystal matched to their own individual personalities and needs. Mine is useful for science work. That is my interest."

"So you have to have other ways of doing things for the ones who haven't got powerful crystals?" said Kevin.

"I haven't got a crystal," said Tracy, "so how is it I can understand what everyone is saying?"

"Good point," said Crispin. "You're all right at the moment because we all have crystals, but you wouldn't be able to understand someone who hadn't a crystal themselves. We must do something about this before we leave."

Crispin stood up and went through to the command cabin and returned after a short time with Larnock.

"I will just go back to the council building," he said. "Perhaps the Master would be kind enough to join Quartok in the command cabin."

He had hardly finished speaking when he disappeared.

"If you would like to go through to the command cabin," Crispin said to Kevin, "I'll tell your friend here a little more of our universe."

Kevin looked at Tracy who seemed quite happy with that and climbed through the hatch into the command cabin.

"It must all seem a bit strange to you," said Crispin to Tracy.

"What do you think?" she replied a bit sharply. "If I told them about this back on Earth no-one would believe me. They'd think I was making it up, or nuts or something."

"Nuts?" said Crispin looking puzzled.

"You know. Off me head, cracked, a sandwich short of a picnic."

Crispin still looked puzzled.

"They might think I was mad," she said as if she was speaking to an idiot.

"Oh, I see," said Crispin. "You must realise that I do not speak your language and I hear what my crystal translates, so some of the things you say sound nonsense to me. You see it can't deal with colloquialisms."

"What?" said Tracy.

"Exactly," said Crispin grinning. "So perhaps we should keep our conversation simple to avoid misunderstanding."

"So, what is all this about Kevin being the Master of the Universe, then?" said Tracy. "What does he know about anything?"

"He doesn't have to know anything to be Master," said Crispin. "He has a crystal that can tell him all he needs to know. No, it is more a matter of his mind being correct for the job. You see we don't have the same sort of governmental system that you have on Earth. In fact, we have very little actual government as such. People do what they were born to do and organise themselves. The Council is really only there to deal with problems."

"On Earth we are told that we should all have the chance to get to the top," said Tracy. "I don't think people would like to be told what they should do."

They aren't told what they should do," said Crispin. "They do what makes them happy, and that is what their species has evolved to do. You have seen the Murin?" Tracy nodded. "Well Kevin was a bit concerned about them. He thought it was wrong that they should spend all their time running around after people and doing things that he thought were uninteresting and tedious."

"Well he's right," said Tracy with some feeling.

"But it is what they want to do. It makes them happy to do what they do, and it makes them particularly happy to do it well," said Crispin.

"Have they been bred specially to do the work?" she asked.

"Well, not exactly," said Crispin. "It's just that over the millennia they have done what they do best and, I suppose it is now in the breeding. But no one made them do it. Everyone finds something that will make them a living doing something they can do well and that they enjoy doing," said Crispin.

"So," said Tracy, "what you're saying is that if they're happy it's OK?"

"Well isn't it?" asked Crispin. "If you chose a career that you particularly wanted to do and which made you happy, you wouldn't want someone else to try and make you do something else would you?"

I suppose not," said Tracy but she didn't look convinced.

"It's just that on your world everyone thinks that the only important thing is to become very rich," continued Crispin.

"Well that seems OK to me," said Tracy.

"Well if you think it would make you happy," said Crispin, "that is what you should do. But I think you will find that most people want more out of life than that."

At that moment Kevin emerged from the command cabin.

"All set for take-off," he said.

"How much do they pay you to do this?" asked Tracy.

"What?" said Kevin startled.

"How much do they pay you?"

"Well, I don't know. Nothing I suppose," said Kevin thoughtfully.

"The Master can have anything he needs," said Crispin.

"I suppose I can," said Kevin. "I had never thought of that. Anyway, I'd don't need paying to do this. It's a bit like a big theme park really, and I can go on any ride for nothing."

"I see what you mean," said Tracy. "I'd never thought of it that way before."

There was a popping sound as Larnock reappeared.

"I think this should be right for you," he said to Tracy holding out a ring with what looked like a diamond mounted on it.

"Wow," she said taking it from him. "Is it a diamond?"

"Oh no," said Larnock. "This is much more valuable. It will allow you to communicate with anyone, whatever language they speak. It will also give you a certain amount of protection and will allow us to communicate with you from a distance. You won't be able to 'jump' with it. It isn't that type of crystal. It will also stop Duros influencing you."

"We're ready to go now," said Kevin. "Quartok has managed to synchronise my crystal with the ship's navigation crystal so I should be able to control the 'jump' to Collandar."

"So, if you would all like to make yourselves comfortable," said Quartok, "the Master and I will get to work in the control cabin."

"Do we have to strap ourselves in?" asked Tracy.

"No. That won't be necessary," said Quartok. "But it may take a little while as we will have to do it in several jumps. Now, after you Master."

Kevin led the way into the control cabin and took his seat at one of the consoles while Quartok sat at the other one. It was a bit cramped for Kevin as it had been designed for a smaller person, but the seat had a little adjustment that made it reasonably comfortable.

Quartok set some of the switches and a screen in front of them started to glow dimly.

"Now I would like you to close your eyes and visualise the place we will be going to," said Quartok making a few more adjustments. "But don't try to 'jump', at least not yet."

Kevin closed his eyes and visualised the landing place that he had prepared the previous evening. The scene drifted into view in his mind and then clicked into sharp focus. The same scene appeared on the screen in front of them.

"You can open your eyes now," said Quartok. "We have locked onto the target."

Kevin opened his eyes and was amazed to see the view that had been in his mind now displayed on the screen in front of them. Quartok was adjusting dials and setting switches.

"Right," he said. "It looks as if it will take three 'jumps' to take us there."

"Why can't we do it in one?" asked Kevin. "I can."

"Yes, I know," said Quartok. "And you can take several people with you. But you wouldn't be able to take the ship as well, at least, not safely."

The screen changed and became black. Quartok rotated a disk in front of him and a large blue planet drifted into view.

This will be our first 'jump'," he said. "It takes us quite close to Optimus in the third quadrant." He pressed a switch and spoke into what must have been a microphone.

"Prepare to 'jump'," he said. "Five, four, three, two, one, now." As he said this he pressed a pad on the console. Kevin grabbed the sides of his seat as the pull of gravity suddenly reduced. There was a yelp from the other cabin from Tracy.

"Sorry about that," said Quartok. "I should have warned you."

Kevin looked at the planet that almost filled the screen in front of him. It was blue and looked very like Earth but didn't seem to have as much land. In fact, there didn't seem to be much land at all.

"Is it inhabited?" asked Kevin.

"Oh yes," said Quartok. "Very much so. Oh, I see what you mean. Not all life exists on land, you know. This is a water planet. The small islands are used for landing space ships. Under the surface are cities and highways. It is a very busy planet."

"Highways?" said Kevin surprised.

"Oh yes," said Quartok. "They are in transparent tubes across the sea floor. Some run at other levels if the ocean is too deep for them. The cities are built in bubbles where the air breathing population lives. The water breathing population lives in the water, of course."

"Of course," said Kevin.

"Time for the next 'jump' I think," said Quartok. The screen went black. Quartok rotated the disk slowly, but this time nothing came into view.

"What's wrong?" asked Kevin.

"Nothing at all," said Quartok. "Just checking to make sure we aren't going to hit anything. This is just empty space. Ideal for our purposes, I think."

"What's that," said Kevin pointing to the screen. Quartok made some adjustments and the faint blemish grew larger until Kevin could see that it was an enormous rock floating in space.

"Just as well that you saw that," said Quartok. "Wouldn't like to hit something like that." He made some more adjustments until he was happy that there was nothing else close by.

"Prepare to 'jump'," he said into the microphone and after a short pause, pressed the pad again. This time there was no change in gravity so it seemed that nothing had happened.

Quartok clicked a few switches and the view of their landing place came back onto the screen. He rotated the disk and the screen rotated too.

"Just checking," said Quartok. "We don't want any nasty surprises when we arrive. I'll move the landing place a little nearer the foothills. We'll arrive at a little above ground level and then I'll land the craft in the usual way. This time you'll feel an increase in gravity so be prepared."

This 'jump' wasn't as bad as the first because he was prepared for it, and he was pulled further into his seat instead of being ejected from it.

Quartok took the controls, which slid out from the front of the console, and lowered the craft slowly to the ground.

"Well so far, so good," said Quartok. "Now for the tricky bit."

Chapter Ten – Confrontation

Kevin and Quartok went back into the main cabin where Crispin had opened up a large screen, which showed the same picture as Kevin had been looking at in the Control Cabin.

"We can use this to see what there is beyond these hills," said Crispin. "Kevin's crystal is linked into the craft's crystal so we will be able to see what he sees."

Kevin closed his eyes and his mind drifted out beyond the walls of the craft and towards the low pass between the peaks. It looked quite easy going, but that didn't really matter as they would be 'jumping'. As the viewpoint slide forward, it was possible to see the sky beyond the hills, and then the treetops.

"Just as well we aren't walking," said Crispin. "Look at those webs."

"I hadn't noticed them," said Quartok. "It looks as if they are there to raise the alarm if anything comes through the pass."

"Ah. There are the buildings," said Lartop. "But which one do we want? They all look the same."

"They are the same," said Kevin, "but this is the one we visited last time I was here." The picture zoomed in on a building in the middle of the town. The viewpoint went towards one of the openings near the top and went inside. Immediately they could see enormous spider type creatures scuttling around. Tracy let out a yelp and clung to Kevin's arm.

"Don't do that, please," said Kevin trying to concentrate on what he was doing. "They can't get at you."

"Where will we find the ones in charge?" asked Quartok.

"Well I met them in the conference room," said Kevin. "I think it was through here." The viewpoint moved forward into a large chamber with humps of fluffy material arranged in a circle.

"No-one here," said Quartok. "Any idea where they would be?"

"No," said Kevin. "They were all here when I arrived. I'll try through here." The viewpoint moved to the end of the room and into a dark recess. It was difficult to see anything, as it was very dim.

"What's that over there?" said Crispin pointing to the corner of the screen. Kevin zoomed in and it was just possible to make out two small white spiders, one each side of an opening in the wall.

"Sentries," said Kevin. "They're smaller than the others but very fast. They're poisonous as well. I think they are the hunters that paralyse their prey before it is wrapped in web and hung up until they're ready to eat it. I don't think the big ones are poisonous, though I couldn't be sure."

The viewpoint moved past the two sentries into a passageway, which seemed to be empty. There were no doorways off the passage, just one at the far end which led into a large room which was dimly lit through openings in the walls which were covered by a fluffy curtain of sorts.

On a hump in the corner of the room was an enormous black spider. He looked very old.

"I think he was the one who seemed to be in charge when I was here before," said Kevin. "Perhaps we should 'jump' straight in while he is on his own."

"I think you're right," said Quartok. "Wait 'til we're all linked up. Right, I think we're ready. Jump now." Kevin 'jumped and quickly opened his eyes. The small group was standing in the middle of the room facing the sleeping spider, which slowly opened an eye, blinked and then opened the other eye.

"So, you've come back, have you?" said the spider in a rasping voice. "We've been expecting you."

Suddenly several little white spiders tumbled out of the dark corners of the room and leaped at them. Tracy screamed which momentarily stopped them in their tracks, which gave Kevin time to point his finger in an arc in front of them drawing a line of fire out of the floor.

The white spiders backed away from the flames.

"You'll be next," said Kevin, "so keep your distance." The old black spider waved a leg and the white spiders scuttled of and disappeared into the darkness.

"Where's Marlitta?" demanded Kevin. "Tell me right now or I'll burn holes in you."

The spider looked uneasy and shuffled a bit. "She's not here," he said.

"Well perhaps you'd better tell me quickly," said Kevin losing patience. He raised his hand and pointed it at the spider.

"We sent her away," said the spider. "To another planet. We had to."

"What do you mean by that?" asked Kevin. "Why did you have to? Was it Duros?"

"Of course it was Duros. You know quite well it was Duros," he hissed. "This isn't something we would do for the fun of it."

"What's that supposed to mean?"

"It means that we are a peaceful people," he continued. "We like to keep to ourselves. This is a very sparsely populated world but we manage to maintain a meagre existence even though food is hard to come by. There are a few migrant herds of creatures that we can hunt for food, but it is a large planet and they don't come this way as often as we would like."

"That explains the space ships bringing in captives for you to eat," said Kevin in disgust. "So you traded Marlitta for captive creatures to eat, did you?"

"Basically yes," said the spider. "But not willingly. If we had refused, Duros would have wiped us out, so we were forced to co-operate with him."

"And what about the people you are eating," continued Kevin. "Don't they have rights?"

"What people?" asked the spider. "We do not eat intelligent creatures. What do you take us for?"

"Well they looked like people to me," said Kevin.

"They were two-legged tree creatures," said the spider, "but not intelligent."

"And what was all that about when you brought me here before?" said Kevin. "Who was attacking you? Was that Duros?"

"No-one was attacking us," he said. "It was a subterfuge to get you to give up your crystal, but it didn't work."

"It wouldn't have done you any good anyway," said Kevin. "The crystal can't be used by anyone other than me. I'm sure Duros would know that."

"I think," said Quartok, "that he just wanted to remove your power. It must mean that he is up to something and doesn't want to have to face you."

"What happened to Marlitta's crystal," asked Kevin suddenly. "Has Duros got it?"

"No," said the spider. "We kept it. We didn't want Duros to get it as we thought it would make him more powerful."

"Do you know what he is planning?" asked Crispin.

"Not exactly," answered the spider. "But we think he is planning an invasion somewhere, but we don't know where."

"Do you know where he took Marlitta?" asked Kevin.

"I assume he will have taken here to our nearest neighbour. I don't know what you would call it but it is the planet next nearest to the sun from here. We're not spacefaring people so I can't tell you more than that. I do know that it is peopled by beings that are closely related to us. I don't think they are helping Duros willingly either, but I can't be sure."

"Do you know whereabouts on the planet they will have taken her?" asked Quartok. "We can find the planet easily enough, but a planet is a big place."

"I do not know personally," he said. "But we have people who can tell you more. Why don't you go back to your ship – I assume you are in a ship? – and return in one hour, our time, and I will have the council convened along with some of our best scientists. They will be able to show you exactly where to go."

"All right," said Quartok. "But first bring us Marlitta's crystal." The spider made some clicking noises and one of the little white spiders appeared and scuttled out of the door.

"It will be here shortly," he said.

"Will the people of this planet be friendly?" asked Kevin.

"They will be cautious," replied the spider. "They won't want to get on the wrong side of Duros. We don't either, so I would hope he doesn't find out that we have helped you."

"Well, he won't find out from us," said Kevin.

The little white spider ran back into the room and placed a crystal on the floor in front of Kevin.

"There is the crystal," said the large spider. "Please take it and return later."

Kevin stooped and picked up the crystal, then all of them linked hands and were instantly back in the main cabin of the ship. As they unclasped hands, Tracy collapsed into a heap on the floor, sobbing uncontrollably.

"What's the matter?" asked Kevin kneeling down and holding her shoulders.

"I think she is in shock from being close to the Collandans," said Quartok. "I noticed that she looked panic stricken while we were there, but I didn't want this to happen there. Leave her alone for a bit and the Murin will get her something to calm her down."

Kevin hadn't realised that there were Murin aboard, but he should have known that they went most places with important people and could disappear from sight completely when not needed. Suddenly four of them appeared from nowhere and carried Tracy into her cabin.

"Will she be OK?" asked Kevin.

"Yes," said Quartok. "I think the Collandans are similar in appearance to creatures from your own planet which she has a phobia of."

"Spiders," said Kevin. "But on Earth they are only very small, but people can be scared of them."

"It is not surprising, then," continued Quartok. "These must seem like monsters to her. It is no wonder she is in shock. Still we must leave her to the Murin. We have other things to discuss. Perhaps we should all make ourselves comfortable and the Murin will bring us some refreshment."

They all sat down in the cabin seats and adjusted them to face inwards so that they could all see each other. Two more Murin appeared and quickly set out food and drink in the centre of the cabin so that they could all reach it. Then they disappeared as quickly as they had appeared.

"Now gentlemen," said Quartok taking charge of the situation, "what do you think?"

"It seems odd," said Crispin, "that those little hunters should rush out as if to attack us. After all, the big black one said that he had expected us back. I don't trust them."

"Nor do I," said Lartop.

"I don't know what to think," said Quartok. "They're such an alien species; it's difficult to know what they are likely to say or do."

"If they have had dealings with Duros," said Kevin who had been thinking, "they would still be under his power and likely to say anything to make us do what Duros wants. I think they are trying to get us to go to that planet knowing that Duros is planning to trap us. I think that if they thought we could beat Duros they would co-operate with us."

"Don't you think that Marlitta is there, then?" asked Crispin.

"I don't know," said Kevin. "Now she hasn't got her crystal I don't know how we could trace her."

"It is possible to detect her presence using her own crystal," said Crispin. "Perhaps you should ask Spectro. You are still linked into the ship's crystal so we'll all be able to hear what he says."

"I'd forgotten about him," said Kevin. "He keeps so quiet for so long I forget he is here. I sometimes wish he would tell me when there are things I should know. I forget that I have to ask him. Right, here we go."

He put the question to Spectro and they all sat and listened to his reply.

"It's like this," said Spectro. "When a person has a crystal of power, it is matched to the mind of the person who owns it and the link cannot be broken. However, the link gets weaker the further they are from their crystal."

"So how can I find out where Marlitta is?" asked Kevin.

"Hold Marlitta's crystal next to your own crystal and try to see her as you would if you were trying to contact her. You won't actually be able to speak to her but you will be able to sense how near she is, and possibly get an idea of direction."

"Right," said Kevin, "let's do it."

He took Marlitta's crystal out of his pocket and held it close to the crystal that hung round his neck on a chain. Then he closed his eyes and tried to contact Marlitta. At first nothing happened but he kept on trying. Soon he thought he could sense her. It was not a sound or a sight or even a sense of touch, but he felt sure she was nearby. Without thinking about it he started to use his mind sight. The big screen in the cabin sprang to life and everyone clung to their seats as the viewpoint raced out of the spacecraft and shot off across the plain outside. The land was flat as far as the eye could see, with little vegetation and a scattering of rocks and boulders lying around. Soon the ground started to rise. It wasn't a hill exactly but the ground sloped gently upwards and then suddenly they stopped at the edge of a sheer cliff.

Everyone gasped. Stretched out before them was a vast sea that reached to the horizon. Waves lapped the rocks far below them but there were no sea birds to be seen anywhere, which Kevin thought was strange. It was hard to imagine the seaside without gulls.

"What is that?" said Lartop. "Out there near the horizon. It looks like land, and is that a tall building on it, a tower maybe?"

Kevin saw what Lartop was referring to and the viewpoint rushed forward, out over the cliff and over the waves at the speed of a jet fighter aircraft. Quartok's knuckles where white where he grasped the arms of his seat.

The point on the horizon grew larger rapidly until it was possible to see quite clearly a small rocky island. There was no vegetation at all, and right in the centre was a tall tower. A very tall tower. Kevin thought it looked like a lighthouse except it wasn't painted like a lighthouse and it didn't have a light at the top.

"I think she's here," said Kevin. "In fact, I'm sure she's here. Shall we 'jump'?"

"No," said Quartok, "not yet. We need to find out more about the place first."

The picture faded and Kevin opened his eyes.

"We need to find out what that place is," said Quartok. "We must keep out appointment with the Collandan Council and find out what they can tell us."

"The hour is nearly up," said Lartop. "How is the girl?"

"I will go and see," said Crispin standing up and going to the little side cabin where the Murin had taken Tracy.

"But can we believe them?" said Kevin. "They could tell us anything."

"You could get Spectro to monitor them and check for truth or lies," said Lartop.

"Could I? Said Kevin surprised. "I didn't know he could do that."

"You didn't ask," said Spectro. "Is that what you want me to do?"

"Yes please," said Kevin.

At that moment Crispin returned.

"It seems she was stung by one of those hunters," he said. "She will have to stay here. I'll stay with her while you go and have your meeting."

"Will she be OK?" asked Kevin suddenly concerned.

"Oh yes," said Crispin. "But it takes a while for the effects to wear off. It wasn't a full sting, but enough to make her feel quite unwell."

"OK," said Kevin. "Look after her. We shouldn't be long."

Kevin, Quartok and Lartop joined hands and 'jumped' back into the council room. Suddenly they found themselves faced by a circle of spider-like creatures. It was difficult to tell, but Kevin thought they all seemed a bit shifty. The old black spider they had spoken to earlier sat on a hump in a central position and on either side of him were lesser dignitaries, or so they seemed to Kevin. Behind these were several of the little white hunters probably acting as guards. Kevin kept a wary eye on them.

"We have returned as you asked us to," said Kevin trying to sound official. "Now, are you ready to tell us how to find Marlitta?"

"Welcome back, Master of the Universe," said the old spider. "May I introduce you to Craa who is head of our scientific scholars. He has studied the universe and has also made a study of other cultures, races and species that have visited us. He is also one of the few Collandans who has actually left this planet and visited another. I will leave him to tell you what you wish to know."

He sunk back onto his hummock and another, smaller spider raised itself and moved forward into the centre of the gathering. It wasn't as hairy as most of the other spiders and had a smooth shiny body of a dark reddish-brown colour and legs of a similar, though lighter, colour.

"Greetings Master," he said to Kevin in a quiet rasping voice. "I am told that you wish to find the female creature who was with you when you visited our planet previously."

"Yes," said Kevin losing his patience. "What have you done with her?"

"We haven't done anything with her," Craa continued. "Perhaps I should tell you the whole story from the beginning."

"That would be a good idea," said Kevin.

"Well, it all started a while back when we had a visit from one of your kind," said Craa.

"Duros," said Kevin.

"Yes, that was his name," continued Craa. "He led us to believe that we were in danger from another planet and said that he could help us. He said they had lain waste our neighbouring planet and said that he would show me. He had a crystal, which he used to travel from place to place instantly, and he used it to take me to the planet he had told us about. It was dreadful. The place had been devastated. He said that we must send an emissary to the Master of the Universe and ask for his help.

"When I asked him how we would do that he said that he would transport whoever we nominated to go."

"That would have been Mondarwi," said Kevin.

"Yes, indeed," said Craa. "He is over there." He indicated one of the spiders sitting at the side by waving a leg at him.

"Oh, I'm sorry," said Kevin. "I hadn't recognised him."

"But we became suspicious," continued Craa. "Who was this creature and what had it to do with him? So, we challenged him and his demeanour changed completely. He said that he had destroyed the other planet and he would destroy ours too if we didn't do as he said. He had tried to get the people of our neighbouring planet to contact you and they had refused, so he had destroyed them. We had no choice but to do as he said. So Mondarwi went to fetch you using the crystal that Duros gave him. I don't think he had another, but we didn't know that at the time.

"When you arrived here he wanted us to get your crystal from you and give it to him, but you wouldn't be persuaded."

"Well it didn't make any sense," said Kevin. "You wouldn't have been able to use it as it is special to me."

"We know that now," said Craa. "He made us capture your friend and take her crystal, which we did, but you escaped. We tried to use the crystal but it wouldn't work for us so we just kept it until you returned. Your friend was taken away in a spacecraft and we were given supplies in repayment, but Duros said that we should not tell you anything or he would return and punish us. We are very worried."

"I don't think he is as powerful as you seem to think," said Kevin. "If you could use his crystal to 'jump', it must have been a very general-purpose crystal, not one that can be used to destroy anything."

"No," said Craa. "But he had allies. The people with the spacecraft were not from our system. He called them the Nagreb. I think they are a race of warriors."

"I have heard of them," said Quartok. "They are from outside the Galactic Federation, but we have had problems with them in the past. Many years ago they mounted an invasion and destroyed many planets before they were stopped. I don't like the sound of this at all."

"Where will they have taken Marlitta?" asked Kevin.

"They said they were taking her to one of the home planets of the Nagreb. Probably to be held hostage," said Craa. "That, I'm afraid is all I know."

Kevin stood and looked thoughtful, but he was actually asking Spectro if they were speaking the truth.

"I think so," said Spectro. "It is difficult to tell with such a species, but I'm fairly sure that is the truth."

"What is the tower on the island just off the coast over there," asked Kevin pointing in the direction of the coast.

Craa looked surprised, or at least Kevin thought that was his expression.

"You mean the Eternal Rock?" Craa asked. "I don't know. It has always been there as far as I know. It was once worshiped by our people in ancient times."

"I think that is where Marlitta is being held," said Kevin. "How is it defended?"

"As I said, it has always been there," said Craa. "It is a large rock. It is solid. Nothing can be inside it."

"He's lying," said Spectro.

"Now you know that I can't believe that," said Kevin. "You must realise that I have a crystal that is very powerful and I will use it if you do not tell me all you know."

"I can't," said Craa.

"Can't or won't?" asked Kevin.

"He will destroy us if we tell you," said Craa becoming very agitated.

"And I will destroy you if you do not," said Kevin.

At that, several of the hunter spiders leapt forward as if to attack him. He acted instinctively and flames blazed from his outstretched hands. He was aiming at the floor but two of the leading hunters ran straight into it and burst into flames. Panic followed and all the other spiders climbed over each other to escape the wrath of the Master as well as the flames that were spreading rapidly across the floor of the room. It seemed that the web material burned well once started.

Kevin pointed again and dowsed the flames with negative energy. He didn't know quite how he had done it but it had worked. The room was now filled with choking smoke so they moved out into the corridor where there was a breeze from the ever-open doors in the side of the building.

"I think you made your point," said Quartok.

"I didn't mean to kill those hunters," said Kevin. "They just ran into the flames."

"I know you didn't," said Quartok. "But if you hadn't they would have got you and they might have killed you. You had no choice. But at least you now know the sort of power you have."

"Yes," said Kevin, "and I don't like it very much."

"Good," said Quartok. "That is the most important lesson you could learn. Now we had better try and get them back again. We need to know how to get into that tower."

When the smoke had cleared from the conference room they went back in and stood where they had stood before and waited until, one by one, the spiders returned.

Chapter Eleven – The Eternal Rock

When all the Collandans had returned, or at least all those who dared, Kevin spoke to them.

"I'm sorry about that," he said. "But they attacked me and I had to defend myself. But you can see that I am more powerful than Duros and you must help me. Duros must be stopped and captured before he does more damage."

"It was not your fault," said the old spider who seemed to be the chief. "They exceeded their orders. We will tell you about the Eternal Rock. As Craa told you, it has always been there, and as far as we know, it is not hollow. It was built by an ancient race that once lived here, but we don't know its purpose. I hope you can believe this."

"Yes," said Kevin after checking with Spectro. "I do believe you. But why was Craa so agitated when I asked him about it?"

"It would seem that Duros knows something about it and told us we weren't to mention it," said the old spider. "It's obviously important to him, but we don't know why."

There was no more that they could learn from the Collandans, so they said goodbye to them and 'jumped' back to their ship where they found Tracy looking a lot more healthy, surrounded by Murin who were fetching her things to eat.

"About time you got back," she said without looking round. "Sniffer wants a walk."

Kevin had completely forgotten about Sniffer who had been left in a side cabin and was lying on the floor with his head hanging out, looking very sorry for himself.

"It wouldn't hurt for him to have a run outside," said Kevin. "Would it?"

"I would have let him out myself," said Crispin, "but I wasn't sure what was out there and if it was safe."

"I think it would be all right," said Quartok. "As long as he isn't too long."

Kevin went to the hatch and opened it and looked out, but before he could say anything he had been propelled forward, landing in a heap outside while Sniffer bounded over him and disappeared into the distance. Kevin picked himself up, brushed himself down, and climbed back into the ship.

"You're right," he said to Tracy. "He did need a walk."

They decided that it might be nice to stretch their legs outside and all climbed out and started to stroll slowly round the spaceship.

"I'm going to have a look at that tower," said Kevin.

"Perhaps you should wait until Sniffer returns and then we all can go," said Lartop. "We could take the ship with us so that we had somewhere comfortable to sit while we thought how we could get into it."

"Well all right," said Kevin. "I don't think Sniffer will be long."

Kevin sat down and leaned against one of the supporting legs of the ship and decided he would have a little chat with Spectro.

"I've been thinking," he said in his mind. "When we first met Mondarwi, on Earth, you led me to believe he was genuine. Why didn't you tell me he was lying? After all, you can tell when people are lying, can't you?"

"Yes, I can, generally," answered Spectro. "But at that time, he wasn't lying. He actually believed what he was saying. Duros is quite clever in that way. He doesn't trust other people to lie for him so he makes them believe what he says is true. That way they are much more convincing."

"Oh, I see," said Kevin. "Now, about this tower, what is it and how do we get in?"

"It is a very ancient object," said Spectro, "and I don't think you can actually get into it."

"But it seems as if Marlitta is in there," said Kevin. "So, it must be possible to get into it."

"It is possible that it acts like a relay station for crystal communications," said Spectro. "Marlitta is probably somewhere else but you are detecting her through the tower."

"Is it possible to tell where she really is, then?" asked Kevin.

"Probably," replied Spectro, "but I don't have any actual data on that. You see, this is right at the edge of our civilised universe and it was most likely created by other beings from outside our universe, using technology that we don't know about."

"What would happen if I went inside the tower using my mind sight?"

"I have no way of telling," said Spectro. "It could be dangerous, but I don't know for sure."

Kevin thought about this for a bit, then closed his eyes and his viewpoint inside his mind swept across the ground, out over the cliffs and across the sea to the island with the tower. He could sense the presence of Marlitta but could not communicate with her. He moved his viewpoint right up to the smooth side of the tower as if he were holding his ear to it. Nothing changed so he moved forward a bit more and it was like pushing through the skin of a large bubble. There was a sudden change in the sound, sight and feel of everything around him. There were strange birds singing and the light was much more brilliant than it had been, and as his eyes got used to the glare he realised that he was inside a walled garden. The walls were made of shining marble that reflected the light and there were archways and alcoves of the same material. Amazing flowers grew out of alabaster pots, flowers he had never seen or could have imagined before.

He turned his field of view round to see what was behind him and was surprised to see another tower, similar to the one on the island, but this time it was gleaming white and only about twice his own height. He looked about him wondering if anyone was about, but there was no one. He could now sense Marlitta's presence very strongly so he moved his point of view towards the source of the feeling.

He drifted weightlessly along the paths, across a lawn, and up a slight rise towards a group of what could only be trees, though they were not like any he knew. They were tall and slender and purple, rather like giant rhubarb, but more delicate. The leaves were more of a blue colour with purple veins branching out across their surfaces.

The ground beneath the trees was covered in what looked like a type of moss with colourful fungi scattered about in small groups, some forming rings.

Beyond the trees was a large lake on which swan birds of various sizes, all very colourful. They were rather like the ducks and geese that he would see at home. As he watched, a small group of them swooped in from the sky and alighted on the water.

Beyond the lake was a grassy bank leading up to a flat lawn in front of a small building of alabaster, gleaming white in the afternoon sun. The unusual thing was that all the grass was green, which stood out among all the other colours.

Kevin was drawn towards the building, so he let his point of vision drift out over the lake towards the building. He had grown quite used to using his 'mind sight' but still felt vulnerable, as if other could see and harm him although he knew that no-one would sense his presence.

As he approached the building he was startled to see someone emerge from an archway at the front and walk slowly across the grass towards him. It was a young woman in a long flowing white gown who looked as if she had been taken straight from a child's fairy story. As she came closer he was amazed to realise that it was Marlitta.

"Marlitta," he exclaimed, but she didn't react. Of course she wouldn't. She couldn't hear him so, without giving it any more thought, he 'jumped' and appeared in front of her, sitting on the grass with his head in his hands and his eyes shut. Leaning against him was Sniffer looking a bit startled.

"Who are you?" exclaimed Marlitta, and Kevin opened his eyes and looked up at her.

"Don't you recognise me?" asked Kevin in surprise.

"Kevin?" she asked tentatively. "Is it you?"

"Of course it is," he said scrambling to his feet.

"But it's been so long," she said, "I thought you had forgotten me."

"Well I came as quickly as I could," he said indignantly. "I came as soon as I could track you down."

"But I've been here for over a year now," she said.

"Don't be silly," he said, "it's only been a few days since you were captured."

Sniffer walked over to Marlitta and sniffed her.

"You remember Sniffer?" said Kevin.

"Oh yes. But I really have been here for a very long time."

"How did you get here?" asked Kevin.

"I was taken in a space ship of some sort to a planet, near the one where we met the Collandans, and was handed over to some people similar to Earth people. They didn't use crystals, in fact I don't think they had them or even knew about them. They moved from planet to planet using tall pillars of stone. There's one down in the garden over there." She pointed to where Kevin had come from. "I tried to use it to get out of here but couldn't get it to work."

"Are these people still here?" asked Kevin.

"Oh yes," she replied. "They treat me quite well and are quite friendly, but they know I can't escape so they don't need to threaten me or anything."

"Do they say why they are keeping you here?" he asked.

"They are returning a favour to someone who helped them," said Marlitta. "I assume it is Duros but they don't say who it is or why he wants me here."

"I think it was to try and trap me," said Kevin, "or keep me occupied while he is up to something else. But I don't know what that is."

Suddenly Kevin noticed that there were two tall people standing outside the white building. They had their arms folded and their feet slightly apart. They were dressed in long white flowing robes similar to the one Marlitta wore.

"I think we have company," said Kevin. Marlitta turned, and seeing the two newcomers, walked towards them.

"I would like to introduce you to a friend of mine," she said. "This is Kevin, Master of the Universe."

"Welcome Kevin," said the one on the left. "To what do we owe this pleasure?"

"I have come to collect my friend," he said. "Why have you kept her here?"

"We were asked to look after her."

"Who by?"

"Someone we have an agreement with."

"So, what's he doing for you?" asked Kevin.

"We have a score to settle with our home planet and he is going to help us."

"And all you have to do is look after Marlitta?" said Kevin. "It doesn't seem a very fair deal. Anyway, where is your home planet?"

"Rather a long story," said the other person in white, "but it is not for us to tell you these things. If you wish to know more you will have to wait and meet the one who controls."

"And what is his name?" asked Kevin losing his patience.

"That is his name, 'The One Who Controls'. I am 'The One Who Serves', and this is 'The Other Who

Serves'." Without another word they turned and walked back into the building.

Marlitta, seeing that Kevin didn't want to leave it there said, "Let them go. We will wait here for 'The One Who Controls'."

"You knew these stupid names, did you?" Kevin was feeling very cross as he felt they had been making fun of him. "I thought they were having a joke."

"No," said Marlitta, "that's something you can be sure of. They do not joke. In fact, I have never seen them smile. They're the most dismal people I have ever met."

"Is this control freak like that too?"

"No," said Marlitta. He's a bit more normal. He does smile, but it's not a happy smile."

"So how long do we wait for him?"

"I don't know," said Marlitta. "He could arrive in a few minutes, or he could be a few hours. Let me show you round the estate while we wait."

Chapter Twelve – The One Who Controls

While they waited for 'The One Who Controls', Marlitta showed Kevin around the gardens and Kevin told her what had happened while they had been separated. Marlitta was amazed at the short time that had elapsed for Kevin while she had been here for over a year, or so it seemed.

"After you escaped," said Marlitta, "I didn't know what was going to happen. I had been stung by one of those nasty little white ones and couldn't move much at all. I must have lost my crystal when I was stung. Eventually I was taken out to a space ship and dropped in the hold. I don't know how long I was there but it seemed an age.

"Eventually, we landed and I was taken out into a building rather like the ones on Collandar, and the web was removed so that I could move about and stand up again. It took rather a long time for my legs and arms to start working again but when I could walk they took me into another room where a large man was waiting. It was a surprise to see someone of human form after all those eight-legged creatures.

"He was very pleasant and said that he had been asked to look after me until someone came for me. I thought it must have been you that arranged it so I went along with him. He didn't have a crystal but he brought me here using the towers. They seem to work like crystals in transporting you over long distances, but that's all they seem to do.

"They gave me a room in that building over there, and I was given new clothes because my old ones had been ruined when they removed the web, and they give me food at regular intervals. I can wander wherever I want to. I even tried to use the tower to get me out of here but it doesn't work for me. You obviously have to know how to work it."

"Did they mention Duros at all?" asked Kevin.

"No, not a word. After you didn't arrive to take me back I began to think that you had deserted me."

"No, I would never do that," said Kevin vehemently.

"And then I thought that you wouldn't be able to find me because I had been brought here using the towers."

"Well it was difficult," said Kevin, "but we got your crystal back and I used that to trace you. It took me to a tower, much bigger than the one here, and I used the mind sight to go through the tower. Then I 'jumped' and here I am. Which reminds me, here is your crystal."

Kevin fished the crystal out of his pocket and handed it to her. Marlitta took it eagerly and hung it round her neck with the gold chain that was attached to it.

"That feels better," she said. "Everything feels empty without it, and now I don't feel so trapped."

"Have you any idea where we are?" asked Kevin.

"Not really, but I think we must be at the edge of the galaxy, a very long way from what we call the civilised universe. It's so far away that I don't know if we can 'jump' that far."

Sniffer growled and bristled up the fur on the back of his neck.

"What is it, Sniffer?" said Kevin looking in the direction that Sniffer was looking. At first there was nothing to see, then a figure appeared and walked towards them. Kevin gave Sniffer a mental command to stay.

"At least we can communicate using the crystals," said Marlitta's voice inside his head. "This is 'The One Who Controls'."

"Greetings," he said as he approached them. Sniffer growled again. "I hope you have that animal under control."

"He'll be OK if you don't threaten us," said Kevin. "He's a very good judge of character."

"Perhaps you would like to accompany me back to the villa," he continued. "And perhaps have some refreshment with me. It will be more comfortable and easier to talk." So saying, he turned and walked towards the white building. Kevin and Marlitta walked behind him and Sniffer walked with them keeping a close eye on the newcomer.

They went into the building and followed 'The One Who Controls' down a corridor and into a room where food had been arranged on a large table in the centre. All the walls were shining white and one wall was made up entirely of glass giving a marvellous view of the gardens and the valley and mountains beyond.

"Please be seated," he said. "I hope there is food here to your liking."

They sat and ate some of the food, which was delicious, and after a while, 'The One', as Kevin now thought of him, looked at each of them and said, "What would you like to know?"

Kevin was a bit surprised by this. "Well, first of all I would like to know where we are," he said.

"We are on a planet that we call Artemis," he said. "It is situated at the very rim of the galaxy diametrically opposite the sector that you come from. We have been here for about five thousand standard years, which was when we left our home planet."

"And where was that?" asked Marlitta. "No one will tell me."

"It is a planet of little importance over in your sector. We called it Earth."

"Earth?" exclaimed Kevin. "But that's where I come from."

"That is what I thought. We were driven out five thousand earth-years ago by the increasing population of savages, your ancestors. After the flood, my civilisation was decimated and we survived in one small region. We gradually grew stronger and built monuments, temples and many giant pyramids which we used to try and communicate with other beings in the galaxy."

"That sounds like ancient Egypt," said Kevin.

"I don't know the name, but that must be what you call it. Are our pyramids still there?"

"Oh yes," said Kevin. "But no one knows what they were built for. Most people think they were tombs for the pharaohs."

"What a quaint idea," he said "No, that wasn't their intention at all. Anyway, as I was saying, the other races that survived the flood were spreading across the land. They didn't make things or grow things. They started off as hunters and then found it was easier to attack and kill those who grew food and made artefacts and take them for themselves. They grew stronger and stronger until they started to threaten our own world. We were not warriors and had no defence against them so we were eventually forced to leave."

"Where did you go?" said Kevin puzzled.

"We all went into the great pyramid and passed through the portal into another world; this one."

"You mean that the pyramid worked like one of those pillars out there?"

"Exactly. And it was that very pillar, as you call it, which acted as the other end of the portal, as we call it. When we arrived here we found a world in a very primitive state. There was no intelligent life but plenty of wild animals and vegetation. Some of the animals were very dangerous, but we survived and made this our home."

"So how did you meet up with Duros?" asked Kevin.

"Duros?" said 'The One'. "Oh, you mean the little man who visited us just over a year ago. He discovered how to use the portals and visited us several times. He learned about our history and offered to make amends for us. In exchange he asked us to keep you here and look after you. He brought you here using the portals."

"So how is he supposed to be making amends?" asked Marlitta. "I don't understand."

"Simple, my dear," he continued. "He is going to destroy the race of savages that drove us from our world and then we will be able to return."

Kevin went white. Duros was going to destroy the earth, but how?

"He can't do that on his own," said Kevin. "Not on his own."

"Who said he was on his own? Oh no. He has made good use of the portals and has met many other races, one of which is an ancient race of warriors. They are going to take a battle fleet to earth and destroy all intelligent life, and there is nothing you can do about it."

"But I have a crystal of power," said Kevin. "And I can stop him."

"I think not. You might like to try out your crystal and see if it works so far from the galactic centre. You may be disappointed."

Kevin tried to zap one of the dishes on the table, but nothing happened. Then he tried to 'jump' to the other side of the table and again nothing happened.

"I think we're in trouble," he said in his mind to Marlitta.

"At least we can communicate, so all the power isn't gone," she answered.

"I'll show you to your room," said 'The One' to Kevin and stood up and walked from the room. Kevin shrugged his shoulders and got up and followed.

"I said Sniffer was a good judge of character," he said. "Didn't I?"

After that they were left to their own devices, as it was obvious that they couldn't escape using their crystals. Kevin examined the pillar, or portal, to see if he could find out how to use it, but to no avail. Even Spectro couldn't help.

"It's weird," said Kevin to Marlitta as they stood before the portal. "I used the portal to get here so we ought to be able to use it to escape."

"How did you do it then?" asked Marlitta.

"Well, I used the portal to see through using the mind-sight. Then when I saw you I 'jumped', so the portal must have helped me get here."

"Well you could try it in reverse," said Marlitta. "Go on, give it a try."

Kevin sat down and put his head in his hands and opened up his mind sight. He could see the portal and Marlitta standing beside it. He moved his viewpoint towards the portal and kept going. As he felt as if he would crash into it the view changed; he was through. Before him was the island and sea with the mainland beyond. He zoomed out over the sea and across the flat land towards the rugged hills where he had left the ship and his friends. Soon they came into sight, or at least the ship was still there but he couldn't see the others. They must be inside the ship.

"I can see them," said Kevin. "Quickly, hold my hand and hold onto Sniffer."

He felt Marlitta's hand grip his and Sniffer lean against his side, so he 'jumped', but nothing happened. He opened his eyes and they were still in front of the portal.

"It didn't work," said Kevin. "I could see the ship so clearly, but when I 'jumped' nothing happened. But it worked the other way when I came here, so why won't it work going back?"

"Perhaps 'The One Who Controls' is right," said Marlitta. "When you were at the other end the crystal worked because you were nearer the source of power that the crystal uses. Here there is no source of power, or very little, so we can't 'jump'. We'll have to find out how to use the portal as it was intended."

"I've tried that," said Kevin. "Even Spectro can't help, so how are we going to find out how to work the portals? He's not going to tell us, is he?"

"He might if we asked him the right way," said Marlitta.

"And how do you intend to do that?"

"Not me," she said. "Not you, but Sniffer. I think he's scared of Sniffer. I'm sure we could get him to talk with Sniffer's help.

Chapter Thirteen – The Way Out

Several days passed and there had been no sign of 'The One Who Controls'. Other people who appeared from time to time doing their various jobs couldn't tell them when he would next appear. They had begun to wonder if he knew what they were intending, but they didn't know that for certain so they would just have to wait until he appeared again.

Kevin had been trying to get the message through to Sniffer and he thought he understood what was needed. They wouldn't know for sure until 'The One' returned.

They filled in their time trying to find ways to work out how the portals worked, without much success. They worked in a different way to the crystals so there was no point of contact. The best he was able to do was to use his mind sight from time to time to make sure that Quartok and the others hadn't left without him, but they seemed to be happy to wait with the ship. He wished he could contact them, but that wasn't possible.

They found that they could walk any distance from the white building, in any direction. There were no fences to keep them in. It just showed that no one expected them to be able to escape.

On the fourth day, 'The One' returned.

"I thought you might like to know that Duros is leading his invasion force to the earth and will be there in about ten days," said 'The One'. "Then your people will be no more."

"So, you would kill millions of helpless people, just out of spite?" said Kevin in disgust.

"Oh no," said 'The One'. "We couldn't do such a thing. As I said before, we are peace-loving people. If your planet is destroyed it will be down to Duros, not us."

"But you want him to do it. You said so."

"But that is a completely different matter."

"I don't see how," said Kevin. "Anyway, if you are so peace loving, why are you keeping us here against our will?"

"We are not keeping you here. You can leave whenever you wish, but while you remain here we will treat you like our guests. That is our way."

"So how can we leave?" said Marlitta.

"You know where the portal is. Use that."

"But we don't know how to," said Kevin. "If you could tell us how to use it we could leave. If you don't tell us, then you are as good as holding us prisoner."

"You have a strange way of looking at things," said 'The One'. "We have no obligation to tell you anything. If you do not know how to operate the portal that isn't our fault."

"Perhaps you could be persuaded to help us," said Kevin. "Sniffer!"

Sniffer leapt forward and knocked 'The One' to the floor and sat on him.

"Now," said Kevin, "perhaps you would like to think again about helping us?"

"No," said 'The One' defiantly. "That is something I will not do. If your animal kills me then you will never know, and what is more, no one will bring you food or give you shelter. You will have to wander in the wild until you either die of hunger or are eaten by one of the fiercer animals that wander there."

It was obvious that they were not going to get anywhere this way so Kevin called off Sniffer who got up grudgingly and walked over to the corner and sat down and sulked.

"I wouldn't have let him hurt you," said Kevin, "but we really need to know how to get out of here."

"And as I said, I cannot tell you. I have given my word that I won't and I always keep to my word. However, I can tell you this, the portals were built many tens of thousands of years ago by a people who have long disappeared. We don't know who they were or what happened to them, but they have left clues which can easily be found and if you are clever enough you will find your way out."

'The One' got to his feet, brushed himself down, and with a sideways glance at Sniffer, he left.

"So much for that idea," said Kevin. "What now?"

"Well at least he gave us a clue as to how we can find the way out," said Marlitta. "This ancient civilisation must have left writings, or something, somewhere where we can find them."

"You mean like statues or large stones with writing on," said Kevin thinking about ancient Egypt. "Where shall we start looking?"

"Perhaps Sniffer could help," said Marlitta. "Give him some mental pictures of what we're looking for and send him off to find them."

"Good idea," said Kevin. He immediately started sending picture messages to Sniffer, who looked slightly bemused. Then with a yelp he was off at a gallop. "Right, now we wait and see."

They strolled through into the room where they ate and sat down at the table and nibbled some fruit. They waited for a long time, but Sniffer didn't return, so they got up and strolled outside. It was a cool day, slightly overcast, but fine. Down by the lake they watched the duck-like birds squabbling over fishing rights. The birds were all very colourful on Artemis, at least all the ones they had seen. Kevin was fascinated to see some small birds with very long beaks, sipping nectar from the deep bell-shaped blooms. They reminded him of humming birds back on earth.

Suddenly there was a sound of something crashing through the undergrowth behind them, and Sniffer burst through in great excitement, then turned and bounded off again. When they didn't follow him he bounded back and tried again.

"I think we'd better follow him before he explodes," said Kevin. "Come on."

They chased after him but couldn't keep the pace up for long and had to stop, panting, to regain their breath. Then they walked on again and Sniffer kept bounding off and then bounding back again to make sure they were following.

They went across the garden and out into the woodland beyond where the tree grew closer together than they did near the garden. Whenever the sun broke through the clouds, it made a dappled pattern on the ground and on the old gnarled tree trunks. Soon they came out of the wood and onto a shelf of flat rock of blue slate. At the edge of the shelf was a sheer drop of several hundred metres, which made Kevin a bit wary. He wasn't scared of heights but he knew the dangers and made sure of his footing.

The shelf narrowed as the rock rose up on their right and formed an overhang.

"Careful where you step," he said to Marlitta. "It's a bit slippy round here."

They went carefully as the path wound round the side of the cliff until it stopped abruptly at the entrance to a cave.

"Watch out for animals," said Marlitta. "Remember what he said about dangerous animals."

"I think Sniffer would take care of that," said Kevin, "and he shows no sign of there being anything to worry about."

Even so, they entered the cave very cautiously. It was dark in the cave and it took a while for their eyes to grow accustomed to it. At the back of the cave they could see a number of large flat stones which looked as if they had been standing up in a straight line at one time. Now they were standing at different angles, and one had fallen face down on the floor of the cave. Kevin knelt down and ran his fingers over the flat face of the stones.

"I think there is some writing," he said, "but I can't make out what it says. It is in strange symbols."

"Can Spectro help?" asked Marlitta.

Kevin went quiet for a few minutes. "No," he said. "Spectro says that they are not anything known in our part of the galaxy so he can't help."

"I thought 'The One Who Controls' said that it would tell us how to get out of here," said Marlitta.

"I think he knew we wouldn't be able to read it," said Kevin. "I think we're wasting our time here, let's go."

They made their way back up the narrow path out onto the wider ledge and finally back onto the flat ground. Sniffer dashed off again, still hunting for more ancient writings.

"Perhaps you should call him off," said Marlitta despondently. "He's not going to find anything useful."

"Well he might as well keep looking," said Kevin. "It can't do any harm."

As they walked back towards the house, Sniffer came back and led them to several other old monuments, but however interesting they may have been, they were no help in finding out how the portals worked. They went back to the portal and walked round it. Kevin looked into it with his mind sight but all he could see was the island on the planet where the others were waiting for him to return.

The next day they walked further afield in the other direction which led out onto a flat grassy plain with groups of small trees dotted around. In the distance they could see herds of grazing animals, some quite small and others rather large. Kevin wondered why they didn't wander into the garden, as there didn't seem to be anything to stop them.

As they passed one small group of trees Marlitta suddenly froze on the spot, staring at the dark shadow beneath the branches.

"What's the matter," asked Kevin using the mind speech.

"There's something crouching beneath the trees."

Kevin looked more closely and thought he could just make out something that looked rather like a big cat crouching, ready to spring. He called Sniffer back, again using the mind call, and before long Sniffer came racing up to them eagerly. Kevin flashed the picture of the crouching animal into Sniffer's mind causing him to turn his head quickly towards the trees. Suddenly a large black animal sprung out of the cover and came menacingly towards them. Sniffer growled and the fur on the back of his neck stood up. If there were to be a fight it looked as if Sniffer would come off worst so Kevin thought he would try his mind control over the animal. He flashed pictures into its mind and it stood there, obviously puzzled. Kevin thought of fire blazing up in front of him and the animal backed away. As it turned they both shouted at it and waved their arms and Sniffer barked. As if trying to save face, the animal loped away into the long grass.

"Perhaps we had better go back into the safety of the garden," said Kevin.

"A good idea," said Marlitta striding off in that direction. Sniffer looked a bit disappointed but followed them closely back to the garden.

As if to make up for not being able to see off the big black animal, Sniffer decided he would chase some smaller ones. There were a number of smaller creatures that seemed to come into the garden; one type was very like the rabbits that Kevin used to see in the field at the bottom of his garden. Sniffer thought these would make good sport, and probably good eating too, so he chased the first one he saw. The rabbit ran off at a great pace, dodging to right and to left, and Sniffer, who was larger and heavier found it difficult to change direction as quickly. Soon the rabbit had escaped.

Next, he tried a subtler approach. He hid under a bush until one came past him and then he darted out and almost caught the first one before it disappeared down a hole.

The next one dashed off through the bushes in the direction of the portal. It was out of sight in no time, but this time Sniffer thought he would use his best feature, his nose, and started sniffing along the ground in the direction the rabbit had gone.

Having nothing better to do, Kevin and Marlitta followed him to see if he was going to be successful this time. He followed the scent around bushes, through bushes and finally out into the open in front of the portal which Sniffer headed straight towards. When he got to it he stood looking puzzled. He looked up to the top of it but it was obvious that the rabbit hadn't gone up there. Then he started sniffing the portal itself and his head disappeared into it quickly followed by the rest of him.

Kevin and Marlitta were left standing there with their mouths open. Then the rabbit shot out of the portal and disappeared into the bushes.

"So that's it," said Kevin. "It couldn't be simpler. You just walk into it."

He stepped forward and continued walking and suddenly found himself on the little rocky island as the sun was setting over the sea. Then Marlitta was beside him. Kevin grabbed Sniffer and took Marlitta's hand and almost immediately they were back at the spacecraft.

Chapter Fourteen – What Next?

Quartok and the others didn't seem too worried when Kevin returned, as in their time, he hadn't been away very long. They were overjoyed to see Marlitta and wanted to hear all about their adventures. They went into the spacecraft and had some food and Kevin told them all about the impending invasion of earth.

"Well if we send a battle fleet," said Quartok, "it will take too long. They will have destroyed earth before we can get there."

"I don't know what sort of weapons they have," said Kevin, "but they don't have any crystals other than the little one Duros has got hold of. In their part of the galaxy they seem to use those portals to get about."

"What are those?" asked Crispin.

"That's how we got back," said Kevin. "Crystals don't work out there but they've got these pillar things on each planet and use them to travel across the galaxy. There's one on an island over there. The spiders called it the Eternal Rock. I don't think they know what it is. Anyway, we know they don't have crystals, so it's possible I could do something to stop them."

"It would be a big risk," said Lartop, "and we can't be sure it would be successful."

"No, but we have to try," said Kevin. "It's my planet they want to destroy so I have to try. Anyway, I'll have an advantage with my crystal. Even if we send some battle cruisers they might destroy them all. We don't know what weapons they have and they might be better than ours."

"You have a point," said Quartok. "But we'll have to go carefully. First we must get to your planet and see if we can locate the battle fleet."

"We can't just go straight to earth. The people there know nothing about all this and we have to keep in secret. Perhaps we could take this ship to the moon and make our base on the side away from the earth."

"What's this about going to the moon?" It was Tracy who was just emerging from a side cabin.

"Are you feeling better?" asked Kevin.

"A bit, thank you," she said, then seeing Marlitta, "who's this?"

"Tracy, this is Marlitta. Marlitta, this is Tracy Bagshot from earth." Kevin felt quite grown up make introductions properly.

"What's she doing here?" asked Marlitta with a hard edge to her voice. "No one from earth should know about you."

"I know," said Kevin. "She found out by accident. Anyway, she's been helping me to find you."

There was obviously a bit of frostiness in the air. It had never occurred to Kevin that they might have been jealous of each other. It was just ridiculous. It wasn't as if Tracy was his girlfriend or anything. Perish the thought. And he hadn't thought of Marlitta as a girlfriend. After all, she was older than he was, especially after the time slips that occurred when they were in different parts of the galaxy. Admittedly she didn't look older than he did as she was from a smaller race.

"Tracy," said Kevin feeling that he should take charge of the situation, "why don't you go back into your cabin and have a lie down? I don't think you've fully recovered from that bite yet and we have a lot to discuss."

Tracy didn't want to be left out of any discussions and she certainly didn't want to leave Kevin with this newcomer. She was far too pretty to be left alone with him. "I'm all right here, thank you," she said and sat down at the side of the main cabin with Sniffer."

"All right," said Kevin. "But don't keep butting in."

"As if I would."

Quartok seemed to think that Kevin had a point and perhaps they should try it his way, while Lartop, who was much more cautious, didn't like it at all. Crispin, having a scientific interest, wanted to know how the technical side was going to work, and Kevin didn't have any answers for any of them.

"We'll just have to play it by ear," he said. The others looked blank. "I mean we'll just have to wait and see what the situation is when we get there and then decide what to do."

"Oh, I see," said Marlitta. "Yes, I suppose that is all we can do. Can we get this tub to the earth system?"

"Tub?" said Crispin indignantly. "This is the pride of the fleet. It has all the latest instrumentation and navigational aids. There is no other like it."

"That I can well believe," said Kevin. Crispin wasn't sure how to take that but said nothing.

"It doesn't have any weaponry, does it?" said Marlitta.

"Not a lot," said Crispin. "That wasn't its purpose. There are some low power lasers and an antipersonnel force field, but beyond that, nothing."

"Well, I don't think we intended shooting it out with the alien battle fleet," said Kevin. "Our main weapon is my crystal."

"I thought that wasn't working on earth," said Marlitta. "That was why I had to come and get you off."

"Spectro says that it should be OK now. Earth has come out of the energy shadow, whatever that is."

"If we can't land on earth," said Quartok, "how will you be able to 'jump' accurately to the moon of your planet?"

"Well, I can visualise the earth from space and 'jump' us to there. Then we'll have to fly to the back of the moon and find a good place to land and wait," said Kevin. "Then I can use the mind sight to scan space around the solar system to see if I can spot the fleet. When we find it I'll be able to find out what weapons they have and what they intend to do."

"I want to go home," said Tracy.

"Not just now, Tracy," said Kevin. "You have to stay with us until we've got rid of Duros."

They spent the rest of the evening discussing the details and then turned in for a good night's sleep. In the morning, Kevin 'jumped' back to the Collandan city to leave a last message with their chief. He wanted to make sure that if Duros contacted them again, they wouldn't give away their plans. Kevin knew that if put under pressure they would tell him anything he wanted to know so he thought it best to tell them a false story to keep Duros off their scent. He told them that they would return to the crystal city and renew their search for Duros from there, as they had no idea where he was. He hoped that would work and thanked the old spider for his co-operation. Then he 'jumped' back to the ship.

He linked up his crystal with the ship's navigation system again and leaned back in his chair, closed his eyes and concentrated his thoughts on earth. Soon the screen in the main cabin cleared and earth drifted into view. Then the viewpoint changed and moved around the planet until its moon came into view, drifting closer and closer until it nearly filled the screen. Then there was a lurching sensation as they 'jumped' and the gravity they felt was the artificial gravity of the ship. The moon was still floating there on the screen.

"Now," said Quartok. "I'll take over and manoeuvre the ship to the far side of the moon. Then we'll have a look for somewhere to land."

The ship started to move, and this time everyone could feel the acceleration. Slowly, the moon seemed to revolve as the little ship moved around it until it was on the far side from the earth. Then Quartok started to bring in closer and closer to the surface.

"It's a bit rough down there," said Crispin. "Craters everywhere. It looks as if this system has had a battering from asteroids or something. I hope it is all over now."

"I think there are meteorites still hitting the earth from time to time," said Kevin. "Does it matter?"

"Yes," said Crispin. Your moon has no atmosphere to protect it, so even small meteorites could be dangerous. I'll have to set up the deflector shields to protect us from above."

"That looks a likely place," said Quartok pointing to a large crater with a flat bottom. "I'll take us down there."

The ship set off again, slowly sinking towards the moon's surface. The crater got larger and larger until there was a jolt and they were down.

"Are we really on the moon?" asked Tracy. "Wait 'til I tell them back home."

"But you won't tell them," said Kevin sternly. "Will you?"

"I suppose not," she said sullenly. "But I wish I could."

"I'd better take a look round," said Kevin closing his eyes again. The screen flickered and then showed the ship sitting in the centre of the crater. The dust had settled, as there was no air to stop it. The outside of the crater was made up of a high wall, which meant that they couldn't be seen except from, directly above.

The viewpoint raced towards the crater wall and everyone gasped, but at the last moment their viewpoint rose up above the wall and out onto the moon's surface. It all looked much the same with rocks and craters everywhere. Then suddenly their viewpoint rotated upwards and shot out into space. For most of the time the screen was black except for a scattering of stars in the distance. As there wasn't much to see, they started talking amongst themselves while Kevin did his search. Every now and again one of the planets would sweep into view and Kevin would have a look at it and then move on. When he found Mars, he went in and had a much closer look at the surface.

"Why are you looking at this one?" asked Crispin.

"This is Mars," said Kevin. "I wanted to see if I could find the missing Mars Lander. It landed on the surface but didn't send any signals back."

"Is that important?" asked Quartok.

"No," said Kevin. "But I was curious. I don't think I'll be able to find it but it was worth a quick look."

The surface of Mars flowed across the screen for a while as Kevin continued his search. He was fascinated to be able to see what no other person from earth had seen as clearly.

"There isn't much chance that you'll find anything," said Crispin, "if you don't know exactly where to look."

"I suppose you're right," said Kevin. "But it's interesting to see the surface of our closest neighbour."

"But you've walked on the surface of planets on the far side of the galaxy," continued Crispin. "Aren't they more interesting than this dust heap?"

"Well, yes I suppose so," said Kevin. "But somehow this is more real. I've seen photos from the Mars Explorer and I can see Mars in the sky at night. The other planets I've been to don't seem real somehow."

"I think I know what you mean," said Marlitta. "But we should really be looking for Duros and his fleet."

The viewpoint slowed, then shot out into space again. They spent the next hour scanning the sky for any sign of the fleet but found nothing. They had the opportunity to study hundreds of asteroids in minute detail and saw the wonders of the rings of Saturn at close quarters, but no battle fleet swept onto their screen.

Kevin needed a rest so they stopped their search and had something to eat.

"You'll have to try a wider sweep," said Quartok. "And don't forget, they may not come in on the plane of the planets. You were following the planets' orbits."

"Yes, I suppose you're right," said Kevin. "Pity we haven't got radar."

"What's radar?" asked Crispin.

"It's what we use on earth to follow the movement of aircraft and ships," said Kevin. "It uses radio waves."

"I don't think that would work at the distances we're interested in," said Crispin. "I think we'll just have to carry on with the crystal."

"It's a pity you can't do this with your crystals," said Kevin. "Isn't there anything we could do, Spectro?" he added in his mind.

"Yes," answered Spectro. "I can link all the crystals to yours and you can all search, except for Tracy. Her crystal isn't powerful enough."

Kevin explained to the others what they were going to do, and soon they were all settled in their flight seats, reclining comfortably with their eyes closed. It was a bit of a novelty to the others, but they soon got used to it, and having divided up the heavens so they each had their own sector to search, they started to sweep the outer reaches of the solar system for any trace of a battlefleet.

Chapter Fifteen – Battle Fleet

They all searched the skies for several hours. Occasionally one or other of them would doze off and sleep for a while, then wake again, refreshed, and continue the search. There wasn't the same feeling of day and night on the moon as they were permanently in shadow. When they felt it should be morning they got up and stretched their legs and had some breakfast.

"This is really boring," said Tracy. "I wish I could help."

"Well you could keep an eye on the screen and see if you can spot anything that we might miss," said Kevin, "and bring us a snack every now and again."

"What exactly are we looking for?" she asked.

"Did you see 'Star Wars'? asked Kevin. Tracy nodded. "Well we're looking for something like a fleet of space ships like that."

"Wow," said Tracy. "Then what do we do?"

"We won't know that 'til we find them."

They continued searching and Tracy watched the viewscreen, which showed a mixture of what they all were seeing. It was very confusing but it kept her occupied.

After another day's searching Kevin thought he saw something glittering in the distance. It might be nothing but he thought it worth a closer look so he zoomed in on it and was astounded and the sight before him. Tracy let out a cry and the others all adjusted their view to look at what Kevin was seeing. It was lucky he had caught the reflection from one of the windows, as the ships themselves were pitch black and very difficult to see in the dim light. There must have been at least a thousand ships apparently hanging motionless in space; huge black monsters.

"When will they get here?" he asked Spectro.

"At their present speed," he replied, "it would take them another three days. However, they will have to decelerate which will increase the time to six to seven days."

"Seems hard to believe they're moving so fast," said Kevin.

"Yes," said Spectro, "but in space it is difficult to sense speed."

They fixed the position of the fleet in their ship's memory so that they could go back to it again without having to search for ages.

"What now?" said Lartop.

"I think I should probe inside some of the ships and see if I can find out what they intend to do," said Kevin.

"Well go carefully," said Quartok. "Make sure you don't 'jump' inadvertently."

"I don't think that is likely," said Kevin. "I've been using the mind sight rather a lot recently. I think I have it pretty much under control."

"Perhaps a rest first," said Lartop, cautious as ever.

"Maybe you're right," said Kevin. So they sat down and had something to eat and relaxed a bit.

Kevin hadn't realised how tired he was so decided to have a little nap after he had eaten.

"What are those things?" asked Tracy.

"What do you think they are?" said Marlitta impatiently.

"Well there's no need to be like that," snapped Tracy. "You might be used to seeing things like that, but I'm not."

"They're space ships," said Kevin trying to prevent a squabble. "Battle ships to be precise and they're heading this way fast."

"What are they going to do?" pressed Tracy.

"Oh, they're just coming to have a picnic," said Marlitta sarcastically. "What do you think?"

"Why can't you two get along with each other?" said Kevin.

"I've had enough of this," snapped Marlitta and strode off into her private cabin.

"What's wrong with your girlfriend?" said Tracy. "Scared of the competition?"

"What are you talking about, Tracy?" said Kevin feeling a bit exasperated. "Marlitta is not a 'girlfriend' as you put it, and for that matter, neither are you. You are here simply because we couldn't risk leaving you where Duros could get to you again. And that battle fleet, out there, is coming to destroy the earth, so we have more to worry about than your petty girlish jealousies."

Kevin got up and went over to Marlitta's Cabin and knocked lightly. He heard a faint voice inside ask what he wanted so he went in and closed the door behind him.

"Now what is all this about?" he asked, sitting down on the bunk beside her.

"Oh, nothing really," she replied. "It just all got a bit much. Firstly, I was captured by those creatures and didn't know what was to happen to me. And then I was taken to a remote planet and held captive for ages, and you didn't come to rescue me. And when you did eventually get round to it, I find you have found yourself a girlfriend from your own planet. How do you expect me to feel?"

"Well I'm sorry you are so upset," said Kevin. "But it isn't like that at all. For one thing it was only a couple of days 'til I caught up with you. I know the time difference made it more like a year for you, but for me it was only a couple of days. And Tracy is not a girlfriend. I don't even like her. She had to be brought with us because she was a danger. Duros had got to her and was using her against us, well me actually, so we had to make sure he couldn't get to her again. And you talk as if you are my girlfriend or something. We are very close friends and I like you very much, but I hadn't thought of you as a girlfriend. I haven't thought of anyone as a girlfriend yet. But if I did, it would be nice if it were you. One day, maybe, when we are older. But now we have a battle fleet to deal with and I think that is enough for me to deal with at the moment."

"Maybe you're right," she said. "Sorry if I'm being silly."

Kevin left her in her cabin to rest and went to his own for a lie down for a bit. In some ways the battle fleet seemed so unreal that it wasn't half as frightening as girls wanting to be his girlfriend. At his age it wasn't cool to be friends with girls.

After he had rested, he went out into the main cabin again and had a drink and another mouthful of food, and then settled himself in his reclining seat ready to probe the battle fleet. He could find it quite easily now, as the position was stored in the ship's crystal. Quartok, Lartop and Crispin were joined by Marlitta to watch the viewscreen in the main cabin. Tracy went to her cabin to sulk.

The screen darkened at first and then the battle fleet swung onto the screen. There were ships of all shapes and sizes, mostly black, but some were dull red or brown, but there was one that stood out from the rest of them, not because of its colour which was a dark violet, but because of its size. It was enormous, especially when you looked at the size of the portholes and access doors which seemed minute. This would be the place to start, so Kevin steered his point of view towards this monster.

At the front near the top was a long viewport, which would most likely be the bridge where everything was controlled from, so Kevin headed towards this. When he got right up close he could see just how big this was, and it was very frightening even though he wasn't actually there himself.

He screwed up his courage and headed straight through the viewport to be met by a vast array of instrumentation with creatures sitting at dozens of consoles, constantly making adjustments. The creatures were like enormous black beetles and there was a continuous clicking sound as they moved their legs, or arms, or whatever they were, to adjust the controls in front of them.

He moved the viewpoint towards the centre of the bridge, and there sitting in a large reclining seat was a man of enormous proportions in human form. He had dark wrinkled skin and was dressed in what looked like shiny leather clothes of mediaeval design, with boots that could have come from a pantomime. But his face looked hard and cold, and it sent a shiver down Kevin's spine just to look at him.

"Definitely outworlders," said Quartok.

Kevin moved his viewpoint slightly and there, standing next to the reclining seat, stood Duros. What made them all gasp was the fact that he only came up to the knee of the seated figure. They were not talking so it wasn't possible to gain any information, and Kevin was about to look somewhere else when another huge figure came onto the bridge and approached the seated figure.

"Excuse the intrusion, Excellency," said the newcomer, "but I have new readings on the target."

"Put them on the screen, Granock."

The newcomer turned and gave instructions to one of the beetles, who immediately started keying in commands on his console. Kevin swung his angle of view round to take in the viewscreen, which was in front of the seated figure, just in time to see the earth float into view.

"Is this it?" he asked Duros.

"That's it," said Duros. "How close do we need to be to destroy all civilised life?"

"From here we could destroy the whole planet if you want, but to pick out centres of civilisation accurately, we need to move in much closer."

"Right," said Duros. "Do it."

The seated figure looked irritated but gave a signal with one finger and Granock moved away to carry out the orders.

"Let us understand one thing," he said. "After we have cleared this world of vermin, we will take control of it."

"Fair enough," said Duros. "As long as you remember that I have agreed with the Atlanteans that they can come back to their own planet."

"Of course they can come back, as long as they realise that we will be in control. We could do with some workers."

"Well Gdanos," said Duros. "I didn't give them any undertaking that they would be the only people there. We just agreed that I'd get rid of the present inhabitants for them."

"Good," said Gdanos. "Now let me concentrate on getting this fleet into position around the planet. We need to have every angle covered so that they don't get any warning. This planet has a moon, I believe?"

"Yes," said Duros. "A rough rock with no atmosphere. Why?"

"Just an obstacle we'll have to avoid," said Gdanos. "We'll have to go into stationary orbits around the planet. That should take us inside the orbit of the moon. Will there be any other obstacles?"

"I believe they've put up thousands of satellites for communication and such, but they're only small."

"Then we'd better make sure we set up orbits in the same direction," said Gdanos. "They may be small but I wouldn't want one of them to hit us at any speed."

"You should be able to plot their orbits when we get a bit closer," said Duros.

"Good," said Gdanos. "Now strap yourself into a deceleration couch. If we don't start slowing down we'll either hurtle straight past this little planet, or we'll crash into it."

Kevin decided he'd seen and heard enough for now so withdrew his point of view back out into space, and rather than just opening his eyes and losing the mind view, he decided to have a look around the earth himself. He could see the earth in the distance with the moon shining to one side of it, so he headed back towards it. The moon grew larger and larger as his viewpoint raced towards it. He was fascinated by the clarity of his view. He could see all the craters in great detail, but what was that? A light flashed but he couldn't make out what it was, so he zoomed in towards it as fast as he could. As he got closer he realised that it wasn't on the surface of the moon but orbiting it. It was a satellite of some sort. When he was looking at it from close up, he realised it was some sort of surveyor satellite that must be photographing the moon's surface in great detail. He wondered if it would be able to see their spacecraft.

He opened his eyes and dropped out of the mind sight.

"There's a satellite photographing the moon," said Kevin. "I don't want it to see us."

"Well perhaps you should destroy it then," said Quartok.

"But it's a scientific instrument," said Crispin. "You can't do that."

"Well let's wait and see if it's going to pass overhead," said Lartop. "If it does you can destroy it then."

"I'll set the ship's control system to track it," said Crispin.

"Good," said Quartok. "Now what are we going to do about this battle fleet?"

Chapter Sixteen – Battle Plans

"Can't I just zap them?" asked Kevin.

"Not enough power," said Spectro. "You could destroy one of the ships, perhaps, but not all of them. The best you could do is disable them, but then they would all crash into the planet causing no end of damage on the ground."

"You also have to take into account that those ships are full of people," said Lartop. "You can't just kill them all."

"But that's what they're going to do to the people of earth," said Quartok. "We can't let them do that."

"Perhaps there's another way," said Lartop. "A non-violent way."

"Well, I saw the size of that brute in charge," said Marlitta, "and I wouldn't like to discuss it with him."

"Nor would I," said Kevin. "I think their whole purpose in life is fighting."

"Well, that's what warriors do," said Marlitta.

"I wonder if the people of earth know what's happening," said Crispin. "Would they be able to detect the fleet, do you think?"

"I don't know," said Kevin. "They seem to be able to detect asteroids and comets and things way out in space, so they might be able to."

"What do you think they might do if they did detect them?" asked Quartok. "Have they any weapons they could use?"

"Nuclear missiles, maybe," said Kevin. "I expect they could send some of those."

"I don't think that would bother this lot," said Quartok. "They would just vaporise them in space. And if they were to wait until they got closer they would need hundreds of the things to destroy the whole fleet. It would be better if they didn't know, I think."

"Is there any way we could stop them using their weapons?" asked Kevin.

"It depends what they have," said Crispin. "If they're going to kill the population without causing damage to the buildings, they would be using some sort of radiation gun, I would think."

"How would we put those out of action?" asked Kevin.

"Not easily," said Crispin. "You would have to jump into the engine room of each ship in turn and fuse the power source using your crystal."

"It would need too much power," said Spectro. "You might not be able to put them all out of action and then you would be stranded on one of their ships."

"Not a good idea," said Kevin. "I'm a bit tired after all that so I'll be in my cabin if you need me."

He got up and went to his cabin. Three Murin appeared and set some food on the little cabin table and then disappeared as quickly and quietly. Kevin helped himself to a piece of fruit and lay back on his bunk taking small bites at it. He wondered what was happening back at home. Did his parents know what danger they were in? He wasn't sure how long he had been away and whether they were worried about him. They were used to him going off on his own, so wouldn't worry until he was overdue. Perhaps he should sneak a peek to see what they were doing, so he closed his eyes and thought of his living room back home. Suddenly it sprung into focus. His father was sitting on the settee watching television while his mother was doing her ironing. The news was on and nothing unusual seemed to be happening. Then he heard something about a new satellite orbiting the moon. It was going to map the moon's surface in much greater detail than had been done before.

"Kevin would be interested in this," said his father.

"What's that dear?" asked his mother.

"This moon satellite thing. He likes that sort of thing, doesn't he?"

"Oh yes," replied his mother. "But you know what he's like. It's all fantasy with him."

"I suppose you're right," said his father. "But I still think he would be interested. I'll tell him about it when he gets back."

Kevin switched off his mindsight and returned to his cabin. He was feeling quite tired now so he drifted off into troubled sleep. Sometime later he woke and got up and went out into the main cabin where Quartok, Lartop and Crispin were talking.

"Ah," said Quartok seeing Kevin enter. "We were trying to decide what to do to stop this fleet. Lartop is all for talking to them."

"He's welcome to try," said Kevin.

"That's not what I meant," said Lartop.

"You mean that you want someone else to talk to them?" said Kevin. He was feeling a bit crotchety, as he hadn't slept very well.

"That's not what I meant either," said Lartop getting a bit flustered.

"So, what are we going to do?" asked Kevin.

"Well," said Crispin, "we haven't got the power to destroy them and there is disagreement about that anyway. Diplomacy would seem the only practical solution, but again we can't agree about how we should go about it."

"In that case it looks as if it's down to me," said Kevin. Marlitta had entered while Crispin was talking.

"Or us," she added.

"What?" said Kevin.

"Us," she repeated. "You and me. We could do it between us. We could jump to the lead ship and I could get his attention while you create a protection field around us. Then we talk to him."

"I suppose that might work," said Kevin. "I'll check with Spectro." After a few seconds of silence, he said, "He

251

says that should be OK, but I'll have to practise creating a force field and holding it in place while we talk. The only problem would be if Duros were there. I don't know if his crystal could override my force field, but he would be a nuisance if we were trying to persuade them to call off the attack."

"Right," said Quartok. "So, what are you going to say to them to persuade them to turn around and go home? They've come a long way with the promise of a new planet to conquer."

"Well, we could tell them that if they attack earth they will be attacking the galactic federation and that we would send a fleet to wipe them out," suggested Kevin.

"These are warriors," said Quartok. "Their warriors' code may not allow them to give in to threats, but it may allow them to do a deal that would be to their advantage."

"So, what could we offer them that would be better than taking the earth?" asked Kevin.

"We could offer them membership of the federation," suggested Marlitta.

"They would have to give up their warrior ways, then," said Quartok. "I don't know if they'd take well to that idea."

"We could always ask them what they want," said Kevin. "Then we could think about it and make them a definite offer."

"That sounds like a good idea," said Lartop. "We would also have to make it a condition that they gave Duros into our custody."

"That goes without saying," said Quartok.

They spent a bit more time discussing the details, had something to eat and then Kevin started to practise creating and holding a force field while talking to someone. At first, he kept losing it whenever he started to speak, but it got better gradually, and they thought that he would probably be ready by the following day.

When he eventually went back to his cabin for another sleep, he wondered what was happening with the satellite that was circling the moon, so he slipped into the mindsight mode again and revisited his home. There was no one in the living room but he could hear his mother doing things in the kitchen. Luckily the television was on. He looked at the clock and realised that there would be some news on in about half an hour, so he decided to take a look at the satellite himself. Seconds later he could see the satellite floating effortlessly above the surface of the moon. Well, actually it seemed to be standing still while the moon's surface slowly passed beneath him. It must have been getting very good pictures as it was very close to the surface.

Suddenly, Kevin realised that the crater that was coming towards them, and was going to pass directly below them, was the one where their spaceship was standing. He couldn't see it yet but he knew he would be able to see it shortly. He had to do something quickly as he only had minutes to go. Without time to think about it, he created a bubble of pure energy about him, and jumped. Suddenly he was floating in space and it was a weird sensation. He could see the crater as it was about to pass under the satellite, and he could see their ship in the middle of it. What could he do? Without thinking he grabbed the satellite and it started to spin around slowly with him clinging on grimly. By the time they had rotated all the way round, the crater had passed and Kevin's air was running out so he jumped back into his cabin on the spacecraft.

He realised that he was trembling and had to lie still for quite a while to calm himself down. When he was more relaxed he used his mindsight again to go back to his home and see what was on the news. The television was still on, but now his mother was sitting watching it. The news had just started and he watched as several topics of no interest were covered.

Then the newsreader said "And now a further report from our science correspondent Ian Williams at NASA space centre. Ian, I believe there have been further developments?"

"Yes," said the correspondent. "I told you earlier that what looks like a cluster of asteroids or meteorites has been detected moving towards us, well it is thought that there is no danger to earth from these as they are not very large, and what is more important, they are not moving fast enough to cause any damage. It is believed they will burn up in the atmosphere about midnight on Thursday coming.

"However, there has been another report, only minutes ago, about the moon surveyor satellite which seems to have gone out of control and is spinning slowly. It is thought that it will not be able to regain control of its attitude for several days, but we'll keep you informed."

Kevin let out a sigh of relief and returned to his cabin to get a good night's sleep.

The following morning, they all gathered in the main cabin for breakfast where Kevin told them of what had happened the previous evening.

"Well it looks as if we won't be discovered by the satellite, then," said Quartok. "But we might have a problem now they've discovered the fleet. How near will they need to be before they will be able to see what they are, do you think?"

"I don't know," confessed Kevin. "But there are some pretty powerful telescopes, even some in space."

"And if they do find out what they are," continued Quartok, "what are they likely to do?"

"In the science fiction films, they would send rockets with nuclear warheads," said Kevin. "But in real life I don't know if they can actually do that."

"I think we'll need to act quickly," said Quartok. "I think it is time for you and Marlitta to try and talk to these people. Perhaps you should have a look and see who's on the bridge of the main ship."

Kevin sat down and closed his eyes and all the others turned their eyes toward the viewscreen. There was nothing for a while as it was taking Kevin a little time to find the fleet as they had moved quite a way since he last looked. Then suddenly they were there; floating apparently motionless against a star spangled black curtain of space. The viewpoint zoomed in towards the biggest ship in the group, and went straight into the bridge, which looked much the same as it had last time they looked. Kevin scanned the deck until he found what he had taken to be the control console, and there it was with the same enormous figure reclining in it.

"I think it's the same one in the control seat," said Kevin. "What did Duros call him?"

"Gdanos," said Marlitta. "It looks as if he is in charge of this lot. No sign of Duros though or that other big fellow."

"I think now would be a good time to 'jump'," said Kevin. "Get ready."

Marlitta took his hand. "Ready when you are," she said.

Kevin had butterflies in his stomach, not because he was about to face a giant warrior, but because he was holding a girl's hand. It was the most frightening thing he could imagine.

"Ready when you are," she repeated.

Chapter Seventeen – Negotiation

Suddenly they were in the alien spaceship, standing in front of the giant warrior. Kevin hastily threw up a force field to protect them. The Warrior looked at them, puzzled, them grinned and finally burst out laughing.

"Well little people," he said. "To what do I owe the pleasure?"

"Greetings, Gdanos," said Kevin trying to sound as grown up as possible and still keep the force field in place. "I am Kevin, Master of the Universe and this is Marlitta, governor of the third sector and we come to negotiate."

"Welcome Kevin," he roared still grinning from ear to ear. "What would you like to negotiate?"

"We would like you to abandon your invasion of earth and hand Duros over to us," said Kevin.

"We know he is on your ship," said Marlitta.

"Did I say he wasn't?" asked Gdanos.

"Well, no," said Marlitta.

"So, what do you have that would make it worth my while to turn my fleet around and go home?" asked Gdanos. "It would have to be very good to match up with the conquest of earth, and of course it would have to pay the cost of coming here and getting back again."

"Well first of all, I believe you are warriors?" said Marlitta.

"And warriors enjoy conquest?" said Kevin.

"Of course," said Gdanos. "And we enjoy the spoils of war also."

"Well I don't think you will be very pleased with earth, then," said Kevin. It is a poor planet and the inhabitants couldn't even give you a fight unless you were to land and let them throw spears at you."

Gdanos looked perturbed. "What?" he thundered. "Duros said they would make great sport."

"I don't think so," said Kevin. "They're a feeble lot, and their planet has nothing to offer either. It was worked out thousands of years ago. A waste of your time I would say."

Gdanos looked worried, then a smile spread across his face. "You're having me on, aren't you?" he said. "You want this place for yourselves, don't you? You're just trying to make me think it's worthless."

"Couldn't be further from the truth," said Marlitta. "But if you'd rather go ahead and blast this meagre little planet out of existence, well don't let us stop you."

"What do you mean?" he said suspiciously. "I thought you didn't want me to destroy this planet? Now what's your little game?"

"No game," said Kevin. "The point is that the federation would like you to join them, but that wouldn't be possible if you attacked a helpless planet. And think of all the trading advantages you'd lose."

"Trading advantages?" he asked. "What trading advantages?"

"Well it's like this," said Marlitta. "When you join the galactic federation, you are then free to trade with any planet in the federation. Think of the money you would save if you didn't have to maintain a battle fleet and fight for everything you want. But maybe you like to do things the hard way. Perhaps we should leave you to think about it for a while."

"Wait a minute," said Gdanos. "Where does Duros come into this?"

"He is a criminal, a liar and a cheat," said Kevin. "He is needed by the federation to face justice for his crimes. He will tell you anything to make you do what he wants. Do not trust him. We will be back in one rotation of that planet to hear your reply. Goodbye."

Almost before Kevin had stopped speaking they were back in the main cabin of their spacecraft.

"Well done," said Lartop. "That was excellent."

"Yes," said Quartok. "Very good. I hope Duros can't persuade him otherwise. I also hope that the earth people don't try to do anything aggressive."

"I'll keep an eye on them," said Kevin. "But I'm sure they won't be able to launch anything that quickly. It normally takes weeks."

"Well I hope so," said Lartop. "It would certainly upset our plans if they were to show any aggression. These are warriors, and so far, it is not important to them if they invade earth or not. But if they are threatened by earth, then that is a completely different matter. It will be a matter of pride to them then, and there will be no stopping them."

Kevin decided that he must keep an eye on things back on earth and foil any plans to attack the fleet, so he went back to his cabin, closed his eyes, and went into mindsight mode. But where should he start? He had heard the news from his home a couple of times and nothing much had transpired, but he thought it worth trying again, so he zoomed in on his home to see if he could catch the news. Unfortunately, it wasn't switched on. He looked around the house and found that there was no one in at all. His mother must have gone shopping and his father would be at work, so he had another look round, just to make sure, and then he 'jumped' back to his home and arrived in the living room. Sure enough, the place was deserted so he switched on the television and waited for the lunchtime news to come on. He kept watch out of the window to make sure his mother wasn't walking up the drive. He would be able to see her from quite a way off, which would give him plenty of time to get out.

Then the news started and there was absolutely nothing about the meteor shower, as they thought it was, or the malfunctioning moon surveyor satellite. He thought that was rather strange as they usually gave reports on this sort of thing regularly. He would have to look elsewhere. If the Americans had found out more about the fleet, it wasn't very likely they would publish it, so he would have to visit NASA, but not in person, he would have to use his mind sight for that.

He 'jumped' back to his cabin in the spacecraft and set about finding NASA. He knew approximately where it was in America, but not exactly. However, it was quite easy to pick out the launching pads, especially the ones with rockets standing ready for take-off, but which building would be the one he wanted?

At the edge of the take-off area he could see a building that he thought might be the control room, so he swept in towards it. Inside were a lot of offices with people busy at desks while others walked briskly from one area to another with folders or papers in their hands, trying to look busy. Further along the main corridor he saw a sign which said 'Control Room C', so he had a peek inside. But there was no one in this room so he moved on to the next, which was very busy indeed. There were people at all the desks operating controls and looking at the computer screens in front of them. Kevin couldn't help thinking of the beetles in the alien craft sitting at similar consoles, probably doing similar tasks.

There was an enormous wall screen which some of them were studying intently while one of them shouted orders to the others who responded immediately by making adjustments on their consoles.

Kevin looked at the screen but wasn't sure what he was looking at so he moved in closer to hear what was being said.

"I think they're decelerating," said one uniformed man standing next to the large screen.

"Confirmed," came a reply from one of the consoles. "If they continue in this mode they will all go into earth orbit on different paths. Some could take up geostationary orbits."

"If we're to intercept them we must act now, sir," said another. "A nuclear blast won't be any use after they scatter. At the moment they are still in a cluster and we could take them all out with three well placed detonations."

"We're still awaiting authorisation from the Pentagon," said the first one. "Until then, make sure the three missiles are ready for launch."

"Right away, sir," said another and turned and made for the door followed by another in the same uniform. Kevin decided to follow them and drifted through the control room towards the door and waited while they came around the vast array of consoles.

In the corridor they headed off in the opposite direction to the one Kevin had arrived from. There was less activity in this direction and eventually they came to a large solid looking door where they had to use their swipe cards to enter. Each ran his card through the slot and waited until a green light showed, then each inserted a key into two adjacent keyholes and turned them. A second green light came on and one of them pushed a lever down and the door swung open and they walked inside and closed the door behind them.

Kevin didn't have to worry about doors, however thick and solid they were. He simply drifted through and followed the two men over to a large console. It was only a small room but was full of equipment, the most impressive being the console that the two men were now seated in front of. There were no windows in the room, which was lit by concealed lighting from above.

"Want a coffee?" asked one of them getting to his feet.

"Yer, why not?" said the other relaxing a bit. "We could be here for a while."

The first man went over to the other side of the room to a coffee machine and filled two plastic cups with hot brown liquid. He sipped one, pulled a face, and walked back to the console where he set down his coffee and handed the other to his friend.

"Thanks. Don't spill it in the works or there'll be hell to pay." The first man moved his coffee to one side and continued setting controls. "Do you think we'll get the go ahead?" he said.

"Don't know," said the other. "Depends whose they are I suppose."

"Don't look like anything I've seen before," said the first.

Kevin wondered what he could do to stop them launching their missiles. What the man had said about the coffee gave him an idea. If he could spill the coffee into the works it might stop them, but he didn't know, and he wasn't sure if he could do it without being there in person, but it was worth a try.

He concentrated his thoughts through his crystal and the cup of coffee leapt off the shelf and fell onto the console. There was a flash and a lot of smoke.

"Hey, what y' think y' doing?" shouted the other man.

"I never touched it," shouted the first.

"I suppose it just leapt off the shelf, then," said the other.

"Well, yes it did. I didn't touch it. Anyway, we'd better do something before the whole lot fuses."

So, it wasn't broken beyond repair. There was nothing for it, he would have to jump in and destroy the equipment himself. Without giving himself time to think about it, he jumped and without waiting to see the reaction of the two men, he blasted the equipment cabinets to a molten mess.

The two men jumped from their seats as if bitten and seeing Kevin standing there, stood with their mouths open.

"Sorry about that," said Kevin and blasted the console they had just moved away from. "You see, it would be a big mistake to launch those missiles."

"Who are you?" asked one of the men moving towards him. Kevin zapped the floor in front of him and he decided it wasn't worth risking it and moved back again.

"I am Kevin," he said. "Master of the Universe."

"You can't escape," said the other one. "This room is sealed. All we have to do is wait until someone comes to find out what has happened."

"I don't think so," said Kevin. "You see, when they come to let you out I won't be here, so what are you going to tell them? Do you think they'll accept the story about aliens beaming in and blowing up your equipment, or will they call for the men in white coats?"

"Don't think you can get away with this," said the first one. "We've got other missiles we can fire at your damned ships. You won't get earth without a fight."

"I think you've got it a bit wrong," said Kevin. "I know you can't launch your missiles without this control room, and anyway I didn't do this so we could take the earth. In fact, I have just made an agreement with the Captain of the battle fleet to leave earth alone, but if you fire missiles at them they'll forget all about that and blow earth out of the universe. So, think yourselves lucky."

Without another word, Kevin 'jumped' back to his cabin in the ship on the moon. The two men stood staring at the empty space where he had been and then looked at each other.

"Did I imagine that?" they both said together.

Chapter Eighteen – Treachery

After that, Kevin felt quite tired so he dozed off for a while. When he woke up again, he thought that he should just check back on earth to see the results of his visit. In the main control room there was a riot. Everybody was shouting into microphones trying to get some remote technician to perform some impossible task. The general, as Kevin thought he was, stood at the front shouting orders and his minions went dashing off in all directions to carry them out.

Then suddenly, the door burst open and two terrified technicians were frog-marched into the room and dragged before the general who shouted at them quite a lot ending with "Well, what have you got to say for yourselves?"

The two technicians didn't know what to say for themselves but just mumbled something about spilled coffee.

"Coffee?" shouted the general. "Do you realise what this means? Do you realise that you have probably condemned the earth to invasion by aliens?"

"Perhaps they aren't going to invade us," said one of the technicians tentatively.

"Do you think we can risk it?" continued the general. "What do you think it is then, a pensioners' outing?"

"I don't know sir," replied the technician more calmly. "But we don't know that they intend us any harm."

"Well that's not the point," said the general calming down a little. "But the President wants them blasting out of the sky, so what do you suggest?"

"If there's nothing we can do," said the technician, "we'll just have to sit and wait. After all, if they're going to blast us off the planet we won't have to worry about what the President says, and if they don't, we'll have done the right thing."

"Can't deny the logic of that," replied the general. "But there's still the little matter of gross carelessness and the destruction of a very expensive facility."

Kevin couldn't help noticing that the general's left elbow was dangerously near his own cup of coffee which stood on the console next to him, so Kevin gave it a little mental nudge, spilling it into the works.

There was a blinding flash and all the lights went out in the control room. After a few seconds, the emergency lighting came on. The general was looking very embarrassed.

"Don't anyone say a word," he growled. "And you two can get out of my sight and think yourselves lucky that I have a kind heart."

So far, so good thought Kevin and closed down his mental link with the control room. He stretched himself, got up and went back to the main cabin where the others were sitting eating whichever meal they were at. Kevin wasn't sure if it was breakfast or supper.

"All's OK now," he said as he sat down with them. "I've disabled their missile launcher."

"How did you do that?" asked Marlitta.

"Had to pay them a little visit."

"I hope no-one saw you," said Lartop. "That could cause a lot of problems."

"Only two technicians," said Kevin, "but they won't say anything. Who would believe them, anyway?"

"Good," said Quartok. "It is nearly time to visit our friends again. This time I think we should make it a full delegation to make it a bit more official.

"I'm not going near that lot," said Tracy.

"No-one asked you to," said Kevin. "You can stay here and look after Sniffer." Sniffer opened one eye to see what he was missing and then closed it again when there was nothing of interest. Tracy scowled but said nothing. She didn't like Sniffer and he didn't like her either.

"Just time to finish our meal," said Quartok, "then we must go."

They carried on eating until they had had enough, and then got up and went to their cabins to get ready for the meeting. Kevin was last as he was quite hungry and the others had been halfway through their meal when he had joined them.

When he had finished he settled himself into his reclining seat, linked up with the ship's crystal, closed his eyes and scanned the sky for the fleet. It hadn't moved as far as he had expected, probably because they were slowing down.

On the bridge of the command ship things were much the same as before. Gdanos was sitting in his command seat and the beetles were either scuttling about or standing at their control consoles doing whatever they did.

As the others came back into the cabin they gathered round Kevin and waited until it was time to 'jump'. When they were all assembled, Quartok told Kevin that they were ready. Gdanos didn't even flinch as they appeared in front of him.

"So, you're back," he said.

"That's right," said Kevin. "May I introduce my colleagues from the Council." He introduced them and they all exchanged greetings. "Do you speak for all your people?"

"I do indeed," said Gdanos. "I am Supreme Battle leader and my word is law."

"Good," said Quartok. "That will save a lot of time. Now, firstly, we require you to pull away from the earth and head back into space."

"Sorry," replied Gdanos. "Can't do that."

"Why not?" snapped Lartop. "You gave us your word."

"I said I would not attack earth," said Gdanos. "And I don't intend to. However, we are decelerating at maximum and turning as much as we can. To turn around and head back to our home system, we will have to pass between the planet earth and its moon. Laws of physics I'm afraid." He grinned broadly.

"That's right," said Crispin. The type of drive used by these ships requires a lot of time and space to turn around in."

"Fine," said Kevin. "What have you done with Duros?"

"He is locked in his cabin," said Gdanos. "What would you like us to do with him?"

"We had better take him," said Kevin. "He has to stand trial for his crimes."

"I could save you a lot of time and trouble if you like?"

"No, thank you very much," said Lartop. "That is not how we behave in the Galactic Federation, and that is something you will have to learn if you are to join us."

Gdanos grinned again. "Happy little soul, your friend," he said to Kevin.

"It is no laughing matter," protested Lartop.

"I think he is joking," said Kevin. Lartop looked scandalised. "Now, perhaps we had better have a look at Duros and make sure he can't get away."

"Fine," said Gdanos. "I'll get someone to take you." He pressed a button on his console and within seconds one of the beetles came scurrying in.

Gdanos told it to take them to inspect the prisoner. "Follow the Drindop," he said. "It will take you to Duros. When you are happy he is in safe hands it will bring you back here."

The beetle clicked and scuttled off followed by Kevin and his strange little party. They were taken down long corridors, up ramps to other levels, through large control rooms and finally down a dimly lit passage to a set of rusty looking iron doors.

The insect clicked some controls and the door opened into a dark room.

"Right Duros," said Kevin. "You can come with us now."

There was no reply.

"Perhaps he's asleep," said Lartop.

Kevin ventured in carefully, ready to zap anything that moved. The room was empty.

"There's no-one here," he shouted out to the others. The beetle clicked in an agitated way and headed of down the corridor. The others had to run to keep up with it.

Back at the main control room Gdanos looked surprised to see them.

"He's not there," said Kevin. "What have you done with him?"

"He was locked in quite securely," said Gdanos. "He must still be there."

"Did you take his crystal from him?" asked Marlitta.

"Of course we did," said Gdanos impatiently. He gave the beetle another order and it scuttled off on its mission. After a short interval it returned and clicked out its message. Gdanos looked perturbed.

"It seems we have a traitor aboard," he said. "This is a matter of honour and I must deal with it myself, whatever you might want us to do in the federation. At the moment we're not in the federation so it will be dealt with my way. Please leave it to me. In the meantime, please make yourselves comfortable in the lounge. The Drindop will take you there."

They followed the beetle to a wide area, which had seats of all shapes and sizes, and large viewing windows that looked out at the star-spangled blackness of space. They found seats near one of the windows and sat down looking out. They could see the earth ahead of them, still very small.

"What do we do now?" said Kevin.

"Not much we can do until Gdanos finds the culprit," said Quartok.

"I don't like the idea of him taking the law into his own hands like this," said Lartop. "It isn't right."

"Well we don't have any say in the matter just now," said Marlitta. "I'm more worried about where Duros is and what he's up to."

"Could he escape from this ship?" asked Kevin looking alarmed.

"It depends on the crystal he has," said Crispin. "If he has got hold of one that allows transportation, he could be anywhere by now. On the other hand, there aren't many that could take him any distance so he would only be able to get to one of the planets in your system."

"That can only mean earth," said Kevin. "If he's there we'll never find him."

"Remember that 'jumping' leaves a trace that can be followed. All we have to do is find where he jumped from and follow him," said Marlitta.

"We did that last time, if you remember," said Kevin. "He may have learned by now that he would have to cover his tracks in some way."

"Well there's nothing we can do until Gdanos sends one of those things to fetch us back," said Marlitta. "Then we'll ask him if we can go back to the cell where he was kept and see if he 'jumped' from there. If he didn't, we've lost him."

"I think I could 'jump' back there and find out," said Kevin. "I can visualise the cell quite clearly."

"All right," said Quartok, "but don't be long. It wouldn't be good for Gdanos to find that you've been wandering around his ship."

Kevin closed his eyes and 'jumped' back to the cell. Once there he probed for a trace of Duros's crystal, but there was nothing, so he 'jumped' back to the lounge. There was nothing more they could do, so they settled down to wait for Gdanos.

After about an hour a beetle thing came and took them back to the control centre where Gdanos was waiting for them.

"I have tracked down the traitor," he said, "and he has been dealt with."

"Who was it?" asked Kevin.

"One of my most trusted people," he said. "One from my own clan, in fact. He wasn't happy with the fact that I have agreed to join the Federation and give up our warrior life. He made a bargain with Duros to continue the invasion of earth if he could have control of it himself. Duros agreed to this as long as his crystal was returned to him, and as soon as he had it in his hand he disappeared, just like you do."

"So, what happened to your friend, then?" asked Kevin.

"As we sweep past the earth," he said, "it will be possible to see what you might call a shooting star in the atmosphere of the planet. He wanted the earth, now he will become part of its atmosphere for ever."

No one said anything, but just stood looking at each other. There was no point in arguing about it as the deed was done and the poor unfortunate was at this moment heading straight towards the earth in his space suit with no means of avoiding his ultimate fate.

"I must get back to our ship," said Kevin. "Marlitta will come with me and the others will stay with you to arrange things with you."

They said their goodbyes and Kevin and Marlitta 'jumped' back to their ship. When they arrived, there was no sign of Tracy. They looked in her cabin but it was empty, as were all the other cabins. Sniffer was in his cabin but the door was shut, which was strange, as he didn't like to be shut in.

"She's gone," said Kevin. "But how?"

"I think we have discovered where Duros 'jumped' first," said Marlitta.

"But why has he taken Tracy?" he asked. "She's of no use to him."

"A hostage, perhaps," said Marlitta.

"What's this?" said Kevin picking up a piece of paper from the control console.

"Looks like a note," said Marlitta. "What does it say?"

"I don't know," he said. "I can't read it."

"Your crystal can translate for you," said Marlitta.

Kevin stared at the paper and as he looked at the strange shapes they seemed to flow into letters that he could recognise.

"It says," he said, "that we mustn't follow him or we won't see Tracy again. What can we do? We can't just abandon her even if you don't like her."

"Of course we can't," said Marlitta. "We must follow them and hope we can stop him before he can harm her. It's probably an idle threat anyway."

Chapter Nineteen – Sand and Camels

As they were about to 'jump' after Duros, Kevin decided that they should be careful that Duros wasn't leading them into a trap.

"Suppose he 'jumped' out into space," he said, "and then on to earth. If we followed him we would find ourselves in space and that would be it. So to be on the safe side, I'll take a bubble of air with us, just in case."

"Right," said Marlitta. "What are we waiting for?"

They jumped, but there was no problem. They found themselves on earth in a place where it was rather hot. It was almost like another planet. There was no vegetation to speak of, just sand.

"Now let's see where he went next," said Kevin, but there was no trace of another 'jump'.

"Must have gone on foot," said Marlitta, "or taken some other form of transport. That makes it more difficult."

"It makes it almost impossible," said Kevin. "Perhaps he just walked a short distance and then 'jumped' again." He looked about him for tracks but there was no sign of any. The sand was so dry that the soft breeze smoothed it out almost immediately. "Let's try round about and see if we can pick up any trace of another 'jump'."

"We should walk in a spiral," said Marlitta. "That will give us the best chance of finding where he 'jumped' from."

They started walking in a small circle about the place they had landed, and gradually moved outwards and all the time Kevin tried to sense traces of energy left behind when Duros made his second 'jump'. It was very hot and after a little while both of them needed to find some shade, but there was none in sight.

"It's no use," said Marlitta. "We'll have to find our way to some shelter or we'll die out here in the desert."

"I'll see if I can find any," said Kevin closing his eyes and using his mind sight. He skimmed over the desert dunes, but the scenery didn't change, so he raised his viewpoint to look far into the distance. Again, there was not much to see until he thought he could make out a dark spot in the far distance. He zoomed towards it and found to his joy that it was an oasis of sorts. There was a small spring with a pool of water surrounded by some palm trees and small shrubs of some sort. On the far side were two tents and a team of camels that were drinking from the pool. A man was with them.

"Quick, take my hand," he said to Marlitta who immediately grasped it firmly. A second later they were both peering through the bushes at the little encampment.

"Now what?" said Marlitta.

"I think we should go over and speak to him," said Kevin. "He may be able to help us."

"Will he be friendly?" she asked.

"I don't know," he replied. "But I have my crystal to protect us. I'll set up a force field just in case."

They walked round the oasis to the open area where the man was tending his camels. He didn't see them at first, but when he did he seemed to panic and ran into the nearest tent shouting something. A moment later, two other men emerged, dressed like the first in long flowing loose-fitting garments. The two newcomers were holding guns.

"What do you want?" shouted the first one pointing his gun at them.

"We need shelter," said Kevin. "We are lost and need help."

"And what do you have to trade for this help?" asked the second man.

"Gold would be good," said the first one. "Or dollars perhaps."

"Sorry, no," said Kevin. "We have nothing with us at all. I told you, we are lost."

"I wouldn't say you had nothing worth trading," said the second man looking at Marlitta.

"What do you mean?" asked Kevin knowing exactly what he meant. "Slave trading is illegal."

"Oh dear, what a pity," said the first man. "And that's how we make our living. Maybe we just take the two of you anyway. What's to stop us?"

"I don't think that would be a good idea," said Kevin raising his hand to point at the ground just in front of the three men. There was a blinding flash and sand flew up all around them. Two of the men fell to the ground and the other ran off into the desert. Suddenly there were bullets flying in all directions but their force field deflected them all. One of the bullets bounced straight back and hit one of the men in the leg and he rolled around yelling.

"Stay where you are and throw away your guns," commanded Kevin. The one who'd been hit threw his gun away but the other clung onto his, so Kevin pointed at it and it became very hot. The man yelped and threw it away. Kevin then made them lie down with their hands out in front of them while Marlitta found some rope, which she used to tie them up. When they were secured, Kevin had a look in the tents. The first one was obviously their living tent so he gathered up some useful things such as a water jar and some dried fruit.

"Come here quickly," shouted Marlitta from the next tent, and Kevin dashed round to the other tent wondering what the emergency was. Inside he found Marlitta untying several ragged looking individuals. There were three men, two women and a young lad.

"They were taking them to sell as slaves," said Marlitta.

One of the men stepped forward and bowed low.

"Thank you for helping us," he said. "We are but poor goatherds. These people have stolen all our possessions and killed some of our people. We have been badly treated and have not eaten for several days."

Kevin led them through to the other tent where they helped themselves to food and water.

"How did you manage to capture these people?" asked one of the women.

"We took them by surprise," said Kevin. "But we need to get to a city as soon as possible. Are there any near here?"

The people looked a bit surprised.

"Of course," said one of the men. "About a day's journey by camel is a big tourist place. People come to see the pyramids and other very old buildings."

"Thank you," said Kevin. "Would you like to come with us and show us the way?"

"I am sorry, but no," said the man who seemed to be the senior one. "We must return to our village as quickly as possible. It is a long walk."

"Well, we will take two of the camels," said Kevin. "You can take the rest if you like."

"But we cannot do that," said the man. "They are now yours by right and we already owe you too great a debt of gratitude."

"But we don't need the camels," said Marlitta. "And we couldn't look after them. It would be better if you took them."

"We would be glad to look after them for you," said the man. "It would be the least we could do."

"You could have the other two as well," said Kevin, "when we get to the city, as we won't need them after that. But one of you would have to come with us to bring them back."

"I think we could do that," said the man realising that they were going to end up very wealthy out of this. "When do you think you will return to reclaim your property?"

"It could be a very long time," said Kevin. "If we do not return within a year, you may keep them as payment for your trouble."

"That is most generous," said the man bowing again. "Abdul will go with you to show you the way to the city and will return with the camels." The young lad smiled shyly and stepped forward. This was obviously Abdul.

"Isn't he a bit young to travel across the desert by himself?" asked Kevin.

"You do not seem to be much older yourselves," said the man.

"True," said Kevin. "Right, let's get going then."

"I think you should find some better clothes," said the man and gestured to one of the women who went over to a bundle and opened it up. Soon she had Kevin and Marlitta looking like something from 'Laurence of Arabia'.

They went out and Abdul picked two of the camels that he thought most suitable and made them kneel down. Then they loaded bundles onto them along with the food and water that Kevin had already collected.

While they were doing that, the others were taking down the tents and stowing them on the camels along with all the possessions of the slavers.

"Can we leave you to deal with these men?" said Kevin.

"Certainly," said the man. "Leave them to us."

Kevin wasn't sure what they had in mind but decided not to ask. When they were loaded up, Abdul helped Marlitta onto one of the camels and then tapped it with a stick and it got to its feet grumbling, as camels do. Then he helped Kevin onto his and showed him how to hook his knee around the saddle post. It wasn't too uncomfortable. Then as the camel started to stand up, Abdul leapt onto the back of Kevin's camel, and they were off.

The motion of the camel felt very strange at first, but they got used to it eventually though it was going to take its toll of their tender backsides. After a couple of hours, they stopped, and Kevin was very glad of this.

"You are not used to riding camels, I think," said Abdul.

"No, we're not," said Kevin. "How much further is it?"

Abdul laughed. "We ride until the sun sets then we rest until morning. Then we ride again nearly all day, and then we see the city."

Kevin groaned. This was not a good idea. "Do you think this is the best way to find Duros?" he asked Marlitta. "It would be easier to 'jump', wouldn't it?"

"Easier, yes," she responded. "But would we find him by doing that? I don't think so. As soon as we find some other travellers, we can ask if they have seen them."

"There are travellers ahead," said Abdul. "They will stop at the oasis tonight I would think, as we will."

"How do you know?" asked Kevin a bit surprised.

"I can see the dust they leave in the sky." He pointed and sure enough, Kevin could see a slight haze above the horizon. "I would never have noticed it. How do you know where they will stop?"

"There is nowhere else unless you want to stop in the desert?"

After they had stretched their legs and eaten some of the dried food washed down with warm water, they set off again and by sunset, Kevin didn't want to sit on another camel as long as he lived. However, Abdul had been right. There was a team of camels at the watering hole and three tents erected nearby. A group of women were tending a fire and bringing cooking pots out to set on it while children played by the water's edge.

The people seemed very friendly and invited them to join them for something to eat. Kevin was pleased to have the company but had heard tales about these people eating sheep's eyes, which he didn't fancy at all. Anyway, he had no choice but to sit down and join them.

They were a very jolly lot and chattered away non-stop. Luckily, they didn't ask too many questions about where they had come from and so on.

When the food was ready, one of the women placed a bowl on the rug in front of them and the head man gestured towards the bowl and said to Kevin, "Please help yourself. The sheep's eye is yours."

Kevin blanched and before he could think of anything to say, they all burst into uncontrollable laughter.

"It is our little joke," said the headman. "We know Europeans do not like some of the delicacies that we relish. It was very funny to see the look on your face. But no, please help yourself. You will find some tender meat of the lamb in there and some vegetables."

Kevin helped himself and found the food delicious. They sat for quite a while by the fire listening to the chatter before taking the offered corner of one of the tents to curl up in and fall asleep immediately.

Chapter Twenty – The Great Pyramid

The next morning, they awoke early and went out to find the traders eating something that looked like porridge. As soon as they appeared they were offered a bowl of the steaming stuff which they took and went and sat down with the others.

It was a type of porridge and tasted quite nice. It was sweetened with honey and was actually quite filling. When they had finished they thanked their hosts and loaded up their camels.

"I wonder if you have seen two people?" asked Kevin. "There was one who you would think was very small and another, an English girl with very short hair."

The man looked displeased. "Yes, I think we have seen them," he said. "They were not very pleasant. They were heading for the pyramids on foot. They wanted to buy camels but had nothing to trade. We refused them and the little man was quite unpleasant. I think they eventually managed to persuade some other traders to take them. I hope they are not friends of yours?"

"No," said Kevin, "but we need to catch up with them. He is a criminal and is holding the girl hostage and we need to save her."

"In that case," said the man, "you must allow us to help you. You must come with us and we'll help you catch them." He gave some urgent sounding orders and people started rushing around striking camp and loading the camels. Soon they were ready and were setting off at a pace that Kevin was not at all happy with.

"I don't like this much," he said to Abdul.

"It is all right, Master," he replied. "They can go much faster than this if necessary."

Kevin hung on and by midday they could see another group of camels ahead of them moving more slowly. After another hour they had almost caught up with them, but as they approached, one of the camels broke from the group and raced away leaving a cloud of choking dust behind.

One of the traders, who was riding with Kevin, whipped his camel into motion and raced after the fleeing camel while all the others came to a standstill. One of the group that they had just caught up with, dismounted his camel and came over to them.

"Thank you for ridding us of that tyrant," he said. "He was forcing us to take him to the Great Pyramid. We weren't intending to come this way at all, and now we have lost one of our camels. We also have an English girl that he seems to have left with us."

"Tracy!" shouted Kevin and a bundle on one of the camels turned towards him. It was Tracy, and she didn't look happy. They all dismounted and Kevin was pleased to be able to stretch his legs again. Marlitta tried to comfort Tracy who was in tears and wouldn't be consoled.

After a while, the trader who had raced off after Duros, appeared around a sand dune riding his camel and leading another one which appeared riderless.

"I have managed to recover your camel," he said as he approached. "I don't know where the rider went though."

"He's escaped again," said Kevin to Marlitta. "What now?"

"What is this Great Pyramid they were talking about?" she asked.

"Oh, it's an ancient monument, one of the wonders of the world," replied Kevin.

"Isn't that what 'The One Who Controls' was talking about?"

"Yes, you're right," said Kevin. "I think he is going to try and use it to escape. If it's still a portal, that is. I can't see how it can be, though. If it was, people would have found out about it by now."

"Perhaps he knows the secret," said Marlitta. "Anyway, we must get there before he can use it."

"Right," said Kevin. "How do we get to the Great Pyramid?"

"We can take you," said the leader of the traders. "The English girl can ride on one of our spare camels."

Tracy was hastily pushed onto a camel and they set off again, even faster than before. Kevin held on for all he was worth with Abdul clinging on behind him, not perturbed at all. Marlitta seemed to be managing very well on her camel, while Tracy looked anything but happy. She was clinging on for all she was worth and sobbing as well, when she managed to find the breath.

After another two hours riding they slowed down to a walk.

"There are the pyramids," said the trader pointing ahead of them. Kevin shaded his eyes from the sun and was amazed by the spectacle. It wasn't that far to go now. "We will travel the rest of the way at a slower pace. We do not want to draw attention to ourselves. If this fellow you are looking for should see us, he will just think we are another trader caravan coming in from the desert and will not try to hide from us."

"I think he will be going into the pyramid," said Kevin. "Will we be able to get in?"

"I do not know," he replied. "Tourists are allowed inside, but they have to pay. Sometimes the pyramid is closed when they are doing research work there. I will find out for you."

They continued towards the pyramids, which were now getting quite close and looked enormous. The Sphinx had just come into view and Kevin was explaining to Marlitta what it was, or at least to the best of his knowledge.

They left the main track and took a narrower winding track that led up to the pyramids. There didn't seem to be many people about. A man with three pack mules was leading his animals away from the Great Pyramid along another track that cut across the one they were on. When they got to the junction they turned up the track towards the pyramid and would have to pass the man with the mules. As they passed him, the trader asked him about the pyramid.

"Sorry, it's closed today for archaeological work," he said.

"Did you see a little man go in?" asked the trader. "A foreigner, perhaps?"

"Yes," he replied. "Said he was an inspector. Never seen him before though. If you wait at the entrance he will be out again soon, I should think."

They carried on up the track to the pyramid and eventually moved into the shadow, which was very pleasant. At the entrance Kevin told the traders that they would wait and thanked them for their help. They said that it was their pleasure and headed off towards the city leaving Kevin, Marlitta, Tracy and Abdul with the two camels they had taken from the slavers.

"Well thank you for your help," said Kevin to Abdul. You can return to your people now and take the camels with you."

"But what about the packs?" he asked. "Do you not want your things?"

"No thank you," said Kevin. "We don't need them anymore. You may keep whatever you want."

Abdul's face lit up. He climbed onto one of the camels, nudged it to its feet, and set off down the track leading the other camel by the rope attached to its harness. As he turned onto the main track he turned and waved before setting off at a brisk trot.

There was no one about at the entrance but there was a notice in several languages that said that the pyramid was closed. Kevin peered into the darkness within but couldn't see very much.

"I want to go home," moaned Tracy.

"Soon," said Kevin.

"I'll keep an eye on her," said Marlitta, "if you want to go on ahead."

Kevin went into the passage and Marlitta pushed Tracy after him.

"I don't like it in here," she sobbed.

"Oh do be quiet," said Kevin feeling annoyed with her. After all, she was two years older than he was and was generally a bully at school, and here she was behaving like a five-year-old.

"Use your crystal to give us some light," said Marlitta.

"Hadn't thought of that," said Kevin holding up his hand. A faint glow appeared as if it were coming from his finger. It gradually got brighter until they could see quite well. "Didn't want to overdo it and blow a hole in the wall."

They made their way into the pyramid and eventually came to a place where the tunnel split and one path went downwards while the other went upwards. There was a sign pointing along each branch, the lower one to the 'Queen's Chamber' and the other to the 'King's Chamber'.

"Which way?" asked Kevin.

"Don't ask me," replied Marlitta. "I'm a stranger here."

"My hunch is that it would be the 'King's Chamber' that would be used as a portal. It's higher up and it in the middle of the pyramid. I saw some diagrams of it once on a programme on television."

They set off up the higher passage that rose quite steeply into a gallery where the roof was quite high. As they came to the top there was an entrance into another chamber, which had a notice outside saying 'King's Chamber'.

"I think there's someone in there," said Kevin lowering the beam of light. "Yes, I'm sure I saw a light in there moving about. It might be the archaeologists that are working here. I'll have a look."

He walked forward into the entrance to the chamber and there was a flash and Kevin had to shield his eyes for a moment.

"What is it?" asked Marlitta urgently. "Are you all right?"

"Yes fine," said Kevin turning towards them. "It was Duros, but he has got away."

They all went into the chamber, which was now empty.

"He just walked through that wall," he said pointing to the far end of the chamber. "He must have reactivated the portal. Wait here, I'm going to have a look to see what's at the other side."

"Be careful," said Marlitta. "He may be waiting for you."

"I will" he said and stepped through the wall. Tracy stood with her mouth wide open, but no sound came out. After a few seconds Kevin reappeared.

"We have to close the portal quickly," he said. "Duros has got an army out there about to come through. How can I close it, Spectro?"

Spectro gave him an explanation in his usual longwinded way, much to Kevin's frustration.

"Right," he said. "Stand back." He pointed at the wall and then turned his hand palm outwards. A dull glow built up slowly. Kevin looked as if he were trying to push something back but was being pushed back himself.

Suddenly, a figure flew through the wall and fell at his feet. There was a blinding flash and then it went very dark.

"What happened?" said Marlitta.

"I want to go home," said Tracy.

Kevin brought back some light onto the scene. The wall now looked very dark and solid and sitting at his feet was 'The One Who Controls'.

"What are you doing here?" said Kevin in surprise.

"We are going to retake our world," he said. "The conquering hordes are assembled and will be coming through any moment now. The time of the 'Old Ones' has returned."

"You had better see where they have got to then," said Kevin grinning.

"What?" said 'The One'. "Where are they?" He turned as if to walk back through the wall and walked straight into it stunning himself.

Kevin pulled him to his feet again and took him to the wall and placed his hand on it. "Look," he said. "Solid as a rock. The portal is closed forever. Good luck in your new world, 'Old One', we're off home now."

At that moment there was the sound of running feet in the tunnel outside the chamber.

"Looks as if we've disturbed them," said Kevin. "Give them my regards."

He grabbed Marlitta and Tracy and 'jumped' back to the waiting spacecraft on the moon.

"Well we didn't catch him," said Kevin, "but he'll be out of the way for a while. I don't think his new friends will be very pleased with him now."

"The Council will have to put out an alert around the peripheral worlds to be on the lookout for him," said Marlitta. "He won't be able to 'jump' from where he is because crystals don't work there, as we found out. He may find his way back eventually by means of the portals, but it could take him some time."

"Well I need to get back home now with this big baby," said Kevin.

"What d'y mean?" said Tracy.

"What I say," said Kevin. "And when we get back, you mustn't mention a word of what happened, OK?"

"Try and stop me."

"Oh, I can, believe me," said Kevin. "Will you take this ship back for me Marlitta? We can't leave it here."

"Of course," said Marlitta. "But next time, come and see me sooner." She gave him a kiss, which made him blush, and made Tracy scowl. "Off you go then and take that hairy brute with you."

"That's no way to speak about this sweet little girl," said Kevin grinning.

"The dog, idiot."

"Oh him," said Kevin. "Come on then Sniffer." He put his hand on Sniffer's head and reluctantly took Tracy's hand, and they were immediately back on the moors above Kevin's home. Sniffer bounded off gleefully, while Tracy moped along behind Kevin as he strode out for home.

"Can't stop me telling," she grumbled.

"Well, actually I can," he said. "I can use my crystal to wipe all your memory of what happened."

"Can't."

"I can," he continued, "but I don't want to. Actually, you can tell whoever you like and see if they believe you. I think you will end up having a visit from the men in white coats if you keep on about it too much. Then there's the other option…"

"What's that then?" she snapped.

"We can keep it as out secret. You can keep your crystal ring and I may call on you to help out again if you want to."

"I think I'd like that," she said smiling. "Can I keep the crystal then?"

"Of course," he said. "It doesn't have the power mine has, but you can use it to contact me any time you want. Just talk to me in your mind and I'll hear you. You'll find it helps you with your language classes. That's what it is good at; translating languages."

"Cool," she said. "OK, I won't tell a soul."

"Great," said Kevin. "See you at school tomorrow."

Tracy set off towards the village while Kevin turned to his left and headed for the field behind his house while

Sniffer raced around wildly, happy to be back. Suddenly he heard a voice in his head.

"Just testing," it was Tracy's voice.

"Receiving you loud and clear," answered Kevin.

He had just reached the wall at the bottom of his garden and was climbing through. His mother waved from the kitchen window and he raced up the garden.

"Had a good time?" she asked.

"Great," said Kevin. "Had a problem with giant spiders and then had to stop an invasion of earth by an alien race."

"Very nice dear," his mother replied. "Now go and have a wash. Tea will be ready shortly."

* * *

Part 3

The Galactic Maze

Chapter 1 – An Unexpected Call

It had been about a week since Kevin had returned from his most recent adventure and he was back at school again. It was strange how being back at school made his strange adventures seem like misty dreams. He could hardly believe that they had been real, but as he pressed his hand against his chest, he could feel the hard shape of his crystal that hung around his neck on a fine chain made of a metal unknown on earth. He could also speak to the crystal, in his mind that is, and Spectro, the voice of the crystal would give him any information that he requested. This aspect of the crystal had been very useful to him at school, though he had to be careful not to get too many questions right as he didn't want anyone to notice him particularly. Since he had become Master of the Universe he had to be very careful that no one found out. He didn't know what would happen if they did; no one had told him, but he thought it wouldn't be what he wanted. He might have to leave earth for good and never see his family and friends ever again, or worse still, he may lose his crystal and return to being a normal unexceptional boy. He didn't like the thought of that either.

He was in a French class doing a translation when he realised that he was doing it perfectly, with no mistakes at all. This was because one of the main uses of all types of crystal was to translate spoken and written languages into one understood by the crystal's owner. There were thousands of different languages throughout the universe and people from all different parts could converse with each other without knowing what language the other was speaking. It just sounded as if they were speaking your own language. So, when he looked at a page written in French, it looked like English to Kevin, so he just had to copy it down. The problem was that he wasn't very good at languages and usually got rather poor marks, but now he had suddenly become very good at it and his teacher had remarked on it.

"I hope you haven't been copying from someone else," said Miss Roach, his French teacher. "That is a remarkably good piece of work."

"Thank you, Miss," said Kevin. "I seem to have got the hang of it since you started teaching us."

Miss Roach looked unimpressed but said nothing.

"Perhaps you should make a few mistakes," said Spectro in Kevin's mind. It made him jump.

"I wish you wouldn't do that," said Kevin, also silently in his mind. "You keep quiet for ages then blurt out something when I'm least expecting it."

"Sorry," said Spectro. "Perhaps I should put some mistakes in for you when you are at school. Do you think that would help?"

"Yes," said Kevin. "Thanks. That sounds like a good idea."

It was even worse in science as Spectro kept wanting to correct the science teacher, Mr Jones. It was just that earth science was a bit primitive compared with science in the rest of the universe. However, it didn't matter as it just made Kevin look as if he didn't understand science very well.

He sometimes got messages in his mind from Tracy Bagshot, a girl a few years older than himself. Tracy had been the unwilling helper in his last adventure and to keep her quiet, he had had to let her keep her crystal. It was only a weak crystal but it allowed her to contact him if she wanted to.

He didn't have a lot to say to her as the less she knew, the less trouble she could cause. When he went outside at the lunch break she was waiting for him and he tried not to look disappointed.

"There's something I need to tell you," she said when there was no one else near them.

"What is it now?" asked Kevin with a resigned look on his face.

"I've been hearing voices in my head," she said. "Not yours. I mean other voices. Do you think it could be Duros again?"

"What do they say?" asked Kevin.

"It's difficult to say," said Tracy. "It is usually when I'm still half asleep and I can't remember what they were saying."

"You were probably just dreaming," said Kevin. "That's the most likely answer. Let me know if you hear anything definite. Anything you can remember."

"Oh, OK," said Tracy looking disappointed. She had thought that there might be another adventure in the offing. Not that she had enjoyed the last one while it was happening, but it had seemed better when she was safely at home again.

On his way home that evening, Kevin thought he ought to mention it to Marlitta or one of the Council such as Quartok, but perhaps he would leave it for a while. But then he thought it would be nice to see Marlitta again, so that evening he went for a stroll up onto the moor behind his house. It was a pleasant evening and the sun was quite warm on his back as he climbed the hill up to his favourite little hidey-hole among the rocky outcrop at the top. When he got there, he sat down in his favourite seat. It was a rock that had been carved out by the action of water over thousands of years, and Kevin thought of it as his control couch. It didn't seem quite so real since he had sat in a proper control couch, but that didn't matter.

He leaned back and closed his eyes and tried to make contact with Marlitta on her planet, way across the galaxy. Her planet was called 'Paradise', which was what it was like now, though it had been far from pleasant when Kevin first visited it.

"Hello Kevin," came Marlitta's voice in his head. "I thought you had forgotten us."

"It's only been a couple of weeks," said Kevin.

"Maybe for you," said Marlitta. "You know time goes at different speeds in different parts of the galaxy. It's been eight months here."

"Look, I need to talk to you," said Kevin. "Do you want to come here, or shall I come to 'Paradise'?"

"Why don't you come here," said Marlitta. "You'll be surprised at how things have changed."

"OK," said Kevin. "I'll just get a fix on you." He let his mind sight follow the link between them until he could see Marlitta. She was walking down a path between some trees. It must have been morning there, at least that was how it looked. Suddenly Kevin was beside her. He had used the power of his crystal to 'jump', as he called it. He had been transported in an instant across the vastness of space and was now walking through this delightful open woodland with Marlitta.

"Where are we?" asked Kevin.

"Not far from the village. The rebuilding work is still going on but the vegetation has just shot up. I love to walk through the woods before breakfast."

"Oh, it's nearly bedtime for me," said Kevin. "Look, I'm a bit worried about Tracy Bagshot."

Marlitta's face fell.

"I thought we'd seen the last of her," said Marlitta.

"No such luck," said Kevin. "I had to let her keep her crystal, and now she's hearing voices."

"You let her keep her crystal?"

"Yes. It was the only way to keep her quiet. It's only a weak one."

"I wonder if someone is trying to get information from her," said Marlitta.

"Could they do that?"

"I don't know. Maybe," said Marlitta. "It doesn't make a lot of sense though, does it? Duros can find you using his crystal. We've established that. So, what could he learn from Tracy?"

"I don't know," said Kevin. "Perhaps it's just her imagination."

Suddenly Kevin realised that he was beginning to recognise the scenery around him.

"The village is near here, isn't it?" he said.

"That's right," said Marlitta. "When we come out of the woods you'll be able to see it."

Kevin was quite surprised at how much it had changed. There were far more buildings now than he remembered from his last visit.

"Who's this hurrying towards us?" he asked.

"Don't worry," said Marlitta. "It's just Rotunda. I wonder what's bothering him this time."

"Is he still here?"

"Oh, yes," answered Marlitta. "He thinks we couldn't do without him. How wrong he is."

Rotunda hurried up to them panting and spluttering.

"Calm down," said Marlitta trying to calm him. "Get your breath back and then you can tell what the problem is."

"Can't," he gasped. "…Urgent … Master .. of .. Universe is here.."

"I know."

"You know?" he gasped. "How?"

"Who do you think this is then?" she said indicating Kevin.

"Ah," said Rotunda. His jaw dropped as he stared at Kevin, then he shut his mouth and went down on one knee. "Your pardon, Excellency. I had not recognised you."

"Oh get up, Rotunda," said Kevin "There's no need for all that. This is only an informal visit."

"I only sent the message back to the village so that some breakfast could be prepared for us," said Marlitta. "No need for any fuss. Just go back and see to it please."

Rotunda struggled to his feet, bowed several times, and scuttled off back to the village.

"He means well," said Marlitta, "but we have to make sure he only deals with mundane things – nothing where he can do any damage."

Back at the village people were scuttling about, obviously preparing for his visit.

"I hope they haven't gone to any trouble," said Kevin. "I've had my tea and I'm not really hungry."

"Well I am," said Marlitta. "So, you can sit and watch me eat. I haven't had my breakfast yet and I'm starving."

They went inside and sat down. Marlitta tucked into a bowl of something hot and steaming that looked rather like porridge onto which she had ladled spoonfuls of something that looked like syrup.

"Sure you won't have some?" she asked.

"Well maybe just a little," said Kevin. "It looks delicious."

After he had eaten a good bowl full he helped himself to some toast, or at least what looked like toast but tasted sweeter.

"I thought you weren't hungry," said Marlitta. Kevin just grinned and continued eating. "I don't think you need to worry about Tracy. She's of no importance to anyone, except you."

"No need to be jealous," said Kevin still grinning.

"Who's jealous of a primitive earth creature?" said Marlitta also grinning.

"Maybe you're right," said Kevin. "But I thought I'd just let you know in case Duros was up to his tricks again. Anyway, I can't stop. I'll be expected home shortly, but it has been nice to see you again."

"Maybe I'll pop in to see you next time," said Marlitta, "and perhaps say hello to your friend Tracy."

"If you must," said Kevin. "See you later."

He closed his eyes and visualised the rocks where he had been back on earth and when he opened them again he was there. Then suddenly he was pushed from behind and fell to the ground. He was panic stricken and tried to turn so that he could see who was attacking him. It was difficult to use his crystal against someone if you couldn't see them. Then something very wet sloshed across his face.

"Sniffer," he cried. "Will you get off me." Sniffer was the large hound he had brought back from his first adventure. Duros used to use animals like Sniffer to literally sniff out people he was hunting, but Kevin had used his crystal to subdue Sniffer who was now his inseparable friend. He must have woken to find that Kevin had gone off without him and followed him up onto the moors.

Kevin set off down the hill towards home while Sniffer raced joyfully about trying to catch rabbits or grouse that might be lurking in the heather.

Back at home, he was met by his mother.

"I think one of your friends has been trying to play a joke on you," she said. "The 'phone rang just after you had gone out and I couldn't make out a word they were saying. It was either a wrong number from some foreign country or one of your friends being stupid."

"I don't know who that would be," said Kevin, genuinely puzzled. "If they ring again I'll take it. I'm sure to be able to recognise their voice.

At that moment the telephone rang. Kevin and his mother looked at each other, and Kevin ran in to answer the telephone while his mother carried on with what she had been doing.

"Hello," said Kevin into the receiver.

"Ah. That must be Kevin," said a voice he vaguely recognised.

"Yes," said Kevin. "Who's that?"

"I thought you'd recognise my voice," said the person on the telephone. "Last time we met you left me with some very unpleasant people in a pyramid."

"The-One-Who-Controls?" asked Kevin though he already knew the answer.

"I don't use that name now," he replied. "No-one here can understand me and I can't understand them. I knew it was you when you answered the 'phone because your crystal allows you to understand what I'm saying and I can understand you."

What do you want?"

"I need your help."

How can I help you?" asked Kevin.

"You can get me back to where I came from."

"I thought you wanted to be here on earth."

"Yes, but not like this. I need to go back and you will help me."

"Why should I?" asked Kevin.

"Because if you don't you won't see your friend again."

"What friend?" asked Kevin puzzled. "Marlitta?

"No, your earth friend. I think she is called Tracy."

Chapter 2 – The Challenge

Kevin was amazed.

"What do you mean?" he demanded. "What can you do to Tracy? You have no power at all. You're stranded here on a planet where you can't even speak the language. How can you do anything to Tracy?"

"Not me," said the 'One-Who-Controls'. "I am just the messenger. I have heard from your old friend, Duros. It is he who has your friend, but you could get her back if you were to accept his challenge. But to do that you will first have to get me back to my adopted planet."

"And how am I supposed to do that?"

"You must meet me and I'll tell you."

"Where are you?" asked Kevin.

"I am not far from where you left me. I have been taken to a large building in the nearby city."

"Is it a prison?" asked Kevin.

"No. I don't think so. It has many rooms, all with beds with people in them. Some rooms have several beds, and there are people moving about and going to the people in the beds."

"It sounds like a hospital," said Kevin.

"But I am not ill."

"They may think you are nuts," said Kevin.

"Nuts?"

"Yes, you know, ill in the head. After all, they can't understand what you're saying."

"Perhaps."

"Do you have any freedom?" asked Kevin.

"I can go from my room to the room with seats and the box with pictures. And I can walk in the garden."

"Good," said Kevin. "Leave it with me. I must talk to some other people and then I will find you."

"Thank you. I will walk in the garden every evening just before sunset."

"OK," said Kevin. "Goodbye for now."

"Goodbye. But don't leave it too long or it will be too late."

Kevin replaced the receiver.

"Who was it?" shouted his mother from the kitchen.

"Oh, just a friend," said Kevin. "He wants me to go on a camping trip with him at half term."

"That should be all right," said his mother walking through to the lounge. "Did you say you would go?"

"I told him I'd ask you first."

"Well it's all right by me," said his mother. "I'll start getting your things together. There's only one more school day. Will you want to leave on Saturday, or will you leave it 'til Monday?"

"We'll probably want to get off on Saturday."

Kevin decided that he had better talk to Marlitta and Quartok rather quickly so he decided to have an early night.

He awoke very early the next morning, before his mother was awake. His father was away on business again so he would have about two hours before his mother would expect him up and about.

First, he contacted Marlitta using his crystal and told her to meet him at Quartok's rooms in the Council building in the crystal city. Then he contacted Quartok and told him he would be coming to see him in a few minutes. Quartok was not amused as it was the middle of the night and Kevin had woken him, but he said he would be ready by the time Kevin arrived.

Kevin closed his eyes and visualised the flat platform outside the large crystal building and suddenly it was dark and cold and he was standing outside the Council building. He hurried across to the steps up to the front entrance. There was no one about except for a solitary person going up the steps in front of him. As he came to the doors he realised it was Marlitta. They went in and went straight up to Quartok's rooms.

Inside, Quartok was looking very sleepy in a silk dressing gown, or at least it looked like silk. Lartop was there too.

"Come in," said Quartok. "What is the urgency of this visit?"

Kevin and Marlitta entered and sat down. A small troop of Murin appeared and served them hot drinks. These were the little serving creatures that seemed to appear from nowhere and disappear as quickly. Kevin had thought it was unfair to have these little folk doing all the mundane jobs, but he had since learnt that it was what they wanted to do. Nothing gave them more pleasure than cleaning, tidying and preparing food.

"Duros is still causing trouble," said Kevin when they were seated and sipping their hot drinks.

"What has he done now?" asked Quartok.

"He has kidnapped Tracy Bagshot," said Kevin.

"Oh, is that all?" said Quartok. "I thought it must have been something important for you to wake me in the middle of the night." He was rather grumpy when woken.

"It is not really a matter for the Galactic Union," said Lartop. "You must remember that your planet is outside the Union and therefore none of our concern."

"But it is my concern," said Kevin indignantly. "And as I am Master of the Universe, it is your problem too."

"So, what is the situation?" asked Quartok.

Kevin told them what had happened and asked what they would recommend he did.

"Well I am rather busy at the moment," said Quartok. "And so are most of the other Council members. You remember that you invited a rather large warrior nation to join the Union. Well, that was the easy bit. We're now having to sort out the details, and it could take some time."

"So, what am I supposed to do?" asked Kevin getting a little impatient with them.

"I don't really think you have to do anything," said Lartop. "As Quartok just said, it is not really the concern of the Galactic Union. It's not as if he is threatening you directly or mounting an invasion of Union territories. No, I think he can wait until he does something more positive."

"So I have to go after him myself do I?" said Kevin.

"I don't think that would be a good idea either," said Quartok. "You shouldn't endanger yourself unnecessarily."

"Well, if you won't do anything, I'll just have to do it myself," said Kevin and stood up to leave.

"I cannot condone that," said Quartok. "You must not put yourself in any danger for no good reason."

"I thought I was Master of the Universe," said Kevin. "So why is it that you can tell me what I can and can't do?"

"You are Master of the Universe," said Lartop, "and that is why we have to advise you as to what you should or shouldn't do. You do not have to take our advice, but I would strongly advise you to do so."

"Well you have given me your advice," said Kevin. "I'll go and think about it. Goodbye!"

He walked to the door and Marlitta got up and followed him out. Kevin felt furious. He had not expected such a reaction from Quartok and Lartop. He was used to them being there to assist him whenever he needed help.

"You aren't going to do anything foolish, are you?" asked Marlitta as they walked through the entrance lobby and out onto the steps.

"What am I supposed to do?" said Kevin. "You don't like Tracy and they don't think she matters, so I'll just have to go after her myself."

"I may not like her," said Marlitta. "But I wouldn't let you go off on your own to try and rescue her. If you want to go, I'll go with you."

"Will you really?" said Kevin, surprised.

"Of course I will," she said. "After all, you have put yourself in danger for me, so I can't be surprised if you want to do it for others, even those you don't particularly like. So, when do we start?"

"I've got to go to school today," said Kevin. "I'll be ready to set off tomorrow morning. I'll meet you on the moor by the rocks above my home. You remember those?"

"Yes," said Marlitta. "I'll meet you there. That gives me several days to sort things out back home. Time moves at a different rate there, as you know, but I'll have all that time to get things organised. So, I'll see you then."

"Yes," said Kevin. "'Bye for now."

They both 'jumped' back to their own planets. 'Jumping' was what Kevin called the power of the crystal to take him instantaneously to anywhere he could visualise in his mind.

Only a few minutes had passed on earth since he had left, so he set about getting his things together for his journey, wherever it might take him. It was not like going on holiday where you knew what you would need. He didn't know where he was going or what the conditions might be like. It could be sweltering hot or freezing cold. He just didn't know, and there was limited space in his rucksack.

The day went slowly at school, and he couldn't concentrate on his lessons, but then, nor could the other children just before the half-term holidays. He hurried home after school to finish his packing and when he got home he was met by his mother at the door.

"Have you seen Tracy Bagshot at school today?" she asked.

"No," said Kevin. "Why?"

"Her mother rang to see if she had come back here after school. I said I'd let her know if she turned up."

"No," said Kevin. "She's not in my class so I don't see her often unless I bump into her in the playground."

Kevin thought it best to say as little as possible at this stage. The last thing he wanted was not to be allowed to go camping because Tracy had gone missing.

That evening he went to his room early and closed his eyes and used his mind sight to see if he could locate 'The-One-Who-Controls'. *I can't keep on calling him that*, he thought. *I'll just call him John.*

He soon managed to home-in his viewpoint on the pyramids. From there he soon found the city and set about finding the hospital. It would probably be a new building, he thought, but all the new building seemed to be offices, hotels or museums. Eventually he had a closer look at one of the older buildings that seemed to be quite large and was rewarded immediately. It was indeed a hospital, but was it the right one? He scanned through the corridors and tried to find a garden leading off any of them. Eventually he found one, a sheltered courtyard garden with palm trees, some shrubs and potted plants. In the corner, in the shade of a palm, was a seat, and there sitting on it was 'The-One-Who-Controls', or 'John' as Kevin had decided to call him. Perhaps this would be a good time to speak to him so without thinking further, he 'jumped' and appeared suddenly in front of the startled John.

"Hello John," said Kevin.

"I am not John," he said. "You know my name."

"Yes," said Kevin, "but I think John is easier. Anyway, you don't control anything now. So, what have you done with Tracy?"

"I haven't done anything with her, as I told you on the telephone. It is Duros that has taken her. All I am is the messenger."

He held out his hand and Kevin saw he was holding something that sparkled. He reached out and took it and gasped. It was the crystal ring he had let Tracy keep.

"So, what have I got to do?" he asked.

"Duros has set you a challenge," said John. "You must find your way through the maze to the centre, and there you will find the earth girl."

"Maze?" said Kevin. "What maze?"

"You remember the portals on my planet?" he continued, "the pillars that can transport you from one place to another. Well, Duros has learnt how to programme the routes between them and you will have to find your way through the portals until you find your friend."

"So how does this affect you?" asked Kevin.

"You must take me back to my planet and I will activate the first leg of the maze for you."

"And how am I supposed to get you back to your planet?" asked Kevin. "The portal in the Great Pyramid is closed now and I don't think it can be re-opened."

"That is correct. So, you must use your crystal to take me by the route you used to get there, last time."

"Yes, I could do that," said Kevin. "Be here tomorrow morning and I will meet you again."

"I will be here," answered John, but Kevin hardly heard him as he had 'jumped' back to his bedroom at home.

Chapter 3 – Into the Maze

The next morning Kevin set off up the hill to the rocks where he was to meet Marlitta. The day wasn't marvellous; it was a bit overcast and there was a chill in the breeze and the sky looked threatening. His mother had tried to put him off going, but he said that it would be all right as he had his waterproofs with him. In fact, the weather was the least of his worries as he was setting out on a journey he couldn't even imagine. Perhaps he was being stupid and putting himself into danger for no good reason. Perhaps Tracy wasn't in any danger anyway, but how was he to know? He would just have to go through with it.

At the top of the hill he turned to see where Sniffer had got to but couldn't see him anywhere. Then, as he went between the rocks, he saw Marlitta making a fuss of Sniffer who had obviously got there first.

"So, what now?" asked Marlitta.

"First we must go and get John," said Kevin.

"Who's John?"

"That's what I call 'The-One-Who-Controls'," said Kevin. "He is in a hospital in Egypt. I know where to find him."

"Why do we need him?"

"If we take him back to his planet he will set us on our way through the maze," said Kevin.

"What maze?"

"Well it seems that Duros has set us a challenge," said Kevin. "We are to use the portals, starting on John's planet and find our way to the centre where he is holding Tracy."

"And then what?"

"We bring her back, I suppose."

"I don't like the sound of this," said Marlitta. "Perhaps Quartok has a point. We are putting ourselves into danger with no guarantee that we'll even find Tracy let alone get her back."

"I know that makes sense," said Kevin. "But I can't just leave her out there not knowing what might happen to her. If you don't want to come I'll just have to go alone."

"Too right I don't want to come," said Marlitta. "But I said I would and I mean to keep to my word. So, are we going or are we going to stand here freezing?"

Kevin smiled and took her hand. It still gave him a thrill to do that. He grabbed Sniffer in the other hand and, in a flash, they were in a dark secluded garden in Egypt. There was no sign of John yet as it was still quite early and Kevin didn't know what time John would be allowed out, so they sat on the seat out of sight of the entrance to the garden and waited. Sniffer curled up under the seat and sulked. He would much rather have been exploring but Kevin wouldn't allow it.

After a while there was the sound of someone opening the sliding door from the hospital corridor into the garden. Kevin hoped it was John. He didn't want to meet anyone else. Then they heard shuffling footsteps coming towards them. Sniffer growled softly in the back of his throat and Kevin put a hand down to quieten him. Then a figure came into view. It was John.

"I thought you would be alone," he said.

"You didn't say I couldn't bring a friend," said Kevin. "You know Marlitta I think, and Sniffer." Sniffer poked his head out from beneath the seat and growled.

"Please keep that beast under control," he said backing away.

"No need to worry," said Kevin. "He won't touch you unless I tell him to. Perhaps we should be off then."

They all joined hands and Kevin closed his eyes and thought of the garden where he had first met John, and immediately they were there. It was either early evening or early morning; Kevin wasn't sure.

"So, what now?" he asked.

"Well you know where the portal is," said John.

"I know where it is, yes," said Kevin. "I know that if I walk through it I will come out on Collandar. We did that last time."

"Not now," said John. "All the portals can be switched to connect with any other portal; a bit like your telephone system back on earth."

"Except the portals don't have a dial," said Kevin.

"Oh, but they do," said John. "But not so obvious."

"Then you had better show us how it works," said Marlitta, "or what was the point of us coming here?"

"Oh, I'll show you all right," he said. "But it will be up to you to decide which way to go."

"And how do we decide that?" asked Kevin getting a little annoyed. Sniffer growled and John gave him a sideways glance.

"I'll give you a little clue, and it's no use threatening me with that animal because this is all I have been told. Duros said 'It never rains but it pours, but after the rain comes sun, but you will find what you are looking for in a colder place'. That is exactly what he said and he didn't explain it to me."

"Right," said Kevin. "Now you can show us how to work the portals."

They walked round the lake into the garden and there, glinting in the early morning sun, was the portal. John walked up to it and placed his hand on the surface at eye level.

"If you do this," he said, "you will be able to look through the portal at what is beyond. And if you slide your hand one way or the other, the picture will change as you look through different portals at the far end. You can't see a lot, but it will give you some idea as to what the place looks like. When you have decided upon one you like, just slide your hand straight down, like this, and lift it off the surface. You can then walk through, but you must all go through within a slow count of ten or the portal may switch randomly to another destination and you may not be able to find each other again."

"I suppose, if that happened, we could just walk straight back again," said Kevin.

"If you did that you would not necessarily return to where you had just come from," said John. "All I can say to you is to be very careful and think before you step through."

"Is there anything else we should know?" asked Marlitta.

"There is a lot you should know," said John. "But I am not the person to tell you. All I can say is that many worlds that were in the old empire, and served by the portals, are no longer civilised. Some sustain no life at all while others have been taken over by wild and dangerous creatures. On many of the planets there are several portals sited near each other, while on others they further apart. Your crystals will be of little use to you in this part of the galaxy, but they may help you find the next portal. You will need to learn to listen to the song of the portals. The old ones could do so in their heads, but you might be able to do it with the help of your crystals."

"Is that all you can tell us?" asked Kevin. Sniffer growled again.

"Well, there is one other thing," he said. "You can only reach certain destinations from each portal, so you might have to pass through several to get to your destination. Also, the routes open to you change from time to time, so you might have to wait until a route opens for you. This portal will be able to take you to your first destination now and will remain open for about an hour. So, I will leave you to plan your route."

He turned and started to walk away.

"Good luck to you," he said without turning. Sniffer growled again.

"Oh all right, Sniffer," said Kevin. "But just a little bite." Sniffer raced after John who, hearing him coming, started to run as fast as he could towards the little white building, but Sniffer was fasted and caught him in mid-flight and brought him to the ground. He had a few good bites of his leg and then turned and walked proudly away. John, pulled himself to his feet and limped away as fast as he could, looking back at intervals to make sure Sniffer wasn't returning for another go at him.

Kevin had placed his hand on the surface of the portal and was peering through the gaps between his fingers.

"Can't see much," he said.

"Try moving your hand," said Marlitta. "It could be dark at the other end."

"Good thinking," said Kevin and slid his hand slowly across the surface. "I can see something now."

There were scenes of desert places, some where there was nothing but water, barren rocks, dense jungle, none of which looked very tempting.

"How are we supposed to choose where to go?" said Kevin. "This is ridiculous."

"Remember what John said," said Marlitta. "It never rains but it pours. Is there a place where it's pouring with rain?"

I haven't seen one yet," said Kevin. "If that's what we're looking for, perhaps we should prepare ourselves first. You know, get into our waterproofs."

They opened their packs and took out their waterproof clothes and clambered into them. Then they put their packs back on.

"Keep a hold of Sniffer," said Kevin. "As soon as I find a place that looks right, I'll lock it off and we go straight through. We won't have long so be ready."

Kevin went back to searching through the portal and eventually he came across a scene of a bleak mountainside where it was teaming with rain.

"I think this is it," he said. "Are you ready?"

"Ready."

He slid his hand downward to lock the portal open and stepped through. Marlitta followed hastily with Sniffer. When they were through they had a quick look round to make sure it was safe. There wasn't a soul in sight, which wasn't surprising as the rain was really torrential. Kevin didn't think he'd ever been in such a rainstorm before.

"Let's have a look for the next stop," said Kevin. "I don't want to stay here too long."

He put his hand on the portal and peered through but it was difficult to see anything with the water pouring down the surface.

"We'll have to find some shelter until it stops," said Marlitta. "It can't do this all the time."

They looked about them. They were on the side of a craggy mountain of bare rock. There was a way down to a flat plateau, but it was difficult walking on the rocks because of the water that was pouring down them, but they managed to get down onto more level ground.

"What's that over there?" shouted Marlitta above the noise of the rain. Kevin looked in the direction she was pointing and could see a dark patch under the looming cliff.

"It could be a cave," shouted Kevin. "Let's have a look." He set off towards the cliff face.

"Be careful," shouted Marlitta. "You don't know what might be in there." Kevin slowed down and crept cautiously to the cave mouth.

It was only a small cave but it looked dry in there. Kevin held up his hand and hoped his crystal could summon up enough power to produce a light and was rewarded with a bright beam of pure white light that shone straight into the cave. It was empty, so they went thankfully in out of the rain. It was quieter inside which made it easier to talk.

"Do you think you could start a fire?" said Marlitta. "There seems to be a bit of debris in here. It must have blown in at some time from some trees higher up the cliff."

"I didn't see any," said Kevin.

"Nor did I," said Marlitta. "I was just guessing." She scraped some small twigs and leaves into a heap and put some loose rocks around to keep of the breeze that gusted in every now and then. Then she broke up some larger pieces of wood and started stacking them to one side.

"You could help," she said.

"Right," said Kevin and started dragging some larger pieces from the back of the cave and breaking them up. When they had finished, he knelt down in front of the prepared twigs and tried to summon up enough power from his crystal to light the fire. There was some power there, but not enough. "You'll have to help with your crystal."

They both focussed all their thoughts into starting a small fire. If they had used as much effort in their part of the galaxy, the whole cave would have exploded, but all they managed to do was to cause a small piece of twig to start smouldering. While Kevin kept the power going, Marlitta blew gently on it and eventually it caught and a small flame appeared.

They fed it more small twigs and some dryish leaves and eventually it grew into a nice little fire. Then they started putting on larger pieces, carefully so as not to put it out and after quite a while of effort, they had a cosy little fire going.

Kevin built up a wall of rocks in front of it to protect it from the weather and to shield the light in case it should be seen from down in the valley, which wasn't very likely while the rain continued, but you never knew what was out there.

Kevin opened his rucksack and took out the few provisions he had brought with him. There was some chocolate, a small pack of sandwiches, and some cake. They shared them out and had soon eaten them.

"We'll have to find something to eat here," said Marlitta, "when it stops raining."

"Or move on to the next place and hope there is some wild fruit growing."

It seemed to be getting dark, so they settled down to rest, though it wasn't really their bedtime yet.

Marlitta put the two packs together to use to lean against. Kevin felt a bit uneasy when she snuggled up against him but he tried not to show it. Eventually they both drifted off to sleep and woke to find that it was light and the rain had stopped.

Chapter 4 – New Friends

Kevin was also quite alarmed to find that he had his arm around Marlitta, so he pulled it away as carefully as he could, then pretended to be asleep again.

"I don't like to bother you," said Marlitta, "but I think we have company."

Kevin opened his eyes and raised his head slowly until he could just see over the rocks they had piled at the front of the cave, and there, just outside the cave, stood three people who could only be described as Neanderthals. There seemed to be a man, a woman and a child of about Kevin's age. They were not small like most of the aliens Kevin had met but were about the size that you would expect them to be on earth. They each held a spear with a wicked looking head on it made from flint. Kevin knew that these were very primitive but were also very effective as they had razor sharp edges. He had seen them being made on 'Time Team' and knew how difficult it was to do.

"I think we should act as if we weren't afraid," said Marlitta. "Let's stand up and look them in the eye, and if they look as if they're going to throw those things at us, dive to the ground again."

They both stood up and faced the newcomers, who, much to their surprise, dropped to their knees and touched their foreheads to the ground.

"Hello," said Kevin, feeling rather stupid.

"Greetings, oh great ones," said the man.

"Could you stand up, please," said Kevin.

The three figures looked up at them but didn't stand up.

"Up onto your feet, please," said Kevin trying to sound authoritative. They got up but kept their heads bowed. "What are your names?"

The man looked up at him in surprise. "Surely you know our names, oh great ones?"

"I do not remember the name of every being in the universe," said Kevin.

"No, of course not," said the man. "We can't be that important to you. I am Nargoo, this is Gleddritt, and this is our son, Boojar. We are of the Narwitt tribe who hunt the dense forests in the valley."

"Why are you up here, then?" said Marlitta.

"We come to pay our respects to the Gods at their totem." He pointed at the portal.

"Have you ever seen any of the Gods come from there?" asked Kevin.

"There are tales of the Gods coming through there in times gone by," said Nargoo. "But there haven't been any for many generations."

"They can't have seen Duros and Tracy, then," said Kevin to Marlitta. "Perhaps they went straight back through the portal to a different place."

"There were two strange people who came down from here a few days ago," said Nargoo, "but they weren't Gods."

"What did they look like?" asked Marlitta.

"There was an evil creature," said Nargoo. "Small but smelling of evil. He had with him a young girl who could have been of our race but had fairer skin and hair. She was bigger than you."

"Do you know where they went?" asked Kevin. "We need to catch up with them."

"I would not advise it," said Nargoo. "They could be dangerous."

"They went to the Eternal City," said Gleddritt suddenly. "It's no use trying to hide it," she said to Nargoo, "they are sure to find out."

"The Eternal City?" said Kevin.

"Yes," said Nargoo. "We couldn't stop them. We know we must be punished, but we did our best. Please be merciful to us. We have guarded the city well for generations untold. It is the first time we have failed."

"You will not be punished," said Marlitta. "But you can lead us there as quickly as possible."

"Oh, thank you," said Nargoo. "We are forever in your debt."

"Oh be quiet, Nargoo, you stupid man and lead the way back to the encampment," said Gleddritt.

"Can I go next?" said Boojar who had been silent until now.

"No," said Gleddritt. "You will take up the rear to protect from ambush."

"Ambush?" said Kevin, alarmed. "Who would ambush us?"

"Not who," said Nargoo. "But what? There are animals that we hunt and there are creatures that hunt us, so we must go very quietly. Please follow us closely." Kevin and Marlitta picked up their packs and followed Nargoo and Gleddritt down the track, which was still wet, and slippery from last night's rain. Boojar followed behind looking important.

At first the going was rough and rocky, much like the English Lake District, and then they came to the tree line and entered a quite dense forest through which the path wound. Underfoot the ground was softer, being covered with dead leaves and pine needles. As they descended, it got warmer and more humid and greener plants appeared at the sides of the path.

Suddenly Nargoo stopped and held up his hand. They all stopped behind him. No one spoke. Kevin couldn't hear anything, but he looked in the direction that the others were looking.

"I think they will pass without seeing us," said Nargoo quietly.

"What are they?" asked Kevin.

"They are the Guardians of the Eternal City," said Nargoo.

"Try the mindsight," said Marlitta so that only Kevin could hear.

Kevin closed his eyes and let the crystal do its work. There was still enough power in it to be able to see things in the distance. Kevin could see the forest ahead of them as if he still had his eyes open, then he moved forward, in his mind so that he could see things further away. It was like having a television camera that he could control using his mind. His point of view moved forward through the trees until he could see a group of creatures moving away from them lower down the valley. There were six figures walking upright and they seemed to be wearing metal armour because the light glinted off it as they walked rather stiffly down the track.

Kevin zoomed in closer. It was still difficult to realise that he couldn't be seen. They were quite bulky creatures who walked in a very clumsy fashion, very unlike the Neanderthal type people they were with. As his view point got closer, Kevin realised that they were completely covered in metal, and when he looked closely at their knees and elbows, he could see that the joints were all metal.

"They're robots," he said aloud.

"What are robots?" asked Nargoo.

"They are not living creatures," said Kevin. "They are machines made of metal."

"I do not know," said Nargoo. "Any of our people who have been close to the Guardians have never returned. I think we can move on now."

They set off again down the path and veered off to the right rather than follow the route taken by the guardians. Soon the forest thinned out and opened into a wide green valley with a stream racing down one side of it, swelled by the recent rain. Further down the valley, Kevin could see smoke rising and thought he could make out some small round buildings.

"Our camp is at the end of the valley," said Nargoo. "Boojar, run ahead and tell them we have visitors and to prepare a welcome."

Boojar set off at a steady jog and was soon well ahead of them. As they passed a rocky outcrop, Nargoo held up his hand again and they all stopped. He raised his spear to shoulder height and crept forward. Gleddritt held Kevin's shoulder to stop him following and signed for him to keep quiet. Suddenly an animal, rather like a small pig, raced out of the thicket where it had been hiding and made for the stream, but Nargoo had already hurled his spear with deadly accuracy. The pig squealed once and then lay still with the spear sticking out of its back.

Nargoo trotted over to it, removed the spear and picked up the animal by its hind feet and threw it over his shoulder and set off again towards the camp.

"Very good to eat," said Gleddritt grinning. Kevin didn't look so sure.

"Don't you eat meat?" said Marlitta to Kevin.

"Of course," said Kevin. "But I don't kill it with a spear. Do you?"

"Not nowadays," said Marlitta. "But we used to before you came. Don't you remember what it was like when you first came to my planet? We had to hunt and kill whatever we could to survive. We even ate those lizards that lived in the desert regions."

The camp, as Nargoo had called it, was getting quite close now. It looked more like a permanent village than a camp. Kevin was expecting to see tents, but these were like Bronze Age round houses with straw roofs.

"I thought you said it was a camp," said Kevin. "This looks more like a permanent village."

"Well it is permanent as long as the Guardians don't find it," said Gleddritt who was walking with Kevin and Marlitta while Nargoo went on ahead. "We have many of these camps, you see, and we move from one to the other as necessary. It would be difficult and unnecessary to take everything with us and set it all up again at the next camp site, so we leave it all and just take ourselves."

"I see what you mean," said Kevin. "How long do you stay in one place?"

"It depends on the hunting, and the Guardians," said Gleddritt. "We have been here for a while, but as there are Guardians about, we will probably move on soon."

As they walked into the camp, a crowd of children ran out and gathered around them chattering to each other. Boojar was there telling the others all about them and revelling in the importance it gave him.

"Please come into our hut," said Nargoo. "We can talk more easily in there away from the noise of the children."

They went in and sat down on bundles of animal skins, which turned out to be quite comfortable. There was a fire burning in the centre of the floor and the smoke curled up and out through a hole at the top leaving the air reasonably clear round the sides where they were sitting.

Gleddritt cut some meat off a large chunk that was on a spit near the fire and gave them each a good portion and a lump of bread. They all sat and ate in silence and as they were finishing Nargoo asked them about their plans.

"We need to know where those other two went," said Kevin.

"The evil ones?"

"Well, one of them is evil," said Kevin, "but the other is his captive. We want to rescue her."

"It is thought they went to the Eternal City," said Nargoo. "I will speak to the elders and storytellers and see if they can help you. It will be very difficult to get you in there as it is guarded by the metal Guardians we passed on the way down from the mountain."

"Thank you," said Kevin. "That would be very helpful. When can we talk to them?"

"There will be a story-telling around the fire, tonight," said Nargoo. "We would be honoured if you would join us. You may put your questions to the Elders and they will tell you what they know in the traditional way through stories."

"Thank you," said Kevin. "That would be great."

After they had finished eating, they went outside to have a look around. Boojar followed them like a pet puppy and kept asking questions that Kevin found very difficult to answer. At least he kept all the other children from pestering them.

"Are you going to kill the Guardians?" he asked.

"I don't know yet," said Kevin. "I need to find out a lot more about them. What can you tell me about them?"

"They are creatures of great evil, I think," he answered sounding very serious for such a young boy. "They guard the Eternal City and will let no one into it. They also search for hunters in the forest and destroy our camps and kill our people if they can catch us. But we are very fast and clever in the forest and can usually escape easily. They lose interest in us if they can't see us."

"What weapons do they have?" asked Marlitta who had been thinking deeply.

"They do not use spears, as we do," he said. "But they point at us, like this." He pointed his finger at Kevin. "Then the person they point at falls dead. I do not know how they do it. I have tried, but it doesn't work for me."

"Laser weapons, I should think," said Kevin. "It's a pity our crystals have no power. We could set up a shield otherwise."

"Does Spectro know what could be done against them?" asked Marlitta. Kevin had forgotten about Spectro, the voice of the crystal. "I'll ask him."

"I heard," said Spectro in Kevin's head. "If they are using energy weapons you could make simple reflective shields. The energy is like light and can be reflected with mirrors."

"And where are we to get mirrors here?" asked Kevin, also inside his mind. "The natives here don't use metal. They only have stone spears."

"Perhaps if you could get close enough to one of these robots," said Spectro, "you could get one of them to throw a spear at it and see if you can disable it. Then you could use the metal it is made of to make a shield."

"Sounds dodgy to me," said Kevin. He told Marlitta what Spectro had said.

"Possible, I suppose," she replied. "But first we could see if there's any other way we could make a mirror."

"I'll ask at the story-telling tonight," said Kevin.

Chapter 5 – Stories round the Fire

After dusk had settled on the camp, all its inhabitants came out of their huts and gathered round the campfire in small family groups. Kevin and Marlitta sat with Nargoo and his family, which included Nargoo's brothers and sisters and their families, so there was quite a group of them. On the far side of the fire sat the Elders, who numbered ten. These were the oldest members of the tribe and were sometimes called the Grandfathers. They seemed to rule the tribe and decide when things should be done and who should do them. They were also the historians and remembered all the stories that were handed down from father to son over the centuries. Some of the very oldest stories had either been lost altogether or had been changed a bit in the telling and retelling.

When they were all settled by the fire, a group of them started singing a strange but compelling chant. Soon others were joining in until the whole clearing echoed with the strains of the chant. Some of the boys had taken up drums and were beating an intricate rhythm to accompany the chant while others played on whistles made out of hollow reeds.

Suddenly the singing and playing stopped as if a conductor had brought down his baton at the end of the piece, and there was silence in the clearing except for the crackle of the fire.

One of the Elders stood up and approached the fire where he stopped and gazed round at the assembled company.

"I would like to welcome our guests," he said. He sounded more like a scholar than a savage. "May your stay with us be pleasant. My first story in the telling of our history goes back to the time before the Guardians. We were a proud and very advanced civilisation and the Eternal City was our capital and was also known as the gateway to the universe. We don't know why. Our ancestors had many machines and we had many mechanical creatures to do our bidding. It is said that we ruled over other worlds, but I don't know how this could be.

"Then there came a time of darkness. It is not told what happened, just that our civilisation crumbled and we were forced out into the forest to fend for ourselves and were not allowed back into the Eternal City and were hunted down and killed if we came too close to it. Now we live in the forest and hunt for our food, and that is our way. We are happy to be hunters and we are happy to live in the forest. It would be better, though, if there were no Guardians to bother us, but that is a small price to pay."

The elder bowed to them and went back to his seat. Another one got up and moved to the fire.

"I tell the stories of leaders and heroes of our tribe," he said. "Is there anything in particular that I can tell you?"

"I really need to know what happened to the two people who came here recently and went to the Eternal City," said Kevin. "Can you tell me about them, please?"

"That is not really part of our folk lore," he said. "But I can tell it from the story of Hadreg the Hunter. Hadreg is of the Hadwitt tribe, who are related to us but who hunt in another part of the forest. Hadreg and his son were out tracking a wounded braglett and were catching up with it, when they came upon a strange pair of people walking through the forest. One was small but had some sort of power that held Haqdreg's hand so that he could not raise his spear. The other was a girl, much like one of our own and was larger than the man but seemed to be in his power.

"Hadreg asked who they were and what they wanted, and the man said that they were just passing through and wanted to find the Eternal City, though he did not call it that. He told Hadreg to take him to the City, but Hadreg told him it was forbidden and that the Guardians would kill them. He suggested they went back the way they had come. They were on the path down from the mountain.

This made the little man very angry and said that they would take them to the City immediately, and however much Hadreg and his son tried to resist, they had no option but to take them. They were very frightened as they went closer and closer to the City, for they expected to see Guardians at any moment.

"When they reached the City, they went to the foot of the steps that led up into the main gate where two Guardians stood, one on each side. Hadreg thought this would be the end of him and his son, but the Guardians did not kill them. The little man held up something shiny and just walked between them and into the City. The Guardians just stood there and let them go in. Hadreg and his son turned and crept away and hid themselves in the forest as quickly as they could. But they weren't followed."

"We will need to go there, then," said Kevin. "Do you know what he held up for them to see? Was it like this?" he showed them his crystal.

"No. It was more like a flat disk, but Hadreg couldn't see very clearly."

"Thank you," said Kevin.

The Elder sat down and another took his place.

"I would like to tell you about our life style," said the Elder. "We live in the forest, as you have seen, and hunt animals with our spears. We also gather wild fruits and some other plants and roots that we can eat. We hunt in a range of one day's walk from our camp and move on to our other camps when the hunting gets poor. There are only a few types of animal that we can kill with our spears as some animals are too fast or too small to hit with a spear."

"Have you tried using a bow and arrows?" asked Kevin. The Elder looked a bit annoyed at being interrupted but decided not to make an issue of it.

"I do not know what these are," he said.

"I could show you how to make them," said Kevin. "And a slingshot is another useful weapon." He would have suggested a catapult but didn't think they would have elastic.

"We would be very grateful to learn of such things," said the Elder. "I will introduce you to the spear makers later. We do not have skills in making things because in the days of the great ones, we did not have to make things. That was done for us by the Servitors. I think they must have been similar to the Guardians, but I am not sure."

"You were served by robots?" said Kevin amazed. "You must have been very advanced. What went wrong?"

"I do not know," answered the Elder.

"Who made the robots that served you?" asked Kevin.

"They made themselves, I think. They made everything that we needed; all our food, clothes, houses and they must have made more Servitors as well."

"It sounds as if they were in control," said Kevin. "They must have decided that they didn't need you and threw you out."

"I suppose that is possible," said the Elder. "Maybe that is why they try to destroy us whenever they find us. They don't want us to get back in control. I don't know why they are worried about us, though. We don't know how to control or destroy them."

"There might be a way," said Kevin. "They use weapons that send beams of light and heat to kill people. What we need is something like a mirror to reflect the light back at them."

"What is a mirror?"

"It is a shiny thing that you can see yourself in," said Kevin. "Rather like looking into a pool of water and seeing yourself there."

"Yes, I have seen that, but there is something better than that. There is a creature that lives in the swamps, that flies. It has a skin that is very shiny. I think that would do what you want. There is only one problem, though. It isn't possible to kill one with a spear. They are much too fast."

"How big are they?" asked Kevin.

"About the size of the animal that we are cooking for the feast, tonight." He pointed at the animal Nargoo had killed earlier, that was cooking on a spit over the fire. It was about the size of a dog, though looked more like a small pig.

The Elder sat down and another stood up.

"Is there anything else you would like to hear about?" he asked.

"What do you know about the shining pillar up on the mountain?" asked Kevin.

"Not a lot is known about it," he said. "It has been there as long as anyone can remember. We think it must belong to the Gods. They use it to visit us from time to time."

"Is that why Nargoo thought we were Gods, then?" asked Kevin.

"If you are not Gods, then who are you, and how did you get here?"

"We came through the pillar," said Kevin. "We come from other worlds, but we are not Gods. The people who built them weren't Gods, either. They aren't magic, but they use a technology that we don't understand. But we can use them. We are looking for another one, similar to the one on the mountain. We need to follow the two you saw going into the city. Could there be one in there?"

"It is possible, but no-one has been into the city and returned, so we cannot tell."

"We thought it might be possible to destroy one of the Guardians with a spear," said Kevin. "Then we could use the metal to make a mirror."

"We have tried that," said the Elder. "But they destroyed our spears in mid-flight and then turned on us. Several people were killed by them. No, the only way will be to hunt the Flying Demons in the swamps."

"Flying Demons?" said Kevin. "What are they?"

"They are the creatures we told you about with the shiny skin. We call them Flying Demons because of their appearance. People used to think they were evil creatures, but in fact they are not dangerous, but they are very difficult to catch or kill. They skim over the surface of the water, very low and very fast, and if we were to hit one with a spear, it would come down into the water and be lost."

"Couldn't we wade out and get it?" asked Marlitta who had been sitting quietly listening.

"No. It is death to enter the waters of the swamp," said the Elder. "There are creatures that live in the water that attack in swarms and will strip the flesh off your bones in seconds."

"They sound like piranhas," said Kevin. "There're fish on my planet that can do that. But if you had a string attached to the spear, you could pull it back."

"Possibly," said the Elder, "but as we have told you, it is very difficult to hit a Flying Demon with a spear. They are too quick."

Kevin told them more about the bow and arrow, and it was decided that he would show the spear makers how to make bows and arrows, the following day. Then the meat was carved up and everyone ate and chatted among themselves. It was the most exciting thing that had happened for a long time, not counting the appearance of the Guardians every now and again.

After they had finished eating there was some spontaneous singing and then the different family groups went back to their huts to sleep. Kevin and Marlitta went with Nargoo and his family to their hut and were given places to make their beds out of animal skins and bracken.

Eventually they settled down and slept, as they were quite tired.

Chapter 6 – The Swamps

The following morning, they woke early. The sun was just beginning to break through the trees and the forest was full of the sound of creatures whistling and calling in the trees. Kevin assumed that most of them must be birds of a sort, though none of the sounds was recognisable to him.

The family was up and about and there was a smell of cooking from the hearth of bread and meat. They all gathered round the fire and ate warm, freshly baked bread and a chunk of meat. There was a wicker basket full of fruit for them to finish up with.

After they had finished, Nargoo took them to another hut, which was partly open at the front. It was a sort of workshop where several people were busy chipping stone and scraping long straight boughs of wood. This must be the place where they made the spears.

"This is Dondig, the Master Spear Maker," said Nargoo pointing out a big burly fellow who was busy chipping rock to make spearheads. "Dondig, these are our guests. I want them to show you how to make a different type of weapon."

Dondig didn't look too pleased. He held his high position in this community by being the main authority on spear making and he felt threatened by the fact that these newcomers knew more than he did. Kevin realised this, as it wasn't too difficult to see.

"Where I come from," said Kevin carefully, "they use other weapons that may be useful to you. But I'm not a craftsman so I will need your skill to be able to do this."

Dondig's expression lightened a little.

"What is this weapon?" he asked.

Kevin explained to him about bows and arrows.

"You see," he said. "The arrows are a bit like spears, but much smaller, and they have feathers at the end to make them fly straight. They are not thrown but fired from a bow which is made of a piece of springy wood which is bent by tying a piece of string between the ends."

Dondig didn't look too convinced.

"You will have to show me," he said. So, they went out into the forest to find some suitable slender stems to make into a bow. They cut several different types to try out and took them back to the workshop. Kevin told one of the assistants how to carve it to make it the right shape for a bow. He had had a go with bows and arrows at a mediaeval fete, once and had a good idea what they looked like. One of the others found some suitable string. They made this from a plant that grew in the open lands beyond the forest. It was a bit like hemp from which rope is made on earth.

While this was going on, Dondig was carving an arrow as Kevin had told him.

"Are you sure this is big enough to kill something?" he asked looking sceptical.

"Oh yes," said Kevin. "It may not be as heavy as your spears, but it will go very fast."

It took quite a time for Dondig to make an arrowhead as he wasn't used to making them so small. The first few attempts ended in rubble, but eventually he managed to produce a usable one.

He fitted it to the shaft in the same way as he did the spearheads, but much smaller and more delicate. Then they had to find some feathers.

They did kill and eat larger birds from time to time but didn't have any use for the feathers except to use as decoration. Hunters would put them in their hair to show how good they were at hunting and none wanted to give them up to be used on arrows. Eventually a few small ones were found and Kevin cut them up and explained how they should be fitted to the arrow shafts, at least to the best of his knowledge.

Finally, it was all finished and Kevin had to demonstrate how it was used. He wasn't particularly good at this, but at least it would show them what to do.

He fitted the arrow to the string, pulled back the bow, and fired the arrow at a tree not too far away. The arrow sped across the clearing, missed the tree but hit one further away and sunk into the bark where it remained, quivering.

There was a gasp from all those watching and one of the boys ran to retrieve the arrow.

"I'm sure you can improve on this," said Kevin. "Then you will be Master Bow maker too."

Dondig looked pleased.

"Thank you," he said. "I will start work immediately."

Kevin took some of the spare string and found some pieces of animal skin that was used for making shoes and belts and things of that sort and started to make a slingshot. He had made them before and they didn't take much skill. Boojar watched him, fascinated.

"How will it work?" he asked eagerly.

"I'll show you when I've finished it," said Kevin. "Go to the stream and see if you can find me some nice round stones about that big." He held his finger and thumb apart to indicate the size of the pebble he wanted. Boojar raced off and Kevin continued in peace to finish the slingshot.

A group of youngsters and a few older members of the tribe gathered round to watch and when Boojar returned with the pebbles, he pushed his way through to the front and proudly showed Kevin what he had collected.

Kevin discarded one or two as being too large or too small and another two because they weren't round enough. Then he took one of the pebbles and fitted it into the leather sling, held the ends together and started to swing it round his head.

Everyone moved back to give him room and Kevin released one end of the sling to send the pebble flying over the treetops and crashing down through the branches.

There was a gasp from the assembled group.

"Can I try?" asked Boojar.

"Of course you can," said Kevin. "But you must be very careful not to hit anyone. You must aim for something and not just send it anywhere."

Kevin made everyone else move back behind the line of fire and showed Boojar how to hold the ends together so that he could release one end. Then he showed him how to swing it around his head, keeping his eye firmly on the target.

"Now aim at that tree down there," said Kevin pointing at a tall slender tree.

Boojar looked at the tree and then started to swing the slingshot round his head. Then he released the end and the shot flew off towards the tree. It didn't hit it but came quite close.

There was uproar, as everyone wanted to have a go.

"First, you'll all have to make one of these," said Kevin. "Take a good look at this one, then go away and find the things to make one. I'll help you put them together, then Boojar can show you how to use them, but you'll have to practise a lot if you want to be able to hit anything."

Kevin went back to Nargoo's hut and left the small group to find string and leather to make slingshots. Marlitta had gone back earlier and was sitting outside talking to Gleddritt. She smiled as Kevin walked up to them.

"Have you got them all working?" she asked.

"Yes," said Kevin. "And I've got Boojar showing the others how to use a slingshot."

"He'll love that," said Gleddritt. "He likes being the centre of attention."

Every now and then, someone would come up to them for advice on making their slingshot, and Kevin would show them. Soon they all had one and had gone off to the river to gather pebbles.

"We'll have to wait until Dondig has made the other weapons before we set off for the swamps," said Gleddritt.

"And they'll have to learn how to shoot them too," said Kevin. "It takes a lot of practice."

"I think they will learn quickly," said Gleddritt. "They are excellent with spears."

And so it was to turn out. Dondig had soon improved the original design of the bows to make them stronger but harder to pull, but the arrows went further. He also used a different type of stone for the arrowhead that would not shatter each time it was fired. He also made some arrows using sharp bone for the tips. These were excellent as they wouldn't stick into wood, but just bounced off, but would cut right into an animal. This meant that if they shot at a bird and missed, they didn't lose their arrows.

Boojar had set up a target made out of an old animal skin draped over a wooden frame and the group with the slingshots was firing pebbles at it for all they were worth. They were soon joined by some of the men with bows and arrows. At first, arrows and pebbles went everywhere, and very few hit the target. But when Kevin and Marlitta walked across to watch them, they were beginning to hit the target most of the time.

The next day a hunting group went out, as they normally would, but instead of spears, they took only the new bows and arrows.

Boojar led another small group of boys, with slingshots, out into the forest to see what they could get.

That evening they ate very well indeed. All the hunters were overjoyed with their new weapons as they were able to fire arrows from concealment without startling the animals when they stood up to throw. The boys brought back some birds that looked rather like colourful chickens and were all puffed up with pride at being able to contribute to the larder.

"I think I'm a great hunter, now," said Boojar handing one of the birds to Gleddritt.

"Don't be too proud," said Gleddritt. "It is very good what you have done, but we all work as a team in this tribe, and everyone does his bit, however great or small."

Boojar looked a bit disappointed but ran off to talk hunting with his friends.

The following day, they decided to set out for the swamps. A group of six hunters were to accompany them as well as Nargoo, Gleddritt, and Boojar, who refused to be left behind. It would take them most of the day to get to the swamps, so the hunters took every opportunity to practise their new skill as well as stock the larder for the evening meal.

It was easy walking as the trees were thinner in the direction of the swamps and the ground was quite flat and the paths grassy and smooth. They walked in silence so they did not disturb any game they might come upon.

As they got nearer to the swamps, the ground got softer and wetter, and eventually became quite soggy and difficult to walk on.

"I think we had better move off the track and find firmer ground for tonight's camp," said Nargoo and veered off to his left. They had to clamber over some rocks and break through some dense undergrowth before coming out onto a flat grassy area overlooking a lake. "This will be a good place to camp."

They took off their packs and started to set camp. They didn't have tents and would have to sleep in the open, but it didn't look like rain and was quite warm, so Kevin wasn't too bothered. He had slept in the open on the moors, more than once.

Gleddritt went to find dry wood for a fire, while Nargoo dug a fire-pit for her. Boojar just got in everyone's way and had to be told to sit down.

When the fire was set, Nargoo lit it very quickly by striking a stone with something he had in his pocket.

"What's that?" asked Kevin.

"This is a very valuable thing," he said. It is my firestone. There are not many of them and I am lucky to have this one." He held it out to Kevin to look at.

"It's iron," said Kevin. "Where did you get it?"

"It was handed down to me by my father, and he got it from his father. Without it we could not start a fire."

"It's made of a metal called iron," said Kevin. "Or it might be steel, that's a very tough type of iron. You can make knives out of it."

Nargoo looked doubtful.

"Look, I'll show you," said Kevin opening his rucksack and taking out his old camping knife. He opened the blade and those watching gasped. "It's just a knife, look."

Kevin picked up a piece of wood and cut chunks off it. It remained the main talking point for the rest of the evening.

Chapter 7 – The Noises in the Night

After they had settled down to sleep, Kevin lay awake for quite a while in spite of the fact he was tired out. It was the noises that kept him awake. The air was full of scratching and scraping and squeaking and whistling, and every now and then there was a deep gurgling sound. In themselves the noises weren't frightening, but as you dozed off to sleep, your mind made strange and frightening things out of them.

After a while he managed to doze off, but was woken again by another sound, not loud, but persistent, like someone whispering nearby. He raised his head slowly to see if he could see what it was, but it went quiet when he did so. He lay his head down again and lay and listened. Shortly it started again. Then there was a sound as if something was moving through the undergrowth nearby. Then it stopped, but the whispering started again.

He decided to use his 'mindsight' with the help of his crystal, so he closed his eyes and could then look out over the camp without moving. He looked into the undergrowth but couldn't see anything. Every now and again the undergrowth would move, but when he looked, there was nothing to see. It was as if the creature were invisible.

After a while he dozed off but woke suddenly. He had heard something but didn't know what. He listened intently. Had it been a twig snapping? He suddenly felt very cold, as if there were a ghost approaching. He lay as still as he could and tried to sink into the ground. He could feel it coming closer, he knew it was there but couldn't see anything.

Slowly, the feeling started to subside, and soon he felt it was safe to sit up and look around. He could see the others huddled in groups about him, sleeping soundly. The two moons had risen and cast a dim light across the marshes, which reflected the light through a thin haze that had gathered over the water. It was very quiet now, rather like it was when a predator was about.

Kevin strained his eyes to see through the mist but could see nothing. He looked all round him but could still see nothing, so he lay down again and had soon dozed off into a troubled sleep where he dreamed of something stalking him through a dark wood. Whenever he walked he could hear footsteps behind him, but when he stopped the following footsteps stopped too. He tried to run but his feet seemed to be stuck to the ground and it was like walking through treacle.

There was a sharp crack and he woke with a start. All was quiet again. He froze and listened but could hear nothing so he raised his head again to look around. Again, there was nothing to be seen. Then he heard a rustling noise nearby but could see nothing. He was now very frightened and began to wish he was safe at home again. Why had he set off into the unknown like this? Without the power of his crystal he was just a twelve-year-old boy. The rest might just as well be a dream.

But it wasn't. It was real and he was lying awake in the dark on a strange world with danger creeping up on him in the dark. Perhaps he should wake the others. But that meant making a noise that might provoke the prowling creature to strike.

He tried to contact Marlitta using his mind speech, one of the few powers of the crystal left to him in this distant part of the galaxy, but he couldn't wake her. He felt about him for something to use if they should be attacked, but there wasn't much to hand. There were no large rocks or sticks, and his knife was in his rucksack, which he was resting his head on. Perhaps he could wriggle his hand inside and find the knife.

He moved as slowly and quietly as he could, but it was very difficult. Eventually, he found the opening and slid his hand slowly inside. Where was that knife? He couldn't find it.

There was another slithering sound nearby. Was it coming closer? He couldn't tell. Where was that knife? Of course, it was in the side pocket, which meant removing his hand from the main flap and finding the side pocket. He had to turn slowly onto his other side to be able to find the side pocket. Now to unzip it. Why was it that zips never wanted to slide easily when you needed them to?

Another crack of a twig breaking followed by more slithering sounds. Kevin froze. How close was it now? He couldn't tell. The zip came open and he managed to wriggle his hand into the side pocket. Now, where is that knife? He felt around in the pocket and forced his hand down to the bottom but couldn't find the knife. It was agony trying to twist his arm without moving his body and now the knife wasn't in this pocket. It must be in the other one.

Another crack and a rustle and then a sound rather like a sigh. It was getting nearer so where was that knife?

He slowly turned over onto his other side so that he now had his back to the approaching menace and he felt sure he could feel its eyes staring at his helpless back. Next, he had to move the rucksack so that he could get his hand into the other pocket. This seemed to take an age and his back ached under the pressure of raising his head just enough to allow the rucksack to move, inch by painful inch until the pocket was within reach.

More slithering noises. Could it be a snake? Kevin didn't think so because of the breaking twig noises. How close was it now?

He started to struggle with the zipper on the pocket and had as much trouble with this one as he had had with the other. It was difficult to do it one-handed but, after a bit of a struggle, he managed it. Now where was that knife? He slid his hand as far as he could into the pocket, which was full of all sorts of useful things, but not the knife. Then, right at the bottom, he found what he had been searching for. It took a bit more twisting and pushing before he could get a grip on it. Then, thankfully, he slid his hand out of the pocket and rolled slowly over so that he could open the knife.

Now he felt a little more secure, but then a thought struck him. Would he face a lion or a rhinoceros armed with just a camping knife? He thought not, but then again, he didn't think it was something as big as that that he could hear creeping up on them.

Slowly he raised his head to see if he could see what was out there. At first, he could see nothing out of the ordinary, but after a time there was another sound and he could now focus his attention on where he thought the sound came from. If it moved, he thought, he might be able to see something.

He waited for what seemed an eternity, and then there was another click followed by a scraping noise. He thought he saw a movement, but it was difficult to tell in the darkness. Then he thought of something. Why not use his crystal to give him some light? He knew that there was enough power available to do that. Why hadn't he thought of that before?

Slowly he sat up and then managed to get into a crouching position. Then he pointed his finger at the place he thought he had seen the movement and focused his mind on producing a beam of light. Suddenly, a bright beam of light shot from his finger, dazzling him momentarily. But when his eyes had adjusted he found there was nothing there. Had it gone before his eyes had adjusted themselves?

He stood up quietly, not wanting to wake the others and crept down to the place where he thought he had seen a movement and examined the ground and plants for breakages or footprints but found nothing. Then he noticed that the ground was a bit wet, as if something had stood there dripping. He followed the wet track down to the water's edge where he noticed some scrape marks in the mud. What could it have been? He thought of an otter, though he knew it wouldn't be like anything found on earth. If it had been dangerous, it would have attacked them, he thought, so he went back and settled down to sleep. He was exhausted so fell asleep almost immediately and slept soundly until almost dawn.

When he woke he wasn't too sure where he was but was aware that his bed was very uncomfortable.

Then he remembered. He was lying near the lake where he had imagined he had heard noises in the night. But then he heard it again. He opened his eyes. It was just beginning to get light and there was a rosy dawn creeping across the marshes, dappling the ground with golden light. The noise came again, but it wasn't quite as frightening in the light.

Slowly he raised his head and could see the tall grass-like plants swaying nearby. There was something creeping through the grass towards him.

Got you now, he thought and grabbed his knife and crept towards the patch of grass, hiding himself behind some small bushes as he approached. He waited behind the last bush at the edge of the grass, hoping the creature would come past him without being aware of his presence.

The grass swayed and rustled and he could now hear a snuffling noise as if something was sniffing to sense if danger were near.

There was a scuttling noise and something came into view at the edge of the grass. Kevin didn't wait to think, he just leapt on it.

There was a scream from it and then a blubbering sort of noise, but it struggled and scratched and bit to try and get free.

"Keep still, will you," said Kevin.

"Leave me alone," it said. It spoke! Kevin was amazed. It was an animal that could speak.

"Then keep still and I won't hurt you," said Kevin. It kept still so Kevin took his weight off the thing so that he could see what he had caught. It was a bit like a huge otter but had soft blue fur.

There was a snigger nearby and Kevin looked up to see that the rest of the camp was awake and everyone was standing looking at him.

"What are you doing to that poor creature?" asked Marlitta.

"It was sneaking up on us," said Kevin. "I heard it in the night, but I caught it this morning."

"Sneaking, is it?" said the creature. "I don't sneak. Anyway, who's the intruder? Not me, that's for sure. It's lucky for you I didn't bite your throat, pouncing on me like that. Now can you please let me go."

"Who are you," said Kevin letting go of the creature.

"I am Plugo of the water people," it said. "Who you are is more to the point."

"We are sorry about this," said Nargoo stepping forward. "This is Kevin. He is a visitor to our world. He didn't know what you were."

"Well, perhaps you could tell him then."

"This is Plugo," said Nargoo. "He is one of the water people who live in the marshes. He is a hunter and we are in his territory."

"What do you want here?" asked Plugo. "I thought you had agreed not to hunt in our territory."

"We are not hunting, as such," said Nargoo. "We are after one of the shining ones that fly over your water."

"What do you want one of those for?" he asked. "You can't eat them."

"We want the shiny skin," said Nargoo.

"Ask a silly question," said Plugo.

"Kevin needs the skin to make a mirror," said Nargoo. "We can use that to protect us against the Guardians."

"The Guardians don't bother us," said Plugo. "They don't like water. One of them fell in once and he exploded."

"Water?" said Kevin. "I hadn't thought of that. They must be powered by electricity and water will short it out. You have been a great help to us Plugo. Thank you very much."

"My pleasure," said Plugo not quite sure how he had been of help.

"Now all we have to do is kill one of the flying things," said Kevin.

Chapter 8 – The Eternal City

They had to wait until the sun had risen for the flying creatures to appear. When they did, Kevin was amazed by what he saw. They were enormous dragonflies that zoomed close to the surface of the water at great speed, the sun flashing blindingly off their shiny skins. It looked as if they were made of glass.

"I don't think we can hit one of those with an arrow," said Nargoo. "They are too fast, and if we tie strings to our arrows they will be much more difficult to aim."

One or two of those with bows and arrows fired at the dragonfly as it passed but couldn't even make a near miss.

"I think I could hit one," said Boojar swinging his sling.

"But how would we get it back?" asked Kevin. "If it lands in the water, the fish will get it, or at least it would get us if we tried to wade out to it."

"I could fetch it for you," said Plugo who had been watching with interest.

"Don't the fish attack you?" asked Kevin.

"No," said Plugo. "They don't like our fur. I'll swim out and if you can bring one down I'll get it for you." He slipped silently into the water leaving hardly a ripple. After a while his head popped up again. "Ready when you are."

Boojar started swinging his sling and let fly as soon as a dragonfly zoomed past, but he narrowly missed it. After a few tries, he hit one on the side of its body throwing it off balance, but it didn't bring it down. However, it did make it angry and it turned and dive-bombed them making them all drop to the ground.

After a few passes it went away. Shortly another one appeared and this time Boojar's aim was better and he hit it on the side of the head and it fell like a stone into the water where Plugo was, and holding it above the water, he swam back with it.

"We'll have to skin it straight away," said Nargoo. "Before it shrivels up." He took out his flint knife and started cutting up the creature. Kevin looked away as it wasn't a very pleasant sight. He thought it would be a good idea to thank Plugo for his help, so he walked across to the water's edge where Plugo was lying in the sun. He thanked him for his help and Plugo looked a bit embarrassed but quite pleased.

"It was a pleasure," he said.

"Are there many of you living here in the marshes?" asked Kevin.

"Not many," answered Plugo. "We tend to live a solitary life. We hunt alone but every year, when it gets hotter, I go and look for a mate and raise a family. Then they all go off to find their own hunting grounds. At this time of year, when it rains a lot, it is good for hunting as the marshes get full of water as they are now. It is nearly the end of the rainy season now. We haven't had rain for a few days, so I'll soon be setting of into the higher ground to find a mate."

"Where do you go?" asked Kevin.

"I follow my stream up into the hills where it is cooler and go to one of the mountain pools where the fish are good to eat and the water is cool and wait for a mate to come along. Then we will catch fish together and build a nest in a burrow at the side of the river. We store the fish in the burrow to feed the little ones when they arrive. When they are a few weeks old we teach them to catch fish and to avoid creatures that would hurt us. We have a very pleasant time until the rains come again. Then we swim down the river on the flood waters and when we get to the marshes we go our separate ways."

"Don't you ever see them again?" asked Kevin.

"Sometimes," answered Plugo. "But often not. The marshes are very extensive and youngsters swim off to find hunting grounds of their own, and sometimes this means going far away from here. But as I said, we are solitary by nature and don't like the company of others except when we are bringing up a family."

Nargoo came over to them proudly carrying the dragonfly skin stretched over a bent piece of twig that he had cut from the bushes nearby. They had sewn the edges with string that was laced across the back. Kevin was very impressed.

"It looks like a shield," he said holding it in front of himself. He had to explain 'shield' to the others because it wasn't something they had heard of before. "We could do with several of these so that we can have one each."

They decided to stay for the rest of the day, hunting dragonflies and making shields. Plugo, despite preferring his own company, seemed quite happy to stay with them and retrieve the dead dragonflies from the water.

By nightfall they had made six gleaming shields and were feeling quite hungry. Plugo had gone off for a while to hunt and had brought them several large fish which were lying on the ground near a fire that Gleddritt was tending. The others had been out looking for wild vegetables and fruit to go with the fish.

"Pity there aren't any potatoes here," said Kevin. "Then we could have fish and chips."

The others looked puzzled, so Kevin had to try and explain fish and chips, but he didn't feel that he had succeeded.

As the sun set they sat round the fire and ate the fish with some cooked root vegetables and followed it with fruit. It was delicious and they all were very hungry.

Plugo said goodbye to them and disappeared into the dark waters of the marsh. Kevin felt a pang of regret as he had quite taken to the strange creature. He thought how good it would have been to take him back to earth but thought that perhaps he would be much safer here on his own world.

That night they slept well and, in the morning, packed their things and set off back to the village. It was a miserable journey as shortly after setting off, the skies opened and the rain torrented down unrelentingly. Luckily it was warm, but not very pleasant. The others didn't seem to mind as they were used to it.

Back at the village they gathered round the fire in Nargoo's hut and tried to dry off.

"You seem to enjoy this weather," said Kevin.

"The good thing about it is that we know we are safe from the Guardians when it rains," said Nargoo.

"They don't like the rain," said Boojar. "They stay in their city when it rains."

"What we need," said Kevin "is a water pump so that we can squirt water at the Guardians."

"I don't know what a pump is," said Nargoo. "But we have water bags that we use for storing water. The children sometimes play with them and squeeze them so that water squirts out. They get very wet."

"Sounds exactly what we want," said Kevin. "How do you carry them?"

"We sling them on our backs," said Nargoo. "Boojar, go and fetch one, will you." Boojar ran from the hut out into the rain again and soon returned with a large bag made from animal skin. It appeared to be about half full of water. Kevin took it and went to the door and experimented with it. He found that if he restricted the nozzle, he could get a good range with it.

"Why don't we go when it's raining?" said Kevin.

"Because they won't come out into the rain," said Nargoo "but they can send their light beams out from the buildings and kill us before we can get close. If we wait until it's fine, they will come out and approach us before shooting."

"How many water bags have you got?" asked Marlitta.

"Quite a few," said Nargoo. "We should have one each when we attack the city."

"It could be quite difficult to squirt the water and hold a shield at the same time," said Kevin experimenting with the water bag. "Perhaps if we added a strap we could hang them over one shoulder and squeeze with our elbows. That way it could be done with one hand."

"I'll see what we can do about that," said Gleddritt and, taking the water bag from Kevin, went out into the rain.

That evening they sat inside and planned the attack on the city.

The following day was still very wet, but it gave them time to make shoulder straps for the water bags. Kevin designed a nozzle out of horn that produced a very powerful water jet when the bag was squeezed.

"I think that should be very good," he said. "I only hope these things aren't waterproof."

The following day, Kevin and Marlitta accompanied by Nargoo and two of the hunters, set out towards the city. Boojar was most disappointed that he wasn't allowed to go and he sat and sulked by his hut.

"Perhaps next time," said his mother. "It will take several attacks before they can get into the city. We don't know how dangerous it is, so it's best if just a few go this time."

As they walked through the forest, Kevin could hardly believe that they were walking into danger. The sun was shining and birds were calling in the trees. It was idyllic, but after a while, Nargoo signalled for them to be quiet, so they crept forward very slowly until they reached the edge of the trees. Beyond was an open plain covered in low stunted vegetation and in the middle was an ancient looking group of buildings, a bit like a fairy-tale castle.

"Is that the city?" asked Kevin in surprise. "It doesn't look much."

"That is the city," said Nargoo. "I think it was larger in the old days but that is where the Guardians stay."

"Right," said Kevin. "Hold your shields in front of you and we'll move out into the open. Stand in a row, side by side and try and make a wall of our shields." He remembered from his history lessons that that was how the Romans fought their battles.

They moved into a line and then started to move towards the city. Nothing seemed to happen for ages. Kevin didn't want to get too far from the trees, as he felt very exposed out here.

"How near can you usually get?" he asked.

"They usually would have come out by now," said Nargoo.

"Perhaps it is because we are behind these shields," said Marlitta. "If we turn the shields sideways on for a moment and then straighten them up again, perhaps they will see us and come out."

They tried it, but nothing happened. They tried it again and this time they moved forward and immediately there were flashes of light as the sun caught the moving metal parts of the robots. After a while Kevin could see them more clearly. There were two of them, heading straight towards them. They hid behind their shields again and the robots slowed and moved from side to side as if searching.

"They can't see us," said Kevin. "How close dare we let them get without our shields up?"

"They don't shoot until they are within a spear's throw," said Nargoo. So, they removed their shields again and the robots returned to their direct path towards them. As they got closer, Kevin could see that they were quite evil looking things carrying what looked like some sort of gun that you might see in a Star Wars film. Those must be the laser guns.

As they got to within what Kevin judged to be a spear's throw, the first one raised its gun towards them.

"Behind your shields," shouted Kevin. There was a blinding flash but no one was hurt but a small bush burst into flames halfway between them and the robots. The beam had been reflected.

Both robots started firing, now, and bushes burst into flames all around. Still the robots advanced until Kevin thought they must be within range of their water squirters.

"Start squirting," he said and squeezed his water bag for all he was worth. A stream of water shot forward and the first robot, thinking it was a spear, tried to shoot it out of the air but failed miserably. The water hit it and there was a blinding flash and it fell over.

In the meantime, the others had opened up with their water cannons, and within seconds the two robots were lying on the ground twitching.

They approached slowly, but there was no response from them, so Kevin went up to the nearest one and tried to move it but it was too heavy. The others formed a wall of shields around their victims so as not to attract any more attention from the city, while Kevin examined the robots. He wondered what Duros had held up to them so that they would let him pass and whether it was something the robots carried. The first lay on its back and there was nothing removable on its front, but the other had fallen face downward, and as he approached it, Kevin could see a sort of panel on its back. It came off quite easily and inside he could see what looked like some controls.

Chapter 9 – Inside the City

"I think this is the control panel," said Kevin.

"What's that?" asked Nargoo.

"These are just machines," said Kevin. "They're not alive, and this is where you can give them orders, and turn them on and off."

"How can anyone do that?" asked Nargoo. "You can't get close enough to them."

"But Duros did," continued Kevin. "You told us that he just walked into the city."

"Yes, but he had something in his hand," said Nargoo.

"Was it like this?" asked Kevin pulling something out of the back of the robot.

"I think it might have been," said Nargoo. "But I'm not sure."

"We'll just have to try it out," said Kevin. "It would be nice to be able to reprogramme one of these, but I think we've broken them. Anyway, I wouldn't know how to do it."

"You could always ask me," said Spectro in Kevin's head. It gave Kevin quite a surprise as he hadn't heard from him for quite a while, and with the crystal's power being so low in this part of the galaxy he had quite forgotten about him.

"Okay, go ahead," said Kevin, still speaking silently in his head.

"Look at the controls," said Spectro "and I will translate for you."

Kevin looked and all the little squiggles and markings changed slowly into English. Spectro then explained to Kevin how to reprogramme the machine to be friendly. It was actually quite easy.

"What you have in your hand," continued Spectro "is the pass key. Each robot must have one to work, and if you appear to have one when you approach the robots, they will think you are one of them. Then you can command them to let you reprogramme them. These two are damaged so it will be quite safe to leave them here."

"I have worked out how to reprogramme the robots," said Kevin out loud. "And this will keep us safe to approach them." He held up the shiny disk.

"I think you might have had some help from Spectro," said Marlitta in his head. The crystals still had enough power for communication.

"What makes you think that?" asked Kevin grinning. The others looked puzzled but didn't say anything. "No, I know how to reprogramme these things so we could convert them all to be helpful."

"You've got to get to one first," said Marlitta. "How do we do that? If we squirt them with water they won't be any use."

"I don't think you're listening," said Kevin waving the shiny disk. "This is our pass key. If I hold this up so they can see it, they will keep still and not attack me."

"I'm glad you said 'you'," said Marlitta. "I don't think I'd want to risk it."

"I'll need you all to hold the shields in case they fire before I can use the disk," said Kevin. "We make a wall of shields again and walk up to the city. Then I use the disk and reprogramme the first one."

"Have we got to do that for all of them?" asked Marlitta.

"I hope not," said Kevin. "I am hoping that I can instruct the first one to reprogramme the next, and then that one will go and reprogramme others until they are all reprogrammed."

"Sounds good," said Marlitta. "Too good."

"They're only machines," said Kevin.

"I know," said Marlitta. "But no-one programmed them to kill humans. They seem to have done that by themselves."

"I'll have to put in a main command then," said Kevin. "That will stop them ever doing that again. And if something does go wrong with one of them, I'll make sure that it is dealt with by the others. That's assuming I can reprogramme them at all."

There was a noise behind them, and turning, they saw that the first robot had recovered and got to its feet. Kevin held up the disk and hoped that it worked. The robot simply stood and looked at them.

"What do I do now?" Kevin asked Spectro in his mind.

"Go over to it and open the panel in its back." Kevin did that. "Now set the switches as follows." Spectro gave instructions and Kevin clicked the switches. "Now you can reprogramme it by speaking to it."

Kevin gave it a set of overriding instructions which included not being able to kill humans or allow anything else to kill them. He also gave instructions as to what they could allow in making new robots or repairing old ones, so that this situation could never happen again. He put the disk back into the second robot and the first robot reprogrammed it. It took only seconds. Then the two robots walked off into the city to reprogramme the others.

"That should have done it, I think," said Kevin. "Now you can make use of them."

"What do you mean?" asked Nargoo.

"They will do whatever you want them to do now," said Kevin. "Just like in the old days. They will grow your food, prepare it for you. You can live in the city and they will wait on you and do whatever you ask them to."

"I think that could get a bit boring," said Gleddritt. "I think I prefer our old type of life. We are hunters and live in the forest. It is good that we don't have to worry about the Guardians any more. But I wouldn't want them to do everything for us."

"Well that's up to you," said Kevin. "If there's anything you need help with, you just have to tell them what you want and they'll do it. In the meantime, perhaps you should tell them just to look after the city. One day you might need to use it."

They moved slowly towards the city, keeping an eye open for rogue robots, but all was quiet until they reached the steps to the main gate. Then two large robots appeared and took up positions either side of the door but didn't look threatening. Then the two original robots, or at least they looked the same as the first two, came out.

"All are reprogrammed," said one of them. "What are your orders?"

"Perhaps you would like to show us around the city," said Kevin.

"Certainly," said the robot. "Please follow me."

"What is your name?" asked Marlitta.

"We do not have names," replied the robot. "We have serial numbers, but that is only for repair records."

"Well I think you should have names," said Marlitta. "Perhaps Nargoo and his people should give you names."

"That would be very pleasant," said the robot. "I will look forward to receiving mine."

They entered the city, which was a sight to behold. You wouldn't believe it had been uninhabited for thousands of years. It was like a fairy-tale castle, everything shining and new looking, but there were no people, just a steady bustle of robots of all shapes and sizes going about their endless tasks, keeping the city in prime condition for the return of their masters. They seemed to have forgotten that it was they who had got rid of their masters in the first place.

They walked through gardens and into large halls crammed full of statues and pictures and the most luxurious furnishings. A small robot came up to them and offered them some food on a gold plate. It was startling enough for Kevin, who had seen a few surprising things since becoming Master of the Universe, but to Nargoo it was too much. He stood with his mouth wide open and stared at everything.

"It is too much," he said.

"You are right," said Gleddritt. "We should not tell anyone about this. They would want to come and laze about and be fed by these things. I don't think we are ready."

"Perhaps you should tell the robots not to allow anyone in, but not to hurt them," said Kevin. "Leave it so that only you can come here. Then when you have learned how to make best use of the city, you could give new orders. You can always call out robots to help in the camps, if you need extra help."

"Thank you," said Nargoo. "That would be a good idea. It will take a long time to get used to this and it is possible that the tribes might squabble over it. We have not had fighting for many years, and I wouldn't like this to be the cause of more fighting. We will go back now and tell the others that the Guardians will no longer harm us, but that we must keep away from the city. If we need help, I will come here and ask for it."

"I think we should say goodbye to you soon," said Kevin. "I think this is the way for us to leave your world. I have enjoyed meeting you."

"You have taught us much," said Nargoo. "Hunting will be easier with the bows and arrows. When will you leave?"

"Tomorrow, I think," said Kevin. "But first we must go back to the camp and collect our things. Sniffer will wonder where we have gone. But first I must find out where the portal is."

The robot led them further into the city until they came to a wide paved square with a small building at its centre. The robot headed towards it but stopped outside.

"We are not allowed to enter," it said. "We will wait for you here."

Inside was a single room with walls of polished marble. There was not much light, but as they moved they had the impression that they could see through the marble to something beyond.

"I think the walls are portals," said Kevin and walked closer to one of the walls. He touched his hands onto the wall and it seemed to disappear though he could still feel it. In front of him was a large expanse of sand stretching into the distance.

"Doesn't look too good," said Kevin. "We're looking for a hot place," said Marlitta. "Don't you remember?"

"Yes," said Kevin. "But this looks a bit too hot. Let's try one of the other walls."

There were actually eight walls and each looked out onto a different landscape, all of which looked hot.

"Let's go back to the camp," said Marlitta. "We'll have to decide tomorrow which way to go."

Back at the camp, everyone was eager to know what had happened at the city, including Sniffer who nearly knocked them over in his joy to see them back. Kevin told them that they had succeeded in taming the Guardians and that it was now safe to approach the city.

That evening, around the campfire, Kevin explained to the whole village that they could now make use of the city's many facilities if they wished to, but he said it was up to Nargoo to decide what they should do. There was much discussion with many of the younger ones wanting to move into the city and have the robots wait on them, but Nargoo stood up and moved to the fire and everyone went quiet.

"I have to advise caution," he said. "Let me tell you what happened to our ancestors. They were a very advanced and clever people who built great cities and traded throughout the universe using the portals through which Kevin and Marlitta came. They built machines to work for them. The Guardians are actually machines built by our ancestors. They used to serve them in every way, bringing them food, clothes, and anything they might want. And they grew lazy and allowed the robots more and more control over what they did. And this included the way they programmed themselves and the new robots they built, and these robots became more and more intelligent until there came a day when the robots, in their cold logical way, decided that the people were wasteful and unnecessary and decided to remove them. There was a great uprising and the robots killed all the people they came in contact with, but a few escaped into the forest to live as hunters. Many died as they didn't have the skills to survive, but some learnt to hunt and made their life in the forest moving from camp to camp to avoid being caught and killed by the robots.

"We have now brought the robots back under our control, but we mustn't fall into the trap our ancestors fell into. If we use them to help us, we must maintain control and, at first, only use them to do things that are necessary to us, but I would urge you to keep our present way of life. It is good and will be even better now we do not have to keep avoiding the Guardians."

An elderly looking man got to his feet and moved to the fire. He looked rather gruff and Kevin thought there was going to be an argument.

"If these things can help us," he said in a deep grumbling voice, "perhaps we could use them to rebuild the camps. We never get much time, what with hunting and such."

"That sounds like an excellent idea," said Nargoo. "I will arrange it."

Another much younger lad leapt to his feet.

"What rubbish is this?" he shouted. "Let's move to the city. If you won't, I will and so will others. You can't stop us."

"That's where you're wrong," said Nargoo. "The robots will not allow you into the city until I tell them to. It is for your own good. If there is anything you need, you can put it to the council, and if they think it sensible, then we will let the robots do it for you."

There was a bit of grumbling but as everyone ate and drank they became more mellow and Kevin felt that things would turn out well for them all on this planet.

Chapter 10 – On into Danger

The next day Kevin, Marlitta and Sniffer left the camp and headed towards the city. There were long goodbyes but eventually they were on their way. Kevin felt a bit trepidatious as they walked to the city. It had been a pleasant time on this planet, and now that the robots had been brought under control, it would have been pleasant to spend some time here. But he knew he had to move on if he was to be able to find Duros and Tracy, and anyway, he had to go on if he was ever going to find his way back to earth and his home.

Back in the strange octagonal room, they scanned the scenes that appeared before them. They were looking for somewhere hot, and most scenes seemed to be of hot places.

"I wonder if Sniffer could help," said Marlitta suddenly. "There might still be traces of their scent here."

"Can't hurt to try," said Kevin. Then he used his mind power through the crystal to communicate with Sniffer. He didn't use words; that wouldn't have been any good. He used visual images. Sniffer growled when Kevin pictured Duros, so he knew they were on the right track. Then he concentrated on the floor and then looked at the walls. Sniffer seemed to understand and started sniffing around the floor. It must have been difficult for him, as they had been in before, leaving their own more recent scent. But this was what Sniffer was good at. His tail was wagging, which meant he was onto something. Suddenly he shot forward and disappeared through one of the walls. Kevin grabbed Marlitta and dashed after him.

They were suddenly dazzled by the glaring sun and had to shade their eyes until they had adjusted. They found themselves standing near a huge rock, which looked hand carved, if a little roughly, or maybe it was just very old.

"That must be this end of the portal," said Kevin.

They were in a dense jungle, which dripped with water, and steam rose from the hot ground. There was incessant noise all around from the denizens of the jungle, but nothing could be seen. The heat was overpowering and they were soon sweating profusely.

"Where did Sniffer go?" said Kevin.

"I don't know," said Marlitta. "Perhaps you should call him back with your crystal."

Kevin tried, but Sniffer didn't appear and he couldn't feel Sniffer's presence through the crystal either.

"I think we've lost even more crystal power here," said Kevin. He tried speaking through the crystal, in his mind, but Marlitta didn't respond. He repeated it aloud and told her that he had just tried to speak to her through the crystal. Marlitta looked alarmed but said nothing.

"We'll have to see if we can follow his tracks," said Kevin looking at the ground around his feet. There were some signs of Sniffer's passage like broken plants and trampled grass.

They followed the tracks into the jungle but it was very difficult for them to force themselves through the thick undergrowth. Also, there were nasty creatures that clung to any exposed skin, like leeches. Marlitta cried out as something dropped onto her arm. It looked like a big spider but had too many legs. Kevin hit it with his hand and it scuttled away into the undergrowth.

They struggled onward but lost any sign of Sniffer's progress. They just wanted to find an open area, but the jungle stayed hot, wet and dense. Although it had been morning when they left the last planet, it appeared to be late afternoon here and would soon be getting dark.

"We must find somewhere safe before it gets dark," said Kevin who didn't like it here at all and was worried what other sorts of creature were about, looking for their next meal. "Look for a tree to climb."

They struggled on but couldn't see any trees that would be easy to climb. Suddenly Marlitta stopped and seemed to be listening.

"What is it?" asked Kevin.

"Shush. Listen."

"All I can hear is creatures screeching," said Kevin. "What can you hear?"

"I think I can hear running water," said Marlitta. "Maybe a waterfall."

Kevin strained to hear but couldn't.

"This way," said Marlitta and headed off to the left. The going was no better but was also no worse. Soon Kevin could hear it too. It did sound like a waterfall or rapids, perhaps. The ground started to slope downwards as if they were at the edge of a plateau, but the trees were too tall to be able to see far. The undergrowth got less dense and there were more rocks and boulders about and the noise of the water was getting very loud now.

Suddenly, they emerged from the dense forest at the edge of a rocky gorge where, deep below them, ran an angry torrent. There was actually some sort of path leading downward, perhaps made by some sort of animal. There was nowhere else to go so they followed it.

The sound of the thundering torrent was now so loud that they could hardly speak to each other without shouting. Kevin tried the mind speech again and found, to his relief, that it did work over short distances.

"What do you think is down here?" asked Marlitta.

"I don't know," said Kevin. "Perhaps a cave or some sort of shelter, I hope."

They stopped for a short rest, as it was impossible to keep going in this heat. They could see out into the distance now, though everywhere appeared to be covered with trees. There was a vast plain below them which was covered with a thinner covering of trees with a few patches of open ground here and there. The sun was getting quite low in the sky now, so they set off again along the path. It wasn't easy going, as the path was very steep and rocky.

Just before it got dark, they turned a corner around a rocky outcrop to find a small cave in the rock. They stopped and looked at it carefully.

"Do you think anything lives here?" asked Kevin.

"How would I know," said Marlitta. "Can you use your mind sight to see inside?"

"I'll try." It did still work, but inside the cave was dark and it wasn't possible to see very far. "Perhaps we should throw something in."

"And see what comes out?" said Marlitta. "Better find something heavy to throw, just in case it's big and angry."

Kevin crept up to the cave mouth and hurled a rock as far inside as he could. Marlitta stood to one side with a large rock held above her head. Nothing happened.

"Better try again," said Kevin and threw another rock inside. There was a squawk and something shot out of the cave and disappeared down the track at an amazing speed.

"What was that?" said Marlitta.

"Search me," said Kevin. "It went too fast to see. I wonder if there are any more of them in there." He threw another rock in but there was no response. "I think it's safe to go in."

They crawled into the cave and made themselves as comfortable as they could. It was too warm to need a fire and they had brought some food with them so they settled down to eat. It was only lunchtime for them though it was getting dark outside.

"I wonder where Sniffer's got to," said Kevin. "I'm getting a bit worried about him."

"He'll find us eventually," said Marlitta. "You mightn't be able to contact him with your crystal, but he still has his nose and I'm sure he'll pick up our scent eventually."

"I hope you're right," said Kevin. "It's just that we don't know what's out there."

"I think he can look after himself," said Marlitta. "How about using your mind sight to see what's about."

Kevin settled down, closed his eyes and focused on the path outside. As it was dark, he couldn't see a lot so he gave up. They talked for quite a long time as neither of them was tired. Eventually they dozed off and slept well into the morning. When they woke, they had something to eat and then shuffled to the front of the cave. Kevin peeked out carefully.

"I can't see anything," he said. "I think the coast is clear."

They crawled out and stood up. The sun was well up into the sky and it was already getting quite hot. As they moved off down the track, Kevin suddenly heard a sound from above them. Some pebbles tumbled down onto the path ahead followed by four strange creatures. They were a bit like baboons but with some feline features. Their faces were rather like the faces of cheetahs but they had hands like those of a chimp. Each grasped a weapon. Two had spears, one had a club and the other had what looked like a knife.

Kevin backed away from them and thought about heading back up the track, but when he turned he found that there were more of the creatures behind them. They were trapped so they stood still and waited to see what the creatures had in mind. They didn't seem too brave, but that didn't mean that they wouldn't attack them.

"Now what do we do?" asked Marlitta.

"I don't know," said Kevin. "They have weapons so they mean business. What do you think they want?"

"To eat us, perhaps?"

Kevin bent down and picked up a rock.

"I wonder if they speak," he said and walked towards the smaller group hefting the rock in his hand. "What do you want?"

The creatures backed off a little, and then one of them moved forward again and held up his spear.

"What do *you* want?" it said.

"We are looking for some other people like us who came through here," said Kevin. "We mean you no harm." The creature looked pointedly at the rock in Kevin's hand. "Just self-defence." He threw the rock down and showed them that his hands were empty."

The creatures talked among themselves for a while then turned back to Kevin.

"You will come with us," it said and headed off down the track. The creatures behind moved forward and waved their weapons at them, so Kevin and Marlitta set off after the leading group.

"Where are we going?" he asked but received no reply.

It was a long way down the slope, but eventually they reached more level ground and entered the jungle again, but at least here there was a path. The creatures walked in a half upright, half all fours posture using the knuckles of one hand to balance with and the other to hold their weapons. Kevin could hear the leading creatures talking in an agitated way but couldn't make out what they were saying.

Soon they came to an open area and the bright light made them blink, but as soon as their eyes became accustomed to the light, they could see that they were in a village of sorts. There were small hut-like structures in a circle, but they looked too small to accommodate all the creatures. Other creatures had come out of the huts and some had emerged from the forest and were now gathering round them, not looking too friendly. One of the creatures moved forward and glared at them.

"What do you want here?" it said in a cackling voice.

"I have already told you," said Kevin. "We are just passing through and are trying to find two people similar to ourselves who have passed through a little while ago."

"But you have no right to be here," the creature continued. "This area is forbidden to you. You will have to wait until we can obtain a judgement from the Kraddock. Take them."

Several of the creatures leapt forward and grabbed them and pushed them off to the edge of the clearing where there was a large wooden cage. One of them held the door open while the others pushed them inside. The door slammed behind them and was fastened.

"You will stay here until the Kraddock comes," said the spokesman and turned his back on them and walked away. The others took a last look at the strange newcomers and loped off to carry on with whatever they had been doing before.

"Now what?" said Kevin.

"How should I know?" said Marlitta. "We'll just have to wait and see what this Kraddock is, won't we?"

"I suppose so," said Kevin feeling a bit dejected. He felt in his rucksack and pulled out the remainder of the food and they sat and ate it in silence. Then they just sat and waited as the sun went down behind the trees and the night creatures started their nocturnal chorus.

Chapter 11 – Riddles at Dawn

Luckily it didn't get too cold at night, even so they found it difficult to sleep. The ground was very uncomfortable and the unfamiliar sounds kept disturbing them, not to speak of the worry about what would happen when this mysterious Kraddock arrived.

Kevin had just managed to doze off when a sound woke him. It was strange really because there were so many sounds out there. But this was a different sound, a close-by quiet sort of sound. He opened his eyes slowly and looked in the direction he thought the sound had come from. At first, he could see nothing as it was quite dark, but then he thought he saw a movement.

"Who is it?" he asked softly not wanting to disturb Marlitta, but Marlitta was awake and alert too. There was no answer.

"Who is it?" asked Kevin again. "I know you're there. What are you scared of? We are in this cage and can't get at you."

There was another movement and something came close to the bars of the cage. It wasn't as large as the creatures they had been captured by, but it was too dark to see clearly.

"I think it is a young one," said Marlitta. "Hello little one. What is your name?"

It shuffled a little and then said in a small voice, "I am Soodar."

"Hello Soodar," said Marlitta. "What are you doing here? It must be past your bedtime."

"I wanted to see the Dring."

"What is a Dring?" asked Marlitta.

"You are," said Soodar. "They said they had caught two Dring and are waiting for the Kraddock to come and test them."

"What is the Kraddock?" asked Kevin.

"Don't you know?" asked Soodar in surprise.

"No," said Kevin. "We are strangers here."

"Perhaps you could explain to us," said Marlitta.

"The Kraddock is the all-powerful," said Soodar. "He flies over the forest and makes sure everyone is doing what they have to do and not wandering into the territory of others. If there is a problem, he flies down and passes judgement. If he finds the person guilty, he eats him and flies off again."

"Eats them?" said Kevin in horror. "What sort of creature is this Kraddock?"

"I do not know," said Soodar. "I haven't seen him, but I am told he is as big as ten people and has great black wings. He doesn't have a face like us but a great sharp pointed thing sticks out where his nose should be."

"Sounds like a bird to me," said Kevin. "How big is it?"

"It is about as tall as two men," said Soodar. "But much broader. It can kill with one strike of its leg. It has big claws."

"I don't like the sound of him," said Kevin. "When will he come?"

"I don't know," said Soodar. "But he is said to visit at sunrise."

"Can you get us out of here?" asked Kevin.

"Of course," said Soodar. "But I am not allowed to. I am sorry. But I can give you this. Now I must go."

There was a scuffling noise and he was gone leaving Kevin holding a small hard object. It was a little flint blade, but it wasn't big enough to be able to cut through the bars of the cage. Kevin had a look at the fastening of the door, but could not loosen it, so they settled down for the night. They didn't get much sleep but did doze a bit out of sheer exhaustion. The night seemed to go on forever, and Kevin wasn't sure if that was a good thing or not. Every time he woke it was still dark and the denizens of the night were still calling to each other. As dawn broke, he had just managed to fall into a deep sleep and the sun was rising into the sky when he woke again. Nothing had happened and the strange creatures were all going about their business and ignoring them completely.

"I don't suppose they'll bring us breakfast," said Kevin as Marlitta rubbed her eyes and sat up.

"Probably just as well," said Marlitta. "We don't know what sort of food they eat."

"Well we'll have to get some new food soon," said Kevin. "All ours has gone."

"Have you tried your crystal?" asked Marlitta. "See if you can get us out of here."

"I don't think it will be any good," replied Kevin. "I've already tried to call Sniffer but can't get any response. Anyway, I'll have a go." He concentrated on the fastening to the cage door but there was no response.

"Not enough power," said Spectro. "So don't waste what there is." Kevin was startled, as he had forgotten about Spectro. He had assumed that because there was no power there would be no Spectro either. He told Marlitta what Spectro had said and then had a closer look at the way the cage was fastened. It didn't seem anything too sophisticated, but he couldn't reach far enough to get hold of the catch.

"What did Soodar give you?" asked Marlitta. Kevin showed her the blade.

"I don't know what use it will be," said Kevin. "Oh, look out. Here comes trouble."

A group of the creatures was walking purposefully towards them. When they reached the cage, one of them opened it and the others grabbed Kevin and Marlitta and dragged them out.

"What are you going to do with us?" shouted Kevin. But no one answered.

They were dragged roughly across to the centre of the clearing where there were two posts sticking out of the ground. Each of them was taken to a post and their hands were tied behind the post so that they couldn't move.

When they were secured, the creatures hurried away looking furtively upwards as they went.

"What now?" said Kevin.

"By the way they were looking at the sky," said Marlitta, "I would think that they are expecting the Kraddock to be arriving at any time. By the way, where's that blade that Soodar gave you?"

"It's still in my hand," said Kevin. "They never bothered to search me."

"Well see if you can use it then."

Kevin tried to manoeuvre it so that he could cut the ropes. It was very difficult, as he didn't want to cut himself or drop the blade. Eventually he had managed to cut through the cords and his hands were free. He turned to Marlitta and cut her bonds as well.

"Better stand against the posts," said Marlitta. "If they see we've escaped they will come and tie us up again."

"They seemed rather nervous, though," said Kevin. "I think they're scared of this Kraddock thing. Perhaps we should be too."

"One of them dropped his spear in his rush to leave," said Marlitta. There was a spear lying on the ground near Kevin's feet. "Perhaps you can grab it at some stage. Not now, it'll be too obvious."

Suddenly the sky darkened as if a storm cloud had covered the sun, and there was the noise of rushing wind. They looked up and were horrified to see an enormous bird-like creature descending in the clearing a short way from where they stood. It was a strange creature, a bit like a vulture but much bigger.

It landed with a bit of a bump and skidded to a halt, shook its feathers and, with as much dignity as it could muster, strutted over to Kevin and Marlitta.

"Bit of a bumpy landing," it said. "Now, who are you?"

"I am Kevin, Master of the Universe," said Kevin trying to sound important.

"Oh, Master of the Universe is it? Pleased to meet you your Highness." It made a noise that could have been a chuckle. "Anyway, whoever you are, I'm sure you will be delicious."

"You can't eat us," said Marlitta.

"And why not, pray?" it said turning to Marlitta. "I'm sure you won't be able to solve the riddle."

"What riddle?" said Kevin.

"The riddle I have to ask you," it replied. "I can't eat you 'til you've failed to answer the riddle. Everyone knows that. Still they can never answer the riddle so they get eaten anyway."

"So, what is this riddle, then?" said Kevin getting a bit impatient.

"All in good time," it said. "Don't rush me. Don't rush me. You'll give me indigestion. One should never rush one's breakfast. Are you in a hurry to be eaten?"

"Of course not," said Kevin who couldn't really imagine being eaten by something as preposterous as this.

"Good," it said. "Now here is the riddle. You can discuss it with your friend if you wish. Take your time, but not too much, and give me an answer. Then I'll eat you."

"You seem very sure we won't be able to answer," said Marlitta.

"Nobody has yet," said the Kraddock.

"Suppose we get it right," said Kevin. "What will you give us?"

"I don't know," it replied. "As I said, no one has got it right yet. What would you like?"

"We would like to know where two others like us went to," said Kevin.

"Two more like you?" it said in alarm. "How many of you are there?"

"Just us and the other two. We need to know where they went."

"Well I don't know," it said. "But if you win I'll find out for you. How will that do?"

"Fine," said Kevin.

"Right. Here is the riddle," it said. "What is it that rules the sky, is admired by all and is feared by all and is the most admirable creature in the universe?"

"That's it?" asked Kevin.

"That's it," said the Kraddock. "Now can I start my breakfast?"

"No," said Kevin. "You said we could have time to think."

"Oh, all right," it said. "But don't be too long." It strode off across the clearing and there was a scuttling of creatures running for cover as it approached them. Then it turned and strode back and forth for a while.

"What could it be?" asked Kevin.

"Could be anything," said Marlitta. "What does Spectro think?"

Kevin asked him and then told Marlitta that Spectro didn't know.

"Oh great," said Marlitta. "We'll have to think of something."

The Kraddock was on its way back.

"Well?" it asked.

"Not yet," said Kevin.

"Well hurry up," it said and strode off again.

"Well I wouldn't be surprised if it was talking about itself," said Kevin. "We could try that, and if he says it's wrong we might be able to get it confused."

"Well that's better than nothing," said Marlitta. "Look out, it's coming back."

"Last chance," said the Kraddock. "What is the answer?"

"You," said Kevin.

"Wrong," said the Kraddock.

"I don't think so," said Kevin.

"What?"

"I think it applies to you," said Kevin. "Don't you rule the sky? Aren't you admired by all? And aren't you the most magnificent creature in the Universe? I think so."

"Well, if you put it that way," it said. "I suppose it does apply to me. But it isn't the right answer so I'm going to eat you anyway."

"So, what is the right answer," said Kevin quickly.

"I don't know," said the Kraddock.

"You don't know?" said Kevin. "So how can you tell if someone gets it right?"

"They never do."

"How do you know?"

"It doesn't matter. Now stand still while I eat you."

Kevin made a dive for the spear and pointed it at the Kraddock while Marlitta ran around the back of it and grabbed its tail and pulled. The Kraddock let out a screech of pain and swung round to try and dislodge Marlitta and Kevin lunged with the spear and stabbed it in the shoulder. It gave another screech and turned back towards Kevin.

"Perhaps that was the right answer," it said. "I won't eat you. Now please ask your friend to stop pulling my tail."

Marlitta let go and walked round to the front of the Kraddock.

"Now keep your side of the bargain and go and find out where those other two went," said Kevin.

"All right," it said. "If I can still fly. You hurt my shoulder you know." Kevin waved the spear again and the Kraddock backed away and tried flapping his wings. "It's very painful."

"You'll live," said Kevin. "Now get off with you." The Kraddock started to run across the clearing in great bounds, flapping his wings for all he was worth. Kevin thought he wasn't going to make it, but at the last moment he rose heavily into the air, just brushing the treetops with his feet. Soon he was just a distant speck in the sky.

"That's the last we'll see of him," said Marlitta.

"Don't you think he'll keep his word?" asked Kevin surprised.

"No, I don't," said Marlitta. "We'll have to find some other way. Perhaps this lot'll help us now they know we are a force to be reckoned with."

The creatures that had captured them were creeping out of hiding and moving slowly closer to them. Kevin turned to look and they scuttled back into hiding except for one small creature that stood there looking at them. It was Soodar. Kevin called to him and he trotted over to where they were standing.

"That was great," he said. "You must be Gods to be able to defeat the Kraddock."

"No," said Kevin. "Just ordinary people, but the Kraddock was a coward. You just had to stand up to him."

"Well, I still think it was great. What will you do now?"

"We're looking for two other creatures like us that came through recently," said Kevin. "We want to know where they went."

"Are there any old buildings or monuments?" asked Marlitta.

"I don't know what you mean," said Soodar. Kevin tried to explain about buildings made of stone and monuments. Soon Soodar's face lit up. "Oh, you mean something like the tower."

"That sounds likely," said Kevin.

"Can you show us where it is?" asked Marlitta.

"Well, I've never seen it," said Soodar. "But I've heard tell of it. It's in the territory of the fierce people, so we don't go there."

"Is there someone who would take us?" asked Kevin.

"I don't know," said Soodar. "We could ask them. We would have to have a meeting."

"Would you like to organise it for us," said Marlitta. "Quickly."

Soodar dashed off towards the hiding creatures at the edge of the clearing.

Chapter 12 – The Quest

There was a lot of activity at the edge of the clearing so Kevin and Marlitta stood and waited patiently. After all, they didn't want to alarm these creatures any more, as they may disappear into the jungle and then they'd be alone. If they were to get help from these timid creatures they'd have to be careful not to frighten them.

After a while they saw the small figure of Soodar emerge from the milling crowd and make his way across the clearing to them.

"They are convening a meeting," he said. "Would you like to eat while you are waiting?"

"Thank you," said Marlitta. "What sort of food do you eat here?" Soodar looked a little puzzled at such a stupid question but he explained what was available.

"Perhaps you should come and look," he said and headed off across the clearing to a large open hut at the other edge, under the shade of the trees. Inside were some of the other creatures; Kevin assumed they were females as their fur was a different colour to the others.

There was an array of food on the table, all of which looked all right and, in fact, quite tasty. There was a vast array of fruits as well of some cooked meats. They tasted some of the things and found them delicious. They were quite happy with the fruits, but thought it was best they didn't know what sort of meats they were.

It was reasonably cool in these open buildings. The roof was made of some broad leaves arranged in thick layers which kept out the direct heat of the sun which was now quite high in the sky and a heat haze was shimmering over the clearing. After a while Soodar came back and told them that the meeting was ready for them. It was being held in another of these open buildings, which situated in a separate clearing a little way from the main clearing.

The heat struck them as they stepped out into the sun and walked across the clearing and the heat was reflected up at them from the baked ground.

At the other side of the clearing, they entered the jungle through a narrow path. They could still feel the heat but the shade made it more bearable. After about a hundred paces they came to another small clearing which was surrounded by tall trees giving welcome shade to the meeting house which sat in the middle.

Inside, there were about twenty of the creatures sitting on the floor in a large circle. Soodar took them in and led them to the middle of the circle where he left them standing. After a short delay while the circle of creatures seemed to be talking amongst themselves. One of them stood and looked at them.

"I am Glugget, leader of the Marn people," he said. "I give you welcome." His manner didn't seem that welcoming though.

"Pleased to meet you," said Kevin. "I am Kevin, Master of the Universe, and this is Marlitta, member of the Grand Council."

Glugget looked unimpressed. "If you are Master of the Universe, it is strange we have never heard of you."

"I am Master of the Galactic Union," said Kevin. "That is only part of the galaxy, so I suppose the title Master of the Universe is a bit exaggerated."

"The Elders of the Marn people would like to know why you are here and what you want?" It was obvious that they were a bit scared of these newcomers, especially after they had got the better of the Kraddock.

"We are just passing through," said Kevin. "Two others, similar to us, passed through here recently and we would like to know where they went. Soodar mentioned the 'Tower'." A murmur went around the circle of Elders. "We thought they may have been heading there. Can you lead us to it, please?"

"It is not in our territory," said Glugget. "We are not allowed outside our territory. The Kraddock decreed it."

"I don't think the Kraddock will be back," said Kevin. "And if he does return, you don't have to listen to him. Just stand up to him like we did. He is a coward and doesn't like to be threatened. Now, who is going to take us to the Tower?"

"Not me," said one of the elders.

"Nor me," said another, and soon there was a full consensus against it.

"I'll take you," said a little voice from the doorway.

"What are you doing here?" demanded Glugget. "Go back to the village at once."

"Is that you, Soodar?" asked Kevin, and Soodar peeked his head into view. "Come here, please." Soodar came in and walked to the centre of the circle where Kevin and Marlitta were standing.

"I'll take you," he said.

"Well done Soodar," said Kevin. "You are the bravest here. You will be the leader of our quest." Soodar looked very proud, but there were many round about who looked angry.

"I will come too," said a rather plump one standing up and trying to look important.

"And so will I".

"Me too."

In no time they were all intent on coming with them.

"I am Nadron, the Elder of this Council," said an important looking fellow in the centre. "I should lead the quest."

"Thank you Nadron," said Kevin. "But that honour goes to the bravest. And Soodar is the bravest as he spoke out first. Soodar will lead. We will all follow."

There were some mumblings of dissent but eventually they had all agreed.

"The quest for the tower will leave as soon as you have gathered provisions," said Kevin. "We'll go back to the village and collect some food for ourselves, if that's all right with you?"

"Certainly," said Nadron. "We'll all congregate there when we're ready."

Kevin, Marlitta and Soodar walked back to the open building in the clearing to collect some of the food that was there. As soon as they were busy packing things into Kevin's rucksack, Soodar went off to gather his own belongings. Kevin packed only the things he thought would keep fresh in the heat. He also filled his water bottle again.

When they were ready, they sat down in the shade to relax until everybody was ready. The first one back was Soodar who was trying to look important. He had in his hand two spears, which he gave to Kevin.

"I thought you might like to have these," he said.

"Thank you Soodar," said Kevin. "That's very thoughtful of you. Have the others got weapons too?"

"Oh, yes," said Soodar. "They wouldn't go into the jungle without them."

There was a noise outside and Kevin realised that the others had all assembled and were ready to go.

"Right," said Kevin. "Time to go, I think. Lead on Captain of the Quest."

Soodar looked very proud and scampered outside where everyone was waiting.

"Lead on," said Kevin, and Soodar took up his position at the front of the column, followed closely by Kevin and Marlitta. As they set off there was a bit of discord amongst the rest of the group as they all thought they should be next in line.

Kevin stopped. "We need the next most important person at the back to prevent stragglers being left behind and to defend us against anyone creeping up on us."

The remaining group immediately rearranged itself with the ones who thought themselves the most important at the back. Then they set off again into the jungle.

It was getting quite hot now in spite of the shade from the trees, but the others didn't seem to notice it. Occasionally, they saw a brightly coloured bird fly off in alarm as they passed by, and there were some tree-climbing creatures that peeked at them from the leafy canopy above.

After walking for about three hours, they stopped for a rest and something to eat. It seemed as if they were intending to stop for quite a while as the others were setting up a sort of camp.

"We must camp for a while," said Soodar. "The sun is too hot to walk in the afternoon. We will set off again when it is cooler."

It turned out that 'a while' meant all afternoon, and they didn't set off again until early evening. The nature of the jungle changed as they walked and soon it was more like open woodland. A cool breeze sprung up and the walking became much more pleasant.

They walked on until it was nearly dark before stopping to set up camp for the night. A fire was lit, probably to scare off wild animals, and palm type fronds were cut for them to sleep on. Kevin found it difficult to even contemplate sleep under these conditions, but he was exhausted, so it wasn't long before he was fast asleep.

He was woken by the sound of movement nearby and sat up in alarm, but it was only Marlitta getting some food from her pack. The others were all up and about getting ready to set off before the sun rose too high in the sky, so Kevin had a hasty bite to eat and hoisted his rucksack onto his back and joined the others who appeared to be waiting.

A little way along the track they crossed some enormous footprints. Several of the others, who considered themselves trackers, bent down to examine the prints. There was a great deal of consternation and it seemed that several were considering going back.

"What is it," Kevin asked Soodar.

"A Mangat has passed this way in the night and is not far away," said Soodar. "Some say we should go back."

"What do you say?" asked Kevin.

"I say we should go on and keep very quiet," said Soodar.

"What is a Mangat?" asked Marlitta.

"It is a sort of giant lizard," said Soodar. "It walks on two hind legs and has many sharp teeth and a long tail. It is covered with scales of armour and cannot be killed with a spear."

"Sounds a bit like a tyrannosaurus rex," said Kevin. "There were creatures like that on earth many millions of years ago. I would quite like to see one."

"I wouldn't," said Soodar.

There was a terrifying roar from the jungle nearby and half of the group fled. Kevin was just going to shout at them to stay, when a huge animal crashed out of the jungle in full pursuit of the fleeing creatures. It was very like Kevin's idea of a dinosaur, but it was faster than he would have expected. His little group was transfixed with fright, which was probably what saved them.

The dinosaur ran on two legs faster than a horse could run and it soon caught up with the last of the fleeing Marn and caught it in one vicious bite and swallowed it in the next. Then it raced off after the others.

Soodar held up a hand to stop Kevin speaking and indicated that they should remain absolutely still. It was just as well, because another of the dinosaur creatures trotted out of the jungle and followed in the footsteps of the first one.

"It is safe now," said Soodar.

"For us, maybe," said Marlitta. "What about the others?"

"There is nothing we can do for them," said Soodar. "The ones that can run the fastest and keep going the longest may escape. But we couldn't do anything to help them. We would just get eaten too."

He turned and set off down the track again, away from the sounds of the dinosaurs crashing through the jungle. The rest followed, but no one spoke.

They walked until it had become too hot, then they settled in the shade of a tree to wait for the sun to lower in the sky. The country was more open here, with trees scattered about a grassy plain. There were a few rocky outcrops here and there and the land rose slowly ahead of them, so it was hard going.

In the distance there were herds of animals grazing. They looked a bit like wildebeest, but, obviously, they wouldn't be exactly the same as the animals found on earth.

"Are any of those animals dangerous," Kevin asked. Soodar looked out across the plain and shook his head.

"No," he said. "Not unless you are a threat to their young. But we won't go that close. Actually, it's good to see animals grazing, because it means there are no predators about, or if there are, they aren't hungry at the moment." He looked up the slope to the right. "We have to go up there, but not until it is cooler."

Chapter 13 – Across the River

As soon as the sun had moved lower in the sky, and it was getting cooler, they set off up the hill. As they went, the trees became fewer and further between and a light breeze sprang up. Soodar kept looking right and left as they became more exposed. The grazing animals had moved further away and there was little sign of life on the higher ground.

"Is it safer up here?" asked Kevin.

"Not really," said Soodar. "There are animals like the Mangat we saw earlier, but smaller. That doesn't mean they are less dangerous. They can run very fast and they have very sharp teeth."

"Won't we see them in the distance, though?" asked Marlitta.

"No. They hide on the ground and look like rocks until you get close to them. Then they dash out and grab you."

"Can they be killed with spears?" asked Kevin.

"I don't know," said Soodar. "No one has ever tried, as far as I know."

They kept well away from rocks in case they weren't rocks but something with teeth, and soon they were up onto a level rocky plateau with only small scrubby trees, which grew out of cracks in the rock.

"We could do with finding a cave to shelter in tonight," said Soodar. "It is too dangerous to stay out here. I think we're being tracked by a pack of joogar."

"What are joogar?" asked Kevin.

"They go on four legs," said Soodar, "and they have a leathery hide and large eyes and large ears, so they can see and hear very well."

"I bet they have large teeth as well," said Kevin feeling a bit like Red Riding Hood's grandmother."

"Yes, they do," said Soodar. "They hunt in packs and will follow their prey for days until it is exhausted. Then they move in for the kill. That's why we need to find a cave where we can light a fire in the entrance to keep them away."

"I take it they don't like fire, then," said Kevin. "Perhaps we could use that against them and maybe drive them away."

"I think they would just come back again," said Soodar.

Eventually they found a rocky outcrop with a cleft in it that would do as a shelter. Soodar lit a handful of what looked like dead bracken, and when it was blazing, threw it into the cave. Nothing happened, so they went in and made the blazing bracken into a more permanent fire. It was a bit of a squeeze for them all to get inside, but they managed it. Besides Kevin, Marlitta and Soodar, there were five of the Marn remaining with them. All the others had fled into the jungle and become lunch for the two dinosaurs. Kevin tried to chat to them but they seemed unwilling to talk much, so they had something to eat and then settled down for the night.

It was extremely uncomfortable and they all found it difficult to sleep, especially knowing that a pack of wolves, with leather hides, were roaming about outside. The Marn were muttering amongst themselves, but Kevin couldn't hear what they were saying. It sounded as if they might have some trouble with them before long.

In the morning, they had something to eat and drink before venturing out of the cave. Outside it was still cool and there was a haze over the plateau.

"They're still with us," said Soodar. They all looked out to see what he was looking at.

"I can't see anything," said Kevin.

"Over there," said Soodar pointing. Kevin could just make out a group of small humps in the grass. Surely, they couldn't be the wolf-like animals that had been following them, could they?

"They have closed in for the kill," said Soodar. "As soon as we move out into the open they will strike."

"What can we do?" asked Kevin feeling more worried than he had for a long time.

"We haven't enough spears to fight them off," said Soodar. "Once they've decided to make a kill there is only one way out, and that is to kill every one of them. They don't know what it means to give up and run. And that's not our only problem."

"Why, what else is there?" asked Kevin getting really worried now. He wished he had the power of his crystal, but it was completely dead.

"Sorry," said Spectro reading his thoughts, "but I can't help."

"There might be a way," said Soodar.

"Mardrig!" said one of the others quietly.

"Yes," said Soodar.

"What is that?" said Kevin.

"Well you will have to help," said Soodar. "We will go out and the joogar will come after us. When they do, you must come out and throw rocks at those two puggets." He pointed and Kevin could see what looked like two rocks sticking up out of the grass.

"Puggets?"

"Similar to those animals that attacked us in the jungle, but smaller and faster."

"What will happen then?" asked Marlitta who had been listening intently.

"I hope that the puggets will attack the joogar," said Soodar. "They hate each other. Now we will set off in that direction and go past the puggets as quietly as we can. The joogar will follow and when they are between you and the puggets, start throwing rocks over their heads and try and hit the puggets. That will annoy them and they will think they are being attacked by the joogar. When they are busy fighting, you must go down the slope in that direction." He pointed at the slope that lay behind where the joogar were crouching. "We'll meet you at the bottom of the slope."

So saying, he set off followed by the others at a slow trot. The joogar didn't move at first, then, one by one, they stood up and moved forward. But they seemed confused, looking in the direction of Soodar and his group, and then turning and looking back at the cave where they seemed to sense Kevin and Marlitta.

"Keep absolutely still," Kevin whispered to Marlitta who hadn't mover a muscle. She glared at him and then looked back at the joogar that were moving forward slowly. If they didn't move soon Soodar would be in real trouble because, the way they were going, the puggets would see them and attack. But luckily, the joogar decided to follow Soodar rather than waiting around in case there was someone left in the cave, and they loped off up the slope. It wasn't long before they were between the puggets and the cave, so Kevin and Marlitta stepped out and started to hurl stones as hard as they could at where the puggets were lying. The first few stones fell short and the puggets didn't seem to see or hear them, but the joogar did and stopped in their tracks and looked towards the sound of falling stones. Then they moved in that direction. The puggets still didn't move.

"Do you think Soodar could have been wrong about those things?" asked Kevin. "If they're just rocks we're in big trouble. But then one of the 'rocks' lifted its head and stared sleepily at the approaching joogar. Then the other one lifted its head also. The joogar stopped and stared back. You could almost hear them thinking "Oops!"

Then they started to back away slowly, still fixing the puggets with their cold steely glare. The puggets, sensing that breakfast was served, slowly got to their feet and moved slowly forward. They were strange creatures with long powerful hind legs, small forelimbs with little hands, a long fleshy tail, which they swept from side to side as they walked, and a mouth full of wicked looking teeth.

Suddenly the joogar fled in all directions and the puggets raced after them. Straight past the cave where Kevin and Marlitta were standing, they raced, and in seconds they were gone. Quickly, Kevin grabbed Marlitta's hand and they raced off down the slope as fast as they could go. It wasn't easy, as the ground was rough and strewn with small rocks. Tough little plants grew between the rocks and could easily have tripped them up if they hadn't been careful.

At the bottom of the slope ran a small rocky river. It was almost like home on earth. The sound of the water splashing over the rocks sounded so familiar it gave Kevin a pang of homesickness.

They looked about them but could see no signs of danger, so they sat down on the rocks by the river.

"Why are we doing this?" said Kevin sadly.

"Doing what?"

"Chasing around the universe on a wild goose chase, and not knowing if we'll ever get back home again."

"What's brought this on?" asked Marlitta.

"Oh, just the sound of the water," said Kevin. "It reminded me of home. And I feel upset that those friends of Soodar's got killed by those creatures in the forest. It must have upset him, but he still carried on to help us. I just wonder if it is all worth it."

"You felt you had to rescue your friend, Tracy, and I felt I had to help you. It just had to be done."

"But I hadn't realised it would cause harm to other people," said Kevin.

"We didn't cause the harm to come to those people," said Marlitta. "That might have happened anyway. It is the world they live in. We didn't cause it. Anyway, we have to go on now. There's no way back."

"I suppose you're right," said Kevin. "But I wish we could go somewhere where my crystal would be of use. I feel helpless without it."

"Perhaps in the next world we go to there'll be some more power," said Marlitta. "Let's hope so anyway."

After a while they heard sounds of movement above them on the hillside. Thinking it might be more of the dinosaur type creatures, they dashed for cover among the rocks. They kept as still as they could until they could see who or what was coming.

"It's Soodar," said Kevin and stood up so that he could be seen.

"It didn't go quite as planned," said Soodar. "But it worked well enough. I am glad you are safe. Now you must cross the river and we must return to our village."

"Aren't you coming with us?" asked Kevin in surprise.

"No," said Soodar. We must return now. The river is the boundary between our territory and the next. We are not permitted to cross it. I am told that if you carry on over that rise you will be able to see the tower in the distance."

"Who lives in this territory, then?" said Kevin.

"I don't know," said Soodar. "I have never met them. But I am told they are creatures much like yourselves, only bigger."

"Will they be friendly?"

"I don't know," said Soodar. "They will probably want to hold you until the Kraddock visits again to pass judgement."

"Well we've met him before and he said he'd help us. We'll just have to play it by ear."

Soodar looked puzzled.

"I mean we'll have to wait and see what happens and then make our decisions."

"Thank you for your help," said Marlitta. "It was very kind of you to help us."

"I'm sorry about your friends," said Kevin.

"It can't be helped," said Soodar. "It was their own fault. They shouldn't have run away. Remember that if you see any large creature. Keep absolutely still and they may ignore you."

"May?"

"Nothing is certain in the jungle. Goodbye. It was a pleasure to be able to help you." He turned and walked back up the hill followed by his friends.

"Well," said Kevin, "I suppose we should move on."

They made their way through the rocks down to the river bank. The water was quite shallow and the rocks acted as stepping stones for most of the way. In the middle was a stretch with no rocks and they had to wade through holding onto each other to prevent the strong flow knocking them off their feet and carrying them away downstream.

At the far side, they removed their shoes and emptied the water. The sun was quite warm so they lay their wet things on the rocks to dry for a while. After about an hour they decided they would have to move on, even though their things were not quite dry.

It was a steady uphill trudge from the river towards the crest of the hill where they were hoping for a sight of the tower. On the way there were small rises and dips, and as they reached the top of one of these, a new vista appeared. It was a shallow valley crossing their path with stunted trees and other vegetation growing in the dip. As they took in the scene they suddenly froze. No more than fifty paces in front of them were two of the dinosaur-type creatures.

"Don't move a muscle," said Kevin.

The creatures were looking at them and had obviously seen them, but they were not moving either. In fact, they were absolutely motionless.

"What are they doing?" asked Marlitta.

"I don't know," said Kevin. "I thought they would ignore us if we kept still and they would just walk away. Why don't they go?"

After a while it was obvious that they were not going anywhere.

"We can't just stand here for ever," said Kevin. "Let's move very slowly towards them. There are some trees over there that we could climb if they looked as if they were going to attack us."

They moved one painful step after another towards the trees. Suddenly, the dinosaurs made a dash towards them.

"Run," shouted Kevin and set off as fast as his legs would carry him towards the trees, but the dinosaurs got there first, and with an agility they would not have believed, they amazingly climbed into the tree.

"They seem scared of us," said Kevin walking up to the tree.

"Leave us alone," shrieked one of the creatures in a high-pitched voice. "Go away."

"I didn't think they could talk," said Marlitta.

"Nor did I," said Kevin.

"We don't mean you any harm," said Marlitta to the creatures.

"They can talk," said one of the creatures to the other.

"No, that's not possible," said the other. They are primitive creatures. They can't communicate.

"Excuse me," said Kevin, "but we thought that you were primitive creatures and could not speak."

"What rubbish is this?" said the first creature. "Of course we can talk. It is you hairy creatures that are primitive."

"Hairy?" exclaimed Kevin. "We're not hairy. Just a bit on our heads, maybe. Look, come down from that tree. We're not going to hurt you."

The two creatures spoke to each other in hushed voices for a while then turned to Kevin and said "Promise you won't hurt us, then."

"Of course," said Kevin. "Just come down."

The creatures climbed down, a bit more slowly than they had gone up and stood nervously looking at Kevin and Marlitta.

"Who are you?" asked one of the creatures.

"We aren't from this planet," said Kevin, "and we're trying to find our way back to our home. I believe there is an ancient tower somewhere near here. Do you know where it is?"

"The old tower," said the other creature. "Of course. It isn't far, but no-one is allowed to go near it."

"No," said the other one. "It is forbidden. You can't go there."

"But we have to," said Kevin. "It is our only way home. Can you take us to the tower?"

"We could take you near to it, but we can't go too close."

"I suppose that will have to do," said Kevin. "Thank you."

Chapter 14 - The Tower

The strange creatures took them further up the hill but didn't go over the crest. Instead, they went along the crest, keeping below the top.

"Why are we keeping below the peak of the hill?" asked Kevin.

"We must be careful," replied one of the creatures. They hadn't been able to discover their names, as they were virtually unpronounceable to Kevin. So he decided to call them Dino One and Dino Two, though it was difficult to remember which was which.

"Why?" asked Kevin.

"The hairy creatures live just over this ridge, in the forest," replied Dino One. "We must skirt the forest and keep out of sight as they are very dangerous."

They carried on along the ridge until they reached a narrow valley cutting through the ridge. A small stream ran along the bottom of the valley and there was a narrow path winding its way down to it. They started down the slope, but Kevin and Marlitta found it difficult going as the path sloped steeply and their shoes did not give much grip, unlike the Dinos, whose feet had long curved claws that dug into the soft ground.

Eventually, after much scrabbling and sliding on their bottoms, they reached the side of the stream. It looked so idyllic it was hard to believe there was imminent danger just over the crest of the hill.

"We must now keep very quiet," said Dino One, "or they might hear us."

They crept along the bank of the stream as quietly as they could, though it was difficult going as the vegetation was quite thick. Suddenly, Dino One froze and held up one of its tiny front feet. They all stopped, straining to see what the problem was. Kevin peered through the vegetation but could see nothing.

"What's the matter," he whispered.

"Keep quiet," said Dino One.

Up ahead, Kevin noticed a slight movement in the long grass. Then a large brown form emerged from the riverbank and started up the slope away from the river. It brought to Kevin's mind, pictures he had seen of 'Bigfoot', the wild man that was supposed to live in the wild lands of Canada, but this one was much bigger. Kevin watched, fascinated as the creature climbed the steep slope and just caught a glimpse of the wicked face as it disappeared from sight.

"We must move quickly," said Dino One, "before any more of them come down to the stream."

They moved as quickly as they could manage until they were well past the place where they had seen the creature and carried on at a more leisurely pace up the valley, which slowly flattened out. They then changed direction slightly and made their way up the slope to the edge of the ridge.

As they reached it, they crept on all fours to the edge and looked over. To the left was the forest where the hairy creatures lived, and to the right was a large sweeping plain. In the middle of the plain stood an enormous tower. It looked a bit like a TV transmitter that Kevin had once seen when he was out with his parents in the car. But he couldn't imagine that that was what it was. Not here in this primitive world.

"What's that over there?" asked Marlitta pointing across the plain.

"It looks like a large animal," said Kevin, "a bit like an elephant." The creature was standing grazing on the lush vegetation.

"Keep quiet," said One of the Dinos. "The hairy ones are coming."

Kevin looked over towards the forest and was surprised to see a group of the hairy creatures emerging from the trees.

"It looks like a hunting party," said Kevin. "I think they are after that animal over there. While they are busy chasing that animal, perhaps we could skirt around them."

"I don't think that would be a good idea," said Dino Two. "They would be sure to see us and hunt us down."

"They certainly would," said Dino One. "We must wait here until they have returned to the forest."

"That would take ages," said Kevin. "We are trying to catch up with two people who will have come this way recently. A small man and a large girl. They would be making for the tower."

"I still think we should stay," said Dino One. "Anyway, how do you know these people haven't been captured by the hairy ones?"

"I don't. But we still have to get to the tower. If they have been captured, there's nothing we can do, unless you want us to walk into the forest and rescue them?"

"Oh, no," said Dino One in horror, "we couldn't possibly do that. They would kill us and eat us. That is what they do."

"Well I'm going on now," said Kevin. "We can see the tower now, so you needn't come if you don't want to." The two Dinos looked at each other.

"Well we would rather not, if you don't mind," said Dino One.

"That's fine," said Kevin. "We can find our own way now and thank you for your help so far. We would have walked straight into the forest and been caught."

"Glad we could help," said Dino Two.

"And remember," said Dino One, "if they see you, don't move a muscle and they will eventually lose interest and go away."

"Thank you," said Kevin. "I'll remember that."

The two Dinos turned and crept away down the slope to the river, and Kevin and Marlitta crept over the ridge and made their way down to the plain below keeping well away from the route being taken by the hairy ones. The vegetation got taller as they got lower and they were able to keep well concealed from the view of the hunting party. They kept moving in the general direction of the tower, and all was quiet for a while.

"What's that?" asked Marlitta suddenly. Kevin stopped and listened. There was a crashing sound in the distance.

"Perhaps it is that big animal trying to escape from the hunters," said Kevin.

"I think it's coming this way," said Marlitta. "We'd better get a move on or we'll get trampled to death."

They set off at a trot. It wasn't easy going as the vegetation was quite thick and was taller than they were, so they couldn't see where the large creature was. As they ran, the sound of the crashing beast got louder and louder.

"It's getting closer," shouted Kevin skidding to a halt. "We're running into its path."

Suddenly, an enormous shape burst through the undergrowth no more than a few yards in front of them. Both were riveted to the spot in horror, but the beast took no notice of them and continued its frantic charge. Kevin and Marlitta continued to where the beast had crossed their path and were stunned to come face to face with a large group of the hairy creatures, who all skidded to halt and stood staring at them. Kevin and Marlitta didn't have to remember to remain absolutely still as they were too shocked to move. After what seemed to be an age, but was actually only about two seconds, the group of hairy hunters all fell to their knees and then fell forward to place their foreheads on the ground with arms outstretched in front of them.

"What are they doing?" asked Marlitta as quietly as she could.

"I don't know," said Kevin. "Perhaps they think we are some kind of gods."

"So, what do they expect us to do?"

"How should I know?" answered Kevin. "Do you think I should speak to them?"

"I thought the Dinos said that they couldn't speak."

"I think they must be able to communicate in some way or they couldn't hunt in a group like this."

"Well you could try," said Marlitta. Kevin took a step forward and took a deep breath.

"Go back to your village," he said with as much authority as he could muster, but it sounded rather squeaky to Kevin. One of the creatures tilted its head slightly to look at him through its hairy fringe.

"What?" it said in a deep growl.

Kevin took a step backwards. "Go back to your village," he repeated. "Now."

The creature at the front rose to his knees and looked at Kevin for a long moment. "Oh, all right then," it said and scrambled to its feet, turned to the rest of the hunting party and said "Back to the village."

They all got back onto their feet and set off through the jungle at a brisk trot.

"I just don't understand this planet," said Kevin.

"Let's not worry about that," said Marlitta. "We need to get to that tower before anything else happens to delay us." She set off at a brisk pace. Kevin, seeing her disappearing into undergrowth ran after her, afraid that if they lost sight of each other they may never find each other again.

The ground rose steeply as they continued and soon they were out of the tall vegetation and only had to contend with stunted bushes of knee height. They turned and looked back over the plain that they had come from, and could see the large creature, that had run across their path, still trotting away from where they had met.

On the other side of the plain they could see the forest where the hairy creatures had come from, but there was no sign of the creatures themselves. In front of them, at the top of the rise, stood the tower. It seemed to be made of some kind of latticework with a large stone building at its base. There was no sign of movement anywhere near the tower, so they continued towards it. The tower must have been much taller than it had at first seemed, as it didn't seem to be getting any nearer as they walked towards it.

"How much further is it?" asked Kevin, stopping to get his breath. "It still seems miles away."

"That tower must be enormous," said Marlitta. "It must be past midday now. I think we'll be lucky to get there before it gets dark."

"Duros and Tracey must be miles ahead of us by now, or we would be able to see them ahead of us," said Kevin. "I can't see how we are going to catch up with them, even if we are still going the right way."

"Maybe we should just concentrate on finding our way home now," said Marlitta, "or we may be stranded out here for ever."

"Well," said Kevin, "if we're going to be stranded away from home, we should find a world that's pleasant to live in."

"That could take for ever," said Marlitta.

"Well we've got forever," said Kevin. "I wish we hadn't lost Sniffer. I would feel a lot safer with him about."

"Maybe he will track us down eventually," said Marlitta.

"I hope so," said Kevin. "I miss him."

After what must have been another two hours, the tower was getting much closer and seemed to be so tall that it reached high into the sky with little wispy clouds around the top of it.

They were having another rest, when Marlitta thought she heard a strange noise.

"What's that?" she asked. Kevin listened.

"It seems like a sort of whooshing noise," he said, "but I can't see anything."

Suddenly, a large flapping object dropped out of the sky and sped towards them.

"It's the Kraddock," shouted Kevin, "and it's coming straight at us."

They both ran for their lives as the frantic object hurtled towards them, flapping furiously. As it approached, it hit the ground and skidded for about twenty paces before lifting into the air again. It repeated this several times before coming to an ungainly stop with its head on the ground and its tail in the air. It scrambled to its feet, fluffing its feathers to remove the dust and bushes, and waddled unsteadily towards them.

"Nice landing," said Kevin trying not to laugh.

"Getting better," said the Kraddock. "There's a difficult side wind across this slope. Anyway, I have been looking for you to show you the way to the tower, but I couldn't find you. Where have you been?"

"We came across that plain," said Kevin pointing in the direction they had come from.

"Well never mind, I have found you now, and there is the tower."

"Yes," said Kevin. "We'd noticed it."

"Ah, yes," said the Kraddock. "But do you know how to get into it?"

"I assume we just go through the door at the front," said Kevin.

"Not a good idea," said the Kraddock. "You would be zapped the moment you were inside."

"Zapped?"

"Yes, the people who built the tower wanted to protect it from others who were not friendly towards them. I don't know the details as it was built thousands of years ago."

"So how do we get in then?" asked Marlitta.

"Well if you go around to the side, you will find a small door that is disguised to look like part of the wall. It isn't easy to see but if you put your head close to the wall and look along it, you will be able to see where it is not perfectly smooth. Press your hand in the middle of the recessed area and it will open. Then just go inside. What you will find in there I do not know as I can't get through the door."

"But how do you know we won't get zapped when we go in by the side door?" asked Kevin.

"Just stands to reason," said the Kraddock. "Why would they put traps on the side door when it is hidden so well?"

"So, you're just guessing," said Kevin.

"Well, yes. I suppose so."

"We'll just have to go carefully then," said Kevin. "We don't have any other choice."

"I wish you well, then," said the Kraddock. "But now I must go. Things to do, things to see to. Goodbye." So saying, he started his long ungainly run down the hill with his wings outstretched, feet paddling for all he was worth.

"I don't think he's going to make it," said Kevin screwing up his face. "He's going to go straight into those trees." The Kraddock was going faster and faster until Kevin didn't know how he could move his feet so fast. Then at the last moment he lifted his feet up and just managed to rise above the trees, flapping furiously. Slowly he gained height and headed off over the forest. They watched until he was just a speck in the distance.

"So, what do we do?" asked Kevin.

"Well first we should locate the door and get it open," said Marlitta. "Then we'll have to poke things inside to see if there are any traps."

They went around the side of the building and ran their hands along the smooth stonework to see if they could feel a difference in the surface. When they were half way along, Marlitta stopped and put her face up against the wall and looked along its surface.

"I think it looks a bit different just along here," she said.

Kevin put his face against the stone to look along the surface, and as soon as he touched the stone a door sprung open revealing a dark passage inside. It gave him such a surprise that he jumped back in shock. The door immediately sprung shut again.

"How did you do that?" asked Marlitta.

"I don't know," said Kevin. "I just put my face against the stone and the door opened." He touched the stone with his hand, but nothing happened.

"Is that the same place that you touched it last time?" asked Marlitta.

"I'm not sure," said Kevin. "I think so."

"Put your hand flat on the stone," said Marlitta. "Then slide it around until you find the right spot."

Kevin placed his hand on the stone level with his face and slid it backwards and forwards. At first nothing happened. Then, suddenly the door sprung open again. This time he stayed where he was and the door stayed open.

"What can we use to poke inside?" asked Kevin.

"I could go and find a tree branch if you like," said Marlitta.

"Good idea," said Kevin, "but don't go too far. There are some small bushes over there. Perhaps you could break off a branch." Marlitta walked over to the bush and pulled at the branches but did not seem to be having much luck. Suddenly, she turned and ran back to Kevin in panic.

"What is it?" asked Kevin.

"There's something coming through the undergrowth," said Marlitta. "Something big by the sound of it."

"Keep absolutely still," said Kevin. They both froze as the sound came nearer and nearer to them. Kevin wondered if it would be better to risk the passage and go inside where the creature couldn't get at them. But before he could do anything, it burst from the undergrowth and threw itself at Kevin, who thought his end had come. But the worst that happened to him was that he got a good licking.

"Sniffer!" shouted Kevin in glee. "Where have you been? I thought we had lost you for good."

Sniffer turned to Marlitta to repeat his slobbering greeting.

Before Kevin could stop him, Sniffer shot into the passage and disappeared from sight. Nothing happened. There was no sound of zapping so Kevin ventured carefully inside. When they were both inside, the door shut with slam and all was darkness.

"Now what do we do?" said Kevin.

"The passage isn't wide," said Marlitta. "Perhaps if we feel our way along the passage we might come to somewhere that is lighter.

"But what if we don't?"

"What choice have we got?"

Kevin put out his hand, and as soon as it touched the wall a dim illumination appeared. It didn't seem to come from anywhere in particular, but was enough to see by, so they started to make their way along the tunnel. After about fifty yards they came to a larger room which was also lit with the eerie light. At the other side of the room were two openings.

"Which way now?" said Kevin.

"I don't know," said Marlitta. "They both look the same."

They walked over to the two doorways and peered into each in turn, but there was no way of telling which they should take.

Suddenly, there was a terrified scream from inside one of the openings.

"What on earth was that?" said Kevin.

"I don't know," said Marlitta, "but it came from this passage."

They both ran into the passage and ran along it until they came to another big chamber. This one was enormous and was brightly lit. They skidded to a halt and looked about them. In the centre of the hall was a cabinet with transparent sides, rather like a large glass case. Next to it was what looked like a control console of some sort. And lying on the floor next to it was Sniffer. At first, Kevin couldn't see what he was doing, but then he realised that there was a pair of small legs poking out from under him.

"I think he's sitting on someone," said Marlitta walking towards Sniffer. Kevin followed. When they got there, they could see that there was a head poking out of the other side.

"Get me out of here," it said.

"It's Duros," exclaimed Kevin.

"Of course it is," he snapped. "Now get this brute off me immediately."

"And what's the magic word?" said Kevin grinning.

"What are you talking about? What magic word?"

"Please," said Kevin.

"Don't be so stupid," snapped Duros. "Get it off me."

"Well before we can do that I would like to know what you have done with Tracy?"

"Nothing," said Duros. "She is here somewhere."

Kevin looked around but could see no sign of the girl.

"Tracy," he called. "Where are you? It's me, Kevin. If you can hear me come out."

They looked around but there was no sign of movement. Then the top of a head appeared over the back of the control console, followed by a very frightened face.

"Oh, there you are," said Kevin. "Come around here."

"But what about the monster?"

"That's no monster," said Kevin. "He's my dog. He's called Sniffer, and at the moment he's sitting on your captor."

Tracy crept around the console and peered around it to see if it looked safe to come out. Sniffer looked up and growled and Tracy disappeared behind the console again.

"He won't hurt you, so come out," said Kevin. This time she did come out.

"Now make friends with him," said Kevin. Tracy gingerly put out her hand towards Sniffer, who looked at it then licked it enthusiastically.

"Yuck," said Tracy pulling it away.

"Now I want you to have a look round and see if you can find some string or cord."

Tracy looked around her. The place looked very clean and tidy despite the fact no one had been in there for years. Along the wall at the far side was a set of cupboard doors, which she thought looked a likely place to find string. She walked across to them and tried to open the first one, but it didn't seem to want to open. So she tried the next one, and that opened easily. Tracy let out a scream and ran back to Kevin.

"What *is* the matter with you?" he asked.

"There's someone in there," she whimpered.

"Don't be so stupid," said Kevin and walked over to the cabinet where he was surprised to see a pair of red eyes looking back at him. He backed away as Marlitta came over to look too.

"What on earth is it?" said Kevin.

"Looks like some sort of robot," said Marlitta.

"Not just some sort," said the robot. "I am a mark ten office staff robot, and it's rude to stare."

"Sorry," said Kevin in surprise.

"Apology accepted," said the robot gliding out into the hall. "I suppose you have made things untidy again."

"No," said Kevin. "We haven't touched a thing."

"Pity," said the robot. "I have had nothing to do for ages. It hasn't been the same since the Masters left."

"Masters?" said Kevin. "Who are they?"

"Now you are being stupid," said the robot. "The Masters are in charge of everything. They built this station and I have looked after it ever since they left. I wish they would return. You aren't Masters, are you?"

Kevin and Marlitta looked at each other and grinned.

"Yes," said Kevin. "I am the Master of the Universe."

"Oh my goodness," said the robot. "Please forgive your humble servant, Master. I didn't realise. What can I do for you?"

"Well firstly, we need some string or cord to tie up our prisoner," said Kevin pointing to Duros.

"I take it your prisoner is the one underneath?" said the Robot. "What about the other one? He shouldn't really be in here."

"It's all right," said Kevin. "He's with me."

"Well I suppose that is all right then. Now to get you something to restrain the prisoner. Please wait here while I go and fetch something for that purpose." He glided off and disappeared down one of the passages. There was a flash and a bang followed by a squawk, and the robot returned rather unsteadily.

"I forgot about the intruder protection," he said "I must turn it off before I can get what you want." He went to the console and flicked a few switches and set off down the corridor again. After a few minutes he returned with a set of manacles.

"If you could remove your animal," he said, "I will secure the prisoner."

"I am not a prisoner," shouted Duros. "I am a member of the Galactic Council. You have no right to hold me prisoner."

There was a whirring noise followed by a whine from the robot. "Oh dear," he said. "I cannot restrain a member of the Galactic Council, but also, I cannot disobey an order from the Master. This could damage my circuits."

"It's all right," said Kevin. "Duros is no longer a member of the Galactic Council. He has been disgraced and is a criminal."

The whirring stopped and the robot looked relieved. "Oh good," he said. "That is a relief. But if he is a criminal he should be terminated."

"Terminated?" squawked Duros.

"Terminated?" said Kevin.

"Oh yes," said the robot. "That was the law of the Masters. Would you like me to terminate him for you?"

"No," wailed Duros. "You can't do this to me."

"Might not be such a bad idea," said Kevin, winking at Marlitta.

"Perhaps you are right," she replied with a grin.

"Good," said the robot. "I will do it immediately."

"No," yelled Duros.

"Well, perhaps we should take him back to the Council for a proper trial and let them deal with him," said Kevin.

"Then you do not want me to terminate him?" asked the robot.

"Afraid not," said Kevin.

"Oh dear," said the robot. "I was really looking forward to that. We haven't had a termination in hundreds of years."

"What you can do," said Kevin, "is to tell us how to work this contraption." He pointed at the control console.

"Contraption?" said the robot indignantly, his voice rising half an octave. "That is the finest transporter portal in the universe."

"Good," said Kevin. "Then perhaps you could set it to take us back to civilisation."

"But this is the centre of civilisation," said the robot. "Why would you want to go anywhere else?"

"Because this is not our civilisation," said Kevin.

"I'll see what I can do," said the robot. "Please get into the cubicle."

They secured Duros with the manacles, and Kevin took his crystal from him and put it in his pocket. Then they dragged him into the cubicle. It was a bit of a squeeze with all of them in there and Sniffer kept turning around to sniff at everything.

The robot went over to the controls and started setting switches and dials. Then he walked over to the cubicle and opened it. "You will be coming back, won't you?" he asked in a mournful voice.

"No," said Kevin. "We don't belong here. We're trying to find our way home."

"Oh dear," said the robot and walked back to the console. He made a few more adjustments before gliding back to the cubicle and squeezing himself inside.

"What are you doing?" said Kevin.

"My place is with the Master," he said. "I'm coming with you."

Suddenly the hall and the cubicle disappeared and they found themselves in what looked like a ruined castle. The roof had gone and the walls were crumbling.

"Where have you brought us?" said Kevin in alarm.

"Oh dear," said the robot. "What has happened here? It shouldn't be like this."

It was beginning to get dark and they just had time to have a quick look round before trying to make themselves comfortable for the night. The place seemed deserted and there seemed to be no signs of life at all. There were no birds singing or anything. A few tufts of coarse grass clung on to life in cracks in the tiled floor.

Darkness came quickly followed by a cool breeze, and they had to snuggle closely together to keep warm, much to the indignation of Duros, who kept complaining all night long.

Chapter 15 - The desert

By the time morning came they were all feeling very cold and hungry. But as the sun rose in the sky it got warmer and warmer.

"Where have you brought us, Robot?" said Kevin.

"It is the planet of Kronos," said the robot. "It used to be teeming with life and was a most desirable place to be. I don't know what has happened to it. It shouldn't be like this."

They walked through the ruins until they came to an archway that led out of the castle, but beyond, there was nothing but barren land. It wasn't sand, as you would expect in a desert, but was fairly hard packed and rock-strewn. There was the occasional stunted bush clinging onto life, here and there, but other than that there was nothing.

"Right, Robot," said Kevin. "Where do we go from here? There must be another portal somewhere."

"It should be here," said the robot, "in this building. But it shouldn't be like this. I do not understand."

"Well I think you should try and find it quickly," said Marlitta. "There are things out there and they're coming this way."

They all looked out over the barren land and were horrified to see dark shapes creeping slowly towards them.

"I knew this decrepit machine was up to no good," said Duros. "Now it has led us to our doom."

"I am not decrepit," said the robot indignantly, "and I haven't led you to your doom. At least not intentionally."

"So that makes it all right then does it?" snapped Duros.

"Be quiet both of you," said Kevin. "Now, do you know what these things are, robot?"

"No," said the robot. "They are not creatures that I am aware of. They shouldn't be here at all."

"But they are," said Duros.

"Be quiet," said Kevin. "We need to do something quickly. Robot, try and find the portal as quickly as you can." The robot stood and looked at him but did not move. "Now!" shouted Kevin, and the robot shot off towards the place where they had arrived.

"They aren't moving very quickly," said Marlitta.

"No," said Kevin. "Perhaps, if we keep moving we can lose them."

"But they seem to be aware that we are here and must have started coming this way before they even saw us," said Marlitta. "If that's the case, then they will keep coming after us however far we go."

"They look like large insects," said Kevin. "Large black insects crawling towards us."

"Ugh," said Marlitta. "Don't say that. I hate insects."

"So do I," said Tracy, who had been standing transfixed by the sight. "I want to go home. Please get me home," she sobbed.

"That's what we all want," said Kevin. "But it won't help by crying."

"You haven't tried your crystal to see if it works here," said Marlitta.

"No. I've been without it for so long I had forgotten." He closed his eyes and tried to speak to Spectro in his mind, but there was no response. "Nothing," he said.

The robot came skidding back. "I can't find anything," it said.

"Well carry on looking," said Kevin. "We'll see if we can find somewhere safe from these things." The robot scurried off again, muttering to itself. "Let's have a look over the other side."

They made their way back the way they had come and then continued on towards the other side of the ruins. The robot rushed around probing stonework, still muttering to itself while Sniffer ran around, sniffing, his tail wagging enthusiastically, thinking that this must be a game of some sort.

When they came to the other outer wall they had to climb up some steps to get onto the higher walkway where they could see over the top. Duros became a bit of a nuisance so Marlitta and Tracy stayed at the bottom of the steps and kept a tight hold on him, while Kevin climbed the steps.

At the top, he could just see over the outer battlements by standing on tiptoe. There was more desert on this side too and, to his horror, he saw a large black mass coming towards him over the hard-packed sand. There must have been thousands of them, and Kevin wondered if they could get in from this side of the ruins as they had not found an entrance yet.

He rushed down the steps to where the others were waiting for him.

"There are more of those things on this side too," he panted. "Let's get back to the centre, where we arrived." They literally had to drag Duros, as he had become a gibbering wreck.

When they eventually reached the place where they had arrived, the robot was still probing the stone work and getting more and more agitated, and Sniffer was still sniffing with great enthusiasm.

"There has to be another portal here somewhere," said Kevin. "Spread out and see if you can find it."

"What about Duros?" asked Marlitta.

"Leave him," said Kevin. "There's nowhere for him to go." They let go of him and he dropped to the ground sobbing, while the others all set to, feeling the stone work for a portal.

Where could it be? Kevin looked around to see if there was an obvious feature in the stonework that could be a portal. He knew from past experience that they were very difficult to find and that Sniffer was the most likely to find one if there was one to be found.

"Keep an eye open for those things, Tracy," he said. "Let us know if they are getting near."

Tracy did not look too sure about that and shook her head.

"Tracy," he shouted. "We need you to warn us when they get close. Now climb up on that broken bit of wall so that you can see the archway."

Reluctantly, she climbed up onto the wall and, kneeling on the top, looked out over the ruins towards the archway.

"Are you sure that there is a portal here?" said Marlitta.

"No," said Kevin, "but I'm sure there must be. What do you think, Robot?"

"I do not know, Master," it said. "I was under the impression that most relay stations had several portals as there would be no point in sending people if there was nowhere else to go. There is a possibility that the other portals are somewhere else."

"Well I hope not," said Kevin, "because there's no way we could get to them. Keep looking."

"They're coming," screamed Tracy climbing off the wall in terror.

"Where are they?" asked Kevin.

"Coming through the arch," sobbed Tracy. "I don't like them. Please get me out of here."

They renewed their search frantically. Suddenly, Kevin noticed Sniffer's head disappear into the stonework where he was sniffing.

"It's here," shouted Kevin, but before he could stop him, Duros leapt to his feet and threw himself at the portal, but instead of passing through, he ran straight into solid stone. There was a nasty sound as his nose was squashed against the stone wall. He stood for a moment and then fell backwards onto the ground and lay still.

Kevin grabbed him and pulled him away from the wall. Then he felt where Sniffer had been sniffing. Near the bottom of the wall, his hand went into the void beyond.

He moved his hand higher and found that the top of the portal was only about a foot above the ground.

"I think it's got buried over the ages," said Kevin. We'll have to dig it out a bit so we can crawl through."

"Stand clear," said the robot. "I think I can do this." It formed its hands into a sort of scoop and started to scrape the soil and debris from the portal.

"Quickly," said Marlitta. "Those things are nearly here."

"I think we should be able to crawl through now," said Kevin. "Robot, you go through first and clear the rubble from the other side."

The robot went down onto all fours and disappeared through the portal.

"You next Tracy," said Kevin. But Tracy did not need to be told and was half way through the small gap. When she was half way through, Kevin thought that she must have got stuck, but suddenly she disappeared with a jerk. Marlitta went next followed by Sniffer.

Duros was still lying dazed on the ground, so Kevin got hold of his hands and pulled him towards the wall. Then he got down onto his knees and squeezed himself backwards through the portal dragging Duros behind him. The creatures were now quite close and he could see them crawling slowly towards him. When he got through, he just had Duros's arms, head and shoulders through the portal, but his midriff seemed to be stuck in the gap.

"Give me a hand to get him through," he shouted, and Marlitta grabbed one arm and Kevin grabbed the other and they both pulled for all they were worth.

Duros let out a yell. He was now fully conscious. "Pull harder you fools," he shouted. "They've got hold of my feet."

They pulled harder and Duros yelled but didn't move. The robot came over to them.

"Perhaps you would allow me," it said. Kevin and Marlitta moved out of the way and Duros started to disappear, shouting and yelling for all he was worth. But before he had completely disappeared, the robot grabbed hold of him and pulled. Duros shot out of the hole as if jet propelled and landed in a heap.

"What are you trying to do?" he shouted. "Get this monstrosity off me. It nearly pulled my arms out of their sockets."

"Would you rather have been eaten by those things?" asked Kevin. "We can soon push you back through there if you would prefer it."

Duros glared at them. "And where are my shoes?" he said.

"I think they are being eaten by those things on the other side of this portal," said Kevin. "Do you want to go back for them?"

The robot made itself busy filling the portal with rocks. "That will keep them from coming through," it said.

Now that the panic was over, they looked around to see where they were. There was long grass all around and some trees nearby, and there was a gentle breeze blowing. Above them, fluffy clouds moved slowly across a deep blue sky. When he looked closer at the trees, he noticed that there were brightly coloured birds in the branches.

"This looks better," said Kevin. "A lot more friendly."

"Do not be too sure," said the robot. "We have no idea where we are. There could be creatures here that might want to eat you. We must progress carefully."

"Oh, thanks for that," said Kevin. "By the way, do you have a name? We can't keep calling you Robot."

"Of course," said the robot. "I am called '1773263-utility-mark 3 alpha'."

"That's a bit of a mouthful," said Kevin. "Do you mind if we call you Alf for short?"

"That would be quite acceptable," said Alf.

They had all been sitting on the ground and could not see beyond the tall grass, so Kevin got to his feet for a better view.

"Wow," he said. "Look at this." The others stood up and joined him with the exception of Duros who found the ground very prickly on his bare feet.

The ground fell away into a wide valley with a river flowing through the middle of it. A group of large animals was grazing nearby and others were drinking in the shallows at the edge of the river.

"Anything dangerous here, Alf?" asked Kevin.

"Large animals can always be dangerous even if they don't want to eat you," said Alf. The smaller ones could be carnivorous, but I can't tell for sure."

"Keep quite still," said a voice in Kevin's brain, which startled him. "What did you say?" he said.

"No one said anything," said Marlitta.

"It was me," said the voice, "Spectro. We are back in the energy field of the galaxy and your crystal is working again. But, as I said before, keep quite still. There are creatures creeping up on you through the long grass."

"Keep still," said Kevin to the others. "There're some creatures in the long grass."

"How do you know?" asked Marlitta.

"Spectro is back."

"Well, let's get out of here then," said Marlitta. "Take us back to the Crystal City."

"Of course," said Kevin. "Link hands."

They all linked hands and Kevin closed his eyes and visualised the platform in the Crystal City.

Two large predators that were crouching in the grass leaped for the kill but found there was nothing there when they landed.

Chapter 16 - Back to the Crystal City

Tracy had seen the creatures leap and had waited for the terrible claws to rip her to pieces. She was too terrified to move, but before they reached her, the light changed and they found themselves standing on the crystal platform outside the headquarters of the Galactic Council. Alf had a firm grip of Duros who was looking a bit the worse for wear in his soiled garments and bare feet. His hands were still constrained by the manacles, which caused some consternation among the passers-by. As always, people were arriving and departing from this platform and Tracy was mesmerised by the scene.

Kevin led them into the Council building, and Tracy stared around in wonder at the magnificent entrance hall. One of the guards stepped forward as if to stop them, then, recognising Kevin, stopped and saluted.

"Welcome back Master," he said. "I will alert the council to your presence."

"Thank you," said Kevin. Tracy stared open mouthed.

"So, you really are what you said you were?" she gasped.

Kevin led them all through to the private apartments around the Council Chamber, and along the corridor to his rooms where he opened the door and let them in. The room was still exactly as he had left it.

"Make yourselves at home," he said. "Not you Duros. You can stand over there. Alf, keep a firm hold of him. I don't want him to escape or cause any mischief." Alf half dragged Duros across the room and stood with a firm hold on his arm.

"You'll be sorry for this one day," said Duros.

"I doubt it," said Kevin sitting down beside Marlitta.

There was a sudden scurry of activity and several Murin arrived from nowhere in particular. Tracy squeaked and jumped to her feet.

"It's all right, Tracy," said Kevin. "Relax." Tracy sat down again looking at the Murin suspiciously.

"Would the Master and his guests like refreshment," asked one of the Murin.

"That would be nice," said Kevin, "but not for that one over there." He pointed at Duros who glared at him. The Murin scuttled off to prepare food for them.

"What are they?" asked Tracy.

"They are the Murin," said Kevin. "They live to serve. It is what they enjoy most and are only happy when they are doing something for someone."

"I wouldn't like that," said Tracy.

"Well you would if you were one of the Murin," said Kevin.

"Well it seems cruel to me," said Tracy.

"They aren't made to do this," said Kevin, "it's what they want to do. It would be cruel not to let them though."

There was a knock at the door.

"Come in," shouted Kevin, and the door opened and in came a small figure a bit like Duros.

"Hello Quartok," said Kevin getting up and walking over to the newcomer. "It's good to see you again."

"It is good to see you too, Master," said Quartok. "We have been worried about you. Where have you been?"

"I really don't know," said Kevin. "We have been to far parts of the universe that the council has forgotten. My crystal wouldn't work out there and we had to use an ancient transporter system to get from one planet to another, and we had no way of telling where we would end up. And we brought this fellow back with us," He gestured to Duros. "Perhaps you could take him and lock him up somewhere where he can't escape."

"Certainly," said Quartok. "And who is this that has such a firm hold on him?"

"Oh, that's Alf. He's a robot. I have got quite fond of him, but I don't think I could take him back to earth with me. He would cause a bit of a stir."

"I must go where the Master goes," said Alf.

"We'll have to give it some thought," said Quartok.

Quartok touched the crystal that hung round his neck and closed his eyes for a second.

"The guards are on their way," he said. "This time there will be no escape for this villain."

"Good," said Kevin. "I don't want to have to chase him all over the universe again. I really thought that I would never see home again."

"It was really very foolish of you to go after Duros and this earth girl," said Quartok. "You should have taken our advice and left them. You are very lucky to have got back safely."

"You told him to leave me with that monster?" said Tracy leaping to her feet and towering over Quartok who backed away from her looking very nervous.

"Sit down Tracy," said Kevin. "Of course he did. It's his job to look after me."

"But you came after me anyway?"

"Of course," said Kevin. "I felt responsible as I let you have the crystal ring, and that put you in danger."

"This time there will be no crystal," said Quartok. "We cannot risk anything like this happening again. And, maybe we should wipe the memories from this earth creature to be on the safe side."

"What?" shouted Tracy leaping to her feet again. "You will not wipe anything. I'm not having it."

At that moment the door opened and Sniffer shot in followed by two guards.

"Sorry sir," said one of the guards, "but this animal was wandering about the building. We tried to catch it but couldn't get our hands on it. It must have followed us here and come in when we opened the door."

"It's all right," said Kevin. "He's with me." He tried to fend off the enthusiastic licking that Sniffer was trying to give him.

"Take this prisoner to the cells," said Quartok indicating Duros. "High security. He mustn't be allowed to escape or contact anyone from outside."

The guards took Duros from Alf who stood back and watched as Duros was escorted out of the room.

"This is not the end," said Duros over his shoulder as he was propelled through the door.

"We'll see about that," said Quartok. "Now I think that we should continue our discussion in my rooms. The earth girl can stay here. There is food set out in the other room."

"So, you want to talk about me behind my back," said Tracy indignantly. "Great."

"You are of little importance to the galactic federation," said Quartok. "We have other things to discuss that don't concern you. So, as I said, there is food in the next room. Please make yourself at home until we return."

Tracy looked dejected until the thought of food took over and she walked though into the next room to see what food there was. When she saw the spread her eyes opened wide and she forgot all about being left alone and went over to the table to decide what to eat first.

The others went to the door to leave but Kevin turned to Alf who was following them. "No Alf," he said. "You stay here and make sure that no harm comes to Tracy and make sure she stays here. Sniffer will stay and help you. The door will not open for her but we don't want anyone entering from outside to let her out." Alf looked disappointed, if it is possible for a robot to show emotion, but he went back and stood by the wall.

Chapter 17 - Decisions to make

When they reached Quartok's rooms, there was food ready for them.

"First let us eat," said Quartok. So they all sat down and tucked into the food. Kevin hadn't realised how hungry he was until then. After they had satisfied their initial hunger, Kevin told Quartok more about their exploits.

"But I don't see what decisions need making," said Kevin finally.

"Well firstly," said Quartok, "we will have to decide what to do about Duros."

"Well, I'll leave that to you," said Kevin, "As long as he doesn't get loose ever again."

"Well," said Quartok. "There will have to be a trial, and as far as I can see, the capture of a creature from outside the Federation is not, as such, a crime."

"What?" cried Kevin. I come from the earth, and as Master of the Universe that makes earth part of the Federation, even if they don't know it."

"In essence you are right," said Quartok. "But in law you are not. To become part of the Federation, the planet must enter into legally binding agreements, and that requires a planetary government. Your world doesn't have that. In fact, it is a hotchpotch of little countries that are mostly at war with each other. In fact, it is too primitive to be considered as a member of the Federation."

"Well, that is not the point," said Kevin. "He only kidnapped Tracy so that I would follow him. I don't know what he planned to do with us, but I suspect that he hoped to lose us in some remote part of the galaxy, or maybe get us killed. He nearly succeeded and would have if it hadn't been for Sniffer."

"Sniffer?"

"His dog," said Marlitta. "Sniffer kept us on his track and eventually overpowered him so that we could take him prisoner. But I think his main crimes are the ones he committed while still on the council. And for those crimes he had been banished to my home planet to help rebuild it. His crime has been to escape, so he should be sent back there and kept under tighter control."

"You have a good point," said Quartok, "but it will be for the High Court to decide. Which brings us to the next point. The earth girl, what are we going to do about her?"

"I don't see we have to do anything," said Kevin. "We have saved her from Duros and brought her back. I will take her back to earth where she belongs."

"But I think you are forgetting that she was the cause of this latest trouble," said Quartok. "She had a crystal, yes I know it was a small one of no particular power, but it allowed Duros to find her and use her to put you into danger. She cannot be allowed anything like that again."

"I suppose you're right," said Kevin.

"Too true," said Marlitta vehemently.

"That's just because you don't like her," said Kevin. "You never have done. I think you're jealous."

"Don't talk rubbish," snapped Marlitta. "She is a stupid little girl who wants all her own way and does anything to get it."

"That is not the point," said Quartok. "This is not personal. It is a matter of security. This is the first time, ever, that the Master of the Universe has lived outside the Federation with no security at all. We rely entirely on the fact that no one will know his whereabouts and therefore he will be safe. After all, he is not without power. His crystal will protect him from most things, except stupidity."

"And what is that supposed to mean?" said Kevin feeling that everyone was getting at him.

"It means that the Master of the Universe must learn wisdom and behave as a Master would be expected to behave. I know you are very young and it is very difficult, but so far you have done well, until this last little episode. So, something has to be done."

"Such as?" said Kevin rather petulantly.

"Well first of all we must erase all untoward memories from the girl Tracy," said Quartok. Kevin thought Marlitta had a rather smug look but ignored it.

"Will that be painful?" asked Kevin.

"Not in the least," said Quartok. "She will know nothing about it. She will be rendered unconscious. The memories will be wiped and then you will transport her back to earth and she will wake up in her own good time thinking she had just fallen asleep."

"I suppose I could take her back to the rocks above our house. I often fall asleep up there. It's very peaceful."

"Excellent," said Quartok. "Now the other factor is that robot of yours. Why on earth did you bring it back with you?"

"Well I didn't actually," said Kevin. "He just decided to come. He had been looking after a transfer station on a planet long after the people who used it had gone, and when I told him I was Master of the Universe, he decided his place was with me. He has been very useful. I call him Alf."

"Alf?"

"Yes. It's short for Alpha. It's part of his type number or something like that."

"Well it can't go with you to earth," said Quartok. "What would you tell people? No, it would cause too much interest, and that's the last thing we want."

"Pity," said Kevin. "I was looking forward to showing him to people, but I suppose you're right. But how are we going to persuade him to stay here?"

"Why don't we tell him his duty to the Master of the Universe," said Marlitta, "is to stay here and look after your rooms and keep things tidy."

"But there's nothing to keep tidy," said Kevin. "The Murin do all that. They would be quite put out if we left a robot to do what they do so well."

"So we tell the Murin that they are to look after your guest," said Marlitta.

"That might work out all right," said Quartok. If it doesn't, we'll just have to make up some special duties for it."

"And finally," said Quartok, "I would like Marlitta to keep a permanent eye on you to make sure that nothing like this happens again."

"What?" said Kevin indignantly, "I don't need a baby-sitter."

"Interesting turn of phrase," said Quartok. "But you do need someone you can talk to before deciding on any unacceptable course of action. I think Marlitta will be able to manage that little job very well. She can be your new special friend. She looks very much like your people do, so she should fit in very well."

But where would she live?" said Kevin. "She can't live with us. What would I tell my parents?"

"Of course not," said Quartok. We will build a special place for her under the hill near your house. No one will know it is there and she can keep in touch with you using your crystals. I think this will work out very well." Kevin noticed that Marlitta was grinning.

"Girls!" he thought. "I'll never understand them."

Chapter 18 - Home Again

Tracy had been taken to a special unit, rather like an operating theatre, where she was lying on a mattress on the floor.

"Is she all right?" asked Kevin.

"Of course she is," said Marlitta rather sharply.

"She is fine," said Quartok. "She is just asleep now but won't wake up until you get her back to earth. When you are there, just leave her for a while and she should wake up on her own. However, if she doesn't, you can wake her by shaking her gently until she responds. She will remember nothing of her exploits and will think she has just gone to sleep lying on the hillside. You must say nothing to make her think differently, as it is possible that her memories could return if you said things to remind her. Make sure you don't."

"Of course," said Kevin. At that moment Alf came into the room looking agitated.

"Hello Alf," said Kevin. "Have you come to see us off?"

"So, you are leaving," said Alf. "I could not believe that you would go without me, but I am ready now if you are."

"But you won't be coming," said Kevin. "I thought Quartok had explained."

"But I must come with you. It is my place at the Master's side."

"It is your place here," said Quartok, "to look after the Master's residence. And you will be able to accompany him on any trip that he might make within the Galactic Federation, but it would be dangerous for the Master if you went with him to his home planet."

"Why is that?" asked Alf. "I would protect him from any danger."

"But no one must know that I am the Master of the Universe," said Kevin. "If you came with me people would think it very strange as we don't have robots on my planets."

"No robots?" said Alf. "That is very strange. I cannot believe it."

"Well it is true," said Kevin. "We have some machines that people call robots, but they are nothing like you. You would serve me much better staying here and looking after my rooms. If you like, you can help Quartok with some of his duties. There must be a lot of things you could do to help him."

"If that is your command," said Alf, "I will do it. What would the Quartok like me to do?"

"Go back to the Master's rooms and I will call you if I need anything doing," said Quartok.

"Thank you," said Alf. "It will be a pleasure to be of service to you." He turned and glided out of the room.

"Thank you very much," said Quartok. "I have enough to do without having to nursemaid a paranoid robot."

"Oh, I'm sure he will be a great help to you," said Kevin grinning.

"I think you had better get yourself back home now," said Quartok.

Kevin took Marlitta's hand and put his hand on Tracy's shoulder. "I'm sure I've forgotten something," said Kevin, and at that moment the door burst open and Sniffer shot in. "Ah, that was what it was." Sniffer nuzzled up to him and almost immediately they were back on the hillside near Kevin's home. Tracy had landed rather awkwardly in a mass of heather with Kevin and Marlitta standing next to her. Sniffer looked startled for a moment and then sped off across the moorland chasing grouse and whatever else he could find.

"She looks a bit uncomfortable there," said Kevin. "Perhaps we should move her to somewhere better."

"Why are you always fussing over that awful girl?" said Marlitta indignantly. "Just leave her where she is."

"I'm not fussing," said Kevin. "It's just that if she wakes up there, she might get suspicious and wonder how she got there. It's not the sort of place you would just doze off, is it?"

"I suppose not," said Marlitta, "But you needn't think I'm going to carry her. She's too fat to carry."

"Wouldn't dream of it," said Kevin reaching for his crystal. "I'll use this."

"Have you tried moving something as big as her with the crystal?" asked Marlitta.

"Well no, actually," said Kevin. "But how hard can it be?" He held the crystal and his face took on a look of concentration. Slowly she began to rise off the ground, then suddenly she dropped back with a thud and Kevin let out the breath he had been holding.

"Wow, she is heavy," he said. "I'll just have a quick word with Spectro to see if I'm doing it properly." He closed his eyes for a while and Marlitta began to wonder if he had gone to sleep, but then he opened them again. "Ah, I see," he said. "No wonder she seemed heavy. I'd got it all wrong, but Spectro has told me how to do it so I'll have another go."

He held the crystal again and put on his look of concentration. For a moment nothing happened, then suddenly Tracy shot into the air and disappeared from sight.

"Oh dear," shouted Kevin. "What have I done?"

"Good question," said Marlitta looking into the sky. "If a passing aeroplane sees that, the pilot will get quite a shock."

"What shall I do?" he shouted in panic.

"Find her with the crystal sight and guide her down again...slowly," said Marlitta. "We don't want her splattered all over the hillside, do we? Well, at least you don't."

Kevin concentrated again. "Yes, I can see her. She is falling back down again now. I'll try and slow her down. I think I've got control. She's slowing."

"I can see her now," said Marlitta. "She's over there." She pointed. Kevin focussed on the falling Tracy and slowly her course swung round and she drifted slowly towards them. When she had moved over a grassy spot, Kevin slowly lowered her to the ground.

He sat down. "Gosh, I thought I'd killed her for a moment then," he said.

"No such luck," said Marlitta.

"Why are you so nasty to her?" asked Kevin.

"Well you didn't like her yourself," said Marlitta, "if you can remember that."

"No, I suppose you're right," he said. "Should we stay until she wakes up, do you think?"

"Perhaps it would be better if we weren't here," said Marlitta. "Why don't we go and have a look at my new home/"

"Will they have done anything yet?" said Kevin. "They haven't had much time."

"With crystal power it doesn't take much time," said Marlitta. "Remember what we did on my planet to turn it from a desert into a fertile place that anyone would be pleased to live in."

"I suppose so," said Kevin. "But we don't know where it is do we?"

"It'll be under this hill somewhere," she said. "Use your crystal sight and see if there are any caverns down there."

Kevin closed his eyes and let his mind sight look into the hillside. First there were rabbit warrens then rock then, suddenly, he was in a great cave with stalactites and stalagmites all around. It was beautiful. Then as he looked further along the galleries he saw a mass of movement. Murin were everywhere, cutting shaping and moving rubble. Others were polishing and cleaning and making the place habitable.

"I think I've found it," said Kevin. "Take my hand." When he felt Marlitta's hand grasp his, he 'jumped' and was immediately in the cavern.

"Wow," she said. "This is fantastic."

They walked along the passage to where the Murin were working furiously, and as soon as their presence was noticed, the Murin disappeared in all directions leaving a larger person who had been directing operations. He turned and, when he saw Kevin, hurried over to him wringing his hands together in a most agitated way. Kevin recognised him immediately as Rotunda from Marlitta's home planet.

"Welcome Master," he said bowing low. "Welcome to the lady's new residence. But I'm afraid that we have not yet finished the work. Please forgive me."

"That's Okay," said Kevin. "We didn't expect it to be finished yet. We just came to have a look at it."

"Oh good," said Rotunda. "Let me show you round."

"Lead the way," said Kevin. Rotunda strode off down the tunnel and Kevin noticed that the Murin reappeared and went back to work as soon as they had gone.

"There are some smaller caverns down here," said Rotunda. "We thought they would make ideal private rooms for the lady. They will be finished shortly, so if you wish to stay here tonight, all will be ready for you."

"Thank you," said Marlitta. "That would be great."

"We will continue with the work out here until it is finished," said Rotunda, "but we shouldn't be in your way. Now, let me show you your private rooms." He walked over to what looked like a flat wall and placed his hand on what looked like a lump in the wall, and a door slid open to reveal an entrance hall already furnished.

"That's amazing," said Marlitta. "Can we go in?"

"Certainly," said Rotunda. "Please make yourselves at home."

They went into the hall, which had several doors leading to rooms on either side. Although they were underground, it was warm and cosy and a warm light seemed to seep out of the walls. They were both speechless.

"Will this be all right for you?" asked Rotunda looking slightly anxious.

"It's marvellous," said Marlitta, "absolutely marvellous." Rotunda beamed at her and his little round body seemed to inflate with pride.

"Won't anybody find it?" asked Kevin. "We wouldn't want anyone to find it."

"Oh no," said Rotunda. "Although this is part of a large network of caves under this hill, it has been carefully sealed off from the more exposed caves. If people come exploring the outer caves, they will never find their way in here. We have also installed some barrier crystals to make sure."

"Barrier crystals?" Kevin looked puzzled.

"Yes, they are crystals specially designed to deflect interest from a certain area. If anyone thought of drilling a tunnel though this hill, for example, their measurements would lead them to believe it wouldn't be possible. So, they would give up the idea."

"But what would happen if they carried on anyway?" Kevin persisted.

"Then we would be warned," said Rotunda patiently. "Then we would come and remove any signs that we had been here. But I don't think that likely. No one will see you arriving or leaving as you will be using your crystals to transport you in and out."

"Seems OK to me," said Kevin.

"Great," said Marlitta. "I'll come back later this evening and settle in."

"Excellent," said Rotunda. "All will be ready for you by then. Now, if you will excuse me I must get on with the work." He bowed to them then turned and strutted off down the tunnel to where he had been overseeing operations.

"This is great, isn't it?" said Kevin. "I think you'll be fine here. I wouldn't mind living here myself. Anyway, we'd better get back to my house or they will wonder where I have got to. We'll tell them that you have just moved to the area and will be starting at my school next term."

"We'd better get back to see if your fat friend Tracy has woken up yet," said Marlitta.

Kevin took Marlitta's hand and 'jumped' back to the hilltop where they had left Tracy.

"She's gone," said Kevin as they materialised on the moor near the rocks. They walked over to where they had left here and could see the crushed grass and bracken where she had been lying.

"There she is," said Marlitta pointing down the hill. Kevin followed her gaze and saw Tracy making her way down towards the road on the side of the hill away from his house. "She should be OK now," said Kevin. "It's probably just as well that we weren't here when she woke up. Right, let's go down to my house. You can have some tea with us if you like."

"If your mother doesn't mind," said Marlitta.

"Are you nervous?" asked Kevin.

"A little," said Marlitta, "but you can let go of my hand now." Kevin dropped her hand as if it were hot. "Sorry," he said.

"Don't be silly," said Marlitta. "I was only joking. Come on. Let's go and meet your parents. Are they much bigger than you?"

"Well yes, I suppose so. I'd never really thought about it."

They set off down the hill and crossed the field at the bottom and climbed the wall into Kevin's garden. The back door was open and a welcome smell of cooking drifted out to meet them.

"This is really very quaint," said Marlitta. Kevin gave her a sidelong glance but did not ask her what she meant.

Kevin's mother came to the door as they walked up the path.

"I was expecting you before this," she said. Then she noticed Marlitta. "Oh, hello." She said.

"This is a new friend," said Kevin "She has just moved to the area and will be starting at my school next term."

"Oh, I see," said his mother. "Would she like to stay for something to eat?"

"If that's all right," said Kevin. "Her name is Marlitta."

"That's an unusual name," said his mother. "Is she Spanish?"

"I don't know," said Kevin turning to Marlitta. "Are you?"

"Possibly," said Marlitta. "My parents are from somewhere far away."

"Well come inside and make yourselves at home."

Kevin's mother had baked a steak and kidney pie, which Marlitta looked at as if it were poisonous.

"What's that?" she whispered to Kevin while his mother was fetching the vegetables.

"Steak and kidney pie," said Kevin. "It's my favourite." Marlitta didn't look convinced.

At last everything was dished up and they sat down to eat.

"Well," said his mother. "How did the camping trip go? Anything exciting happen?"

"Oh yes," said Kevin. "We travelled all over the universe trying to catch up with Duros and we nearly didn't get back."

"That must have been fun," said his mother. "You really do have a vivid imagination."

* * *

Happily Ever After?

For the next few years, Kevin continued his school work during term-time, but went off with Marlitta, during the holidays to carry out their duties for the Galactic Council.

Marlitta spent some time in her underground home, but went back to her home planet, quite a bit, to see that all was running smoothly there. Nothing dramatic happened, with the exception of the occasional problem with one of the warrior races that had been allowed to join the Federation.

The years rolled by and Kevin found himself having to make a decision. He had now turned eighteen and his parents were trying to persuade him to go to university but Kevin couldn't see the point as his future lay elsewhere.

The choice was between continuing his life here on Earth and disappearing every now and then to attend to his other duties as Master of the Universe.

"You really aught to make you position in the Council your major priority," said Marlitta, one day. "I would like to spend more time on my home planet with my family. Why don't you come back with me and forget about Earth for good?"

"I know I haven't any real connections here," he said, "but how would I explain it to my parents? I know they don't give me much of their time, but if I were to just disappear they would be really upset."

"How about emigrating to Australia?" suggested Marlitta.

"But I don't know anyone in Australia," he replied, "and I would need a job to go to."

"No, you wouldn't be going there," said Marlitta impatiently. "That would be your story. You would actually come back with me. You could keep in touch with them on the internet. I'm sure we could tap into that from 'Paradise'." Paradise was her home planet.

"Well, I suppose so," said Kevin.

"Then, of course, we could get married."

"What?" said Kevin. He had always thought that he would like to marry Marlitta but had never had the courage to speak about it. "Would you marry me?"

"I thought you'd never ask," she said.

A few days later, during one of the gaps in his father's travels, Kevin announced that he would be taking a job in Australia. His parents were shocked. How could he get a job in Australia? He didn't have any qualifications.

But after much discussion they accepted that he would have to do as he pleased. They left it for a month and then he said goodbye to his mother and left for good. His father was on one of his business trips so Kevin emailed him to say goodbye.

Back on 'Paradise', Rotunda was overjoyed to see them both and set about organising the wedding for them. The whole of the Galactic Council was invited, though only a few could find the time to actually attend.

Alf was already on 'Paradise' to welcome his master, and Kevin decided that he would make him his best man. Weddings were not performed in the same way as on Earth, so they ended up with a bit of each.

After the wedding, they had a honeymoon in a remote part of 'Paradise' before settling in to his new life as the Master of the Universe. They moved into a very nice home that Rotunda had organised for them, with the help of Alf, and Sniffer seemed to approve of it too, as he could now spend all his time with Kevin and Marlitta.

Strangely, Kevin didn't miss Earth one little bit.

* * *

31337692R00239

Printed in Poland
by Amazon Fulfillment
Poland Sp. z o.o., Wrocław